THE FACE

At first she tho[...] against the windowpane in flight—it had happened several times before, startling whoever was sitting by the window, then landing stunned or dead on the sidewalk outside—so it took her a few seconds to realize that whatever had struck the window was still there, pressed to the glass. She stopped speaking and turned to it, mouth open, and then she saw it clearly and realized what it was—

—a mangled, broken face.

"Paul!" she screamed, backing away from the table and lifting her hands to her jaw, curling her fingers over the flesh of her own face, as if to reassure herself that it was still there, still unbroken and smooth. *Paul Kragen!*

Don't miss these other exciting horror titles from Bantam:

THE BRIDGE by John Skipp and Craig Spector
DARK JOURNEY by A. R. Morlan
HOUSE HAUNTED by Al Sarrantonio
NIGHT by Alan Rodgers
OTHERWORLD by Kenneth C. Flint

DARK CHANNEL

by
Ray Garton

FALCON™

®

BANTAM BOOKS
NEW YORK • TORONTO • LONDON • SYDNEY • AUCKLAND

DARK CHANNEL

A Bantam Falcon Book / May 1992

ISBN 0-553-29190-4

Published simultaneously in the United States and Canada

Bantam Books are published by Bantam Books, a division of Bantam
Doubleday Dell Publishing Group, Inc. Its trademark, consisting of
the words "Bantam Books" and the portrayal of a rooster, is Reg-
istered in U.S. Patent and Trademark Office and in other countries.
Marca Registrada. Bantam Books, 666 Fifth Avenue, New York, New
York 10103.

PRINTED IN THE UNITED STATES OF AMERICA

RAD 0 9 8 7 6 5 4 3 2 1

*Dedicated to
my loving and patient wife Dawn,
whose support got me through this book
and continues to get me through everything else.*

ACKNOWLEDGEMENTS

Any writer who tells you that he or she wrote a book without a bit of help or support from anyone else probably has a bridge to sell you, too. I'd like to thank those who helped me with *Dark Channel*.

Scott Sandin, Derek Sandin, Sarah Wood, Dave Yeske, Paul Meredith, Dr. Evan K. Reasor, Sharon Shepherd, Sid Ayers, Dean R. Koontz, my editor Amy Stout, my friend Francis Feighan, who put up with countless late-night phone calls and always had the answers to my obscure—sometimes bizarre—questions, my wonderful agent Lori Perkins, my sister and brother-in-law Sandy and Bill DeWildt, my parents Ray and Pat Garton, and God. I couldn't have done it without them.

WHEATLAND, CALIFORNIA
OCTOBER, 1962

On the day Lizzie Dayton got a glimpse of hell, the playground of Prairie Grammar School was dark beneath the shadow of rain-threatening clouds.

Before releasing her students for recess, Miss Randall, the fourth-grade teacher, looked out the large rectangular window that gave a clear view of the playground. Drumming her fingernails on her desktop, she said, "It looks pretty cloudy, but the weatherman says it won't rain. If it does, though, I want all of you to hurry back inside. At the first drop, understand?"

The class replied with a chorus of nods and uh-huhs.

"And be sure to wear your coats," she added. As the children hurried toward the door and forty minutes of playful freedom, Miss Randall said, "Lizzie, could I see you a moment?"

Lizzie was still seated at her desk, as usual. She always waited for the rush to end before getting up to leave. She stood and approached her teacher's desk, wondering if she'd unknowingly done something wrong.

As if reading Lizzie's thoughts, Miss Randall smiled reassuringly and stood, coming around to the front of her desk. She folded her arms and crossed her thin ankles and said, "How would you like to do a favor for me, Lizzie?"

Smiling up at her teacher, Lizzie said, "Sure, Miss Randall."

"Have you noticed that Hester is limping today?"

Her smile fading, Lizzie nodded.

"Well, she hurt her ankle over the weekend and she can't do any running or jumping for a few days. I've noticed you don't play in many of the games during recess and I thought you'd like to keep Hester company.''

Lizzie was no longer smiling. She had a sinking feeling inside all of a sudden, as if her stomach were oozing down into her legs.

"Do . . . do I have to?'' she asked quietly.

"Well, you don't *have* to. But I think it would be a *nice* thing to do.''

Lizzie looked down at her shoes.

"In fact,'' Miss Randall said, leaning forward, "you two might even become good friends.''

That almost made Lizzie laugh; instead, she nodded, said, "Okay,'' and got her coat.

Lizzie Dayton hated recess; the playground was littered with bad memories, and it seemed every time she went out there, another was made. She preferred the classroom, where, safely seated at her desk, she could quietly and confidently do the things she did best: solve math problems, spell words, write book reports or answer quiz questions.

She was a smart girl—the school had suggested she skip the fourth grade that year, but her mother would not hear of it—but for all of her spelling and writing and mathematical abilities, for all of her "book sense,'' as Mom called it, she was unable to fathom the politics of recess.

If she refused an invitation to join in a game of kickball or dodgeball, the other children branded her a "chicken''; they laughed at and ridiculed her for not participating. If she played, however, she was ridiculed for her inabilities and inexperience.

Lizzie was a chubby girl, round-faced and pink-skinned, and lacked the speed and coordination required to be any good at the games the other children played. Her size not only made sports difficult; Lizzie's entire life seemed a chore simply because of the way she looked. She did not understand how a person such as herself—a girl who had never hurt anyone and who was so willing to share her belongings and talents—could be the target of so much cruelty.

Grown-ups seemed to see in Lizzie something special.

"A gifted child,'' they'd say.

"Such a *bright* girl.''

"She has *so* much potential.''

Praise from adults made her swell with pride and think that

perhaps someday, when *she* was a grown-up, she would be accepted and appreciated. But that day was a long way off. In the meantime, grown-ups made lousy playmates.

Lizzie had learned that if she were to avoid the tormenting laughter, the name-calling, and the pointing fingers of her classmates, she had to avoid her classmates altogether.

She especially had to steer clear of Hester Thorne, the most hateful of the lot.

Hester was probably the most popular girl at school. She had the admiration of students and teachers alike. Her shiny blond hair and big blue eyes were magnets that pulled in the attention of everyone around her. Hester was always smiling, always seemed in a cheerful mood, and was never seen without a small entourage of friends.

Lizzie was not, however, among her admirers. In fact, there were times when Lizzie was overcome with a burning hatred for Hester that was strong enough to bring tears to her eyes. It also brought a pang of guilt and the echo of her mother's voice saying, *Hating our enemies just lowers us to their level, sweety; we mustn't hate them. Remember the Golden Rule that Jesus gave us: "Do unto others . . ."*

Usually, Lizzie had no problem living by that rule. When others made fun of her or excluded her at school, they sometimes angered her and always hurt her, but she never lashed out at them. Only Hester Thorne could stir in her such trembling hatred. Sometimes that hatred was so fierce it made Lizzie want to kick or hit her, claw at her eyes, do *something* that would cause Hester enough pain to take that smile from her lips. Maybe it was the smile that did it. . . .

Hester's smile never went away. Even when she was angry or being cruel—and she'd been cruel to Lizzie more times than Lizzie cared to count—the smile remained as if it were a permanent feature of her face. The smile brought a glimmer to her eyes, as if she enjoyed every single thing she did.

But everything Hester did was not good. . . .

Hester had quietly tormented Barry Walker, who was slightly cross-eyed. It was barely noticeable, really; in fact, Lizzie thought Barry's eyes were nice, crossed or not. He wasn't at Prairie anymore; he'd left the second week of school. While he was there, not a day had gone by that Hester did not, at least once, say something to him during recess or after school, only loud enough for her friends to hear. Lizzie never heard what Hester said to him, but she knew by the laughter that always followed that it was something awful. Barry had complained to Miss Randall, but it was useless; Hester and her friends always denied it and Miss Randall always believed Hester. Miss Randall was really a very nice lady and Lizzie liked her very much in spite of her allegiance to Hester. It had nothing to do with her character; *everyone* believed Hester. Everyone but Lizzie.

One day, Lizzie approached Barry after Hester and her friends had walked away in a chorus of derisive laughter. She smiled and tried to sound cheerful as she said, "Try not to pay too much attention to them. They're nobody. Really."

But Barry did not return to Prairie after that day and Lizzie had not seen him since.

At the beginning of the year, Miss Randall had brought a pair of hamsters into the classroom for the students to observe. She'd put Hester in charge of the animals, making her the only student with permission to feed and handle them. When Miss Randall was around, Hester always seemed to take great care in changing the hamsters' food and water and cleaning the cage. But when the teacher was out of the room or busy in her office, Lizzie sometimes saw Hester pinch her thumb and forefinger over the nose and mouth of one of the hamsters until its little body began to wriggle and thrash desperately, all of which got a burst of stifled laughter from Hester's friends.

There were other things, too, small things that seemed insignificant when considered individually but, when added up, were very unsettling.

Like the stray cat that used to hang around the playground waiting for scraps from the children's lunch bags. Lizzie found the cat one day on her way to catch the bus after school; someone had used a firecracker to blow the cat's backside into a glistening black-red mess. Normally, Lizzie would have thought even Hester incapable of such a thing. But the day before, she'd seen Hester huddling in a corner of the playground with her friends, passing around a small bright red object and laughing with corrupt delight. . . .

What mystified Lizzie was everyone's apparent blindness to Hester's cruel nature. It was obvious enough to Lizzie, but no one else seemed to notice. Even those students not given the honor of joining Hester's entourage treated her as if she were a misplaced princess accidentally enrolled in a small-town grammar school. Every teacher in the school knew Hester by name and gave her a smiling "Hello" when they passed her on campus—even the principal, Mr. Drummond, who never remembered *anyone's* name.

Although adults saw great potential in Lizzie, they seemed not to see her at *all* when Hester was near by. No one did.

Hester captured and held the attention of everyone.

Except Lizzie. That was why Lizzie dreaded this particular recess more than she had any other.

When she stepped outside, a game of kickball was already well under way.

Three girls were taking turns skipping rope on the sidewalk. When they saw her, they giggled and one of the girls began to chant as she skipped: *"Liz-*zie *Day-*ton *gained* a *ton*, *eat-*ing *can-*dy *just* for *fun*! *Al-*ways *hun-*gry, *nev-*er *full*, she's *got-*ta *bot-*tom *like* a *bull!"*

Lizzie turned away from them and tried to shut the sing-song voice from her ears.

Two boys were playing catch with a softball on the other side of the playground and directly across from the sidewalk where Lizzie stood, Hester Thorne sat in one of the swings, lolling back and forth in the seat. Her honey-colored curls were jostled by the cool breeze and she kicked at the gravel beneath her with the toe of one shoe.

Hester smiled across the playground at Lizzie, but it was not a smile of welcome; it was a challenge.

Rather than crossing the playground and drawing attention to herself, Lizzie walked around it, first along the sidewalk that ran near a row of classrooms, then along the tall chain-link fence that separated the playground from the school's ballfield. As she walked, Hester's smiling gaze followed her every step. The piercing squeak of the swing's chains grew louder as the distance between the two girls closed.

I'm not doing this for Hester, Lizzie thought firmly. *I'm doing it for Miss Randall.*

Lizzie stepped off the pavement and into the large rectangular graveled area that held the slide, monkey bars, teeter-totter, merry-go-round and swing set. She seated herself on the empty swing beside Hester and tried to smile as she met her eyes, tried to think of a pleasant greeting, something friendly. She could do neither. Instead, Lizzie turned her gaze to Hester's left foot, which was wrapped in an Ace bandage.

"How did you hurt your foot?" she asked.

"Fell off the back of my daddy's new pick-up truck," Hester replied through her smile.

Lizzie blinked with surprise. "Was it *moving*?"

"Of *course* not, dummy. I'd probably be *dead* if it was moving."

Still staring at Hester's foot, Lizzie said, "It must've hurt."

"Not really. I only sprained it a little."

"Oh. That's good."

"Good?" Hester snapped.

Startled, Lizzie looked at the girl and saw anger in her smiling eyes.

"You think it's *good* that I hurt my foot?"

"Oh, no, I just meant that—"

"How would you like it if *you* got hurt and *I* was glad?"

You always are, Lizzie thought, suddenly wanting to burrow into the gravel beneath her and disappear.

"I didn't mean that," Lizzie insisted, closing her eyes so she didn't have to look at that smile. "I only meant it's good that your foot was just sprained a little, that it wasn't hurt worse."

"I'm sure that's what you meant, Lizzie Dayton."

"Well, it is." Her eyes were still closed.

"What do you want, anyway? You don't like me. Why did you come over here?"

Lizzie's eyes opened then and she stared at Hester in disbelief, momentarily forgetting her intimidation.

"I don't like *you*? But you're the one who's always making fun of *me*, saying I'm fat. *I've* never done anything to—"

"But you *are* fat."

Lizzie stared at her lap, feeling the familiar pain again, the pain that would slowly grow into self-hatred. She whispered, "See what I mean?"

"You think that I don't like you because I say you're fat?" Hester laughed a moment—a laugh that came from the pain of others—then said, "That's just stupid. You *are* fat! I'm just telling the truth when I say that, I didn't *make* you fat." She laughed again and began swinging back and forth, her small hands wrapped tightly around the squeaky chains.

The chanting voice of the girl jumping rope across the playground drifted around on the breeze. ". . . she's *got*-ta *bot*-tom *like* a *bull*!"

"See?" Hester giggled. "Don't get mad at *me* because you're fat."

Lizzie remained still in her swing, gulping back the tears she felt stinging their way to her eyes. She wanted to get up and leave but knew that, if she moved, she would reveal too much; she would cry or run away and Hester would know how much she'd hurt her.

Lizzie didn't want that, so she stayed put.

"So how come you came over here, Lizzie Dayton?"

She still said nothing.

"Huh? How come?"

Lizzie wondered if she should tell the truth or say that it was her idea. If she took the credit, Hester might feel a bit guilty for returning a kindness with cruelty.

Then again . . .

"I thought you might like some company," Lizzie said. "That's all."

"Oh? That's all, huh?"

"Yes."

Before Hester spoke again, she let out a little shriek of pain and stopped swinging.

"What's wrong?" Lizzie gasped, turning to her.

Hester was leaning forward, wincing as she massaged her injured foot.

"Kicked my foot. I can't use my foot to swing," she said impatiently. Hester sat up, faced Lizzie, and said, "Come here and push me."

It was at that moment that Lizzie realized exactly what was so unsettling about Hester Thorne.

She had the eyes of an adult. She spoke with the authority of someone accustomed to being obeyed. She did not make requests or ask for favors; she gave orders.

Lizzie slowly moved from her swing, got behind Hester and gave her a gentle push.

"So you thought I'd like some company, huh?" Hester said.

"Yes."

"Are you sure it wasn't just because *you* wanted some company? You always spend recess alone and you never play. Because you're too fat." She giggled.

Lizzie felt her nostrils flaring.

"Or maybe you just think you're too *good* to play with the rest of us. If that's what you think, you're the only one who thinks it."

Go away, Lizzie told herself, *just go back to the classroom and read a book. Before you start to feel too bad.*

She could feel the beginning of a hard lump in her stomach and it grew as Hester went on.

"Is that why you came over, Lizzie Dayton? Because *you* wanted company?"

"No. I told you." She hated the way Hester called her by her full name.

"No, that's probably not it," Hester continued, her voice growing and fading as she swung back and forth, back and forth. "Maybe . . . maybe you did it for Miss Randall. Yes, that's probably it, because you *know* Miss Randall likes me so much. Much better than she likes you."

The hatred was coming back, and with it came tears, drowning the hollow whisper of her mother's reminders to be kind even to her enemies. Lizzie pushed harder, sending Hester higher into the air.

"She probably told you to come talk to me because I can't play, but *you* did it to make her like you. Not because you wanted to. Right?"

Lizzie gave another push, harder still.

"You know how much Miss Randall likes me, don't you, Lizzie Dayton? *Everybody* likes me. But I can't think of a single person who likes *you.*"

The chains squealed like angry rats.

"Think about it. You're out here alone every day at recess. Miss Randall has never asked me or anybody else to keep *you* company. Has she?"

Hester laughed as she swung upward, her legs outstretched before her as she swung even higher than before, arms hugging the chains. When she spoke again, her voice was firm and even a little frightened.

"Hey, don't push so hard!" she snapped.

Lizzie knew she should stop; the anger in Hester's voice almost frightened her into stopping. It was the *fear* in her voice that made Lizzie want to push harder. Making Hester angry took no effort at all; it happened every day without provocation. But to make Hester Thorne afraid was something else altogether. Something like victory . . .

As Hester swung backward, Lizzie stepped back, raised her arms, pressed her palms flat against Hester's back, and shoved so hard she grunted with exertion.

"I'm getting *dizzy!*" Hester cried with a small tremble in her voice. "Stop!"

Lizzie felt her own lips, salty with tears, curl into a smile that she knew she should be ashamed of—

—*we mustn't* hate *them*—

—but she could not fight it.

When Hester swung back—

—"I'll tell!"—

—Lizzie readied herself—

—"I *swear* I'll tell!"—

—and pushed.

"Noooo!" Hester shouted, but the shout quickly became a whimper as she rose up higher and higher, stopping at a height almost level with the top of the swing. On her way back down, Hester babbled, "You're gonna get into so much trouble for this, Lizzie Dayton—"

Lizzie took a deep breath—

"—so much trouble!"—

—gave another powerful shove—

—and Hester was airborne.

She flew from the swing and, as if in a slow-motion dream, floated silently through the chilly air, her limbs splayed helplessly in four directions. She seemed to take forever to land and during that long instant, Lizzie's mouth dropped open and she sucked in a gasp of air and noticed, oddly, that the dark clouds overhead were moving along at a normal pace and everyone on the playground was playing and shouting as they were just an instant before. Only *this*—this one particular event in this corner of the playground—had slowed to a sort of underwater ballet in Lizzie's eyes and she knew why. . . .

Lizzie knew that when Hester Thorne hit the ground, Lizzie was going to be in *so . . . much . . . trouble. . . .*

Hester landed with a thud, a whoosh of knocked-out breath, and a scattering of pebbles.

Lizzie froze.

The empty swing bobbed and swayed in Hester's wake, the chains chattering like gossiping metal teeth.

Distant thunder stomped through the clouds.

Lizzie waited for Hester to cry, to scream for Miss Randall. To do *something*.

But she lay still as sleep on the ground.

"Heh . . . Hester?" Lizzie breathed, moving slowly around the swing. "I'm . . . I'm sorry, Hester." She stopped two feet away from the girl and looked around, expecting to see teachers and students rushing across the playground toward her, hurrying to see what had happened to Hester . . .

. . . to see what the fat girl had done to their little Hester.

No one was coming; no one had noticed.

"Hester?" she whispered again, stepping forward and bending over her. "Hester, I didn't mean—"

Hester's body suddenly erupted in a fit of convulsions. Her arms and legs began to flop like fish on land; her back stiffened and her pelvis jutted upward again and again. With eyes bulging and her mouth a yawning *O*, Hester began to gag. Her head tilted back and foamy saliva began to gather at the corners of her mouth.

"Hester!" Lizzie cried, kneeling down and reaching for her but afraid to touch her. "Oh no, Hester, *stop*!" Glancing over her shoulder, Lizzie realized that they were still unnoticed by the others on the playground. She feared the trouble she knew would come if she called for Miss Randall, but she feared even more that Hester was dying. She filled her lungs with air to cry for help, but Hester's convulsions suddenly stopped.

Lizzie's voice caught in her throat; she was certain Hester was dead, that her last push had somehow killed Hester, that—

Hester rose up.

She did not sit up. She did not pull herself up. It was as if an invisible arm had lifted the top half of Hester's body into a sitting position, bringing her face less than an inch from Lizzie's.

Lizzie suddenly felt helplessly off balance and found herself groping fearfully for something to hold onto, as if she were teetering on the very edge of a pit, as if . . .

. . . as if she might fall into Hester's no longer smiling eyes.

Hester slapped her hands to each side of Lizzie's skull and held it in an iron grip as the playground seemed to fade around

them and Lizzie tried to scream but could not find her voice
and—

—when she looked over Hester's shoulder, she could not find
the playground.

The moment Hester's hands began to squeeze Lizzie's head,
the playground and school buildings melted away like boiling
wax and they were suddenly someplace else, someplace dark and
cold in spite of the flames that were spitting from gaping craters
all around them. The fire shot upward forty or fifty feet to lick
the soot-black sky, rising nearly the height of the buildings
around them, skeletal buildings with supports and girders jutting
like splintered bones from enormous holes torn into the walls.

The sickening-sweet reek of burning meat cut through the icy
air and distant screaming voices rose to the sky with the belching
flames.

Other craters shot fire in the distance and one of them—far
beyond the patch of land that, a moment ago, was the grassy
playing field—was surrounded by a circle of people in tattered
white robes streaked with soot, their hands lifted upward. Although her vision was blurred, either by tears or by the heat
from the fire—

—*Or because this is a dream,* she thought, *that's all, I'm still
in bed having a nightmare*—

—she saw one of the robed figures step forward holding something bundled in a blanket. The blanket was peeled away cere-
moniously and tossed aside and a flesh-pink lump with four
struggling limbs was lifted above the figure's head.

Lizzie squinted, struggling to see better.

No, no . . .

A baby.

Chanting voices murmured like ghosts on the breeze and with
them came the frail, distant cries of the infant.

Lizzie took a breath to cry out but the child was already tumbling
through the air, head over feet, swallowed by the fire before it even
began its descent.

Cries of agony came from every direction, piercing the darkness in which vague shapes writhed and shifted, and there was
an odd sound from overhead, a sound like wings flapping, very
big wings. Lizzie looked up at the thick, greasy darkness, but
saw nothing. When she lowered her eyes, they fell on something

in the darkness to her left. It looked like . . . could it be . . . a pile of *bodies*? She looked closer, squinting and—

—Lizzie screamed, a keening wail, uncontrollable, clutching at her lungs like rat's claws and she looked into Hester's dead eyes again and—

—the two girls began to rise, leaving the corpses below them, lifting weightlessly on the black air and hovering over the fire-breathing craters, unnoticed by those below, some of whom ran for cover, always looking upward, while others fought, beating one another with spiked clubs and heavy chains, while still others walked through the darkness slowly and at ease, the hems of their dirty white robes slapping gently at their feet.

Dim lights glowed in the windows of battered houses while black smoke billowed from others.

Cries of pain and death rose toward them in voices young and old.

They began to move faster and faster until all below them was a dark, muddy blur and Lizzie managed to stop her screaming, lower it to a few deep, gripping sobs, and when she looked down again, they were slowing, descending over a mountain topped with red-streaked snow and on the other side of the mountain was—

—a house.

It was a pretty house, a big white *U*, filled with light, but it made Lizzie want to vomit because—

—the light was black. It was not real light, not good light, not the light Lizzie knew, that you could read by or warm to, but a light that was made of darkness, a cancerous light, thick and smothering, and as they drew closer to the house Lizzie began to cry harder, on the verge of screaming again, because coming from the house, she heard—

—laughter.

But it was not happy laughter.

They passed over the clean white roof of the house until they were floating over dense, dark green woods, falling lower and lower until—

—they were below the high tops of the trees, darting back and forth to avoid them, lower and lower until—

—they were just inches above the ground and ahead of them, Lizzie saw—

—a cave filled with blackness, and they shot through the opening, plunging deep into the darkness until—

—Lizzie saw a faint blue glow ahead of them that grew brighter as they shot deeper into the cave and the light made her ill, made her tremble because, like the light in the house, it was wrong, it was *unnatural*, and she began to scream as she turned and looked into Hester's eyes, lifeless flat eyes with something lurking behind them, something that slithered and settled, waiting patiently and—

—through Hester's mouth, it spoke:

"The child is mine, and through her I will bring about what is to be. Let . . . her . . . *alone!*"

Hester released Lizzie's head and Lizzie fell back in the gravel, limp as a stringless puppet.

The playground was suddenly as it had been an instant before.

Children were playing.

A gentle rain began to fall.

Lizzie Dayton wet her pants. . . .

From the Redding *Dispatch*, July 1972—

REDDING MAN STABS MOTHER
INSTEAD OF WIFE

Dispatch staff reporter

In an apparent attempt to murder his wife, Michael Lumley accidentally stabbed his mother yesterday, putting her in critical condition in Redding's Memorial Hospital.

According to Redding police officer Keith Muldoon, Lumley had been waiting for his wife, Hester, and handicapped son, Benjamin, to return from a drive, intending to kill them both. When Lumley's mother let herself into the darkened house, Lumley mistook her for Hester and stabbed her four times.

68-year-old Beverly Walton was walking her dog by the house when the stabbing occurred and, after hearing Dolores Lumley's scream, notified the police.

"Mr. Lumley's been hysterical since we got to him," Officer Muldoon said. "He's been screaming, over and over, 'I'm sorry Momma, I thought you were Hester, I meant to kill them, kill 'em both, I'm sorry Momma,' stuff like that."

Dolores Lumley is suffering from a punctured lung and kidney and, although critical, is in stable condition.

Michael Lumley is in Memorial's psychiatric ward, where he remains heavily sedated.

When asked if he knew why Lumley wanted to kill his wife and son, Muldoon said, "He kept saying they were evil, that they weren't human, something like that."

Hester Lumley was unavailable for comment.

ANDERSON, CALIFORNIA
JANUARY 17, 1993

The yellow glow of sodium lights bled through sheets of pouring rain, bathing the Peach Tree Motel parking lot in a glaring mist. The splash of the windblown raindrops rose two inches from the flooded pavement, creating the illusion of a ground fog.

Eight cars were parked in the lot, and light glowed through the closed curtains of three motel rooms. A holly wreath framed the number on each door and, in the window of the office, multicolored lights blinked on the branches of a small Christmas tree that stood crookedly on its stand, weary after the long holiday season. An empty white Pontiac idled in front of the office, its wipers sweeping futilely over the windshield.

Interstate 5 ran behind the motel and was busy with late-night travelers, but the road in front of it was deserted. Even the shopping center across the way seemed empty in spite of the bright twenty-four-hour Safeway.

The night seemed defeated by the storm, cowed by the beating rain. Distant lightning occasionally flashed in the western sky, as if on the look-out for some form of resistance, some hint of rebellion from its battle-weary captive.

The office door opened with a jangle of sleigh bells and Harvey Bolton rushed to his car, got inside and parked it in front of one of the darkened rooms. The curb was painted red with white stenciled letters that warned NO PARKING UNLOADING ONLY. Harvey backed the car under one of the sodium lights, then splashed across the lot, clutching a briefcase under his left arm. The wind whipped the hem of his coat madly around his legs and slicked his hair against his skull. By the time he got to his room, the shoulders of his tan overcoat were soaked through.

Inside, he groped for a light switch, flicked it, and light oozed through a gawdy gold-colored lampshade that hung by a chain from the ceiling. Beneath it was a round table with two chairs that matched neither one another nor the rest of the garage-sale furniture in the room.

It had been the only motel along the interstate with a vacancy, so he couldn't complain. Decor was the last thing on Harvey's mind, anyway.

His eyes had spent half their time on the rearview mirror all the way back from Grover. He suspected—he *hoped*—it was just a mild case of paranoia brought on by the distinct sense of un-welcome he'd felt while he was there, but there *had* been the van.

It was gray, no windows except in the front, and the glass was tinted so he wasn't able to see the driver or passenger, if any. Four times he'd noticed it parked across the street from him, or down the block. He was positive it was the same van. Every-where he looked, it seemed, there it stood, parked with the engine off. It might have been empty. But then again . . .

Whether or not his suspicions were valid, he was taking no chances. He knew he might very well have annoyed someone with his questions. The Universal Enlightened Alliance wasn't exactly the Rotary Club. It was a very big, very powerful or-ganization. So he'd kept an eye to the rear all the way, and had felt uncomfortable—no, *vulnerable* was the word—when he pulled over to a rest stop to remove the chains from his tires.

There had been no van in sight the whole trip, but even so, he was happy to be nestled securely in a motel room, however garish its decor might be.

Still . . . he couldn't shake that feeling of being observed.

He dropped the briefcase and his room key on the table and peeled off his coat, tossing it to the bed with a weary sigh. He quickly seated himself at the table, opened the case, took out a manila folder fat with papers and hunched over it, shuffling through the papers urgently.

The papers were covered with his hurried scribbling, notes written quickly during interviews with people who were reluc-tant to speak, perhaps even *afraid* to speak if Harvey's suspi-cions were correct. There were more papers stuffed in the glove compartment of his rented car, but the ones before him now were the most recent. These were filled with information gathered in the last twenty-four hours.

Harvey stopped scanning his notes long enough to remove a microcassette recorder from the case. He placed it in the center of the table and punched PLAY. Pinched, metallic voices began to speak through the tiny speaker as Harvey's eyes returned to his sloppy writing. They were the voices of the people he'd interviewed in Grover earlier that day and the day before, cautious voices speaking well-chosen words. . . .

A young woman standing behind her front screen door, a baby in her arms, another in her swollen belly: "I'd really rather not talk about it. Really. I've, um, got to take care of the kids." Then, quietly, she added, "They don't much like being talked about, you know."

A bartender with dark bushy eyebrows, leaning on his bar: "Some of my best customers belong to that woman's group. What I think about 'em ain't important. Now, pal, the first one's on the house if you'll turn off that damned recorder."

An enormous rosy-cheeked woman in a drugstore: "Does *she* know you're writing about them? That woman?"

That woman.

Her.

The leader.

Most of the people he talked to knew of her—all of them, in fact—but none of them spoke her name. A coincidence, perhaps, but it could mean something. Harvey wondered if the people of Grover were afraid of the Universal Enlightened Alliance or of the woman who'd founded and now led the organization.

Only two people appeared perfectly comfortable talking to Harvey about the Alliance. One was Joan Maher, a waitress in the Lemurian Diner. She smiled at his questions and said, "If you're looking for muck, I'm the wrong person to ask. I used to be a member. I'm not now, but I'm very happy. My life is better than it's ever been and a lot of the credit for that goes to the Alliance. What's your question?"

"Well, are they honest? Is it an . . . ethical organization?"

"Is it *ethical*?" She shook her head, took a deep breath and sighed, "You know, for *years*, televangelists have been falling right and left. Whoremongering, misuse of funds, hidden homosexuality, you name it. But nobody raises an eyebrow anymore, it's just another story on the news. Now, I admit that I no longer believe in a lot of the mumbo-jumbo that goes along with the Alliance, but they're good, sincere, well-meaning people who have done wonders for me, who have made me a better person. So if you're looking for a scandal, why don't you go investigate the Reverend Barry Hallway, huh?''

The other was Bill Coogan who ran a small gas station and convenience store in the middle of Grover, Coogan's Fuel Stop. He was congenial and willing to chat, but even he was a bit reluctant.

"Son, I don't understand the Universal Enlightened Alliance—" He spoke the three words as if he were repeating a rumor he didn't believe. "—and I don't really like 'em much. But my daughter's a member and she claims they've done okay by her, so I guess what I think don't matter a whole lot. But I'll tell you this: if I had my druthers, they'd have their headquarters someplace other than here."

"Why is that, Mr. Coogan?"

"Not really sure. Not really sure." He frowned slightly, pursed his lips and leaned forward on the counter, his weight on his elbows. "What, uh . . . what's your interest in the Alliance?"

"I'm writing an article about them. For *Trends* magazine?"

Coogan chuckled. "You say that like we don't read up here in the mountains." He turned to the small magazine rack behind him and said, "Proud to say I carry your magazine right here. Read it myself. Fine piece of work you folks do. Where you from?"

"Los Angeles."

"Mmm. Well, being a reader of your magazine myself, can't say I wouldn't mind seeing my name in it, but I'll tell you what. I don't really think the Universal Enlightened Alliance—" That subtle distaste in his voice again. "—deserves your attention, you ask me. Course, that's just my opinion, but I'll bet you a tank a gas most people in this town'll feel the same way."

Harvey silently agreed.

"So why don't you go on home and write about something else. Something that deserves looking into."

He'd looked at Harvey then with a smile on his lips, but a firmness in his eyes, a firmness that, Harvey thought, seemed to silently add, *For your own good.* He realized that might be nothing more than a projection of his hopes for a hot story, but still . . .

Water dripped from Harvey's soaked hair and plopped onto the paper before him. He swept his hair back with a flick of his hand then turned off the recorder. He stood and began pacing at the foot of the bed, massaging his stiff neck. Noticing how lumpy the mattress looked, Harvey felt a sudden urge to get back in the car, drive the remaining four hours to the San Francisco airport, and fly home that night, home to his big bed in Los Angeles and his new wife Josie.

As much as he'd hated to leave Josie only four months after their wedding, Harvey was in no position at *Trends* to turn down this assignment. Now that he realized he was onto something much bigger than he or anyone else at the magazine had thought, he was thrilled he'd come. His position would soon change. This was going to lead to things far better than working on fluffy pieces about celebrity out-of-the-body experiences and the latest eccentricity of this week's hottest rock star.

Harvey checked his watch. It was a few minutes after one in the morning. His editor, Tom Gleason, would not appreciate a phone call at such a late hour, but he called anyway.

"Yeah?" a woman croaked through the swirling hiss of long distance.

"Deb? Sorry to wake you. This is Harvey."

"Harvey, what's—is anything—"

"Nothing's wrong, I'm fine. I'm still up north. I need to talk to Tom."

There was a shuffling, some thick sleepy mumbles, then Tom Gleason said, "Harvey? Everything okay?"

"Better than okay, Tom. Fantastic. Fan-fucking-*tastic*!"

"Where are you?"

"Peach Tree Motel. Anderson."

"Anderson? But that's—why aren't you *back* yet?"

"That's why I'm calling. I need a couple more days. At least."

"Mmm. No can do, Harvey. You know that. The story is due on—"

"Run something else."

"What do you mean, run some—"

"What about the TV evangelist story you've been sitting on? The guy in Anaheim?"

"Old news. That's why I'm sitting on it. I need that story, Harvey."

"It's not the same story anymore."

"Not the—what?" Tom was fully awake now, speaking clearly.

"I mean, it's *not* the *same story*. I've learned some new stuff, *big* stuff. I think. There's more here than any of us thought, Tom, I'm sure of it. I need just a little more time."

A thoughtful silence, then: "You're sure, Harvey? I mean, this isn't just wishful thinking or—"

"*Yes*, I'm sure."

"What is it?"

"Well . . . I'm not sure of that yet. But I know it's *something*."

"Well, *that* won't do us any good. I mean, we can't just run some—"

"Then maybe, I could interest *Newsweek*," Harvey barked. "Or the *Times*. I'm not fucking around here, Tom. I've got my ass on the line. I may—" He chuckled suddenly, more with tension than humor. "—hell, I may have pissed some people off already. And if I'm not mistaken, and I don't think I am, they're *not* nice people."

"You're serious."

"Damned right, I'm serious!"

"We're not a news magazine, you know."

"But you're getting this *first*."

Harvey could hear the *click-click-click* of Tom tapping his front teeth with a thumbnail, something he always did when he was thinking fast.

Tom finally said, "Wait a sec while I change phones."

Harvey heard a hushed, "Hang it up for me, honey," then silence as he waited.

Wind pressed hungrily against the curtained windows and raindrops slapped the pavement outside.

"Harvey?" Tom said as his wife hung up the other extension. "Okay, *what* are we getting first? Talk to me."

"The Universal Enlightened Alliance."

"Yeah, that's what you're there for. So tell me something I don't know."

"Well, we all thought it was just another one of those New

Age money-grabbing scams preying on spiritually starved yuppies, right? Well, it's more than that.''

"So what is it?"

"I . . . well, like I said, I'm not sure." Before Tom could speak again, Harvey added, "But I know *something's* going on up there, Tom. Look, I Fed-Exed some stuff to you today, it should be in your office in the morning. Go over it and you'll see what I'm talking about."

"What'd you send me?"

"A couple of interviews, lots of notes, some ideas I've had."

"Ideas?"

"Like I said, I'm not sure what's going on yet, but I've been speculating. People up there in Grover are afraid of something, Tom. I talked to one family that's planning to move. Just up and *move* because of the Alliance. Some already *have*."

"C'mon, Harvey, there's always something weird going on up there. Little people living in Mount Shasta, flying saucers, Bigfoot."

"No, this isn't like that. They *talk* about those things, they're good for the tourist trade. This is different. They don't *want* to talk about this. They're afraid."

"So if they won't talk, why do you need more time? What're you going to do? Why don't you just come back and work with what you've got?"

"Uh-uh. Not yet. There's this woman. Name's Elizabeth Dayton. She lives in Wheatland. At least, she *used* to. She's kind of disappeared. I think she pissed them off. I'm trying to track her down, get her to talk to me."

"What makes her so special?"

"I found an old newspaper article that mentions her. I sent you a copy. I think she knows something."

"Like what?"

"I think she's got some dirt on—"

Three rapid clicks severed the connection and left Harvey with dead silence. He lowered the receiver and started to swear, when thunder exploded overhead and the room's lights flickered, then died.

"Son of a bitch," he groaned, replacing the receiver. He sat on the lumpy bed a moment, hoping the lights would come back on. In the meantime, he waited for his eyes to adjust to the new darkness.

Even the streetlights outside were gone. Harvey went to the window, tugged the curtain aside and looked across the street at the darkened Safeway; through the store's glass front, auxiliary lights shimmered like ghosts, made misty by the rain. He dropped the curtain as harsh sheet lightning cut through the darkness for an instant.

There was nothing to do but wait, maybe sleep, but he felt like doing neither. He felt like rum. Inside the suitcase he'd left in the car was a bottle he'd bought earlier that day; he needed some of it inside *him*, could almost taste it on his lips. There was also a small battery-powered reading light in that suitcase.

Harvey decided he'd sip his rum, read over his notes, and prepare himself for tomorrow. If he managed to find Elizabeth Dayton, he wanted to be ready to catch her off guard with some pointed questions, because he didn't expect her to be too anxious to talk.

Reluctant to face the weather, Harvey slipped into his wet overcoat and left his motel room. He took in a deep breath of cold damp air and let it out slowly as his shoes clapped on the wet blacktop.

The darkness was smothering. A trickle of light came from the motel office; beyond it, from Interstate 5, the lights of the passing cars cast an upward glow that came and went rapidly.

A police car drove slowly by the motel and pulled into the Safeway parking lot; a produce truck was parked at the side of the store, its lights glowing like bright orange pinpoints.

Harvey fumbled with his keys as he neared the Pontiac, stiffening against the cold breeze. When the trunk popped open, a small light came on inside and Harvey reached for his suitcase with one hand, his garment bag with the other, then—

—he heard a sound.

It was a door slamming. Sliding first, then slamming shut.

He let the garment bag drop back into the trunk and stood, setting the suitcase down beside him. He hadn't heard a car drive up. Just the door. And it sounded close.

But when he looked around, he saw nothing new in the parking lot. Of course, it was dark. . . .

Rainwater dribbled down his neck and chilled him.

Harvey turned to the car again, removed the garment bag and slammed the trunk, hitched the bag over his shoulder and carried the suitcase to the front of the car, where he put it down again. As he was unlocking the passenger door—

—something splashed.

As if something had been dropped in a puddle . . .

. . . or someone had *stepped* in a puddle.

Harvey opened the door, activating the dome light, and looked around again.

Yes, it certainly *was* dark. But it wasn't so dark that he wouldn't see someone standing near by or coming toward him.

The faint light from inside the Safeway didn't get far. Harvey could see it, but it bled over the sidewalk in front of the store and no farther.

The dome light in the car was no help.

And the rain was coming down harder, thickening the night.

But I'd see someone, he thought. *Yeah, sure, I'd see if someone was coming.*

Harvey tossed the garment bag over the front seat and leaned into the car, opening the glove compartment. As he reached for the manila folder inside, it slipped out and fell to the floor, spilling its papers.

"Shit."

Three of the papers fluttered by his legs and out the door, into the rain.

"Shit, shit, *shit*!" Harvey spat. He backed out of the car, turned, and squatted down to retrieve his notes and—

—found himself looking at two very large dark shoes.

First he saw the shoes, then caught the smell. Even in the damp gusty air, the smell was powerful.

Then Harvey was off the ground, lifted high. The darkness tilted around him, something slammed into his throat and he heard a crunch, then was thrown on top of the car, landing on his back and rolling down the rear window and over the trunk, falling to the pavement with his face in a puddle.

It was the cold water that kept him conscious; it was the footsteps slopping over the pavement—frighteningly heavy, stalking footsteps—that made him move.

Harvey crawled first, his feet kicking up water, palms scraping over pavement. He made two attempts to stand, nearly falling on his face, succeeded the third time, and realized he was running away from the motel, toward the supermarket.

The police car was there, parked beside the sidewalk, its parking lights on. Harvey couldn't tell if it was occupied, but he tried to scream anyway, tried to scream, *Police! Help! Police!* but—

—nothing came out.

Not a rasp, not even a breath.

It was broken.

His throat was broken, closed, useless.

And he couldn't breathe.

Clutching his tight chest with one hand and holding out the other arm for balance, Harvey began to make a wide turn to head back to his motel room and—

—he collided with a wall, bounced back, and fell to the ground, sitting upright, legs splayed.

Harvey tilted his head back slowly, looking up as the wall moved forward.

It wasn't a wall.

But it wasn't human; it couldn't *possibly* be human.

Can it? he thought. *God, no, Jesus, it can't be, no. . . .*

Crawling backward clumsily, his feet tangling in his coat, Harvey managed to make a slight, insect-like sound in his shattered throat before the beast bent down with massive arms outstretched, and mit-like hands—each with only three pipe-thick fingers—closed on his lapels, lifted him high in the air, where he remained suspended for a moment, floating, until—

—Harvey shot downward and hit the pavement with sparks behind his eyes.

He was deaf for a few seconds, unable to hear through the thunder in his skull, unable to distinguish the lightning in the sky from that in his eye sockets, and for a brief but blissful time, his entire body was numb. Then the pain rolled over him like a boulder, crashing through his daze and returning clarity to the night and Harvey saw—

—the monster bearing down on him, a falling building with one glaring, dribbling eye visible and two tree-trunk legs and before the thought to fight back had even crystallized in Harvey's mind, he swung a leg up and his foot connected with the creature's jaw.

The beast reared back, suddenly upright, but did not make a sound, didn't even release a startled gush of breath.

Harvey crawled backward again, his lungs beginning to burn

now despite his efforts to drag some air down his smashed throat and—

—it was coming again, moving fast, straddling him, reaching down, and—

—Harvey kicked again.

The crotch.

He felt the hulking body stiffen, then stagger back, and Harvey rolled and was on hands and knees, then on his feet, running in spite of the pain, molten pain *everywhere*, especially in his right arm because it was broken and flopped at his side, a useless tube of bone and tissue, but he ran anyway—swaggered, really—lurching from right to left as he tore at his collar, dragging hard for a breath, just one merciful breath, head craned back, mouth yawning desperately, but it wouldn't come, and—

—it was coming for him again, the leaden footsteps gaining momentum as they splashed through puddles and occasionally scraped the pavement, but—

—the motel-room door was growing as he drew nearer, smeared by the hot tears in his eyes and jostling back and forth as he stumbled and swayed, but there just the same, giving him hope, even taking his mind, for a moment, off the blazing flames in his lungs that threatened to burn their way through the crushed cartilage in his throat, and he reached out his left hand, aiming it for the doorknob as—

—the footsteps came relentlessly behind him, no other sound in the rain but his own movement and pain, and—

—Harvey's toe caught on the curb, plunging him onto the sidewalk, and a single mousey squeak pushed up through his throat when his chest hit the concrete, but his outstretched hand was touching the door, was only a couple of feet below the knob, and he crawled forward, leaning on the door, straining his arm, trembling fingers rigid, and he pushed once more with his knee until his hand closed on the doorknob, and then—

—something terrible happened.

It happened even before Harvey turned the knob, although he turned it anyway, but to no avail, because the door was locked.

The terrible thing was that, before he tried the door, Harvey closed his eyes for an instant and, in his mind, he saw it, his room key, exactly where he'd left it: on the table in the room, right beside his briefcase full of notes, right beside his micro-cassette recorder filled with quiet, nervous voices.

Harvey's left arm dropped, suddenly limp as if it, too, were broken.

The footsteps came.

Harvey rolled on the door, turning, as the mountainous figure bounded up on the sidewalk, splashing water in Harvey's face.

Well, Harvey thought with weak finality, wishing it could be a heroic thought, but unable to find any heroism in his fear, *they won't get everything. They won't get the notes in the room. That's what they want. But they won't get them.*

Lightning flashed on the beast's face and, if he had a voice, Harvey would have screamed. The smell enveloped him, clinging like honey, and a three-fingered hand pressed down over his face, closed on his skull, and lifted him like an empty cloth sack from the sidewalk. The fingers squeezed hard . . .

. . . harder . . .

. . . and Harvey thought, *I'm going to die, sweet savior Jesus, I'm gonna die!*

But he didn't. Not yet.

1:18 a.m./P.S.T.

Elizabeth Murphy was torn from her sleep by the sound of her own ragged scream. The bed jostled beneath her considerable weight as she jerked upright, her fists clutching the blankets, shoulders heaving with each desperate breath. She felt sweat trickle down her back beneath her nightgown; her hair clung to her moist forehead in wet strands. The bed sheet was damp.

After giving herself a couple minutes to catch her breath, she pulled the covers aside and got out of bed. As she slipped her robe on her muscles ached with a craving for a drink, a strong drink, something to put some distance between herself and that nightmare. She could even feel slight tremors in her hands, a familiar sensation. As she held her hands out before her, the trembling grew worse until her arms began to quake. She clenched her fists and held her arms stiff at her sides until the quaking stopped.

She'd experienced that before—that and worse—but only after drinking binges, only when she was trying to dry out; she'd gone without a drop for about three years now. She still had cravings at times, but only in times of stress. The nightmare she'd been having caused her *plenty* of stress, and the cravings were strong enough to make her imagine exactly which kitchen cupboard she used to keep her bottles of vodka in and on which shelf and how they'd been arranged. The cravings made her miss knowing that those bottles were in that cupboard whenever she wanted them.

In her small bathroom, she splashed cold water on her face and, when she closed her eyes, she saw that face, the face from her nightmare, so full of hatred and corruption that it hit her like a blast of heat from an opened furnace.

There was still some cooking sherry somewhere in the kitchen. . . .

She padded barefoot over the cold floor. There were several homeless people—at her request, the staff of the Freeway Chapel and Shelter referred to them as guests in an effort to help them retain some dignity—sleeping in the nightroom, but she didn't hear so much as a snore as she went into the kitchen, moving as quickly as possible, before her conscience could catch up with her.

Her hand trembled as she turned on a single light over the large grill, as she opened two cupboards before she found the one she wanted. But the sherry was gone and in its place was a warped, stained noted that read "I dumped it just in case. Bea." It was dated; the note was two and a half years old.

Her shoulders sagged as she released a heavy sigh and smiled with relief. She decided that when she saw Bea in the morning—Bea was one of the cooks and always made breakfast—she was going to give her a big hug.

"Thank you, Bea," she breathed. "And thank you, Lord."

Instead of having cooking sherry, she put a mug of water into the microwave and heated it up for tea.

When she'd stopped drinking, she'd decided to leave behind, once and for all, the frightened and confused little girl she'd been for far too long. She'd been Lizzie Dayton back then. Everyone still called her Lizzie, although she'd married and become a widow since, but when she'd decided she'd taken her last drink, she'd also decided she was going to be a new Lizzie, more dependent upon God and, therefore, stronger. For the most part, and only with the Lord's help, she had succeeded.

But, oh, that nightmare . . .

Lizzie had been having the nightmare for about a month now and each time it grew worse. It made her feel, once again, like that frightened little girl paralyzed with fear in that chamber of

horrors everyone else had called a playground. When she had
the nightmare, every year that had passed since that awful cloudy
day on the playground faded away as if it had never been, making that day seem immediate, making that hellish experience feel
only minutes old.

She returned to her bedroom with her tea and sat on the edge
of the bed. The face from her nightmare remained burned in her
mind, hateful, malignant and horribly familiar, stirring those
cravings for liquor, renewing those old fears. It was too vivid
and powerful to be just another nightmare. It left her with the
feeling that something was coming, something frightening and
important that would involve Lizzie and—

—something that would involve the deadly face from her
nightmare.

Hester Thorne.

Whatever it was, the nightmare made her feel it was coming
fast, that it was unstoppable and there was no way she could
step out of its path.

Lizzie's hands shook again and some tea slopped onto the
carpet. She felt the familiar tightness in her throat that only vodka
could relax. Vodka and something else.

She put the tea on her nightstand and knelt beside her bed.

"Dear Lord," she whispered, "trouble's coming. And I'm
afraid. I need your help."

ONE

THE UNIVERSAL ENLIGHTENED ALLIANCE

1.

Everything was going perfectly.

Jordan Cross sat in the back of a taxicab headed for the wharf wearing tortoiseshell glasses, a blond mustache and a straw fedora over his dyed hair, smiling like an idiot, nodding his head up and down, up and down, like one of those fuzzy sequin-eyed plastic dogs they sell in tacky souvenir shops.

He was sitting by the window behind the driver—a boney Vietnamese man who kept clicking his teeth together—and beside Jordan sat Wendy Frye.

Wendy was slightly plump—rather attractively so—with rosy cheeks beneath her big ocean-blue eyes. She wore a teal silk dress and giggled a lot behind tightly pressed lips, as if she were doing something naughty—which she was—and kept squeezing the arm of the man beside her to her pillowy breast.

The man beside her was T. C. Braddock, a man nearing fifty, on his way to being fat, with rusty hair and an immaculately trimmed beard. A big ring glimmered on his left pinky and a gold ID bracelet dangled from his right wrist. The worst thing about T. C. Braddock was his cigar; it was just one of those small ones, but it might just as well have been a long fat stogie because it smelled just as bad, so bad that the cracked window didn't help.

Jordan hated cigars.

But he just kept smiling and nodding and listening to Braddock's endless monologue until he came to a conclusion: the worst thing about T. C. Braddock was not his reeking cigar, but his inexhaustible mouth.

". . . so when my poppa finally passed on—and I don't care *what* the doctors said, it was from a broken heart 'cause he missed Momma so much—I took over the business. And I did it proudly. That's the problem with young people today, so ashamed of their mommas and poppas, ashamed to fill their shoes. But I knew, see, I *knew* how hard my poppa had worked to build that business, and I was *proud* to take it over. Nothing to be ashamed of, selling men's suits. 'Specially when they're suits of such high quality, know what I'm saying? Like I said before, this suit I'm wearing now? Took it right off the rack in my Daly City store." The Daly City store was where Wendy worked, where they'd met. "Proud to wear it. S'a fine suit." Braddock puffed.

Wendy giggled.

Jordan smiled and nodded.

" 'Course, things have changed a lot since poppa died," Braddock continued. "I've worked hard to make the business grow. Poppa'd be proud of me, I think." Puff, puff. "I don't think he and momma ever dreamed his little business would grow so big. We do a lot of television now, you know? Commercials, stuff like that. A lot in prime time. Mostly independent channels, you know? They wanted me to do my own commercials, but, you know, I like to keep a low profile." He nudged Wendy.

Wendy giggled.

Jordan produced a very convincing knowing chuckle as he glanced at the fat wedding band on Braddock's finger.

Braddock said, "You'll probably see our commercials, you watch any TV in your hotel room. What hotel you staying in?"

"The Hyatt."

"Good hotel, good hotel. I stayed in the Hyatt in Dallas last, what was it, October? I was there for the—" He suddenly leaned forward in the seat. "—oh, here, drop us here, boy."

The cab lurched to a stop and Jordan quickly got out, treating his lungs to a long drag of cool salty wharf air. He hitched the strap of his traveling bag up over his shoulder as the cab roared away, then he joined Braddock and Wendy on the crowded sidewalk.

The sunlight was beginning to fade and dusk cooled the July air. The steamy aroma of crab was quickly replaced by the strong odor of fish, then a gust of sea air, more crab. . . .

The smells were the best part of Fisherman's Wharf, the part Jordan liked. It was the tourists he hated, parading around with their balloons and their babies and kids and their overpriced packages from Ghiradelli Square and Pier 39, stopping to watch jugglers and clowns and caricature artists who drew the same picture over and over again. He'd asked to see the wharf because he knew they wouldn't mind going; there was little chance of seeing anyone they knew there.

"Bet you don't get a smell like *that* anywhere in Kansas, do you?" Braddock laughed, waving his cigar. "Where was it you said you're from?"

"Kansas City," Jordan said with the drawl he'd rehearsed to perfection. He'd told them he was on a business trip.

"My husband had a cousin used to live in K.C.," Wendy said. "He used to come visit every—"

"Well," Braddock interrupted, "we're very proud of our wharf here in San Francisco."

"Don't blame you." Jordan looked around and smiled.

"I promised dinner," Braddock said. "Hope you like seafood."

"Well, if you don't mind, Mr. Braddock, I'd like to look around a little."

"Oh, please, call me T.C., and hell, no, I don't mind. Be proud to show you around. I've lived here thirty years. This is my city!" He beckoned Jordan as he put his arm around Wendy and the three of them walked along Beach Street past the cable car turntable, then down Leavenworth to Jefferson, Jordan craning his neck this way and that, looking at everything as if it were his last day on earth, just like those tourists he hated so much.

They walked the streets, slowed by Jordan's meandering sightseer's pace. He kept a smile on his face as he browsed the tables of the street vendors. He watched a man with long graying hair wearing a Grateful Dead T-shirt bend a strand of copper wire into an eagle with moveable wings; he stopped as a trio of young

boys did a dance number on a corner; he let a street magician
with breathless patter outwit him with a card trick. All the while,
T.C. kept up a steady stream of trivia about the shops and restaurants they passed. They kept on like that for a while, maybe
fifteen minutes, as the evening grew darker and the lights came
up.

Then the moment came.

A little Hispanic boy stepped in front of T.C. and Wendy. He
had a camera and a big smile and said, with a heavy accent,
"Take your picture? You and the lady? Five dollars?"

"No, no," T.C. grumbled, gently pushing the boy aside.

"Hey, *that's* an idea," Jordan said, grinning with tourist enthusiasm. "How about a picture? I've got my camera—" He
started fishing it out of his bag. "—and if you don't mind, Mr.
Braddock, I'd like to be able to say I met you."

T.C. laughed modestly. "Well, I—"

"I mean, I know this is really a silly tourist thing to do, but,
if you don't mind . . ."

"Oh, sure," Wendy giggled. "Let him take a picture."

Jordan had the camera out—one of his Polaroids, because he
didn't want to waste time—and they crossed the street to a corner
that afforded a nice view of the lights of the piers, and Jordan
had them stand close together—"Just a little closer, if you don't—
yeah, that's good"—and snapped one picture, plucked it from
the camera, then another, and on the third, something happened
that made Jordan smile.

Wendy giggled, stood on tiptoe, and gave T.C. a big sloppy
kiss on the cheek.

"*Thank* you," Jordan said with a grin and five minutes later,
before T.C. could bring up dinner again, Jordan lost them.

At nine thirty the next morning, he was in his office, sans
glasses, mustache and hair dye, looking across his desk at Andya
Frye, a wiry thirty-two-year-old construction worker from Daly
City, who was examining the Polaroids.

"That little cunt," Frye whispered.

"It wouldn't have taken so long if they hadn't been so careful," Jordan said. "They were never together in a place where
it was possible to take pictures."

"That little cunt," Frye whispered.

"So I had to do a little fancy footwork. Followed them into

a bar and started up a conversation with Braddock. Said I was a small businessman from out of town, I'd seen him in *Business Monthly*, was an admirer of what he'd done with his business, Braddock Clothiers, and he took it from there. He couldn't resist. Wanted to show me around a little and, *voilà*."

"That little cunt," Frye whispered, then, glancing up, asked, "Was he? In *Business Monthly*?"

"Sure."

"You knew that?"

"Of course not. I had to find out. I do my homework before I leave my office, Mr. Frye."

"How'd you find out it was him? You hardly been on it for a week, how'd you find out it was him?" He didn't look up from the pictures this time.

"That's what you hired me to do. I found out. Took those. Satisfied?"

"That little cunt. Yeah. Yeah, this is fine. All I needed. Thanks." He sat at the desk and stared at the three pictures. "That little cunt."

"Well, if you don't mind, um, I've got some work to do, and . . ."

He shook his head as he stared. "That little cunt."

"Mr. Frye? Was there anything else you wanted me to—"

"Oh, no, no. Fine. That's . . . little cunt . . . that's fine."

They were always like this, the husbands, when they found out.

Jordan slid the bill across the desktop.

"That . . . little . . . cunt."

He put the bill on top of the pictures and Frye looked up, blinked a few times.

"Your bill."

"Oh, yeah, yeah." He glanced over the bill, got out his checkbook and scribbled as he muttered, ". . . cunt, that little . . ." He tore the check out violently, stabbed the pen back in the pocket of his blue chambray shirt, and stood, shaking his head and muttering.

Jordan stood, too. "If it's any consolation, Mr. Frye, I'm sorry. I've been there and I know how it feels. It hurts."

"You know what hurts?" Frye asked quietly, and chuckled, pocketing the pictures. "I'll *tell* you what hurts. What I'm gonna do to that goddamned son of a—"

Jordan was around the desk quickly, leading Frye to the door with a hand on his shoulder, saying, "That's not the right attitude, my friend."

"Whatta you mean? That son of a bitch's been fucking my wife. He's been—"

Jordan held up an index finger and raised his brows, silencing his client. "Remember. Your *wife* has been fucking *him*, too."

Some of the anger left Frye's face and he took out the pictures, looked at them again thoughtfully, his eyes darkening, not with anger, but with pain.

"Yeah," he said. "Yeah. Guess you're right." Then he left.

Lari Parker, Jordan's secretary, looked up from her small desk and watched Frye leave.

Jordan turned to her and said, "They always want to beat up the wrong person," then he turned to go back into his office, but Miss Parker stopped him.

"Um, there's a man named Fiske on the phone. Edmond Fiske?" She cocked a brow.

Jordan mused over the name a moment. It was a familiar name, an important one—even Miss Parker seemed to realize that—but he could not remember why. He said, "Okay," and went into his office and picked up the phone. "Jordan Cross."

"Mr. Cross, thank you for your time. My name is Edmond Fiske." He said it as if Jordan should recognize it, even paused, as if waiting for the recognition.

"Uh-huh. Your name sounds very familiar, Mr. Fiske, but I can't say that I know you. Should I?"

"Oh, no, not personally. Do you read *Trends* magazine?"

It clicked.

Edmond Fiske owned *Trends* magazine, which was on every grocery store checkout stand across the country, on the rack between *People* and *Us*. He also owned a nationwide cable network, one of those artsy channels that showed foreign films with subtitles and documentaries about old lesbian war correspondents and the invention of the bomb. But what kept him in the gossip columns was the very prestigious and astronomically expensive apartment building he owned in Manhattan; the residents moved in by invitation only and included some of the weightier names in society, politics and show business and being a weighty name in all of the above, Mr. Fiske himself lived in the penthouse.

"Mr. Fiske," Jordan said, "my apologies. Of course I know who you are. It just didn't occur to me that you would be—"

"Oh, nevermind, please." He had a deep voice that sounded young and healthy and pleasant. And important. "Look, the reason I've called you is this: I'm in L.A. right now, but I'm coming to San Francisco tomorrow and I'd like you to have lunch with me tomorrow afternoon."

Jordan waited a moment for the punch line. "I'm sorry?"

"I said, I'd like you to have lunch with me tomorrow afternoon."

He was tempted to tap the receiver on the desktop to knock the bugs out of the connection. "May, uh, may I ask why?"

"Of course. Because I want to hire you and I'd like to talk with you first. I sent a package to your office that should arrive today. I'd like you to look that over before we meet. Say, one o'clock? Stars?"

"Stars? The restaurant, you mean?"

"Yes. I'll be staying at the Mark Hopkins so, should anything come up, you can reach me there."

Jordan still didn't believe it, not for a second, but he spoke as if it happened every day. "Sure. One o'clock it is."

"Great. See you then." Edmond Fiske hung up.

Jordan sat behind his desk frowning for a few minutes, trying to remember the last time he saw the *real* Edmond Fiske on television and trying to decide if the voice on the phone bore any resemblance to the one on television and wondering why anyone would pull such a lame prank and if maybe it wasn't a prank at all. Finally, he got up and stepped outside his office.

"Miss Parker? Who just called?"

"An Edmond Fiske. Um, was that . . . *the* Edmond Fiske?"

He worked his jaw, thinking a moment, then looked at her as if she'd asked a stupid question.

"Yes. Of course it was. By the way, has a package—"

She held it up, a thin manila envelope. "It just came. It's from—" She looked at the envelope's label. "—Fiske Enterprises."

Taking it into his office, Jordan said, "Yes. Of course it is."

At his desk, he cut the envelope open and an issue of *People* magazine slid out. It was two weeks old and there was a small quickly scribbled note paper-clipped to the cover that read, MR. CROSS—PLEASE READ COVER STORY.

There was a picture of a woman on the cover. Pretty, blond, smiling, and probably forty or so, Jordan guessed, although she looked younger. He knew who she was, had seen her everywhere lately. But he couldn't imagine what interest Edmond Fiske could possibly have in Hester Thorne, or why that interest would require Jordan's services.

In bold white letters beside her face, the cover read, WHO (OR WHAT) DOES THIS WOMAN THINK SHE IS?

Jordan opened the magazine, skimmed the long article, then picked up the phone and placed a call.

"Ackroyd Security, may I help you?"

Lowering his voice: "Pete Lacey from the IRS calling Mr. Ackroyd."

A pause. "Just a moment, Mr. Lacey."

After a few moments of silence, someone picked up and hesitated before speaking.

"This is Marvin Ackroyd."

"How about lunch, Marv?"

"You son of a bitch. You son of a *bitch*."

"Hey, it got me through, didn't it? Your secretary hates me."

"*Your* secretary hates you. To what do I owe the steaming lump of shit I'm now sitting on?"

"Lunch?"

"Sure, I could use a bite. You paying?"

"Bring sandwiches."

"Aw, c'mon. I gotta look at your office again? Can't we meet somewhere?"

"I want to talk to you about something and I'd rather do it here."

"Couldn't you come to my off—yeah, yeah, I know, my secretary hates you. What kind of sandwich you want?"

"Surprise me."

Jordan read the article again, very slowly this time, including all the captions under the photographs. When he finished, he was frowning and Marvin still hadn't arrived, so while he waited, he opened his closet door and threw darts at his ex-wife.

2.

It was her day off.

Lauren Schroeder could not afford a day off, but the Message Line Answering Service refused to work its employees the eighteen hours seven days a week Lauren needed if she and Mark were ever going to get back on their feet.

But that was okay because on her two days off each week, Lauren was able to avoid thinking about how much money they needed and concentrate, instead, on Nathan, their five-year-old son.

After taking the job at the answering service more than nine months ago, Lauren had been able to spend far too little time with Nathan, and she was afraid it showed in his behavior. Of course, Lauren was fully aware of the fact that she was such a consummate worrier, she sometimes searched for things to worry about just to keep in shape. She knew it might very well be her imagination.

Nathan seemed quiet lately, that was all, and it worried her. He struck her as rather lethargic, too. At least, when he was with *her*. He was much livelier when Mark was around; something happened to him, he became more animated, more interested in things.

That was what *really* worried her: those things that so interested Nathan.

Then again, she kept thinking, it could be her imagination. Maybe the changes in Nathan had nothing to do with the fact that she could spend so little time with him.

God knew he had plenty of *other* reasons to be disturbed. . . .

"Mom?"

Lauren blinked her thoughts away and glanced at Nathan, tucked behind his seat belt in the passenger seat. "What, sweetie?"

"Can we go to Chuck E. Cheese?"

"But you just ate."

"I don't wanna eat. I just wanna play the games."

"No, honey. We can't."

He clicked his tongue and sighed. "Just to watch the Chuck E. Cheese show?"

Lauren wanted to roll her eyes and groan when she thought of the giant mechanical animals on stage at the pizza parlor, moving stiffly to loud, badly recorded music. She would be glad they couldn't afford to go there anymore if it weren't for the fact that Nathan always had so much fun. It always made him laugh, that loud mechanical stage show.

Maybe that was what bothered her so much; Nathan didn't laugh very often anymore.

"You can't just go in and watch the show, Nathe. They want you to buy something."

"Couldn't we just get a Coke?"

"Please don't do this, honey. I've told you we can't afford Chuck E. Cheese anymore. We can't afford *McDonald's* anymore. For a while, anyway. But when things get better—"

He interrupted quietly, sinking into the seat a little. "But when do things get better?"

That is the sixty-four billion *dollar question,* Lauren thought. "I don't know. When they get better, I guess."

He looked out his window, silent.

"But look at what we got to do today," she tried. "We went to the park this morning, ate brunch by the pond. We fed the ducks and the fish, too, didn't we? And that was all *free!* See, sometimes free things are just as much fun as *any*thing." *You just have to have the rug jerked out from under your feet to notice,* she thought.

Nathan said nothing, just folded his arms in his lap and stared out the window.

It was as if he just got up and walked out of his body. That's the way it always was lately. He didn't really look unhappy; he looked thoughtful, reflective, but as if his thoughts were unsettling.

"Want to listen to the radio?" she asked.

He shrugged.

She turned it on and found a station playing a Weird Al Yankovich song. Nathan liked Weird Al. But he didn't seem to notice.

He'd been fine in the park, laughing at the ducks, running with a dog—a little terrier that belonged to an old man sitting on a nearby bench—even finding amusement in the simple act of eating tunafish sandwiches and Dorritos on the grass.

And now he'd gone, just up and left, leaving his little four-limbed vehicle parked in the car seat.

Well, she was taking him to see Dr. Puccinelli tomorrow. Mark thought she was being paranoid—

—"He seems just *fine* to me," he'd said—

—but she wasn't going to take any chances. Maybe the doctor would have a few thoughts. If nothing else, Nathan always got a good laugh out of the man's name.

She looked at him again. He didn't even seem interested in the scenery. There wasn't much to see on Highway 17, but normally Nathan would *find* something.

"I'll make a deal with you," she said, and waited for him to look at her before going on. "If you promise, for the rest of this week, to be understanding when Mom or Dad says we can't afford something, we'll get a scoop of ice cream before we go home."

He smiled.

"Do you promise?"

"Promise. Cross my heart." He crossed it sincerely.

There was a Thrifty Drug on the way. They had the cheapest. She was ashamed to have to think that way; it would be nice to take Nathan to Swensen's or Baskin-Robbins, or even to see those damned mechanical animals.

But they—along with so many other things, nearly *everything*—had disappeared up her husband's nose. . . .

Unlike other people she'd heard about—and one person she actually knew—Lauren had not seen the symptoms first, she'd seen the *problem*. It had been, you might say, right there under her nose. But more importantly, it had been under Mark's nose—

—at five-forty one cold winter morning almost two years ago. She was awakened by the bathroom light. The door was only open a crack, but being a light sleeper, the single bar of light that fell across the bed was enough to jar her. First she looked at the clock and wondered why Mark was up twenty minutes early, then she listened. He was rattling around in there, doing something. He cleared his throat three or four times, exhaled slowly, then—

—the first long wet sniff.

Lauren rubbed her eyes and sat up just before the next one. There were three quick coughs, a few staccato sniffs, then a sigh, and Lauren thought of Lynda Petersen. Just for an instant.

"Mark?"

He dropped something.

"Mark?"

"Yeah?"

"What're you doing?"

Shuffles, rattles, and clanks, all with a certain ring of guilt to them.

"Just getting up."

"It's not time."

"Couldn't sleep."

Lauren got out of bed and went to the bathroom door, wide awake now. When she pushed it open, Mark was slipping his black leather shaving kit under the sink. He stood, sniffed, flicked a finger under his nose, and smiled.

"I've got an inspection at the plant today," he explained. "A little nervous, that's all."

"You were doing coke." She didn't say it accusingly or ad-monishingly; it was spoken more as an absurd realization, with a little chuckle behind it. It *was* absurd. The only time they did any drugs was at parties, and that was almost always marijuana. She could only remember a couple times they'd done cocaine; she hadn't liked it and Mark had seemed rather indifferent. And in the first year of their marriage, they'd agreed that, if they did indulge, it would only be when they were together, because they'd gone to a party that year, gone separately, Mark first and Lauren about two hours later because she had a baby shower to attend and, as it turned out, she'd arrived *three* hours later to find Mark stoned on weed and engaged in some serious flirting in the dark phone nook in the hallway, the kind of flirting you go someplace private to do, the kind of flirting that does *not* lead to a hand-shake and an invitation to do lunch sometime. She'd been furious at first, but then agreed that, when you're high, you sometimes do things you'd never do while straight, so they'd decided. They would only do it together.

"It's five-forty in the morning," she said, "and you're doing coke." She had a surprised smirk on her lips.

"Oh, c'mon, hon, just one line. Like I said, an inspection, you know? I've been nervous about this for weeks. Tony gave me the coke, just a little. When we had dinner with them last week, remember? It was just for this, just for today. So I could go to work, you know, feeling . . . confident. Believe me, Lauren, I need to feel confident today." He spoke fast, but sounded a little hurt, as if she'd falsely accused him of something.

"Okay, honey, okay, I just—" She chuckled tiredly and rubbed her eyes, going back to bed. "—I was just surprised, that's all."

"There's a little left in there," he said. "I mean, if you want to finish it off later. You go back to sleep. I'm gonna take a shower. You want me to fix breakfast?"

She shook her head, crawling back between the covers where it was warm and she could get a little more sleep.

A little more sleep, she'd thought bitterly many times since. *About eight months more.*

That's how long it had taken her to wake up.

Oh, she noticed things, little things, like the way Mark was always sniffing.

"You gotta cold, Dad?" Nathan asked at dinner one night.

"No. Just allergies, is all."

"Maybe you should see Dr. Puccinelli," Lauren said, thinking, once again, of Lynda Petersen.

"Nah, they're not that bad. Besides, he'd probably want to give me a shot, and you know how I feel about needles."

Maybe it's not needles you should be worried about, Lauren thought, but she didn't say it. Then she put her suspicion away, thinking perhaps he did have a mild allergy, even though she knew he'd never had so much as a cold since she'd known him, and if he didn't, if he was doing a little too much nose candy now and then, he was a big boy and could handle it. He was breaking their agreement, but that was no big deal. He was too busy at the plant to have *time* to do any more serious flirting. He barely had time to flirt with *her.* She didn't worry.

Then the first past-due notices came.

Lauren had always been clumsy with numbers so, when they got married, it was agreed that Mark would handle the finances. So when a past-due notice came now and then, she handed it to Mark and he slapped his forehead and muttered, "Shit, I completely forgot," and she would forget all about it. They were small ones at first, a phone bill or cable bill, so it was no big deal. Then they got bigger.

First, there was a threat to turn off the water if the bill was not paid promptly. Then a threat came from the electric company, which held to its word and turned off the power one week later.

"I told you about the power bill, Mark, how could you *forget* about the *power* bill?"

"I told you, I'm up to my ass in work this month, and I told you I would take care of it."

"You should've taken care of it a *week* ago! Now we've got flashlights and candles and no heat until they turn it back on!"

He sniffed and ran a hand through his hair and sniffed again, then said, quietly and with a tremble, "I'm sorry, okay? I mean, what do you want me to do, huh? I'm *sorry*. I promise it won't happen again."

He looked guilty, but sorry, too, so much like Nathan when he was sorry, and she apologized for shouting and wrapped her arms around him, and that was the first time she noticed that he was thinner. Much thinner. Mark was tall and had never been heavy, but he'd always been substantial, and he didn't feel that way anymore. He didn't look it, either. His chest was getting boney and his arms had thinned. His naturally narrow face looked even longer than usual and that tiny patch of skin that puffed a little when he pulled in his chin—gravity's first real hold on his face—was gone, leaving a sharp jawline and a sinewy neck.

She held him for a moment, her frown growing, then looked up at him and asked, "Honey . . . you okay?"

"Sure I'm okay," he sniffed.

"You're feeling all right? I mean . . . well, have you been doing co—"

"Oh, *listen* to you. It was a mistake, okay? Just a little mistake. Now. Get off my back." He went upstairs and didn't talk to her the rest of the night.

The following month, the cable was shut off.

"Do we really need it?" Mark asked. "I mean, by the time a movie comes on Showtime, we've already seen it on video, right? And we don't watch any of that other stuff, do we? Tell you the truth, I'd rather Nathan not be exposed to MTV. He's at a very impressionable age and I don't want him watching that crap."

Then a check bounced and Lauren found out they had only one hundred and twelve dollars in the bank.

"Remember when I had to go into San Francisco a couple

weeks ago and stayed the night because it was so late? Well, I had to pay for all of that, the hotel, the meals. I just haven't been reimbursed yet, that's all. But don't worry—'' Sniff, sniff. ''—I will be. Everything's fine, I promise.''

Lauren knew everything wasn't fine, she noticed he was sniffing more and eating less and getting thinner, and she knew what the problem was, but she didn't know what to do. In her sudden panic she was watchful, but silent. Just to be safe, she started working part-time at the answering service.

When she caught a strange man driving their BMW out of the garage one afternoon the following month, she ran out of the house screaming, first Mark's name—''Mark! What've you done, Mark, *damn* you, Mark, what've you *done*?''—then she shouted, ''Wait!'' running down the walk waving a dishtowel. ''Wait, what're you—who're you—*what the hell do you think you're doing?*''

''Taking the car, lady. You're four months late.''

''But we didn't get a notice! They didn't send us anything! Don't you understand, they didn't *tell* us!''

''I don't send the bills,'' he said through the window as he drove away, ''I just drive the cars.''

Suddenly Lauren was living in a movie of the week. This was the part where the wife realized it was up to her to do something about her husband's drug addiction/alcoholism/(fill in other appropriate popular social problem) and, if she didn't, her family would be destroyed. They usually broke for a commercial about this time.

But not Lauren. She just went into the house, called Mark at work, and screamed at him until her throat was raw. When he got home that night, they talked about it. They shouted, but they talked, too, and Mark, his eyes teary, just like in a movie of the week, agreed to get help.

''Gonna have to,'' he said quietly, one half of his mouth twitching, ''or we're gonna have to find someplace else to live.''

''Whuh . . . what?''

''I'm a little bit, um, behind on the house payments.''

''There've been no notices, not one, I haven't seen—''

''I've been driving home during lunch . . . while you're at work, and . . . and I've been going through the mail . . . taking all the bills.''

He cried then and apologized again and again.

Lauren's parents loaned them some money and a car.

They couldn't afford a drug clinic, so Mark went, instead, to a counselor who charged on a sliding scale.

Lauren was thankful for one thing: they did not end up like the Petersens. Almost, but not quite. Mark came out of it and so did she and they were trying hard now to get out of their financial hole. They still had their home—although that was the biggest burden of all—and they could still say they lived in Shady Hills Colony, even though they were flat broke. Things were going pretty well. Not as well as they might in a movie of the week, but certainly better than they'd gone for the Petersens.

Then Mark found another addiction, one that frightened Lauren even more because it was completely out of her realm of experience. She had no friends who'd faced this problem and knew of no counselors or clinics that treated it. *Donahue* hadn't even covered this one. She had no one to talk to about it and nothing to read. It was not something she could see or touch and it wasn't illegal.

Mark's second addiction was the Universal Enlightened Alliance.

By the time they got home, Nathan had finished his scoop of rocky road and was crunching on the soggy sugar cone.

Lauren had meant to go grocery shopping while they were out, but she'd forgotten to make out a list so, while she was thinking about it, she got a pen and notepad and began jotting down the things she knew they needed before going through the cupboards and refrigerator.

"Mom?"

"Hm?"

"Can I go out back and feed the 'coons?"

"Uh-uh."

"How come?"

"You know how come."

Nearly every day, a few raccoons wandered up from the ravine behind the house and loitered at the edge of the backyard, waiting for the scraps that Nathan used to throw them until Lauren had read an article about wild animal attacks and had learned how vicious raccoons could be. She made him stop.

"Awww. Oookay." He paused, chewing a bite of cone, then: "Mom?"

"Hm?"

"Are you and Dad gonna be yelling again tonight?"

She turned from the cupboard and looked at him, put her list down and reached out to touch him, reminding herself to smile. "No, honey, we're not. I promise."

"Cross your heart?"

She crossed her heart.

Lauren worked on her list and was inspecting the contents of the refrigerator when she realized she didn't have the slightest idea what to fix for dinner.

"What would you like to eat tonight, Nathe?"

"Chuck E. Cheese pizza!" he shouted with enthusiasm, nearly dropping his cone.

"You promised. . . ."

"Oh. Yeah." He calmed, became quiet. "Sorry."

"That's okay. How about spaghetti?"

"I don't care."

"Some chicken, maybe? Fried?"

"I don't care."

"Well," she sighed, frustrated, putting her hands on her hips and staring thoughtfully into the refrigerator. "Do me a favor?"

"What?"

"Call your dad at work? Before he leaves for lunch? I want to find out what he'd like for dinner."

Nathan brightened and said, "Yeah!" then blinked and said, "Thought we weren't s'posed to call Daddy at work."

Mark was a shift supervisor at Diego Nuclear Power Plant and a phone call was usually more bother than it was worth, so he'd asked her not to call unless it was absolutely necessary and asking what he wanted for dinner did not fall under the heading of "absolutely necessary." But she was feeling down; they'd had another big fight last night and, although they'd made up that morning before he left for work—he'd done it grudgingly, but that was okay, as long as it was done—she still felt edgy about it and wanted to make sure he was coming home in a good mood. After all, she *had* promised Nathan they wouldn't fight.

"Well, today," she said, "we make an exception."

" 'Kay!" He hurried into the living room.

"The number's on the pad beside the phone!" Lauren called. "Remember to dial slowly!"

"I 'member."

As she scribbled new items onto the list, Lauren listened to Nathan and smiled.

"Hi, is my dad—I mean, um, is Mr. Schroeder there? Mr. Mark Schroeder? . . . Oh. Yeah . . . Nathan . . . 'Kay. Thank you."

He came back into the kitchen chewing on the last piece of his cone.

"Gone to lunch already?" Lauren asked.

"Uh-uh."

"Oh." She turned to him, a little surprised. "Well, is he away from the phone, or something?"

"Kinda."

"Well, what did she *say*, Nathan?"

"The lady said Mr. Schroeder don't work there no more." He licked his fingertips. "Hasn't for 'bout three weeks."

Lauren dropped the pad and pen and stared at Nathan.

"You sure that's the right number, Mom? Huh? Mom?"

She was gone, running for the phone.

3.

"You didn't bring sandwiches."

"And you didn't redecorate—no, pardon me, decorate—you didn't *decorate* your office." Marvin Ackroyd took in the room and shook his squarish, balding head. "My favorite. Art Messo."

"So where are the sandwiches? I'm hungry."

"They're being delivered. I got held up by a phone call and didn't have time."

"Liar. You knew if they were delivered here, my secretary would pay for them."

Marvin's small eyes twinkled behind his tinted wire-rim glasses. "And probably with pleasure, knowing it's your money, because she—"

"—hates me, yeah, I know. Move aside a stack of something and sit down," Jordan said, waving at the chair Andy Frye had occupied less than an hour before.

Marvin bent his stubby frame and lowered it into the chair with some caution, gently tugging on the sleeves of his dark suit coat. "How can you live like this, Jordy? Don't your clients complain?"

"Number one, I don't live here. Number two, they don't complain nearly as much as they would if I spent time cleaning instead of giving them their money's worth. And number three—"

"There was no number three."

"—number *three*, I'm sick of hearing about my office, so let's have a *real* conversation for a change."

The office *was* a mess. When Jordan was doing some quick research, he tended to get careless. The office was cluttered with books and magazines and newspaper clippings, some scattered over the desk, floor and shelves, others stacked haphazardly in boxes waiting to be thrown out. But the research notes he milked from the books, magazines and clippings went immediately into his files—which were always kept in perfect order—so Jordan felt it all balanced out.

The small office was made even more claustrophobic by the clutter, but the rectangle of smoky mirrored tiles on the south wall helped a little. Unfortunately, the tiles only reflected the opposite wall, which was bare; the lower half was covered by two packed bookcases, but above that, the paint on the wall was peeling and chips of dull grey were gathering on top of the bookcase.

There was a window behind Jordan's desk that afforded a view of another window in a red brick building across a narrow alley. Jordan often thought that was for the better because the Tenderloin—although his office was located in its better half, a qualification that always got a chuckle whenever someone asked for directions—was not much to look at.

There were no pictures in Jordan's office. There were no family photographs on the walls, no framed portraits of a wife or children on his desk; he had none.

There was, however, a life-size cardboard standee tacked to the back of Jordan's closet door. It was a beautiful auburn-haired woman, naked, with a towel draped over the more private parts of her body; her eyes were closed, her lips slightly parted in a gentle smile, and she was holding a bar of soap to her cheek lovingly. Four darts were stuck in the woman's body; a fifth had missed and hit the soap.

The standee had been cut from a store display advertising a

brand-new hand soap called Sensua. The model was Teri Cole, Jordan's ex-wife.

"I see you've been sticking it to Teri again," Marvin said.

"My aim's getting better. See? I got her twice in the towel. All the really painful spots are under the towel."

"I saw her new commercial yesterday. The one for the stockings?"

"Yeah."

"Seems to be doing very well. Teri, I mean."

"That's not surprising."

"No. No, it's not. She's a very beautiful woman."

"No, that's not it. I thought I told you. She's the Antichrist. She sold her soul to the devil. Signed the contract in blood. Probably menstrual blood. God knows she's got no shortage of that." Jordan kicked the closet door shut and the darts all clunked to the floor on the other side. He leaned forward and tossed the *People* magazine across the desk at Marvin. "What do you know about her?"

"Very rich, for one thing," Marvin said immediately, adjusting his glasses as he looked at the woman on the cover.

"What else?"

"Well, what do you want to know?"

"Is there something between her and Edmond Fiske?"

"What're you, high? As rich and famous as Hester Thorne is, you know what kind of publicity that would be for a financial and social god like Fiske? I mean, can you see him bouncing around with the leader of some New Age religion, or cult, or . . . or whatever they call it?"

"The Universal Enlightened Alliance."

"Yeah. I mean, maybe I'm wrong, because if I knew as much about getting and staying as big as Fiske is, I sure as hell wouldn't be sitting here talking with *you*, but I've gotta tell you, I can't see, realistically, Fiske getting chummy with a woman who charges people twelve hundred bucks a pop to spend the weekend with her and her fifty-thousand-year-old—what is he, a king?"

"He was a king in one incarnation, a warrior in another. And a religious leader and a queen and—"

"A queen?"

"It's all in that article."

"So what's the deal here, you called me because you wanted

to know if Edmond Fiske is boinking this—here, here it is, a *channel*—if he's boinking this channel? That it?''

"Well, part of it.''

Marvin snorted good-naturedly. "Who am I, now, Liz Smith? You want me to give Fiske a call and ask him?'' He held an imaginary receiver to his ear. "Hey, Ed, buddy. What's the deal with you and this Thorne babe? You poking her, or what?''

"You don't have to. I'm having lunch with him tomorrow.''

"Shit and fall back in it.''

Marvin stared at Jordan for a while and Jordan nodded his head slowly.

"Get outta town,'' Marvin said.

Another slow nod. "He just called me about an hour ago. Said he wants to hire me.''

"You're serious?''

He nodded.

Through the closed door, they heard voices and paper bags being crumpled.

"Okay,'' Marvin said, "the sandwiches are here. We'll eat, we'll talk and . . . you're really serious?''

Another nod.

Miss Parker brought the sandwiches in and the office filled with the smell of spicy pastrami and pickles.

"Okay, Jordy. If this is no shit, *I'll* pay for the sandwiches.''

So Jordan told him about the phone call. . . .

Since he was a boy, it had been Jordan's ambition to be an actor. He'd never sold his parents on the idea. They were strict charismatic Christians—the kind who rolled on the floor and spoke in tongues—and the profession of acting fell under the condemned heading of "frivolous.'' They were so opposed to it, in fact, so anxious to discourage him from pursuing it, that they refused to attend any of his school plays, even the Christmas play in which he played Joseph.

Their absence cut him deeply. His pain was made even worse when, after each play, he came home and tried to relive it for them, share with them every delightful detail of the evening's show, only to be silenced or assigned some chore, as if his account of the evening's show would somehow contaminate the air like a germ. They'd seen only one of Jordan's performances and he'd had to sneak that one on them.

It was on the day his mother had discovered his stash of *Mad* magazines in his bedroom closet. She'd lectured him on the damage such reading would do to him, how it would prevent him from growing into a stable, serious-minded, God-fearing young man, at which point Jordan said, in a display of uncharacteristically brave defiance, that he didn't *want* to grow into that kind of young man and he didn't want to grow up fearing *anybody*.

"Oh," she said, her voice trembling with shock, "and what kind of young man *do* you want to be?"

"An actor."

She lost all color in her face and stared at him, horrified. When she recovered enough to rush through the house and find Jordan's father, she told him what Jordan had said and they decided to call Reverend Belcher.

The reverend's name was funny, but that was *all*. He was tall—enormously tall to Jordan—with a thick neck, broad shoulders, and hands that hung like anvils at the ends of his arms. His flat round face was riddled with deep pockmarks and his tiny eyes were set deep in two dark oval pits. The reverend's name made Jordan laugh, but the reverend himself terrified him.

When he arrived, Reverend Belcher talked quietly with Jordan's parents for a while, then came into the living room where Jordan waited on the sofa and lectured him on the evils of pursuing a career as worldly, as fraught with immorality and godlessness as acting.

As he listened to the towering preacher's gravelly voice, Jordan got an idea. It was a risky idea, but it tickled him inside. He considered it a while, tuning Reverend Belcher out, then decided to go through with it: his first acting performance in front of his parents.

Jordan dropped to the floor and began to roll around and convulse as he'd seen his parents do so many times. He shouted in tongues—actually, he just rattled off bits of old Little Richard songs and part of "The Name Game"—and he received his first standing ovation. His parents shot to their feet and began shouting praises.

Then Jordan stopped, got back on the sofa and smiled up at them, saying, "See? I'm a pretty good actor, don't you think?"

A major earthquake could not have been as powerful or frightening as the horrible silence that followed. Then Reverend Belcher leveled a thick finger at the spot between Jordan's eyes—it was like staring down the barrel of a shotgun—and said in a low voice that grew steadily into a terrifying roar, "Drop . . . to . . . your knees . . . and ask God . . . and Jesus . . . and all that's *holy* . . . to *save* your *blas*pheming *ass* . . . from the *fiery pits of hell* . . . into which it *so deserves TO BE THROWN*!"

And Jordan had done exactly as he was told, trembling as he prayed for forgiveness of his mockery. His parents had never mentioned it again; Jordan had resented them for allowing Reverend Belcher to terrify him, and for still refusing to acknowledge that he had a talent—a God-given talent—and not encouraging him to nurture it.

His parents had never failed to provide for him, but their attitude toward his passion for acting had never changed, and it had instilled in him a seemingly unshakable bitterness toward the beliefs of Christianity, which he considered arbitrary and dictatorial.

Prodded by the practical urgings of friends and family, Jordan went to college to major in business. But his schedule allowed him to take a few theater classes, which were sometimes bizarre; they never bored him and he learned a few things, but for the most part they simply weren't challenging enough. His favorites were the two makeup classes he took. He enjoyed, and became quite proficient at, transforming himself into different kinds of people.

He never quite finished college. Having nearly ruined his health by working constantly to pay his tuition and spending his nights with books, he decided to take a temporary break, work a while, and save some money. Although, for a while, he entertained fantasies of supporting himself by acting, he once again followed the advice of friends to do something more practical, something more secure and profitable.

So he went into real estate.

Back to school he went, but only for a short time and this time focusing on only one subject. Then he got a job at a small firm in Redwood City, Kiley-Jessup Realty. He tried hard to involve himself in his work and, for the most part, succeeded. But he still wanted to act, more than anything, and talked about it passionately whenever someone bent an ear.

One of those someones was Marvin Ackroyd, who also worked at Kiley-Jessup. Marvin was ten years his senior and not at all interested in acting, but was intrigued by Jordan's boyish enthusiasm for the profession.

"If you're so hot on acting, Jordy," Marvin said one day over burgers at Carl's, Jr., "what the hell're you doing in real estate?"

"Well, I've got to make a living. I figured I'd stick with this awhile, see how it goes, and maybe try out for a part now and then, you know. Lots of plays around here. In fact, San Francisco's sort of become a—"

"Listen to me," Marvin interrupted. "Just listen a sec, okay? There was this guy—an old guy—at Kiley-Jessup name of Arvy Barbour. He retired just before you came. We threw a little party for him, you know, so long, good luck, all that hot comedy. We pitched in together and bought him this tacky little plaque—even *I* thought it was tacky and *I* got no taste—and we gave it to him at this party. It came time for him to give a speech and he stood up and I remember exactly what he said, he said, 'All my life, I've wanted to paint. Anything. Houses, fences, pictures, anything. But after college, I realized I had to pay the rent, so I got into real estate because everyone told me it was profitable. So I've been in this business forty-five years, at this firm for twenty-three, and now, looking back over those years, I've realized something. I've realized that, while my children were growing up, while my wife was raising them, and later, while she was slowly wasting away, I had spent my life selling a bunch of houses. Now I am going to leave you sorry sons of bitches to go home to an empty house and my hands are too shaky to hold a brush. That, ladies and gentlemen, sucks. I hope those of you for whom it is not too late will not wait until your house is empty and your hands are too shaky to hold a brush. Now. Thank you for this lovely plaque. This plaque—' And then he held up that cheap little piece of junk and said, 'This plaque is what I've lived and worked for.' Then he left. Just left. And you could've heard a gnat sneeze, the place was so quiet, everybody just sitting there like they'd been hit over the head with a Buick. Because you know why? All us sorry sons of bitches knew he was right."

After a long pause, Jordan asked, "Why did you tell me that?"

"Because you needed to hear it. Real estate's one of those things, it's like waitressing, the kind of work nobody really wants to do, but they say they're just doing it until they can do what they really *want* to do, whatever that is. Except they never get around to it. They get all cozy in real estate and they stay with it until they've got nothing left in them.''

"Okay. Okay, so what do you want to do? What are *you* hot for, Marvin?''

"You really wanna know?''

"Sure.''

"Well . . . I like to sneak around.''

Jordan laughed. "You sure as hell can't do *that* for a living.''

"You wanna bet?''

They didn't bet, but if they had, Jordan would have lost. . . .

Eighteen months later, without the benefit of much formal training and no professional experience, Jordan got a part in a play.

It was small, but it was great. The play, set in a deceptively utopian future society, was about two men, one young, one old. In need of some extra money, the young man takes a job living with and caring for the old man, who is very rich and who is the product of a very different world. It didn't sound like much, but the development of their relationship—in which the old man tries to show the young man the truth about the decayed, corrupt, godless and falsely "enlightened" society in which he lived—moved gradually from contempt to a deep respect, was powerfully written. Jordan was certain he'd been chosen for the part of the young man.

He was wrong. He played the *old* man, and he played it well. The play was a critical success, and Jordan was singled out, but despite good reviews, it closed after only a few weeks. But Jordan learned something.

He learned that he never wanted to step foot on a stage again. He'd hated each and every tense, sweaty, tedious second of it.

But he didn't feel any differently about acting itself; it was just the work involved in being part of a play that he'd hated. He enjoyed—even loved—the acting itself, the process of remaking himself into someone else—a stooped, trembling old man—and fooling the audience into believing him. It was like putting on a magic show, performing sleight of hand, but instead of using cards and cups and balls, he used his behavior, his speech, and his body. It was that which he loved and wanted to do, but didn't know how to do it without getting on stage.

That was when Marvin did something that, had they made their bet, would have made him the winner.

"You're doing *what*?" Jordan asked him one day nearly a year after his experience on stage.

"Quitting," Marvin said, emptying his desk drawers into a cardboard box. "*Adios, au revoir*, goodnight."

"But, you can't just . . . you mean you're just . . . quitting?"

"Just quitting."

"Why?"

"Because I'm too *good* at this shit. It's too easy. Before I know it, my hands'll be too shaky to hold a brush."

"So what're you going to do?"

"What I've always wanted to do. I'm gonna sneak around."

"For a *living*?"

"For a living." He got the last of his things out of his office, then slapped Jordan's shoulder and said, "We'll be in touch. I'm gonna be pretty busy for a while, getting things set up, but I'll—"

"Getting *what* set up?"

"Well, if I told you, I wouldn't be sneaky, would I? Take care, Jordy."

Six weeks later, Jordan was offered a better job at a bigger real estate firm on Van Ness and took it.

Jordan's father had died suddenly of a heart attack when Jordan was in high school, but his mother's end was lonely and gradual and he made frequent trips from San Francisco to Redding to spend time with her until her death of kidney failure.

Shortly after starting his new job, Jordan met and fell flat on his face for Teri Cole. She was an aspiring model, tall, shapely, silky and exactly the kind of woman Jordan knew did not fall for guys like him.

Jordan had never had much luck with the opposite sex, for which he blamed the strict religious upbringing that had given him a sort of nagging fear of all things real and imagined, a cowardliness, a painful shyness that lent him the appearance of a puppy with its tail tucked between its legs. And, just as a cowed pup is more likely to be kicked than an aggressive one, Jordan had been the target for a lot of pain in his relations with women from high school onward. He'd worked hard to overcome his insecurity and thought that perhaps he'd succeeded enough to attract and have a healthy relationship with Teri Cole.

He put his all into the pursuit, approaching it the same way he might approach a performance.

They were married eight months later.

They were divorced three shaky years later—years in which he'd never felt truly loved by his wife, years filled with suspicions and more fears—after he came home early from a daylong business trip to find her in bed with a male photographer and another female model.

After his divorce he buried himself in his work and spent much of his spare time going to plays—alone. He envied the actors their opportunity to act, but did not envy what he knew they had to endure to do it.

He grew restless, sometimes wondering if he was living in the wrong city, if perhaps he should move to Los Angeles and take a shot at movies and television or to New York to try the stage. Ultimately, such thoughts led to the same conclusion: he would stay where he was and keep doing what he was doing. Maybe his life wasn't a thrill a minute and maybe he wasn't completely happy, but he was getting by and doing fine, and who was ever completely happy anyway.

Nearly four years after quitting Kiley-Jessup, Marvin showed up in Jordan's office, looking dapper in a dark suit and tie, his old horn-rims replaced with tinted wire-rim glasses.

"Marvin, *look* at you. You're not even Italian. What do I call you now, the Weasel? The Icepick, maybe? How about Guido?"

"You got lunch soon?"

"Just leaving."

"Come with me."

Minutes later, they were getting out of a cab.

"The Tenderloin?" Jordan asked. "What are we here for, a hit? We gonna rough somebody up a little?"

"Don't be a smartass. In here."

He led Jordan to the top floor of a dimly lighted grey three-story building and to a door with a small sign on it that read:

ACKROYD INVESTIGATIONS

"You sneak around!" Jordan exclaimed with genuine surprise.

"That's right. C'mon in, I'll order lunch."

The office was small and a little dingy, but neat and tidy.

"Do you actually have clients?" Jordan asked over pizza.

"Hell, yes. I do some process serving, too. No secretary yet, but I've been interviewing. Look at this." He handed Jordan a catalog of security and surveillance equipment.

"You can actually buy this stuff? I mean . . . *anybody* can?"

"Sure. Look at here." He opened the bottom drawer of his desk and removed a long thin black tube with a microphone shaped like a sausage on the end. "Directional mike." Cracking the window behind him, he aimed the microphone at two elderly women on the sidewalk across the street, then handed Jordan a small earphone plugged into the base of the tube.

"Oh, no, no," one of the women was saying, her voice insect-like in Jordan's ear, "*she* didn't have diabetes, she had *glaucoma*. Was Mrs. *Gasper* had the diabetes . . . fat old sow . . ."

"Amazing. Do you use it a lot?"

"Well . . . I haven't yet. But I will."

"Amazing. *All* of this stuff." He thumbed through the catalog some more.

"Big business, too. I know the guy runs this mail-order place—" He gestured toward the catalog. "—right here in San Francisco. Name's Jim Raley." He took the magazine from Jordan and browsed slowly, a small fascinated smile on his lips. "Such toys . . ."

Jordan took a big bite of pizza and said, "So, what's happening? How's business?"

"S'okay. Business is . . . okay."

"You don't sound too enthusiastic."

"Well . . ." He shrugged, thumbed the pages. "Look at this. A little thinger that goes on your phone and disguises your voice when you talk. That something?"

"Amazing. So what's wrong? I thought this was what you wanted to do."

"That makes it all the worse. See, it's like you and your play. You found out you didn't like all the stuff you gotta do in a play—except for the acting—but even so, you were *great*, you really were. Now, me, I find out I don't much like all the stuff involved in *this*. I don't think I'm even any *good* at it." He slapped the magazine down on his desk.

"Well, you must've sunk a lot of money into—how did you afford this?"

"My dad died."

"Oh. I'm sorry. You should've—"

Marvin waved a hand. "Hardly knew him."

"Oh. Well, I am sorry."

Smiling suddenly, Marvin lifted his hands and said, "Oh, well, I got what I wanted and maybe it won't work out. Maybe it will. We'll see. Maybe I'll do something else.'' He picked up the catalog again. . . .

They didn't see each other for four months after that.

One day, Marvin called him at his office.

"Hey, Jordy, I've got a problem you can help me with."

"Need a house?"

"No, no. I need an old man."

"Come again?"

"Actually, what I need is an operative."

"A what?"

"Let me talk, okay? I've got this client, see, an old lady in her eighties, one Elizabeth Carmichael. Name sound familiar?"

"Vaguely."

"It should. She owns a chain of restaurants that stretch from coast to coast, plus she's got her shriveled little fingers in just about everything else you can imagine. I've only talked to her once, but that was enough to know she's a nasty old broad, real mean-spirited. The rest of the time I deal with her lawyer—a fellow named Tomkey—because she's bedridden. And rich, needless to say. She's filthy rich. Aside from her restaurants and who knows what else, she's got a bundle of money stashed in her house. A *lot* of money. You know, stuffed in mattresses, that kinda thing. Tomkey's been trying to convince her to invest it, put it someplace safe, but apparently she wants it close to her, like maybe she's planning to take it with her. Anyway, one day she gets the idea her husband's taking her money a little at a time. You know, just whittling it away. So she had Tomkey call me."

"Why didn't she just call the police?"

"Who knows. Anyway, Tomkey doesn't sound too thrilled with the situation, because, like I said, he's been trying to get her to put the money away. But she doesn't *want* to put it away. She wants to catch her husband red-handed. Tomkey didn't come right out and say it, but I think she's gonna go so far as to press charges, really let the old man have it. Vindictive biddy. So . . . that's where we come in."

"We? What *we*?"

"He's old, this guy, eighty-seven, but he gets around, really active for his age, hangs out with a bunch of old guys just like himself. They spend all day walking around, sitting on park benches, feeding pigeons, having a beer here or there. At least, as far as I can tell.''

"You followed them?"

" 'Course. But the problem is, I can't get at him. I mean, I can't just walk up and say, 'Hiya, I'd like to have a word with you about your old lady's money.' I don't exactly fit in with his little crowd, you know, so . . . that's why I need you.''

"You want *me* to go up and say, 'Hiya, I'd like to have a word—'.''

"No, no. Remember your play a couple years back? You were so damned good, Jordy, you really were. I mean, if I didn't know you, I'd have *sworn* you were really an old man, *really*. And I just thought, since you were so good—''

"No.''

"—but wait, if you'll just listen, I'll—''

"Uh-uh.''

"—just gimme a second to—''

"Marv, I can't do that. In front of an audience it's one thing, but just one guy, or a few guys? In a park, for crying out loud? Or on the street? Trying to pass myself off as an old man? Come *on*.''

"There's no stage. No director. Nobody else to fuck up their lines. No long rehearsals or hot lights. If I remember correctly, you didn't much like all that.''

Jordan mulled that over for a moment.

"Think about it,'' Marvin went on, "you did what you thought you wanted to do—acted in a play—and hated it, but you still want to act. So maybe this is a way you can have the best of both worlds, you know? Acting for a private audience, your own boss, none of the other bullshit. And like I said, I'm not so good at this myself. I could use some help. I've got a couple operatives here and there, I use them once in a while. But none of them can do what you can. Maybe . . . maybe you could just, you know, give it a try?''

Jordan thought.

"It would be a big help to me. Even if it was just this once.''

Jordan thought some more then said, "Okay. Sure. Why not? I'll give it a try.''

First, he spent the next morning with Marvin, trailing Mr. Carmichael and four of his cronies. When they reached Golden Gate Park, Jordan asked, "Is that the bench they always sit on?"

"Same one every time."

"They stay here long?"

"A few hours, the rest of the afternoon far as I can tell. I haven't stuck with them all day."

Then he gave a shopping list to Marvin, who returned the next day with the two bags of makeup supplies necessary to transform Jordan into an old man.

Jordan was up at dawn the following morning, and within three hours, he was eighty years old. He put on the green pants, yellow shirt and brown sweater Marvin had bought at the Salvation Army, all baggy and faded; he used the cane he'd kept from the play as a souvenir, and spent an hour hobbling around his living room, getting into it, until he was ready.

He waited for them on the bench in Golden Gate Park, first feeling nervous and foolish, then more and more confident, until—

—they came.

And it worked.

The old men—there were five of them—were like little boys. They acted giddy, as if the simple act of sitting on a park bench was no less fun than going to a carnival. They accepted Jordan as one of their own and invited him to spend the rest of the day with them.

"Oh?" Jordan said. "What're your plans?"

"Sit here awhile," Mr. Carmichael said, "go have a beer at the pub, maybe a coffee at the diner, then—" He grinned like a mischievous child. "—off to the tracks."

"Tracks?"

"Racetracks. *Horses*." Mr. Carmichael's small round face brightened when he said those two words. His eyes opened wide and sparkled as if he had just uttered two magic words that could wipe away any problem known to man. Then he chuckled behind a gnarled, liver-spotted hand.

It was contagious; Jordan almost laughed with him. "Ah. I see. Well, no, I, uh . . . I'm on a pretty small pension, y'know, and I—"

"Don't worry about it." Carmichael nudged him with an elbow. "I got an allowance."

They did have a beer, and then coffee, and each of them had a slice of banana cream pie, talking about the horses all the while, about sports and a little politics.

And Carmichael picked up the tab.

They took a cab to the track—all of them talking at once as they piled in, like schoolchildren boarding a bus—Carmichael paid the fare, and when they were outside the gates at Bay Meadows, the others gathered around him expectantly, and Jordan followed suit. Carmichael handed each of them a twenty-dollar bill.

"Good luck, boys," he laughed.

"That's some allowance," Jordan said.

Carmichael waved a hand and said, "Enjoy."

When he left them, Jordan was frowning through his makeup. Suddenly he did not feel right about what he was doing. They were such kind old fellows, so innocent. They had been so good to Jordan, so eager for him to join them in their harmless fun. How could he tell Marvin what he'd learned? Marvin would then pass the information on to Mrs. Carmichael who, from the sound of it, would then try to press charges—and probably press hard, from what Marvin had said—against her husband. Against that round-faced little fellow who probably had more fun on his jaunts with his buddies than he'd had during his entire marriage.

Then again, Marvin was his best friend and had asked him to do this for him. Jordan would have to lie to get out of it. He frowned all the way to Marvin's office.

Still in makeup, Jordan caught Marvin preparing to leave his office that evening. "You were right, Marv," he said.

"Look at you, you're great, Jordy, *great*! You look—whatta you mean, I'm right?"

"You *aren't* any good at this. You didn't stick with them long enough."

"Huh?"

"They go to the track. Every day, late afternoon, they go blow their money—excuse me, Mrs. Carmichael's money—on the horses."

"No shit?"

"No shit."

The phone rang and Marvin held up an index finger for Jordan to wait a moment as he took the call. He listened for a moment, then grinned and said, "Mr. Tomkey, you're just the man I wanted to talk to. One of my operatives has just come back from—"

Jordan began waving his arms and silently mouthing, *No, no, no.* He made a cutting motion across his throat with a finger and shook his head frantically.

"Uh . . . could you hold on just a moment, Mr. Tomkey? Thanks." Marvin pressed a palm over the mouthpiece and whispered, "What in the *hell* is wrong with you?"

"Don't tell him anything yet," Jordan said.

"Why?"

"Well . . . I got to thinking on my way here . . . think about it, Marvin, who's the old guy hurting? Not his wife. She can't get out of bed, what's *she* gonna do with the money? He's not even using that much. I mean, what's a few beers, some coffee and a little fun at the track, huh? It makes him so happy. And *he* doesn't have long to go, either, but at least he's healthy enough to enjoy it. And besides, they're *married*, for crying out loud, so isn't this money his just as much as hers? What's the crime here? I figured . . . well, I was just thinking that . . . oh, I don't know what I was thinking."

Marvin stared at him a moment, then said softly, "Jordy, it's not my job to decide what is or isn't best for my clients. My job's just to do whatever they ask me to do."

"Yeah," Jordan said with a shrug, "yeah, I know. I was, um, out of line, I guess."

Marvin thought for a long moment before taking his hand from the mouthpiece. "Mr. Tomkey? Sorry about that. Uh, as I was saying . . ." He rubbed the back of his neck, frowning. ". . . uh, one of my operatives just returned from observing Mr. Carmichael's activities. As you know, I've been on this for a while now, and . . ." He glanced up at Jordan. "I have to tell you I think Mrs. Carmichael is wasting her money. I'm not turning up a single thing."

Jordan leaned his back against the wall and smiled. It wasn't long after that he decided to say goodbye to the real-estate business. Before his hands got too shaky.

Marvin read the *People* article about Hester Thorne, grunting occasionally, shaking his head, as Jordan sat silently behind the desk.

The desk, as well as the office, used to be Marvin's when he started Ackroyd investigations. After Jordan had worked under him for three years—the amount of time required before he could obtain his license as a private investigator—Jordan took over.

Marvin now owned Ackroyd Security and Surveillance, the mail-order business once owned by Jim Raley. "Such toys," he often said to his clients with a whimsical smile.

Jordan waited patiently. They had always discussed each case before taking on a client in the past; they still did, even though they worked in separate businesses.

"So," Marvin said, closing the magazine. "What's the deal?"

"Hell if I know. He wants me to bring the magazine when I have lunch with him tomorrow."

"Edmond Fiske. Son of a bitch. Where you going?"

"Stars."

"I take it you're buying."

"Smartass. Any ideas?"

"Yeah. A good one. Listen to him closely. Nod your head a lot and look very professional. And order the most expensive thing on the menu. He can afford it."

4.

Lauren punched in the plant's number three times before her trembling fingers hit all the right buttons, then she waited through the rings, each of which seemed to last an eternity.

She'd decided to call on the bedroom phone so Nathan wouldn't see how upset she was. She could hear him downstairs, talking to the raccoons outside the window.

"Diego Nuc—"

"Betty?"

"No, this is Jan. Betty no longer works here. Can I help you?"

"Oh, thank God," Lauren sighed, thinking, *Betty quit, that's all, of course, Mark said she was quitting weeks and weeks ago,* that's *what Nathan heard, that's all, a misunderstanding.* "Could I speak to Mark Schroeder, please? This is his wife calling."

"Uuhh, I'm very sorry, Mrs. Schroeder, but . . . well, surely you . . . surely you know your husband doesn't work here anymore, either."

Silence.

"Maybe . . . maybe I should transfer you to Mr.—"

"Wait, just *wait* a second." Lauren clawed her right temple with her nails, closing her eyes tightly. "This . . . can't . . . be.

I mean, it just *can't*. My husband left for work this *morning*, he leaves for work *every* morning, he's—"

"Let me transfer you to Mr.—"

"You transfer me to my goddamned *husband*, Jan, transfer me right *now*!"

There was an icy pause, then: "Please hold."

Lauren's hands began to quake as she waited and her lower lip was hurting because she was chewing it.

Suddenly: "Lauren?" It was a man, but not Mark.

"Who's this?"

"Travis Bissel. 'Member me?"

All she could remember was a beer belly being carried around on pencil legs at the last plant function she'd attended with Mark.

"Yes, yes," she said quietly, impatiently, striving for control, "of course I do, Travis, but I really need to talk to Mark right now, really."

He chuckled and said, "Is he supposed to be here today? He said he might drop by to—"

"Where is my husband?" she shouted, pounding a fist on the bed, then immediately said, "I'm sorry, Travis, really, I am, but that woman I talked to just said, she said—" She coughed up a sob, surprising herself. "—she said that Mark doesn't work there anymore. That . . . that's not true, is it? He left for work this morning, so please, Travis, please tell me that isn't true."

"Oh. Oh, boy, Lauren, you mean . . . you mean you don't know yet?"

"Don't know what?"

"Well, God, Lauren, I can't believe he didn't—why wouldn't he—you mean he didn't tell you?"

Her voice was hoarse when she whispered, "Was he . . . fired, Travis? Laid off? Are th-they . . . closing the plant down again?"

"No. He quit."

The plastic crackled in her hands as she twisted the receiver.

"Three weeks ago," Travis went on, "maybe a little more. He let us know way in advance."

"Whuh-why . . . would he . . . quit?"

"He said you were moving. Up north somewhere. Near Mount Shasta?"

Ice water coursed through her and her mouth became dry. "Mo . . . moving," she muttered.

"You *are*, aren't you? Moving, I mean?"

"Oh, God," Lauren breathed, covering her eyes with a clammy palm. "Oh, my God, what's happening?"

"Laur-uh, Mrs. Schroeder? You all right?" Travis's voice was suddenly somber and respectful.

"No, Travis, no, I'm . . . I'm not all . . . all right."

Lauren hung up gently, her knuckles white as she held onto the receiver and stared at the telephone until a tremor rolled through her body, so powerful that she hugged herself to stop it but couldn't and she tipped over on the bed, shaking and sobbing, until the tremor passed.

What has he been doing? she thought, staring at the ceiling. *Where has he been going every day? And why would he say we were moving? Up there? To that place? With that* woman? *That awful woman . . .*

After a few slow deep breaths, Lauren struggled to sit up and called Glenda Carey, her best friend and Nathan's baby-sitter.

"What's wrong?" Glenda asked immediately after hearing Lauren's voice. Her three sons played loudly in the background.

"We have to talk, Glenda, right now, we have to get together and talk, please."

"Calm down, sweetie. What's wrong?"

"Can I see you?"

"Well, I was just taking the boys out for lunch. You want to meet us?"

"Where?"

"Chuck E. Cheese."

Lauren laughed; it was a giggle at first, then became a genuine belly laugh that hit so hard it scared her.

"Lauren, what's the matter with you?"

Between her laughs, Lauren said to herself, shaking her head, "Fuck . . . the money. Fuck . . . him and his . . . money. *Fuck* him." She fought to kill the laughter, then said, "I'll see you there in about an hour," and hung up to wipe away her tears.

She washed her face and brushed her hair before going back downstairs to Nathan.

He was kneeling at the coffee table thumbing through a book.

"I've got a surprise, Nathe," she said with forced cheer.

"What?"

"We're going to—" She saw the book he was reading and the

others stacked beneath it. "Where did you get those?" she asked, no longer cheerful.

"They were right here."

Lauren's teeth crunched in her skull as she ground them together, moving forward quickly and plucking the book away from Nathan.

"But-but, *Mom*, it's just the magic crystal book, that's all, it's not—"

"I've told you not to read them, I've *told* you! Haven't I?" She pulled at the hardcover book until the dusk jacket peeled off and slapped to the coffee table with that woman's face smiling up at Lauren from the torn cover, then she began ripping the pages out, clumps of them at a time, wadding them in her fist and tossing them aside, growling, "And I've told *him*, that son of a *bitch*, I've *told* him not to leave this *trash*, this *shit*, lying around the *house*, *damn* him!" When all the pages were scattered over the floor and the strip of glue on the spine flapped uselessly from the front cover, Lauren lifted it high with both hands and slammed it down hard on her knee, cracking it in half. She bent down to grab the next one, planning to do the same to each of them, books about crystals and channeling and the all-knowing entity that spoke through that awful woman, that crazy bitch, that money-hungry *monster*, but then—

—she saw Nathan.

He was huddled on the floor, his back against the sofa, hands locked over his chest, eyes so big and scared, lips quivering.

Lauren forgot the books instantly and dropped to her knees, taking Nathan in her arms and whispering, "I'm sorry, honey, I'm so sorry, really. It's not you. You didn't do anything. I'm just . . . just a little upset, that's all."

"Are you and Daddy gonna fight?"

She cried against his small shoulder. "Probably, honey."

"But . . . you promised. You crossed your heart."

"I know, and I'm sorry. I shouldn't have, because I didn't know."

His tense body relaxed in her arms.

She wiped her tears, then leaned back and smiled at him. "How would you like to go meet Glenda and the boys at Chuck E. Cheese?"

"Can we?" he gasped, eyes brightening.

"You bet. Let's go."

She had to stop at the bank for some money first and left the car running while she hurried to the automatic teller. She slipped her card into the slot, punched in her code, and waited for the screen to clear so she could hit the proper buttons to make a withdrawal.

But it didn't clear.

The small screen blinked, then flashed five glowing amber words:

**ACCOUNT CLOSED
PLEASE REMOVE CARD**

Her card slid out of the slot and the machine beeped as it waited for her to do as she was told.

Lauren stared at the screen.

Her face was reflected in the screen and a few strands of her blond hair were blown over her eyes by a soft breeze.

She removed the card, slipped it back in, and punched in her code number.

The same thing happened. But her card did not come back out.

"No," she whispered, punching buttons frantically, then said it again—"No no no no"—as she slammed the bank door open and hurried to the closest free teller. She slapped her palm on the counter and said firmly, "There's something wrong with the machine. It says the account is closed, and it wouldn't give my card back."

The woman—a petite Asian smartly dressed in red and black—smiled condescendingly as she said, "Well, we'll just see about that, won't we? Your account number?"

Lauren gave her the number impatiently.

"One moment." She disappeared behind a divider beyond the window and returned seconds later. "I'm sorry, but this account *has* been closed. Would you like to open a new one?"

Lauren gaped at her. "That . . . can't . . . be. What about savings? We have a savings account here, we've got—"

"Your name is Schroeder?"

Lauren nodded, jaw slack.

"I'm sorry, Mrs. Schroeder, but you no longer have an account here. If you'd like, I can—"

Lauren spun around and jogged out of the bank, crying before she reached the door, and when she got in the car, she pounded both fists on the steering wheel, sobbing. When she finally calmed, Nathan spoke in a whisper.

"Whasmatter, Mom?"

She tried to respond, but words would not form in her mouth. She backed the car out of the parking slot and her tires squealed as she sped away from the bank, heading for Chuck E. Cheese.

The cocaine had been bad enough.

Aside from the fact that it shook them as a family, Mark's abuse of the drug had endangered the plant, and for a while, once word got out, they held their breath waiting to see if he would lose his job. Fortunately, everyone at the plant was understanding; not only was Mark able to keep his job, he was offered as much time off as he would need to get himself straightened out.

So he took two weeks off and saw Dr. Helen Burbage in San Jose five days a week. Lauren attended half the sessions with him at Dr. Burbage's request. She was a soft-spoken woman in her late forties, tall and rather thick, but strangely graceful. She told them that later she would want to see Nathan, but for the moment she would work with them, specifically with Mark.

Dr. Burbage instilled in Lauren a calm she had not felt in many months and as they neared the end of their work with her, Lauren was confident that things were different for good, that they would go on and not look back.

Then, a few months after they finished seeing the doctor, Lauren and Mark attended the plant's Christmas party, and her confidence was stolen from her.

They mingled at the party, but stayed close together and touched one another often, drinking only mineral water because they were afraid to even sip anything stronger. Lauren was talking to one of the wives about Christmas dinner plans when a small balding man with thick glasses approached Mark. His name was Arnold Grossman; he worked in public relations and bore a striking resemblance to the late Wally Cox. He timidly proffered a colorfully wrapped gift the size of a paperback book and said, "This is for you, Mark."

"Oh. Well. I didn't think we were exchanging presents. If I'd known, I would've—"

"No, no, it's not like that. We weren't supposed to bring gifts, but I want you to have this. Really. Take it."

Mark took it.

"Open it later. At home. And when you open it, please, watch it."

"Watch it?"

"It's a videotape. And you may be skeptical at first. But please, as a favor to me—and to your*self*—please watch it."

"Sure, Arnold okay. I will. And thank you."

"I know exactly what you're going through. I went through it, too, and . . . well, maybe this will help you as much as it did me."

When they got home, Lauren was tired and went straight upstairs to change her clothes. When she realized Mark had not followed her, she went back downstairs to find him kneeling in front of the television watching an attractive blond woman standing on a stage; the woman wore what appeared to be a pair of white silk pajamas with dolman sleeves and large stones glittered on her fingers and around her neck. She held a microphone and moved energetically from one end of the stage to the other.

"I know that none of this will sound right to most of you," the woman was saying, "and you're probably going to be skeptical at first, but that's okay. The fact that you're here is a good sign. It means you're searching for something your life is lacking right now, something to fill that empty spot. And I am going to give it to you."

"Mark?"

He didn't respond.

"Mark?"

The woman went on: "Most of you here tonight were probably raised in a Christian home. Or perhaps a Jewish home. You might be Buddhist or Hindu or atheist or Seventh-day Adventist or Scientologist or any one of a thousand different beliefs, but whatever you are, I guarantee you that what I'm about to share with you is going to sound completely . . . entirely . . . *absolutely* . . . wrong. And I guarantee you something else. It's *not*. And if you don't agree with me when you leave here tonight, go home and think about it awhile, and you'll change your mind."

"Are you coming to bed, Mark?"

His head jerked around and he blurted, "Huh?"

"Are you coming to bed?"

"Uh . . . yeah, sure, yeah, just a—I want to—yeah, I'll be there in a minute." He turned back to the television again.

Lauren stood at the foot of the stairs, watching the woman on the screen.

"What I'm going to share with you tonight," she continued, "is a truth that has been kept from you until now. *The* truth. And it will go against everything you've been taught, no matter what religion or faith you come from, because, quite frankly, everything you've been taught is wrong, and if that offends you, I'm sorry. It's the truth."

"One of those," Lauren murmured as she went to the kitchen for a glass of milk, then back through the living room, headed for bed.

The woman was still talking, louder now, more animated.

"—supreme arrogance in teaching you that Jesus Christ was God's one and *only* son. Yes, I know, the Bible says that God gave His 'only begotten Son,' but tonight, we're going to look at that—and many other things—from a completely different angle, and I promise that you will see the lie—and that's exactly what it is, sweet souls, a *lie*—that has been passed down from generation to generation to generation and will *continue* to be promulgated from now until this planet's final dying gasp unless we *stop* it, and learning *how* to stop it is the *truth* that can finally *fill* that emptiness in your life."

"Why are you watching this?" Lauren asked.

Mark jerked around again, as if startled. He shrugged and said, "Well, I promised Arnold I would. I'll be up in a minute, honey." Then back to the television.

Lauren went to bed and fell asleep almost immediately.

When the alarm went off the next morning, she sat up and found herself alone in bed. She put on her robe and went downstairs.

Mark was still in front of the television, sitting Indian-style on the floor and scribbling in the notebook that lay open on his lap. He had not changed his clothes and the videotape was still playing.

The woman was sitting on a cushion on the stage now, sitting exactly as Mark was, her eyes wide and her voice now deep and curled by an odd accent.

"—to worship one true god is a lie. There is no one true god. There is one Godbody, as it is, but the Godbody is made up of many parts and each part is equally important as the next. *You*, my dear seeking souls, are those parts. *Each* of you is a god, each being one part in a greater whole, as it is and forever shall be. Embrace your Godness, children. Live it, nourish it, and share that Godness—share that *one true God* that you are—with the souls around you. . . ."

As she spoke in her strange voice, the woman moved her arms in jerky motions, up, down, out at her sides, as if she were performing some odd stationary dance.

Lauren said, "What are you doing, Mark?"

Mark was so startled that he shot to his feet and the notebook flopped to the floor. He glanced at Lauren, then his eyes darted around the room, coming back to her again. A smile tried to break through, fluttering the ends of his mouth rapidly, like batwings, and he said, "Lauren, you scared me. I thought you went to bed."

"I just got *up*. It's six o'clock."

"Really? Jeez, I guess—" He chuckled. "—I sort of lost track of time."

"Have you been watching that thing all night?"

"Oh, that. Yeah."

"Why?"

"Well . . . it's interesting."

Lauren crossed the room and picked up the notebook. "You've been taking notes?"

"Well . . . it's *interesting*."

"I can't believe it," Lauren whispered, staring at the screen. "You stayed up all night watching this *shit*? Over and over?"

He looked hurt. "It's not shit. Do you think I'd stay up all night watching it if I thought it was shit?"

"Well, it looks like shit to me."

"Maybe it wouldn't if you watched it."

"How many times does she ask for money? Is there a toll-free number?"

"She doesn't ask for any money."

"Well, I wonder how much the people in the audience had to pay."

"It was a free seminar."

She shook her head and went to the kitchen to make coffee.

Mark showered and dressed and went straight to work without waiting for breakfast.

When she got home from work that afternoon, Lauren watched some of the tape and tried—she honestly *tried*—to make some sense out of what the woman had to say, but could not. It was all parapsychological out-of-the-body pseudo-metaphysical double talk, the kind of thing that went over big in Marin County and certain parts of Los Angeles, but not with Lauren Schroeder. She had been raised in a home that clung to no spiritual or religious beliefs; her father had been chairman of the science department at Stanford and had always taught her that if she couldn't see it and it couldn't be proven beyond a doubt, then it wasn't worth her time.

On the back of the videotape was a picture of the woman with a short paragraph below it. "Hester Thorne, founder of the Universal Enlightened Alliance, lives in Grover, California, where all are welcome to come visit or live in unity and harmony to discover and celebrate their individual Godness at the foot of majestic Mount Shasta."

When she looked for Mark's notes, she shouldn't find them. He'd taken them to work with him.

The subject did not come up at dinner that night, and Lauren hoped it never would again; she hoped that Mark's interest in the tape had been fleeting, the result of a tiring evening talking to too many people about things in which he had no interest.

She was wrong.

Later that week, she found another videotape in the bedroom. It had that woman on the box, Hester Thorne, but was a different tape entirely. It was titled, *Messages from Orrin: Finding the Light*.

"Where did you get this?" she asked Mark when he came upstairs.

"Arnold."

"Why?"

"Because he offered to loan it to me and I wanted to see it."

"That's what I mean. Why would you want to see it?"

He sighed and thought about his answer before he spoke. "Because I think she has something to say that I need to hear."

Lauren wanted to say, *What could she possibly say that* anyone *would need to hear? Surely you don't take any of that malarky* seriously! *Surely you're more intelligent than* that! But she didn't because she didn't want to sound like a nag.

Then he began to bring home the books. He didn't talk about

them, but she saw them, saw him reading them. Each of them was written by Hester Thorne and each had the symbol of the Universal Enlightened Alliance in the top right corner of the cover: a silver sphere impaled on a golden crescent moon in the center of an oval crystal.

Mark was behaving differently, too. He seemed preoccupied, distant, and talked little at the dinner table, which was not like him at all.

Worried, Lauren called Dr. Burbage.

"I wouldn't worry if I were you, Lauren," the doctor said soothingly. "In fact, what Mark is going through right now is quite natural. He has just recovered from a very serious addiction, an addiction that took up a very big space in his life. Now it's gone. That leaves a very big *empty* space, and Mark is looking for something to fill it. Now, I'm not advocating any of these New Age philosophies, but neither do I scoff at them. If it works, don't fix it. What videotapes has he been watching, anyway?"

"Some woman named Thorne, Hester Thorne. Um, The Universal, um—"

"Universal Enlightened Alliance, yes. You mean you haven't heard of it? It's become quite popular since Sheila Bennet has become involved."

"The actress?"

"Mm-hm. She's brought it into the public eye and it's taken off. Maybe Hester Thorne's philosophy has something that appeals to Mark. Maybe if you found out what that is, you'd understand it and wouldn't worry so much."

But Lauren didn't understand it and she certainly had no desire to waste her time trying to figure it out. Dr. Burbage said there was a very good chance Mark's interest in the Alliance would pass, so she decided to wait for that to happen.

It never did. In fact, it got worse.

The books Mark continued to bring home were filled with colorful pictures and illustrations that caught Nathan's eye. He began to page through them carefully, reverently, asking Mark endless questions about them, all of which Mark answered gladly. Nathan was especially fascinated by what he called the "magic crystals" pictured in the book and by the idea that a man who had lived and died countless centuries ago could speak through a woman who was alive today.

Lauren had nothing against Nathan indulging in entertaining

fantasies; she read to him nightly and his favorites were the Oz books and the *Chronicles of Narnia*. She was happy to know that Nathan had an active and healthy imagination and she wanted to keep it alive. But she made sure he knew the difference between fantasy and reality and didn't confuse the two.

Mark, it was beginning to seem, did *not* know the difference and he was passing his confusion to their son.

"Mark, I don't like it."

"Why not? It's not hurting him, or anything, there's nothing—"

"Look. If you want to believe in this . . . this . . . *stuff*, that's your business. You haven't pestered me with it, and I appreciate that, Mark, I really do. But Nathan is very impressionable and you're his *father*. He'll believe anything you tell him."

"Why shouldn't he believe it?"

"Because it's—" She started to say *bullshit*, but decided that was too harsh. "Because he shouldn't. You know that, Mark. He's just too young."

Mark shook his head slowly. "You know, when I was growing up, my parents thought the same thing. They were confirmed atheists and they stood between me and anything . . . spiritual. They didn't want me exposed to or polluted by any of the things they thought were bullshit. So I grew up without it, all of it, church, Sunday school, prayer, all that stuff. The other kids around me, though, they had something . . . *special*. They went to church on Sundays and they said their prayers at night and at Christmas they celebrated the birth of Christ. I felt I was missing something. I've *always* felt that way. And now I've found this, the Alliance, and . . . it works for me. It all fits up here—" He tapped his temple. "—I wish I could make you understand that. Nathan asks me questions about it and I'm not going to tell him to go away, you want me to do that? He wants to know. I'm going to tell him."

"But he doesn't understand it, Mark. He takes it all so seriously, the magic crystals and the channeling and—"

"*I* take it seriously."

Without choosing her words, Lauren snapped at him: *"Then you've got a problem, Mark, and I don't want you to give it to Nathan!"*

It turned into a shouting match that lasted late into the night, and Mark would not speak to her the next morning, a Friday.

So, naturally, she was surprised when he called her that evening, sounding cheerful, and told her to pack a few things because they were going away for the weekend.

She thought it was odd, but hoped it was just a way for Mark to apologize indirectly, maybe even a good sign, a sign he was trying to close the small gap that had been caused by his new-found spirituality.

She packed a few things, Mark came home a couple hours early, and they drove north. Mark would not tell her where they were going, saying he wanted it to be a surprise, but the farther north they drove, the less surprised Lauren thought she would be when they arrived.

Ninety minutes after sunset, they passed a sign that red GROVER—33 MI., and Lauren could barely get the question out.

"Mark? Are we . . . by any chance . . . going to Grover?"

He grinned. "You guessed!"

Nathan leaned forward in the backseat and exclaimed, "That's where the magic crystals are!"

"That's right, Nathe."

"No," Lauren said quietly. "We're not going there."

"But I already made reser—"

"We are *not* going *there*, Mark."

"I made reservations at a beautiful hotel. And it's inexpensive, too. It's gorgeous up there, you'll see. Just wait till we get there."

She said no more, for Nathan's sake, but her stomach was in knots and she decided that if Mark tried to push the Alliance on her for a whole weekend, she and Nathan would take a bus home.

The hotel was located on the north side of Grover, a small, quaint mountain town scattered with patches of snow left over from winter. Mark drove through a white wrought-iron gate and down a narrow road that curved through a dark sanctuary of pines. Lauren saw glimpses of light between the branches and tree trunks. The light grew and grew until they rounded the final curve, and—

—Lauren gasped.

The hotel was bathed in light, a massive Gothic building with turrets and spires; it formed a *U* surrounded by sheets of bright green grass and a forest of fragrant pines. Behind the hotel stood Mount Shasta, still draped in white; when viewed from the proper angle, the mountain resembled a robust woman lying on her back, knees hugged to her chest, hence the hotel's name: Sleeping Woman Inn.

But that was not what made Lauren gasp.

In front of the hotel at the center of the U-shaped drive stood an enormous sculpture. It was an oval crystal, ten, maybe twelve feet tall, and inside it glimmered a flawless silver sphere impaled on a golden crescent moon. Words were carved into the well-lighted granite base:

THE UNIVERSAL ENLIGHTENED ALLIANCE WELCOMES YOU

With fear trembling her voice, Lauren whispered, "They own the hotel."

"Isn't it beautiful?" Mark asked, smiling, as he slowed the car to a stop in front of the entrance. "Okay, Nathe, let's go. We're here."

"Yaaaay!" Nathan shouted, excited, scrambling out of the car.

Their bags were carried inside by a man in a grey uniform, smiling, silver-haired, and pleasant.

But Lauren didn't care how pleasant he was. She hated him because he was a part of what she saw as a sort of conspiracy against her, against all she believed in, and most importantly, against the way she wanted to raise Nathan, who was foremost in her mind. She was afraid he would be tainted by their visit there, and she intended to get him out.

They went to their room, which was beautiful—

—"I thought you said this was *inexpensive*," Lauren grumbled as they unpacked—

—then Mark said, "Anybody hungry?"

They were *all* hungry, and Mark led them downstairs. Lauren thought they were going to a restaurant, but no . . .

They went, instead, into an expansive ballroom where there were tables of food, and—

—tables of crystals and tables of literature and tables of videotapes.

A convention, Lauren thought, *this is a fucking convention!*

When she was a little girl, Lauren's brother, Carl, was a science-fiction fanatic and dragged her to a science-fiction convention once. It was crowded with fat smelly people who clogged the hotel elevators and crowded around dealers' tables selling plastic ray guns and *Star Trek* insignias and back issues of *Famous Monsters of Filmland* magazines. Some of them were just kids, but many were older, in their twenties and up, and most of *those*, Lauren was willing to bet, still lived with their parents, didn't have jobs or ambitions or even enough drive to get off their asses and *bathe*. They probably spent all their time stuffing their faces while they devoured science-fiction magazines and books, comic books and watched reruns of old sci-fi television shows as if they were documentaries. They had torn down the wall that separated fantasy and reality and turned their backs on the latter.

She suddenly had the same feeling as she walked into the ballroom of the Sleeping Woman Hotel, and she wanted to leave more than ever, but desperate to keep peace in her family, she vowed to give it a little more time.

The ballroom was crowded with people who seemed to take all of this seriously—which made it even worse for Lauren—who stood around eating cold cuts from paper plates and talking about discovering their Godness and healing themselves of serious physical ailments. She stayed close to Mark and held tightly to Nathan's hand as they stood in line for food and she resisted the temptation to shout at Mark for leading them to believe they were taking a weekend vacation when they were really attending a gathering of genetically defective people who thought so little of themselves that they felt the need to turn to a system of belief that was nothing more than a elaborate and expensive fantasy contrived by a woman who was tired of spending her days washing dishes and slicing vegetables.

As they walked away from the buffet table, Mark stopped suddenly and Lauren sensed his tension. She looked up to meet the eyes of a tall blond woman who smiled first at Mark, then Lauren, then Mark again

"Welcome," the woman said, holding out her hand.

Mark took it, shook gently, smiling stupidly like a schoolboy with a stomach-churning crush on his teacher.

"I'm Hester Thorne," the woman said.

"Yes," Mark replied nervously. "I know. It's . . . a pleasure, um, to meet you."

Lauren stiffened.

"Where are you from?" the woman asked.

"We're from Los Gatos. Near San Jose?"

"Ah, yes, the Silicon Valley. Do you work with computers?"

"No. I work at the Diego Nuclear Power Plant."

Her eyes brightened. "Really? How interesting."

"Um . . . Mark, my name is Mark Schroeder and this is my wife Lauren. And my son Nathan."

"You're the lady in the magic crystal books," Nathan said, awestruck.

The woman laughed and hugged him to her.

Lauren's blood chilled and she gently pulled her son away from the woman.

"It's a pleasure to meet all of you. Thank you for coming." She turned to Mark. "I'd like to talk to you for a while before you leave. I'm very interested in your work. It's such an *important* part of our time."

Then she walked away.

If that had been all, Lauren might have done nothing, might have stuck it out like a trooper, telling herself she was just indulging her husband's hobby, as she'd indulged her brother's as a child. But when she looked at Mark, she saw him staring after the woman, saw his eyes glinting with awe and admiration and—

—*No, no*, she thought hopefully, *you're just imagining it, just pushing your anger onto him*—

—was that *affection* in his eyes? Was that the way he used to stare at *her*, at *Lauren*, before they were married?

She began to tremble and leaned toward him to whisper, "Will you excuse me for a second?"

"Sure, honey," he said, his eyes never leaving the woman's back as she disappeared into the crowd.

She hurried to the room, called a cab, packed her things and Nathan's, leaving Mark's, and carried them down to the lobby, dropping them at the desk. She returned to the ballroom to find Mark deeply involved in a conversation about Orrin with one of the other visitors, took Nathan's hand and whispered, "Honey, Nathe has to go to the bathroom."

"Yeah, okay," he said impatiently.

Nathan looked up at her and said, "No, I don't, Mom, I'm—"

She quickly dragged him away.

The cab took them to the tiny bus station in Grover where she bought two tickets to Los Gatos, charging them to her MasterCard, and they waited until the bus came to take them away. When Nathan protested, she hushed him firmly.

When they got home at nearly four in the morning, she put Nathan to bed and did not answer the phone when it rang.

Mark returned the next day.

They had been fighting ever since.

"I'm telling you," Glenda said as she ushered her sons into her car in the parking lot of Chuck E. Cheese, "dump him. He's a goner."

"Look, Glenda," Lauren said, ignoring the advice, "I swear I'll pay you back for the pizza. I'm going to—"

"Will you forget about the damned pizza. What, you think it's gonna break me? Listen, why don't I take Nathan for the night. You're going to bring him over in the morning anyway, and I don't imagine things are going to be great when Mark comes home tonight. *If* he comes home."

"That's okay, Glenda. Really. I'd rather . . . well, it may sound stupid, but I'd rather have him close tonight. But thanks. And thanks for listening."

"Anytime. See you in the morning, huh?"

"Yeah."

On the way home, Nathan asked hesitantly, "Mom? What'd Glenda mean when she told you to dump Daddy?"

Lauren started crying again; she couldn't help it. "Nothing, honey. She just . . . we were just talking. That's all. That's all."

She could tell he didn't believe her; he stared silently out the window all the way home, looking troubled, worried.

When they got home, the phone was ringing and Lauren picked it up quickly, snapping, "Hello?"

"Hi, hon. It's me."

She said nothing.

"Just wanted to tell you not to hold dinner for me. I'm gonna be late."

It took courage to speak. "Late from what?" she whispered.

He chuckled. "From *work*."

She started quietly, but her voice rose to a scream as she pressed the receiver hard to her ear. "From work? From *work*? What's going on, Mark? Will you tell me that? *What the hell have you done, you son of a bitch?*"

There was a long crackling silence over the line, then he hung up.

Lauren put Nathan to bed early, spending more time than

usual at his bedside. She was scared. For herself. For Nathan. But not for Mark. She realized, as she huddled beside Nathan's bed, watching him doze off, that she no longer felt anything for Mark but contempt.

At least tonight, she thought. Mark had a way of changing the way she felt.

She drank an entire bottle of wine by herself that night, waiting on the sofa for Mark to come home. By two in the morning, she could stay awake no longer and trudged upstairs, undressed, and fell asleep immediately, drained by the alcohol.

Lauren awoke thirty minutes before the alarm went off the next morning. She looked around the room blinking, still dazed from the amount of wine she'd had, unused to its effect. She checked Mark's side of the bed; it was cold and untouched.

Immediately depressed, Lauren went to the bathroom, washed her face with cold water, then headed out of the bedroom to wake Nathan, stopping in the doorway. She backed up.

The closet was open.

Mark's side was empty.

She stared for long seconds, certain she was not yet awake and only dreaming.

But she was awake.

A thought struck her. Hard.

She bolted from the bedroom and ran down the hall, shouting, "Nathan? *Nathan!*"

When she entered his room, she stumbled to a halt in front of his closet. It, too, was open and mostly empty.

Lauren rounded the corner toward Nathan's bed, sickened.

Nathan was gone.

5.

"Mr. Cross, it's a pleasure to meet you."

"*My* pleasure."

Edmond Fiske and a short balding man at the table with him stood as Jordan was led to the table in a secluded corner booth. Fiske was about six two or three, darkly tanned with sun-lightened brown hair and clear hazel eyes. He was casually dressed in a powder-blue V-neck cashmere sweater over a cream-colored shirt, and smoothly pressed pleated grey slacks. He looked physically powerful as well as financially; his shoulders were broad, his arms sizeable, and even his hands were large. Jordan tried not to let the man's grip make him wince as they shook hands.

Jordan sat down and put the *People* magazine on the table. Somehow, it clashed glaringly with the table's elegant setting.

"Hungry?" Fiske asked.

"As a matter of fact, I am." Jordan opened the menu. "What do you recommend?"

"Well, everything is good, but if you like, I can order for both of us. It will save time, and—" He smiled, exposing two strips of perfect ivory-white teeth. "—I want to see that you have the best meal on the menu."

"Sure."

"I hope I didn't interrupt your schedule."

"Not at all, Mr. Fiske. I usually break for—"

"Please, call me Ed. If we're going to be working together, let's drop the formalities. And this is Tom Gleason, editor at *Trends*."

Gleason smiled and Jordan nodded at him, then said, "Well . . . I'm still not sure what you want from me or if I'll be able to help you. And I'm *especially* not sure why . . ." He glanced at Gleason whose silence made him uncomfortable. "Well, I don't mean to sell myself short, I'll be the first to tell you I'm very good at what I do, but—"

"You're wondering why I called *you.*"

"Yes."

"We'll get to that in a minute. I ordered wine," he said as a svelte young waiter approached the table with a bottle, removed the cork and poured some in Fiske's glass. Fiske tasted it, nodded thoughtfully and said, "Perfect, thank you, Des." The waiter poured for each of them. Fiske breezed through their order efficiently, his sharp eyes darting up and down the menu, then dismissed the waiter with a sniff. "I chose you for three reasons, Jordan," he said. "Your reputation, your location, and the fact that your license expires in a month."

Jordan blinked. "My license?"

"Yes. I'll explain in a minute. Did you read the article?" He nodded toward the magazine.

"Yes."

"Aside from what you read, what do you know about Hester Thorne and the Universal Enlightened Alliance?"

"Not much, really. Just what I've read and heard. And each article seems to cover the same territory. It's the most popular group in the New Age movement, endorsed by some big names in show business and even politics, particularly Sheila Bennet, who's always writing a best-selling book about it between her movies and that nighttime soap she does, um . . . what's it called? *Empire*, I think. Uh, let's see, Hester Thorne was a lowly housewife who was visited by an ancient entity named Orrin, who now uses her as his mouthpiece. That sort of thing."

"Yes. She was a housewife in your hometown, by the way. Redding."

"That's right. Um, you seem to know a lot about me, Mr. Fis—uh, Ed."

"I do, but don't worry. Just business. I always check out potential associates."

Fiske smiled again, disarmingly, and Jordan believed him. Fiske glowed with wealth and power, but was without threat. For the moment, anyway.

"Tell me, Jordan, do you read *Trends*?"

"Yes, I do."

"Good. I'm very proud of that magazine. I've worked hard to choose the right people—" He cast a smile of approval in Gleason's direction. "—to make it something more than the average grocery-store fare." He gestured vaguely at the *People* by Jordan's elbow. "A little glitz, a little gossip, but only glitz and gossip not touched by the other magazines. We don't do publicity pieces, we do *stories*. And we do them differently than everyone else. It's not going to win anybody a Pulitzer, but I'm proud to say that, when you've read all the latest, you can pick up *Trends* and read something new. That's why, when I told Tom, here, that I wanted an article on the Universal Enlightened Alliance, I knew I wouldn't get the same old tripe everyone else has written about the group. Tom heads up the Los Angeles bureau. He put several people on the story. One of them was sent to Grover." Fiske turned to Gleason and cocked a brow, signaling him to take over.

"His name was Harvey Bolton," Gleason said. "He was a good reporter. I knew he'd—"

"Was?" Jordan interrupted.

"I'm getting to that." Gleason frowned and scratched the shiny patch of skin atop his head, choosing words carefully. "See, the reporters who work for *Trends* . . . they're good reporters, all of them, don't get me wrong. But I knew that if there was something odd about the Alliance, something that wasn't right, Harvey would find it while another might not. I thought it best that those working on the story not know that Ed's intention was to—" He glanced at Fiske cautiously before going on. "—to find something . . . *new* about the Alliance."

"You were looking for dirt," Jordan said.

Gleason quickly replied, "Not necessarily dirt."

"My opinion of the Alliance is not a favorable one, Jordan," Fiske said. "I was curious to see if we might be able to confirm it. But we didn't want any of the reporters to find things that weren't necessarily there. We didn't want a biased story. We wanted them to find it on their own, so we thought it best not to tell them my reasons for requesting the story. That's all. I'm not in the business of mudslinging."

Jordan nodded.

"Harvey was hungry for something big," Gleason continued. "Something that would draw attention to him. He was married recently, starting a new family, and, well . . . he needed to improve his income. So I told him we wanted to cover the Alliance and sent him to Grover. As far as he knew, it was just another assignment, but I knew if there was something to find, he'd find it."

"And he did," Jordan guessed as Gleason sipped his wine.

"That's right. He called me at home from Anderson at about two o'clock on the morning he was supposed to return to L.A. He was excited, said he'd uncovered something big, although he wasn't quite sure what. Not yet. I wanted to make sure it was for real before I gave him the go-ahead to pursue it, but we were cut off. I found out later there was a bad electrical storm that night, so I'm guessing that was the cause. Before we were cut off, though, Harvey told me he might be in some danger."

"Did he say why?"

"Said he might have pissed some people off, but he didn't say how. Later that morning, about seven or so, he called again." Gleason reached beneath the table and brought up a briefcase, put it on his lap, opened it and removed a microcassette recorder. "I recorded most of the call," he said, putting the recorder on the table and turning it on.

The tiny speaker crackled and a rasping, strangled voice spoke through the long-distance hiss: "—got me, Tom . . . puh-please, Jesus, help me . . . th-they've—"

"Harvey? Is that *you*, Harvey?"

The voice dragged in a desperate breath. "Yuh-yes, Tom, please, Jesus Christ, you guh-gotta help me, *please*!"

"Where are you?"

"A monster, Jesus, they sent . . . a fucking . . . *monster*—"

"Where *are* you?"

Silence.

"Harvey? Answer me, where are you?"

Nothing.

Gleason turned the recorder off.

"That's all there is," he said.

Jordan asked, "Is that the last you heard from him?"

"Not quite." Gleason opened the briefcase again and removed a thick manila envelope. "The day before, Harvey had Fed-Exed this to the office." He handed it to Jordan.

Inside were Xeroxes of magazine and newspaper clippings, handwritten notes and photographs, and two microcassette tapes. A quickly scribbled note was paper-clipped to the top of the stack.

> Tom—
> Read these carefully in the order I've stacked them, then tell me: what's wrong with this picture? Please don't laugh this off. Give it a chance. We'll be in touch.
>   H.B.

"I take it you've read these," Jordan said.

"Every one of them. Several times."

"And what *is* wrong with this picture?"

With a glance at Fiske, Gleason shrugged and said hesitantly, "I'm . . . not really sure. It's obvious Harvey was convinced something was wrong, but I just don't see it."

Jordan turned to Fiske. "How about you?"

"I'm afraid I don't see it, either."

"Did you go to the police with this?"

"The police sniffed around for a couple months, said they went to Grover and questioned some people. I have no reason to believe otherwise, but they found nothing and closed the case.''

''You don't think they did enough.''

''I think they did what they could. The police are limited in what they can do. Limited by time, their work load, money, and most of all, by the law.''

''Which is why you've called me.''

Fiske nodded and smiled as he took a piece of bread from the basket on the table and buttered it slowly.

''You want me to find him.''

''Oh, I think he's dead.''

''Why do you say that?''

''No reason. Just a suspicion. I want you to find out if I'm right.''

''And if you aren't?''

''Find him, bring him to me, and I will deal with whoever is responsible. If he's dead, I want you to find out who did it, how, and why.''

''What about you, Mr. Gleason? Do you think Harvey Bolton is dead?''

Looking at the recorder, Gleason said, ''Well . . . he didn't sound too healthy the last time he called me.''

The waiter brought their salads and all three men spread their napkins on their laps.

''Let's finish our business after lunch,'' Fiske said.

As they ate, no one mentioned Harvey Bolton; they chatted, instead, about sports and politics.

As soon as they finished their dessert, Fiske turned to Gleason and said, ''You mentioned some business you had in town, Tom.''

''Oh, yes, yes.'' He glanced at his watch. ''In fact, I'm late already.'' He quickly gathered his things together, and when Jordan handed him the manila envelope, he shook his head and said, ''No, that's yours. You'll need it.'' He scooted out of the booth, stood, and shook Jordan's hand. ''It was nice meeting you, Mr. Cross.''

As Gleason left, Jordan thought the abrupt departure must have been planned ahead of time. He wondered why Fiske wanted to be alone with him.

Removing a thin silver cigarette case from the shirt pocket beneath his sweater, Fiske said, ''I think it would be best if you let go of all your other clients, Jordan.'' He offered Jordan a cigarette, then lit it for him before lighting his own. ''Providing you decide to take this on, that is.''

''It's not going to be easy.''

''No, it's not. But I have faith in you, Jordan. You're a chameleon. You're very resourceful, responsible, and loyal to your clients.''

''If you don't mind my asking . . . how do you know that?''

''My people have looked into your work. Your reviews are all glowing. Your clients are very pleased with your work.''

''I keep the names of my clients confidential. How did you—''

''Nothing, Jordan, is truly confidential.''

''I see.'' Jordan stiffened; he made no attempt to conceal his anger. ''Well, if your people are so fucking effective, why do you need me?''

''Because you can do what it would normally take half a dozen of my people to do and you can do it better because you're only one person. You're very . . . creative.''

''You've watched me.''

''Yes. A little. That shouldn't upset you, Jordan. You do it, too. You know it's just business. And you were only observed while working.''

Jordan said nothing. He knew how completely one's privacy could be stripped away, and he didn't like the idea of some— *any*—of his being invaded. It angered him, offended him, even more so because Fiske did not even try to keep his surveillance a secret. He flaunted it with a smirk and his arrogance made Jordan grind his teeth.

''I would never hire someone without checking them out first, Jordan, whether it be an investigator or a gardener.'' Then, casually, after taking a long drag on his cigarette, he added, ''Especially considering the amount of money I plan to spend on you.''

Jordan nodded slowly, suddenly feeling a bit less hostile toward Edmond Fiske. ''You understand this is going to take time. Months, maybe a year or more. I can't make any guarantees.''

''I realize that. That's why I suggest you concentrate solely on this and release your other clients.''

''Even then,'' Jordan said, ''I might come up with nothing.''

''I understand. But I have faith in you.'' He gave Jordan a brilliant smile. ''How does one million sound?''

Jordan fingered his napkin, allowing no reaction to show on his face. "One million," he said flatly, nodding.

"For starters, of course. And absolutely all expenses will be covered."

Jordan nodded again. He told himself silently to stop nodding like an idiot and accept the offer. But something was wrong. He couldn't put his finger on it yet, but something about the whole thing was slightly off center.

"Jordan? That's not enough?"

"Oh, no, it's not that. I'm just . . . thinking."

"Ah."

"If you don't mind, Mr. Fiske—"

"Ed."

"—Ed, I'd like to know exactly why you don't like the Alliance."

Fiske cocked a brow and his tanned forehead creased. He said nothing for a moment, sweeping his tongue around inside his mouth, seeking out stray bits of food. Then: "Let me put it this way. I'm very rich. I've worked hard for what I have, I wasn't born to it. I've done a few things that were less than generous, less than compassionate, in acquiring what I have. Even some things that I regret now when I look back on them. But I'm happy to say I've never actually hurt anyone and I've always been very honest about my intentions. Under the leadership of Hester Thorne, the Universal Enlightened Alliance has become a very wealthy and powerful organization. They have taken money from people hungry for spiritual fulfillment and meaning in exchange for the tallest pile of steaming fly-eaten bullshit I have ever heard in my life, and believe me, I've heard some good ones. A centuries-old entity speaking through a woman who barely finished high school? Come on, Jordan, if you were an all-knowing being who had some great truth to share with the world, would that be your first choice for a spokesperson? And crystals that are supposed to heal cancer and heighten one's psychic abilities? Crystals that also cost a *lot* of money? I think they are damaging lives, and though I have little sympathy for anyone who would buy into such a ridiculous philosophy, I am offended by all the Alliance stands for. Maybe I'm wrong. Maybe Orrin *is* going to save the human race from itself, as Miss Thorne claims. Maybe not. That's irrelevant. What is relevant is the disappearance of one of my employees who was investigating them. I think maybe he came across something that might prove the Alliance to be a fraud. Maybe not. He's gone. That's the only important thing right now.''

Jordan did not think it was the only important thing; not to Edmond Fiske, anyway. He suspected there was another reason behind Fiske's interest in the Alliance.

"Why do you ask?"

"Just curious," Jordan said. "That's all."

"Nothing wrong with that. Listen, Jordan, I'm a little pressed for time. Did you drive here?"

"Took a cab."

"Let me give you a lift. We'll talk more in the car."

In front of the restaurant, a black limousine glimmered in the sunlight. The uniformed chauffeur opened the door for them; Fiske got in first and Jordan followed.

The sounds of the city were not allowed inside the limousine; sunlight and curious eyes were barred by the dark smoky glass. They sat opposite one another, Jordan facing the rectangle of thick glass through which he saw the driver get behind the wheel. The driver's black sunglasses beneath the bill of his cap were reflected in the rearview mirror.

"Where to?" Fiske asked.

Jordan gave him the address of the office and Fiske repeated it into an intercom on the divider over his shoulder.

"You mentioned my license earlier," Jordan said. "It *does* expire soon. Why is that important?"

"Can't you guess. Were you going to renew it?"

He was not. "Well, sometimes it can be a bit limiting. . . ."

"Exactly. I don't want you to be limited. For that, I could go back to the police. If you find it necessary to do something that your licensed status would prohibit, I don't want you to hesitate. Of course, I don't expect you to compromise your integrity, but I know there are things your license restricts that are otherwise legal. Barely legal, perhaps, but legal."

Fiske was right, and that was exactly why Jordan had no intention of renewing his license; he was tired of having his hands tied by a laminated card and a certificate.

"Of course," Fiske said, lighting another cigarette, "I don't have to tell you that this should be handled with extreme confidentiality. The press seems to be fascinated by my every move. I'd hate to read about this in the papers."

"You said nothing was confidential."

He nodded with assurance. "This will be."

"If I take the case, I'll need help. I'll have to share certain facts with my operatives."

"I trust your judgment." He watched Jordan for a moment, as if inspecting him. "You seem uncertain. Well, you don't have to decide right now. I'll be in town until tomorrow." He removed a wallet from his back pocket and opened it. "Here, take this." He handed over a small card. "When you've decided, call this number. They'll contact me immediately and I'll get right back to you. I'd like an answer within twenty-four hours."

As Jordan took the card, the limousine slowed to a stop. The ride had been so smooth and quiet, he'd forgotten they were in a car.

"Here we are," Fiske said.

The door opened and the chauffeur stood patiently beside the car.

"It's been a pleasure talking with you, Jordan. I hope you'll call me soon with good news."

"You'll hear from me tonight."

"Good." As Jordan started to leave the car, Fiske said, "Oh, by the way. Hester Thorne is giving a free seminar tonight at the Sheraton. You might want to attend, just to have a look. Call me afterward and let me know what you think."

"I'll do that," Jordan said, then got out and headed into his building.

6.

The ballroom in the Sheraton was warm and growing slightly humid from the noisy crowd shuffling around to find seats. Soft music played over the PA system. It was the sort of white noise that record stores categorized as New Age music; not music so much as an audible mist that throbbed with something resembling a beat, touched with the faintest ghost of a melody, soothing but empty.

A large flower arrangement gave a burst of color to each end of the stage up front and the backdrop depicted a luminescent Mount Shasta crowned with an airbrushed rainbow. In the center of the stage stood a dais decorated with the emblem of the Alliance and on the floor before it were several white cushions; below that, four steps led from the stage to the ballroom floor.

Jordan and Marvin stood just inside the door, out of the way of the people still filing in. They were all ages, from small children holding their parents' hands to stooped senior citizens leaning on canes and walkers.

"Pulls in just about everybody, doesn't she?" Marvin said, raising his voice to be heard above the music and the drone of voices and laughter. He removed a pack of cigarettes from his coat pocket and shook one out.

"Looks that way. What do you say we get a seat before they're—"

"Excuse me, sir."

Jordan and Marvin turned to the man who had appeared to their left. He wore an expensive-looking cream-colored suit and stood with his hands joined behind his back, smiling as he spoke.

"We ask that you smoke in the lobby only," the man said.

"Yeah, sure," Marvin said with a nod, putting the cigarette back.

Jordan saw a plastic name tag on the man's lapel; it sported the Alliance emblem and his name, STEWART. His tie tack was a small crystal cut in the shape of an eye.

"May I help you find a seat?" Stewart asked, still smiling.

"No, thanks," Jordan replied. "We're fine."

As they moved into the crowd and toward the stage, Jordan noticed others dressed exactly as Stewart, all of them smiling like shoe salesmen. None were especially tall, but although it was not readily apparent, Jordan could tell they all had sturdy, muscular builds beneath their creamy suits.

They found two seats together in the middle of the fourth row from the front and scooted in, stepping over feet, excusing themselves politely.

Neither man looked himself. Marvin wore an old brown corduroy sport coat that had been hanging in his closet since he was in the real-estate business, a pair of tan chinos, and his old pair of horn-rim glasses. Jordan had on a pair of John Lennon specs with clear lenses, a baggy white sweater, and blue jeans; his brown hair was combed straight back, slicked down with a little mousse.

"Sheesh, you look like Mickey Rourke," Marvin had said earlier when they met in the hotel lounge.

"Just as long as I don't look like me."

They sat in their chairs, silently watching the people around them, those wearing crystals on chains around their necks with the light of belief bright in their eyes, and others who moved with the caution of interested skeptics.

The young men in vanilla ice-cream suits quickened their pace in seating those still wandering around the ballroom as the music faded.

As the lights dimmed, the voices silenced, and soon the only lights in the room were directed toward the stage.

They waited there in the darkness as the room cooled down a bit.

Hester Thorne hurried onto the stage toward the dais to a sudden storm of applause, arms raised high. She wore a shimmering white gown—it looked more like a comfortable house robe to Jordan—and the flowing sleeves bunched up around her shoulders, revealing the pale smooth skin of her arms until she lowered them, clutched the sides of the dais, flashed a beaming smile and said, "Good evening, sweet souls!"

The applause rose until she waved for it to stop.

"I can't tell you," she said, "how happy I am to see so many of you here tonight. It gives me hope. It give this *world* hope! First of all, I want you to know that there is only one truly important person here tonight, a person overflowing with unrealized potential and untapped power. A person who can find happiness, fulfillment, and success with help from no one, from nothing. That person . . . that *powerhouse* . . . that one true god . . . is *you*."

Hester Thorne wasted no time in gripping her audience. She spoke with animation and breathless enthusiasm, her words gaining momentum as she spoke, the cylindrical crystal that rested between her breasts catching the light as she moved and flashing like a diamond. Seeing her in person for the first time, Jordan understood her success; unlike most of the others like her—transchannels and crystal healers and meditation gurus—Hester Thorne had tremendous charisma all by herself, without the aid of any New Age trappings. She hadn't even mentioned Orrin yet, and the audience was huddled in her open palm.

"I am not here," she went on, "to share with you *my* philosophy or worldview, but the truth that has been *given* to me. And the admission to this seminar tonight is free because the *truth* is free. It will fall on many deaf ears, but to anyone who pursues this truth I give this warning: learning to *live* the truth is not free. There is a price. It is not entirely a monetary price—" she chuckled good-naturedly. "—although nothing of true value is free. It is a *life* price."

She removed the microphone from its stand and walked around the dais to the edge of the stage.

"Your life must change, you must take a new path, and leave behind everything you now know to evolve into a higher, more aware, *complete* being. You must find the god within you and release it. And when you do—"

She spread her fingers wide, holding the microphone between flat palms, then—

"—magic will be yours—"

—she slowly pulled her hands away and the microphone remained suspended before her, steady, motionless.

"—and miracles will happen. But before I go on, I must tell you this. Everything you have been taught up to this moment—"

She plucked the microphone from the air.

"—is wrong."

Jordan had read of the tricks she performed during seminars and personal appearances. She never spoke of them, explained or defended them—although her critics were quick to point out her blatant chicanery and juvenile parlor tricks—she simply performed them inconspicuously as she spoke, almost as if she wasn't aware of them herself.

Returning to the dais and replacing the microphone, Hester Thorne went on to tell how Orrin came into her life, speaking at a slower pace now, calm and soothing.

She told of the nights she was awakened from a sound sleep by a distant voice.

"At first, I thought I was losing my mind," she said, "maybe having some sort of breakdown. I had been under a great deal of strain in the years preceding my first contact with Orrin and still was. My son, who had been born severely . . . impaired . . . deformed . . . was failing and required constant care. My husband was under a lot of stress, too, both at home and at work, and he was growing more and more unstable. So I was in dire need of what Orrin had to give me."

The voice of Orrin became clearer as time passed and Hester realized he was telling her to go to Mount Shasta.

"As it turned out," she said, "I had spent my honeymoon in Grover, which is just below Mount Shasta. I was raised just a few hours south of there and had grown up admiring that beautiful mountain from a distance. I would spend hours in my backyard staring at it, thinking about it, almost as if I were *drawn* to it. But I had never been there, so my husband arranged a week in Grover for our honeymoon. Even then, I had no idea of the spiritual awakening that was going on in that area, and continues to go on. People yearning for the meaning of our existence here and hungry for communication with our galactic neighbors were gathering there long before I ever arrived.

"At Orrin's request—still half believing I might be crazy—I returned to the small town with my son, who was almost too infirm to travel, but whom I could not leave behind. And there, my communication with Orrin was crystal clear, almost as if he were sitting right in front of me holding a conversation. But he wasn't. He was speaking *inside* me."

There, she learned that Orrin had had countless incarnations as a philosopher and warrior, both on earth and on distant worlds, in cultures totally alien to any that had come and gone on this world.

"Throughout his evolution," she continued, "Orrin has grown in knowledge and awareness. He has seen the endless procession of lies and subtle distortions of the truth that plague this—and *all*—planets. But only one truth remains. It outlives all the falsehoods, but it does not always defeat them. Throughout the universe there have been worlds populated by beings who have either ignored or refused to accept this truth, and as a result, they have died away. Ceased to exist. Not from crime and disease and war, but from the ignorance that results in all of those things. And I am here tonight to tell you—and you are here, sweet souls, to *learn*—that this earth is fast becoming one of those worlds. A victim of ignorance. *But*. It's not too late to *stop* it."

She paused for a while, as if to give her audience time to absorb what she'd said.

Jordan glanced around him and saw only attentive eyes facing front, steady and undiverted. The room was solid with silence.

"Until now," she said quietly, her voice soft as sun-warmed grass, "Orrin's message has been one of peace and encouragement, promoting community among all reasoning beings in the universe. But in every lighted place, there are shadows.''

She lowered her head for a moment and when she lifted it again, her face had changed, become troubled, worried.

''My most recent communications with Orrin have been touched by that shadow. He has told me things that are . . . unpleasant. And even, at times, frightening. They are things I would rather not hear, but *must* hear. And you must hear them, too. I have no idea what Orrin will say when he speaks to us tonight, but some of it may be unsettling to you. I urge you, *please*, do not be discouraged. He may bring to our attention some negative things, but only because he knows we can prevent them. We can *create* the future, a new, bright, and warm future for this earth and for all humanity in this level of existence and those yet to come. Do not be disturbed; be *enlightened*. Later, we'll have a question-and-answer session and talk more about these things, but now, if you will be patient with me for a few moments, I will open the channel. And Orrin will speak with us.''

She took a lapel microphone from the dais, snapped it on, and stepped around to the cushions on the floor, where she settled in a lotus-like position, leaned back her head, closed her eyes, and took a long deep breath. After letting it out slowly, she inhaled again, and this time the breath was louder, thicker, more guttural; her shoulders rose high, stopped, lowered so slowly the movement was almost invisible, then rose again with a third, and deeper, breath.

As Hester Thorne's breaths echoed in waves over the still audience, Jordan realized something, then marveled at it. Without any preliminary explanation, she had begun talking about channeling an age-old being who knew the ''Truth'' as if everyone in the room would accept it as fact without question or doubt. There was no self-effacing prologue, no ''Now, I know you might find this hard to believe, *but* . . .'' She had simply told her audience that everything they had learned up to now was wrong, then had begun talking about Orrin.

And yet, when Jordan looked around him again, there were no doubtful looks on the faces bathed in the glow of the stage lights. They were simply watching, silently and with interest, some with *anticipation*, as if they had no doubt they were about to hear from an invisible, immortal entity.

As she inhaled and exhaled slowly, her breaths growing in volume and length, Hester Thorne's face softened, relaxed, took on a tranquillity that all but glowed from her alabaster skin.

It went on for several long minutes: in deeply, shoulders lifting, breasts swelling, then out with a long deflating sigh.

Jordan leaned toward Marvin to whisper some smartass remark—*Live! On stage! Hester Thorne* breathes! or something like that—but before he could speak—

—the breathing stopped.

She was perfectly still on the cushions for a moment, then her body jolted, as if in pain, and the tendons along her neck stood out like piano wires taut beneath her skin. Her chin dropped and eyes opened, revealing only rolled-back whites and her throat gurgled, then—

—a long miserable groan rolled up from deep in her chest and her body quaked, back rigid, as if she had been entered violently and unexpectedly by a man of unaccommodating proportions. Her hands slapped onto the cushions, bunched into fists, nails clawing the soft white material, and a whisper of gasps and murmurs rose from the audience.

It happened again, then a third time, that orgasmic convulsion that flowed over her, liquid—no, *gelatinous*—and then her eyes rolled back into place and she faced her audience, opened her mouth and began to sing. It was a single high note, unwavering, in a clear and steady voice. Her voice.

But that changed.

The voice darkened; it became broader, richer. Deeper. It became male.

Jordan cocked his head to listen for the disguise, for the trace of Hester Thorne remaining in the velvety baritone. It was not there.

Very good, he thought.

The note, sung in an open-mouthed *Aahhh*, wobbled, changed shape, then faded, becoming spoken words.

"It is Orrin who speaks to you through this vessel of flesh and blood and I come to you in the spirit of love that bind you all, that brings you together and sets you free, that transforms you from the many into the one, the love that is the blood that flows through the veins of the Godbody, as it is and forever shall be. *Greeeeetings*, sweet souls!"

It was all spoken rapidly and in one breath, with a sing-song rhythm that somehow did not sound childish; perhaps because of the full, melodious voice and the strange accent, apparently a mixture of many accents, some vaguely familiar to Jordan, others completely alien.

Some in the audience, already familiar with the routine, responded—"Greetings, Orrin!"—almost simultaneously.

Jordan and Marvin exchanged eye-rolling glances.

As she continued, Hester Thorne's eyes moved back and forth over the audience, massaging the body of attentive listeners before her. She waved her arms in odd, jerky movements as she spoke in the voice of Orrin, fingers rigid and pulled together tightly; each movement seemed to have meaning, as if she were performing some obscure sign language to interpret her words.

"I come to you in the body of the entity you call Hester Thorne so that you may know that other beings live and function outside of the body, without the encumbrance of flesh, as you shall also be in a future existence and have been in existences past. I bring you the truth that has been denied you, the truth that calms all fears and soothes all pain, the truth that will set you free from the bonds of this weary, close-minded planet of disease and despair. If you embrace it, this truth shall fill you with happiness and hope. But also . . . fear."

Orrin—*No, not Orrin,* Jordan chided himself, *Hester Thorne*—Hester scanned the crowd a moment, frowning, lower lip tucked out like a pouting child's.

"For some time now, I have shared my message with countless souls on this level. I have spoken of immortality, of incarnations past and to come, of worlds known to you but not remembered. But time grows short for those of you in this existence and now I must reveal the *whole* truth: a future that may be prevented, but a future dark and frightening. I beg you take heed, and take heart. Armed with the truth, you will find within you Godness and further assemble the Godbody, as it is and forever shall be. This future I have spoken of holds much grief for this vessel known as Hester Thorne. I ask that you show her love and support. Surround her with Godness. Give to her your love. But above all, follow her, for her words are *my* words, and my words are *truth*."

Jordan leaned toward Marvin and whispered, "What is *this*?"

"Got me. Every time I've heard about her, she's talking love and peace and enough saccharine to give you diabetes. This is new stuff, far as I know."

"Many will persecute the vessel Hester Thorne," she went on, and they turned again toward the stage. "Followers who have been faithful and instrumental in spreading the truth shall denounce her, call her a spreader of lies; they shall accuse her of inflaming fear in the masses, and some will call her mad. But they shall be wrong. Many of them will see their errors and recant. Many, however, will not and their stubbornness and ignorance shall be their undoing. Already the wrath descends. Not the wrath of their empty god but the wrath of their *ignorance*. Even as we meet here tonight, the shadow of that wrath is growing over one disbeliever in particular who has repeatedly attacked this vessel Hester Thorne before millions. The wrath of his own ignorance is falling on Reverend Barry Hallway and with every passing moment, the reverend's end approaches. Only if he acknowledges the truth and withdraws his hateful words and false accusations will he be spared."

A smattering of gasps rose from the crowd as heads leaned together and voices murmured.

Jordan tried not to gape at the woman in shock. "Are you *hearing* this?" he hissed at Marvin.

"This woman's got *balls*," Marvin whispered back. "She's kicking a hornet's nest with *that* stuff. Hallway's been denouncing her for quite a while, but he's never said she was gonna *die*."

"You, sweet souls, must aid her with all your strength," she continued. "To do this, your path must be made clear by laying waste to one of the countless lies imposed upon you by your leaders, your clergy and lawmen. The lie of right and wrong, the falsehood of morality. There *is* no right and wrong, only truth and falsehood."

Jordan fidgeted in his seat, disturbed as much by what he was hearing as what he was seeing: eyes locked on the woman in front, necks stiff with attention, faces like sponges that absorbed every drop of what they were hearing.

"Lawmen," he breathed, feeling a headache coming on.

There is no right and wrong . . . no right and wrong. . . .

Good Lord, he thought, *does she know what she's doing? What she's saying?*

The rattle of a door being pushed open came from the rear of the ballroom and sibilant whispers slithered through the silence.

"That which is true," Hester Thorne/Orrin continued, "must be uplifted and followed. That which is false must be discarded. The test is simple. If it does not further the spread of this message, if it does not coincide with and support that which is relayed through the vessel Hester Thorne, it is false."

Jordan felt a cigarette craving crawl up his throat and begin to knock against his teeth. Surely, he hoped, no one would take her *that* seriously.

The whispers from the back continued, became more urgent.

"Many will try to undermine the truth, for ignorance is the only—"

A female voice suddenly cut through the room, coming from the back: "Will you get the fuck out of my *way*!"

The voice was followed by a powerful slap—a hand meeting flesh—that bounced off the walls.

As if directed by one mind, every head in the ballroom turned toward the commotion, including those of Jordan and Marvin.

One of the vanilla-suited men was hunched on one knee, his hand massaging the side of his face, while two others hurried by him in pursuit of a woman who stalked through the shadowy room toward the front, light playing off her tear-streaked face. Her dark blond hair was flat against her skull with a dull sheen to it, as if unwashed, and although she moved quickly, her shoulders looked heavy, tired. She wore a long-sleeved plaid shirt that was improperly buttoned so that it hung crookedly on her lean frame, black acid-washed jeans and sneakers. Her fists were tight at her sides, swinging rhythmically with each step, and her cheeks puffed with furious exhalations.

The two men behind her closed in.

Voices whispered, questioned, and complained.

Jordan spun around to look at Hester Thorne. He expected the intrusion to have jarred her out of her performance, but she remained in character, on the cushions, face blank as an untouched canvas, her eyes following the woman along the center aisle toward the stage. Not even the vaguest hint of surprise infiltrated her calm. Jordan looked to the rear again.

The first man to reach the woman gripped her elbow firmly and was about to speak when she swung around, pulling her arm behind her, and caught him in the jaw with her right fist. The man stumbled backward, falling across three laps in the audience, and several people stood from their seats, surprised and curious.

She was ready for the second man and stepped forward to meet him, kicking up her right foot and hooking it between his legs. The man's mouth yawned open and his tongue curled out, eyes bugging as he doubled over with retching sound and fell hard on his behind.

Jordan was impressed; the woman's movements, although effective, were untrained and held no expertise, only raw energy, a lot of rage and a good deal of luck.

Beside him, Marvin chuckled, "Whuh-*hut* the hell . . ."

"Where's my son?" the woman demanded in a cracked but strong voice, heading up the aisle with long angry strides, not missing a step as she brushed some strands of hair from her forehead with the back of a hand. "What have you done with my *son*?"

The audience abandoned their murmuring and broke into full voice, chattering as they stood from their seats and looked around, wondering, perhaps, if this was part of the program.

Jordan stood, too, keeping his eyes on the woman, who seemed not to notice the crowd at all.

Hester Thorne remained unfazed.

"Whatever you seek, sweet soul," she said, "you must know that—"

"I didn't come for your fucking show, I came for my son! You can *keep* my *husband*, but I want my *son*! *Now!*"

"I ask that you would cease to—"

"I won't cease *shit*, lady, until you—" The woman swallowed her voice and broke into a run and there was an explosion of activity, so sudden that Jordan's head darted bird-like all around to take it all in.

Within seconds, and all at once:

Hester Thorne's face lost its serenity as the intruder bounded toward the stage; her eyes widened first, then narrowed as her eyebrows swooped downward and she slapped her hands onto her thighs, elbows jutting outward, and stood so smoothly she appeared to grow out of the floor like a tree, suddenly seeming taller and broader than before and—

—doors slammed open in back and three more ice-cream-suited men came in, running toward the woman as—

—more people stood and shouted and—

—the woman reached the steps that led up to the stage where Hester Thorne stood, her eyes flaming indignantly as she opened her mouth as if to yawn and—

—the rectangular fluorescent shop lights suspended from chains overhead began to flicker like strobes and Jordan looked up to see several of them swaying left to right. From Jordan's far left there was a sound like an air-filled paper bag popping and one of the swaying light panels blinked out as an explosion of sparks rained over the audience and one end of the light broke away from its chain and dangled precariously as—

—another light blew out and showered sparks and another and several more, and screams rang out from the confused and frightened crowd and chairs clanged together as sparks shimmered overhead like fireworks on the Fourth of July, but—

—Jordan noticed that the sparks were not falling downward but were fluttering horizontally like fireflies bobbing on an evening breeze and—

—then Jordan felt it and he turned to Marvin, who was now standing beside him, and *he* felt it, too: an icy, strangely damp breeze that grew in strength to become a hefty wind that blew the sparks around the room, tossed papers and mussed hair. But there was something else . . . perhaps a coincidence that had nothing to do with the inexplicable wind . . .

Jordan felt nauseated and light-headed and gripped the back of the chair in front of him, closing his eyes for just a moment, but—

—horrifying images flashed behind his eyelids, hazy grey images of butchery and death that came and went so quickly they barely registered, and Jordan opened his eyes with a gasp, and—

—he saw the others around him reacting to the wind, their arms raised, hair blowing, women clutching children to their sides, some people covering their ears or eyes with their hands. Even the ice-cream suits seemed stunned and confused; one stood with his arm shielding his face while another stood beside him, simultaneously wearing a frown and looking startled as he stared at the stage. And then—

—the wind stopped.

"Jordy," Marvin said, gripping Jordan's elbow, "what the hell *is* this?"

Jordan simply shook his head as he looked around.

There were a few lights still on, but the room was considerably darker than before. The audience was scattering, knocking chairs over and pushing one another out of the way. Several of the ice-cream-suited men were trying to calm people down and get them to return to their seats.

The woman who had burst in and apparently started the confusion, however, seemed unaware of it. She bounded up the stage steps two at a time, shouting words that could not be heard above the voices of the crowd.

Jordan looked to his left and saw three men coming, one in the lead, two behind, and those two, at the same moment, pulled aside their lapels with their left hands and began to reach inside their coats with their right.

It was an unmistakable movement, one Jordan had seen before.

They were reaching for guns.

"Something?" Marvin barked.

"Looks like it. C'mon," Jordan said over his shoulder, loudly so Marvin could hear him above the voices, and they moved forward, shoving their way down the clogged row toward the center aisle.

The woman on the stage halted, two feet in front of Hester Thorne, who clutched her lapel microphone and tore it away. Her mouth worked silently, violently, and somewhere, a window shattered. Then another, and another. As shards of glass chimed, screams rose from the audience, and the woman, her back to the audience now, fell down the steps. Although she had not been touched, she plunged backward as if she'd been struck hard in the stomach, bent in the middle with her arms and legs following her outstretched.

Jordan reached the center aisle as the three men stopped just a few feet away from him. The one in the lead spun around and held up a hand. It was a gesture of command and both men behind him dropped their hands from their coats. The center aisle was crowded with people heading for the rear exits, but Jordan and Marvin jogged around them toward the woman lying on her back at the foot of the steps. He didn't know what he was going to do, but he was certain of what he *didn't* want to do: draw attention to himself. Maybe this woman was just some lunatic who had come in off the street, but if not, he wanted to hear what she had to say, and he wanted to get to her without being noticed.

She was propped up on her elbows, staring at Hester Thorne, who stood at the edge of the stage, right arm outstretched rigidly, lips squirming.

Glancing over his shoulder, Jordan saw the three men closing in and said to Marvin, "Hold them off."

Marvin immediately fell to the floor in the path of the three men; one of them tripped over him and Marvin bellowed "Sonofa*bitch*, you tryna *kill* me? I'll sue you bastards from here to—"

Jordan bent down, scooped his arms under the woman's shoulders and lifted her to her feet. Without hesitating, he turned her to the right and began pushing her along the stage toward the side exit.

Walking crab-like along the edge of the stage above them, arm still held out, Hester Thorne jabbered on, her lips writhing madly, her voice a senseless buzz in all the noise. And her eyes . . .

From their distance, it might have seemed like little more than anger to the audience—those paying attention, anyway—but what Jordan saw in Hester Thorne's eyes looked more like steaming, bilious hatred. Perhaps even more than that, something more threatening, more *violent*.

Something went off inside Jordan, an internal fingersnap; he'd found *something*, even if he wasn't sure what it was yet.

Then the lights went out and something passed swiftly through the air, something invisible that went rapidly from the stage toward the back of the room, like a wave of static electricity that stiffened the hairs at the base of Jordan's skull. It was hard to tell in all the confusion, but it sounded like a couple more bulbs had blown. There were screams in the darkness and chairs clanged as they were knocked together.

The auxiliary lights kicked on a few seconds later, glaring and harsh, dancing shadows through the room like marionettes controlled by madmen, and Jordan pushed forward, swinging his arm around the woman's shoulders. She moved clumsily, as if in a daze, pulling away then slamming into him, then pulling away again.

Jordan looked over his shoulder for Marvin, but couldn't see through the crowd scattering for the exits; he figured Marvin had succeeded in holding off the suits because no one was coming after them.

He got her out of the ballroom, into the corridor and down the bank of elevators where he punched the DOWN button.

The woman didn't struggle or protest, just frowned as she stared, open-mouthed, at the gold- and rust-colored hexagonal patterns in the carpet, shaking her head pathetically.

"She has my son," she breathed as Jordan looked around for signs of trouble. "She has my son and—"

"We'll get downstairs, miss, and—"

"—and she's going to do some-something horrible to him."

"—we'll talk, okay?"

He removed his arm and took a step away from her, not looking at her anymore. She was crying and tears made him fidget. He swiped a hand down his face, sighing, wishing Marvin and the elevator would hurry up and hoping this disturbed woman wasn't one of those greasy-haired people he saw so often roaming the streets around his office, picking invisible lint from their ragged clothes and rambling on and on about relatives who owed them money and ex-spouses who owed them apologies. He stuffed his hands in his back pockets and stared at the elevator doors, and was caught completely off guard when the woman threw herself at him and clutched his sweater in her fists, pleading in a whisper, "You've gotta help me. Please. You've gotta help me get my son back. My Nathan. Please."

Jordan lifted his hands to touch her but didn't, not quite; they stopped an inch from her shoulders and he tried to speak but couldn't, suddenly wanting to be home, away from this woman and the Universal Enlightened Alliance.

"Look, lady," he began, but Marvin hurried around a corner and down the corridor, huffing, with the hum of a crowd not far behind him.

"Whatta you say we get the hell out of here," he gasped.

The elevator doors rumbled open and they got in.

7.

"The police said there's nothing they can do. I talked to them this morning, as soon as I discovered that . . . that . . . Nathan was missing. Mark took all the money from the bank, everything we *had*. *And* my *son*. But it's not a police matter, they said. I'd have to get a lawyer, they said. 'He's your husband's son, too,' they said. For all I know . . . hell, he might have sold the *house* out from under me."

The woman's name was Lauren Schroeder and she'd knocked back three shots of Johnny Walker within minutes of entering the nearly empty bar they'd found a few blocks from the hotel. Then she'd ordered another. She was still trembling from her experience with Hester Thorne.

As she drank, they asked her questions, tried to get her to talk, but she didn't hear them, or ignored them. She drank and stared at the candle flickering in a squat red bowl in the center of the table, her hands fluttering; the fingers of her right hand clawed the gold band on her left, nails clicking against it like dry bones, and the red candlelight spilled over her fingers like blood. She shook her head, muttered, looked like she was going to cry again, then drank some more. That went on for a while until, during the minutes between her third and fourth shots, she began to respond to Jordan and Marvin. Starting slowly, then speaking fast, running her sentences together, she told them everything.

"Why are you so sure he's with Hester Thorne?" Jordan asked.

"Because that . . . that *religion*, or whatever it is, is all he's been talking about, *living*, for the last, I don't know, months, over a year maybe, I'm not sure. And he's tried so hard to pass it on to Nathan, tried to get him to believe in all that . . . *shit*. Crystals and extraterrestrials . . . *all* of that. And of *course* Nathan believes it, he's just a little boy, he'll believe *anything* his father tells him. And I . . . I tried to tell him . . . I wanted to make him understand that . . . well, you just can't take a boy like that and . . ." She sighed abruptly, a sudden expulsion of breath that put the candleflame in agony, then putting her face in her hands, she breathed, "I have nothing now. He's taken it all. And after we worked so hard . . . first toward his career, then with the cocaine . . . oh, God, what we went through with that, I mean . . . and deciding how to raise Nathan . . . that's not easy, you know, you can't just . . ." She reached for the glass on the table, but it was empty. "What am I going to do?" Her voice was nearly inaudible. "What . . . am I going . . . to do?"

Jordan looked at Marvin, who raised his eyebrows high as if to say, *So, what now?*

"Not that I doubt what you've told us," Jordan began uncertainly, "but do you have any proof at all, Mrs. Schroeder, of your husband's attachment to the Alliance?"

She laughed coldly and without smiling. "What do you think I am, some kind of lunatic? Running into that place, screaming at that woman? Do you think I did that because I thought *maybe* my husband had run off to live with that . . . *soothsayer*?"

Jordan took a deep breath and closed his eyes a moment, fighting off his impatience. "I said I don't doubt you. I'm just wondering if you have some proof."

She began slapping her hands over the plaid shirt, slipping her fingers in the breast pockets until she found a small piece of paper. "I found this in the bedroom this morning," she said, unfolding it. "A letter. A note, really." When she handed it over to him, her fingers were quivering.

It was written on a page from a palm-sized spiral bound notebook:

> *Mark,*
> *Have courage and be strong. The worst is almost over. Until S.F. . . .*
>
> *Yours in Godness, H.*

Marvin squinted at the note, adjusting his glasses, and mumbled, "He might've written it."

"Might have," Jordan whispered. "But why?"

Marvin shrugged.

"The handwriting looks very . . . feminine. Don't you think?"

"Mm-hm."

"Are you *cops*?" Lauren asked.

"No, we're not. But we have, um, an interest in the Alliance," Jordan said, looking at the note, then at her. "You said your husband led you to believe he was going to work every day for three weeks after he quit his job. What did he do for a living?"

"He was a shift supervisor at Diego Nuclear Power Plant."

"He just . . . *quit*? Just like that?"

"He told them some story about us moving north, up toward Mount Shasta."

Frowning, Jordan studied the note again. "I know it's none

of my business, but . . . did your husband make good money at his job?''

She shrugged. ''We . . . did okay. In fact, we did very well. At least, we *were* . . . doing very well. Before she came along and took it all away.''

''So, other than the money, you can think of nothing about your husband that would especially interest Hester Thorne?''

She shook her head and closed her eyes, whispering, ''I don't know why she wants him. And I don't care. I only want my son.''

After tossing a glance at Marvin, Jordan said, ''During those three weeks after your husband had quit his job, do you think he could have been seeing Hester Thorne? Meeting with her someplace?''

''He could have. Maybe. Probably. I don't know. And I really don't care. I don't care if they're *married*, really. All I want is my son and my share of the money he took.''

'' 'The worst is almost over,' '' Jordan read quietly.

''Sounds like they were . . . well, planning something, maybe?'' Marvin said.

''Have you looked at your phone bills lately, Mrs. Schroeder?''

''What?''

''Your phone bills. To see if he's been making any calls to Grover.''

''He takes care of all that. It never occurred to me to—'' Her eyes narrowed slightly as she leaned toward Jordan and asked firmly, ''Look, who *are* you? Why are you asking all these questions?''

''I'm a private investigator.''

''Really?'' she whispered, then louder, hopefully: ''*Really?* Could you . . . would you help me get my son back?'' She clutched his wrist and squeezed. ''Please? I *need* help. I don't think I can do it alone. And I'm afraid something horrible will happen to him if I don't get him soon. Right *now*. She's awful, that woman, she's—''

Jordan pulled his hand away and cleared his throat loudly.

She stopped speaking but stared at him imploringly, closing her hand into a fist on the table, then relaxing it. Closing, relaxing . . . closing, relaxing . . .

"Why do you think something will happen to your son?" he asked.

Her eyes darted back and forth between them. "I . . . well, I . . . I'm *afraid*. That woman . . . those people . . . there's something wrong with them." She grabbed Jordan's wrist again, her voice wet, lips trembling as she hissed, "Please, Mr. Cross, you *have* to help me!"

Jordan snapped his hand away abruptly this time, making no effort to hide his discomfort at her touch.

Marvin patted his arm, muttered, "Take it easy, Jordan," then took Lauren's hand and smiled, "You're upset, Mrs. Schroeder, and with good reason. But think about it; he's with his dad, right? Sure, you're angry at your husband right now, but you don't think he'd let any harm come to the boy, do you? I don't think so. And Mrs. Schroeder, in our business—" He nodded toward Jordan. "—we've found that missing persons, more often than you think, turn up on their own. I mean, they just come back. I don't think you have anything to—"

She tore her hand away and slammed a fist on the table. "Don't bullshit me! This is something he's been *thinking* about, not a whim. He took all of our money and he quit his job three *weeks* ago! She knew who I was and what I was talking about, couldn't you *tell*? She went crazy! She . . . she was, I don't know, babbling something. Like she was speaking in tongues, or something. And she *knocked* me off that stage! I . . . I think. It felt like it, anyway. I couldn't breathe for a while. It was like . . . well, it almost felt like she . . . like maybe she . . ." Lauren slapped a hand over her eyes and her mouth twisted as she began to cry. "Listen to me, I—I'm starting to sound like *him*. Believing all that . . . that . . ." She scrubbed her face and pushed her chair away from the table. "Forget it. Just forg—I'll find him my—just *forget* it." She spun and swayed a bit, then started out of the bar.

Jordan watched her leave, then looked around; a man and woman sat at opposite ends of the bar, a fat couple sat at a corner table hunched over their drinks, and the bartender was talking quietly on the telephone behind the register.

She was right; Hester Thorne had gone crazy. And in front of an *audience*. The note implied a plan between her and Schroeder; it even sounded like she'd been encouraging him, pressing him, perhaps, to leave his wife. It was impossible, of course, to be sure of anything with just a couple of quickly written lines to go on, but Jordan had no doubt that the two men in the hotel ballroom had been reaching for guns, and he was sure that Lauren Schroeder—whether she was right or wrong— would go to Grover and stir things up to find her son. If Fiske was right and Harvey Bolton had been murdered for learning too much, Grover would not be a safe place for Lauren Schroeder, either.

Whatever Hester Thorne's involvement with Mark Schroeder was—if, indeed, there was an involvement—one thing was certain: the Universal Enlightened Alliance had done some damage to the Schroeder family.

Edmond Fiske would like to hear that.

Better yet, he would *pay* to hear it.

She had reached the door when Jordan called, "Mrs. Schroeder."

No one in the bar noticed.

She stopped, turned slowly.

He held up the note she'd left behind.

Wiping her puffy eyes, she returned to the table, took the note, and stuffed it back into her pocket. "Thuh-thank . . . you."

"Uh, look, Mrs. Schroeder," Jordan began, not quite looking at her, "I can't make any promises, okay? I mean, I'm not saying I'll get your son back, but . . . I think we might be able to help each other. I've—"

She dropped back into the chair and gasped, "Oh, God, thank you, thank you so *much*, Mr.—"

"I *said* I wasn't *promising* anything," he snapped, and felt Marvin's disapproval, knew that Marvin was frowning at him for being so abrupt and uncompassionate. "But . . . I'll see what I can do." He stood and said, "I'll be right back."

"Where you going?"

Taking Edmond Fiske's card from his pocket, he said, "To make a phone call."

8.

The Coke from the machine down the hall hissed as Mark poured it over crackling ice. CNN was on the television and Mark sat at the table by the long window; San Francisco flickered in the night below.

"Is Mom coming later?"

"I . . . I hope so, Nathe."

"You mean you don't know?"

"Well, I'm not sure."

"Does she know where we are?"

That was a tough one. Mark didn't want Nathan to know that they'd sneaked away from the house leaving Lauren no clue as to where they had gone or if they would be back; he didn't want him to know for a while, anyway. He'd made a game of leaving the house without waking up Mom and Nathan had played along happily. Later, he would tell Nathan the truth, when he thought the boy would be able to understand that they *couldn't* tell his mother why they were leaving or where they were going, that she felt nothing but hostility toward everything Mark believed. But for now, he was uncomfortable with that question and chose to ignore it until Nathan moved on to something else. He quietly sipped his fizzing Coke.

"How long'll we stay here, Dad?" Nathan asked, tired of the silence that had followed his previous question. He fidgeted on the edge of the bed, picking at the fringe on the bedspread.

"You mean here in—don't do that, Nathe, it'll tear—you mean here in the hotel?"

"Here in San Frisco."

"San *Fran*cisco. I don't know. Miss Thorne is giving a talk here in the hotel. We might leave tonight when she's finished. Maybe tomorrow."

"Can we hear her talk?"

"Afraid not, kiddo. She wants us to wait here in the room."

"Do you think Miss Thorne is pretty, Dad?"

"Sure do," Mark chuckled.

But that was not his reason for being there, of course. Hester Thorne was a beautiful woman—much more than just physically beautiful—and Mark had come to feel very close to her during their many meetings over the past three weeks. But his attraction to her was not sexual—

—*Not completely*, he thought, *no, certainly not* completely *sexual*—

—it was something much deeper than that, something that had little to do with the physical body—

—*But God knows Hester Thorne's physical body is just fine, thank you very much*—

—and what frustrated Mark even more than Lauren's hostility toward the Alliance and her stubborn rejection of his newly awakened spirituality was knowing that as soon as she learned where he'd gone, she would most likely accuse him of having an affair with Hester. She would accuse him of taking all their money to run away and live with Hester; she would probably divorce him without hesitation and take him to court for custody of Nathan.

It would probably never occur to her—not for a second—that if she would just open up to the things Mark had discovered in the Alliance, if she would just give them a fair *chance*, maybe she would find in them the comfort Mark had found and they could be *together* now, instead of playing these ridiculous, hurtful games.

"Lower plane games," Hester called them, because, she said, "They are played only on this plane, the physical plane, one of the lowest. Other more spiritually and psychically developed beings on non-physical planes have outgrown these games and lead a pure, uncluttered existence. You can outgrow them, too, Mark," she'd told him one afternoon during their first meeting in a coffee shop in Dunnigan, midway between Grover and Los Gatos. "I can help you outgrow them and begin your ascent to a higher level of existence. If you'll let me. You have to *let* me."

"How do I do that?" he'd asked quietly. His voice was low and his words came slowly; he'd had a fight with Lauren the night before—and the night before that and nearly every night for the past several weeks—and he felt low. Mark had finally found something that felt right to him, a belief system that gave his life meaning beyond his status as a husband and father, and Lauren's constant rejection of it, her relentless scathing attacks on it hurt him deeply. He realized for the first time how she must have felt during his addiction to cocaine; she'd adopted the same close-minded denial that had kept *him* from seeing his problem for so long. He saw no signs of improvement between them and decided he would have to take some sort of action. As much as he loved Lauren, Mark could not cling to her while she continued to resist growth; he had to get his own life in order. And Nathan: Mark would not allow the weight of Lauren's bitter stubbornness to drag Nathan down with her.

After the warm reception he and Nathan—and even Lauren, with her sour face and cold manner—had gotten from Hester Thorne during their visit to Grover, Mark decided to try calling her for some advice. He called from work one day and left a message with her secretary, not really expecting to hear from her.

Not only did she call back, she *remembered* him.

"You're the gentleman from the nuclear power plant, aren't you?" she asked pleasantly. "How nice to hear from you."

Mark stalled with small talk for a while, unsure of how to turn the conversation to his personal problems, uncertain if he even wanted to. He was rambling about the weather in the San Jose area when Hester interrupted him with a warm whispery voice.

"What's troubling you, Mark? What can I do?"

And he told her.

She suggested they meet and Mark took a day off that week and drove up to Dunnigan. It wasn't much later that he quit his job at Hester's request to meet with her every day and plan for his future. Also at her request, he kept his actions secret from Lauren. From everyone.

"It would only make things worse," Hester told him. "Especially with your wife. It wouldn't be your fault, of course. She simply insists on playing these lower plane games with you. You're doing the best you can, Mark. You're doing fine."

Nathan went to the window and looked out at the city, silent for a while. Then he turned to Mark and asked, "Do you think Miss Thorne's prettier than Mom, Dad?"

Mark winced, finishing his Coke. "Why don't you change the channel, Nathe? Maybe there's some cartoons on."

" 'Kay."

Nathan occupied himself in front of the television as Mark went to the bathroom and washed his face with cold water, noticing that his hands were trembling. It wasn't an easy thing he was doing, but it was necessary.

He suddenly wanted a drink.

That's not what you need and you know it, he thought, looking at his reflection over the sink. *You know what you need and you've come for it. You've done the right thing. The right thing . . .*

There was a gentle knock at the door and Mark dried his face quickly, crossed the room, and opened the door to Hester Thorne. She smiled at him, but it was a troubled, unsteady smile.

"Hello," Mark said, "come in, please."

She entered the room with forearms folded below her breasts, as if she were chilled, and Nathan scrambled to his feet and ran toward her grinning.

"Miss Thorne!" he shouted.

"Calm down, Nathe," Mark said.

"No, Mark, don't. He's fine." She bent down and hugged him tight, kissed his head. "You can call me Hester, okay Nathan? I don't call you Mr. Schroeder, do I?"

"Okay, Hester. I didn't think you was *ever* gonna come. There's nothin' on television."

She laughed and hugged him again, but Mark saw the reserve in her movements, the tense lines around her eyes.

"Tell you what, Nathan," she said, holding his face in her hands, "why don't you try some more to find something on TV while your dad and I take a little walk down the hall, okay?"

" 'Kay." He returned to the television happily and began turning the dial.

Hester turned to Mark, took his arm, and led him to the door. "Do you mind?" she whispered.

"Not at all. Is something wrong? You look upset."

As they stepped into the corridor outside the room, she shook her head, hooked her arm in his and squeezed. "I'm tired. I always am for a while after a long trance."

"So you're all finished here?"

She nodded. "Mark, I came to tell you . . . your wife was at the seminar."

"Lauren?" He stopped and faced her, pulling his arm away.

"She was . . . upset."

"She talked to you?"

"She *screamed* at me. We had to end early. There was . . . well, a commotion."

She took his arm again and led him around a corner to a small room in which a bright red Coke machine and a cumbersome ice machine both hummed dully.

"Was she hurt?" Mark asked, with a small jolt of fear.

"Don't worry, Mark, nothing happened to her. But . . . well, your wife is a very hostile woman."

"What happened?"

"She came while I was in trance. I don't remember any of it, of course, but one of my men told me. She was very angry, screaming obscenities . . . and I guess she tried to attack me."

"*Lauren?* She would never do that!"

"She injured some ushers. Not badly, but one of them was—"

"Where is she now?"

"A man took her away. Dark hair . . . maybe brown, but they said it was hard to tell because it was slicked back. Little round glasses, maybe six feet tall or so. A mustache. Sound familiar?"

"No, no, that doesn't . . . a man? No, doesn't ring a bell. A *man* . . ." Mark turned away from her and chewed the knuckle of his thumb, quickly calling up the names of all the men they knew who might fit that description, but could think of no one. Someone he didn't know about, perhaps?

A strange and disturbing question was asked rather loudly by his inner voice, so loudly it made him blink hard:

When was the last time Lauren and I made love?

Maybe six, eight months ago. Surely not a whole year . . .

He wondered for the first time since he and Lauren had been married if she could be seeing someone else. . . .

"Mark, I didn't mean to upset you," Hester said. "I just thought you should know."

"Yeah," he whispered. "Yeah."

"I'm a little concerned."

"Why?"

"It's just a . . . just something I'm feeling . . . an impression . . . maybe from Orrin . . ."

"*What?*" he snapped, immediately shaking his head in silent apology for his tone.

She placed her right hand on his chest, over his heart. "Something's coming, Mark. Something . . . bad." Putting her other hand on his shoulder, she added, "And somehow, your wife will be a part of it."

"What? What are you—"

"She'll try to take you away."

"Away from—"

"From your beliefs from what you now know to be the truth.

She wants your son, too, Mark. She wants little Nathan. But you listen to me, Mark. You listen. . . .''

Vaguely, Mark noticed that Hester was standing much closer to him now, so close he could feel her breath on his chin, and her left hand was squeezing his shoulder, gently at first, then with slowly growing strength, until she was kneading it, clenching it between her strong fingers and thumb. But it didn't hurt at all because he hardly felt it, and he could no longer hear the hum of the ice machine or even see the glowing red of the Coke machine behind Hester. The room was filled with her alone: her face, her blue eyes sparkling like wet crystals, and her voice, almost a whisper, flat as a Kansas plain but somehow musical, like one long endless note played on some exotic instrument, and *soft*, so soft he longed to touch it, as a child might a butterfly's wing . . .

. . . but he only listened because he could do nothing else.

"You cannot—are you listening, Mark?—you *cannot* let her take Nathan. She will bury that boy in ignorance like a corpse in a grave. She'll stunt his spiritual growth. Do you know what a gift you're giving Nathan? So few are given the truth so early in life. Most people are exposed to lie after lie for so long that when they finally find the truth they let it pass right by them and grow old in their ignorance. Nathan is young, his mind is open, and you have given him the *truth*, Mark. Don't let *her* take it away from him.''

"Buh . . . buh . . .'' Mark forced himself to blink once, again, slowly. He took a deep breath and tried to smile, but his lips only trembled. "But you have to understand,'' he said, "she's his mother. She's worried about him. About me, too, probably.'' Quietly, he added, "I . . . hope. It's natural for her to be upset. When we get to Grover, I'll call her and—''

"Be careful.''

"I won't tell her—''

"She's waiting for an opening, Mark. Don't give it to her.'' The words could have been spoken maliciously, but they weren't; she was simply stating a fact in a low, smooth voice, a voice as massaging as her hand on his shoulder.

He had forgotten she was doing that and suddenly became aware of it again, of how good it felt . . . and of how close her face was to his . . . so close that if he moved only slightly, head bowed just a bit . . . their lips would touch. . . .

Mark heard the walls collapsing around him and stiffened,

stepped back away from Hester, away from her hand and lips and eyes, away from her voice, but—

—it was only ice cubes falling in the machine and—

—for half a heartbeat, he was seated on the edge of his bed and Lauren was kneeling before him, both of them crying, Mark saying, "I'll get help, I promise I will, Lauren, just, please, *please*, don't leave me," and Lauren holding his head in her hands and saying, "How could I, how *could* I now? I love you too much to leave you now," and—

—the electric rush of adrenaline that had suddenly coursed through him slowed and became a thick coating of guilt that clung to him like grease, clogging his pores, oozing between his fingers.

"I should get back to Nathan," he said in a cracked voice, turning to leave.

She took his hand and held him back.

"You've done the right thing, Mark. You *know* you have. Let yourself be used. Let Nathan be used. Like Orrin uses me. They will, you know. Use you."

Massaging again . . . holding him with her eyes . . .

"They have such plans for you and Nathan. You're different than most. There is . . ." She paused, tucked her lower lip between her teeth and thought a moment, then went on: "There is something called the Inner Circle, Mark. A core group that . . . well, a group that is closer to the other levels of existence. You could be a part of the Inner Circle. You and Nathan. You can't let her stand in the way of that. Can you, Mark?"

He knew he couldn't. The guilt was still there, clutching at him, but what he knew—what he *wanted*—so deep inside him was stronger.

"No," he said. "I can't."

As they returned silently to the hotel room and Nathan, their hands stayed together, fingers locked tightly, arms intertwined, and Mark noticed that although her hand was smaller than his and fit nicely in his palm, nearly disappearing within his fingers, it was *she* who held *his* hand, not the other way around.

9.

Jordan and Marvin spent the next two weeks poring over the material left behind by Harvey Bolton. They went over it again and again, went to the library to find other articles that would back up the material with new information.

They talked with local television and newspaper reporters who had done stories on the Universal Enlightened Alliance, who in turn gave them leads on people whose spouses or relatives were living at the Alliance complex in Grover and were not allowed to have any contact with family or friends. Those people had no legal recourse in retrieving their loved ones because the Alliance was doing nothing wrong according to the law; those living there did so by choice and were not being held against their will.

Although the law could find no fault with the Alliance, the people Jordan and Martin spoke with were certain that there was something insidious about the organization and that something horrible—and perhaps permanently mind-altering—was being done to their loved ones . . . they just didn't know *what;* they all shared this gut reaction, and although they could not specifically define it or prove it, they did not doubt it. Jordan and Marvin found that interesting, but not helpful . . . yet.

Along with the other information Bolton had gathered was a computer printout of a segment of the membership of the Alliance. Although it was an incomplete list, Bolton also included a handwritten note giving the Alliance computer's modem number and password; he pointed out that the password was changed often, but always seemed to be the name of an Ascended Master, a complete list of which was available in Hester Thorne's book *Masters Among Us*. Each name on the printout was followed by a great deal of information about that person's financial, religious, educational, and, if any, criminal background. Some of the names listed were followed by the word WITHDRAWAL, which Jordan and Marvin took to mean that that person had left the organization, but even the withdrawals were followed by a block of information about that person. Except for one: Simon Ketter. His name was circled in black ink and a question mark was written beside it. The entry read simply:

Simon Ketter—WITHDRAWAL

It was odd, but neither of them could come up with a logical explanation for the difference in that one entry, but it wasn't the only mystery in Harvey Bolton's collection of information.

Jordan read Bolton's note over and over—

> Tom—
> Read these carefully in the order I've stacked them, then tell me: what's wrong with this picture? Please don't laugh this off. Give it a chance.

—but was able to draw no solid conclusions from the stack of material. Only one thing stood out. . . .

"Her son," Jordan muttered one evening, hunched over the material on his office desk.

"What about him?" Marvin asked from his chair where he was going over some notes.

"This guy underlined every mention of Hester Thorne's son Benjamin in all these articles."

"And?"

"The only *other* thing he underlined has nothing to *do* with her son."

"What is it?" Marvin asked, standing to lean over the desk.

Jordan pointed to a headline in a tabloid called the *Global Reporter*. It read:

BIGFOOT SIGHTING IN NEW AGE PARADISE
TOURISTS TERRIFIED BY HULKING BEAST
NEAR ALLIANCE HEADQUARTERS

Marvin grunted and shrugged. "I dunno. According to Hester Thorne, her son is dead. Maybe this reporter guy was a nut case, you ever think of that? Maybe he had a history of drug use. We never thought to ask any questions about *him*."

"I don't think so. I think he really saw something in all of this. Even if it was just one little thing, he must've thought it was important. I just wish he would've pointed it out instead of expecting everyone *else* to see it, too. He's got interviews here with people who are pissed off at the Alliance, afraid of the Alliance and indifferent toward the Alliance, but . . ." He leaned back, away from the pool of light his desk lamp cast over the stack of papers, and sighed wearily, "*I* don't know. What have we got? Um . . . well, there's an article that mentions some woman named Elizabeth Murphy who says she grew up with Hester Thorne and thinks she's evil or satanic or something. But then, she's a *Christian*," he said, tossing the last word off his tongue like a thick lump of phlegm, "and they think *everything* is evil and satanic."

"Aw, c'mon Jordy," Marvin said gently as he returned to his chair. "Just because you had some lousy experiences with your parents and their church doesn't mean they're all the same, does it?"

Jordan made a derisive snorting sound.

With a mischievous smirk, Marvin asked, "You mean you don't believe in God at *all*? Not even Satan?"

"Oh, sure. We get together every once in a while for a few beers. Sometimes Santa Claus and the Easter Bunny show up and we play poker. You know damned *well* I don't believe in that crap. I don't *need* to because I don't need an explanation for every little thing that happens."

"You think that's why people cling to those beliefs?"

"Of *course* it is," Jordan snapped, beginning to sound bitter. A frown darkened his face and he was clearly upset by the topic. "If something *good* happens, it comes from God. If something *bad* happens, it's God's will and Satan's pleasure. And everything that can't be understood or explained is evil."

"And your belief?"

"*My* belief? I am a baptized member of the First Church of Shit Happens." He waved his hand as if to dismiss the topic, then began looking through the stack of papers again.

"So, what do you think we ought to do with Mrs. Schroeder?" Marvin asked.

"I don't know." Jordan sounded exasperated. "She calls a dozen times a day, and when she's not on the phone, she's dropping by here."

"You can hardly blame her. The poor woman's understandably upset."

"Yeah, yeah, but what the hell does she expect *me* to do?"

"Anything you can, I think. You need to go a little easier on her. I know she's annoying, but jeez, Jordy, she's no more like your ex-wife than Elizabeth Murphy is like your parents, I'm sure."

"Well, now she wants to go to Grover with us."

"You're kidding. What're you gonna do?"

"Keep saying *no*, what do you *think*?"

"I think we ought to look this Murphy woman up and see what she has to say," Marvin suggested to change the subject.

"Yeah, you're right. That'll be your job. I'm not up to talking to one of *them*."

Marvin chuckled and shook his head. "If she's still in Wheatland like the article says, I'll be able to kill two birds and see Hester Thorne's parents, too."

"Great. First, though, make up a list of all the surveillance equipment you think we might need. Fiske is gonna pay for all of it, of course, so—" He grinned. "—don't be stingy."

"When do we go to Grover?"

"Well, I figure I'll go first and get a feel for the place while you're in Wheatland. Then, once you've talked to everybody you can find there, you join me. In any case, I want to get there before the crowds gather for that damned, uh . . . *festival*, or whatever the hell she's having up there." The five-day-long New World Festival was to begin two weeks from the day Jordan and Marvin had attended Hester Thorne's seminar in San Francisco and it was sure to be terribly crowded.

The media had been covering the festival extensively for nearly two months, always comparing it with the Harmonic Convergence of 1987. But each time Hester Thorne assured them that the New World Festival would be very different from, and far more effective than, the Harmonic Convergence. She pointed out that her festival had a single location, rather than several all over the globe, and would therefore generate more positive energy, which would, she hoped, help to heal the earth's many wounds and speed up the coming of the New Age of Enlightenment.

The media made a big deal of the fact that many of the residents of Grover were less than excited about the upcoming event, but none of them seemed hostile toward the Alliance itself. In fact, Jordan found it interesting that no matter how hard the reporters tried to stir up anger in the residents—usually with blatant questions like, "Doesn't it make you *angry* that these people have moved into your town and are now bringing even *more* people into your town?"—their responses were cautious and carefully worded; it reminded him of some of Harvey Bolton's notes, in which Bolton pointed out that it was obvious the people of Grover were afraid of the Alliance, they just refused to *admit* it.

Neither Jordan nor Marvin were looking forward to the festival—they knew it would be crawling with what Marvin called "crystal zombies"—but it was unavoidable.

While they were preparing for their investigation into the Alliance, Lauren Schroeder was certain that she was losing her mind. She couldn't stay by herself in the house, so she accepted Glenda's invitation to stay at her place. Glenda's husband Pete was sympathetic and generous and treated her like a member of the family even though he and Lauren really didn't know one another well at all.

Lauren felt uncomfortable at first, felt as if she were imposing, but that passed after a few days, mostly because she had no other place to go. She could call her parents in Sacramento or her sister in San Diego; she knew they would do anything they could for her. But she didn't do that. Not yet, not until after she'd learned what Jordan Cross had in mind.

So she stayed with Glenda and her family. The only problem was that every time she saw Glenda's two children, every time she heard them laugh in another part of the house or saw one of them run through the room, she felt sick and had to fight not to start sobbing. Since she'd discovered Nathan's empty bed and closet, every child she saw was Nathan and every child's voice was his calling for her.

She feared for Nathan's welfare—for his *life*—but her feelings toward Mark were very different. When she thought of Mark, she became angry . . . *furious*. When she thought of Hester Thorne, she thought only of revenge. She craved it almost as much as she craved getting Nathan back . . .

. . . which she intended to do whether Jordan Cross helped her or not.

As Lauren looked forward to her revenge and the rescue of her son, Mark and Nathan were being introduced to their new surroundings in Grover.

They were separated the first day, something Mark wasn't expecting and didn't especially like.

"It's standard procedure here," Hester told him smilingly. "You're both going to be doing a lot of studying, and you can't possibly study on the same level, so you'll be separated. Then you'll see him whenever you like."

"But . . . couldn't I at least see him for a little while each day?" Mark asked hopefully.

"Not during the initial courses. It's a very concentrated period of study and training. You'll see what I mean when you begin. You won't have time to think about anything but your work. But when you're done, you'll be glad because you'll be a different person. A *completely* different person.''

Mark was uncomfortable with the separation, but he trusted Hester. He *had* to; he'd left behind everything to go with her and immerse himself and his son in the spiritual belief that he felt was the final truth. Mark thought of people he'd known in the past who had been converted to Christianity; their lives had gone through drastic, and quite sudden changes, which made perfect sense. So why shouldn't *his* life go through some changes? It made perfect sense . . . didn't it?

And as Mark and Nathan were initiated into the Universal Enlightened Alliance, Lizzie Murphy was spending the better part of her nights with eyes open and mind alert. It wasn't just because she was afraid of having the nightmare again—although she admitted to herself quite readily that that was certainly *part* of it—but because she was not tired. By the time she got to bed lately, she felt like she'd just drunk a whole pot of coffee—and *not* her usual decaf.

Instead of sleeping, Lizzie would sit up in bed, sip tea, read her Bible and pray. Eventually, she would fall asleep for a few hours, but when she awoke, she would feel refreshed, as if she'd gotten a full night's sleep. She would be able to go about her work at the shelter without feeling tired. In fact, odd as it seemed, she'd been feeling better than usual, more energetic and somehow . . . cleaner.

Then, at night, she would go to bed and, once again, spend hours sitting up, reading her Bible and praying.

It was as if she were being compelled to study for a test. Perhaps it was more appropriate to say that she was in training. Yes .. she liked that idea: in training. She was getting in shape, not physically but emotionally. It was her soul, not her body, that needed to be fit, because the battle that was coming would not be a physical one.

And Lizzie Dayton had no doubt in her mind that there *would* be a battle.

===== **TWO** =====

GROVER

1.

Bill Coogan sat up in his bed, tangled in sweat-dampened sheets, and tried to drag himself up from sleep, but the nightmare that had jolted him off his pillow clutched at him tenaciously, sank its thorny claws into the gelatinous tissue of his brain, and pulled down hard and he swung his legs off the bed and stood, gasping for breath as he staggered toward his bedroom window to scream for—

—what?

He couldn't remember, but it was important, desperately urgent; he could feel that even as the nightmare dispersed in dying ripples from his memory.

Screaming. There had been screaming, he remembered that. It was the first time he could remember *anything* from the nightmare and he'd been having it every night for weeks. He knew it was the same each night even though he remembered none of it, because it held onto him when he woke, pulling, trying to drag him back to its center, and it always left him with the same empty feeling, as if he'd been sucked hollow and hung by his neck in a hot dry wind. The feeling usually left him after an hour or so, but Coogan suspected that today, it would stick with him awhile.

The screaming would, anyway, because the voices had been familiar ones. Dear ones.

Putting his big hands on the sill, Coogan pressed his sweaty forehead to the cool windowpane, closed his eyes tightly and whispered, "Gettin' too old for these damned nightmares."

Daylight was spreading in the sky, glowing on the undersides of a few white summer clouds that hovered like fat puffs of whipped cream high above the tall pines. It was going to be a warm clear day, and a busy one. The Fourth of July tourists would start pulling into town today. A few early birds had come in yesterday to beat the rush. In the winter, the town was overrun with skiers, and during this week every summer the area was flooded with partyers. Normally, they would come in their campers and trailers and motor homes and fill the hotels and motels and bed-and-breakfasts.

This year, however, would be different because along with the Independence Day crowd would come the followers of Hester Thorne to attend the New World Festival. This would be bigger than most Alliance events; people were coming from all over the country—even from *other* countries—for this one. It was going to be busier and more crowded than ever . . . so crowded, in fact, that Coogan expected more tempers to rise than spirits.

Coogan had no complaints. Like all of Grover, he thrived on the business of outsiders. He sold them gas and snacks and cigarettes; he gave them directions and answered their questions about the area. In fact, he supposed his voice would be hoarse by the time the partyers and festival goers left.

Some, though, would not leave. Some might stay because they found Grover to be a quaint and inviting little town and they might imagine their lives to be simpler and more serene if they settled down there with visions of Mayberry and Currier and Ives winters in their minds. Those people were few and far between and didn't stay long; if the boredom didn't run them out first, the icy-cold winter would. No, the reason that usually kept them in Grover was just outside of town in a big white castle of a hotel: the Universal Enlightened Alliance. Coogan couldn't figure for the life of him what it was about it that made some of them stay. There were more each year, and those who didn't give in to the temptation right away sometimes came back later, with their bags packed. Sometimes an entire family, sometimes a single person passing through. And sometimes, a husband or a wife would come back alone and leave the other behind. Something about it grabbed them, embraced them, and changed them.

When Hester Thorne came to Grover and started the Alliance, Coogan paid her no attention. He saw her as the purveyor of just another crackpot philosophy. But when she began to get statewide, then national attention, and when she began to appear on television and obtained the endorsement of Sheila Bennett—

someone he'd always admired—Coogan felt he had to cock an ear and listen to what Hester Thorne had to say.

He was not a religious man, Bill Coogan. Oh, he and his wife used to go to church before she died, but they did not go there because they thought the church was their end-all answer. They went to be with others who had feelings similar to theirs and because Sunday was just about the dullest day of the week in Grover.

They believed in God and they put great stock in the Bible as a source of good sense; but to the Coogans, organized religion was just another man-made institution that had countless branches, each of which interpreted the Bible in such a way as to back its own particular theory. It worked for some, they granted that much, but not for them. Coogan was saddened to see, as he grew older, that many of those for whom religion did not work were rejecting God because of it, rejecting the very possibility of His existence.

He condemned none of them because the world was nothing if not a flurry of confusion; he even looked into some of the various new churches with curiosity and an open mind. But to Bill Coogan, they ultimately made no sense, because they all turned out to be the invention of leaders just as confused and desperate as their followers or, at their worst, the invention of leaders out to make a quick and easy buck.

Of them all, the Universal Enlightened Alliance—and the so-called New Age movement in general—was the most confusing. And the most disturbing. After he'd examined its beliefs as closely as he could, it seemed to him to have no focus, no center . . .

. . . except *self*. To Coogan, *that* was unsettling.

As if the Alliance itself were not disturbing enough, it had embraced, like so many other people, his daughter. Now he almost wished that she'd gone to the city like she'd planned, just taken the kids and moved into some hellhole apartment with a dozen locks on the door and done whatever it was she thought she'd be able to do better in San Francisco than in Grover.

As Paul Kragen, a writer for the Grover *Sentinel*, had written several weeks ago in one of his scathing articles about the Alliance, "What it comes down to is this: the Alliance is hip and therefore it is big, and these days, anything that is big only gets bigger, because it is hip." Paul made no secret of his feelings about the Alliance and wrote about them often, so often that no one seemed to pay him any attention anymore. He was right, but Coogan sometimes questioned the man's judgment in being right so loudly, especially with the Alliance getting bigger all the time. . . .

Coogan walked back to his bedside, round and white-skinned in nothing but a baggy pair of boxers; his bones ached and his arthritic fingers threatened mutiny as he tried to fish a Camel out of its pack. He stuck it beneath his walrus-like mustache and lit it with an old chrome lighter dulled with age and speckled with dings. His lungs went through their usual morning convulsions and hacked and wheezed as he slipped on his old brown terrycloth robe and his wire-rim glasses, then shuffled barefoot through the cramped bedroom, down the hall and into the kitchen. He put on some coffee, put a couple eggs in a pot of water on the stove, then went through the curtained doorway in the living room to the store in front. He turned on the pumps and flipped the switch that started the Chevron sign rotating outside, coughing and harrumphing all the way, the Camel dangling from the corner of his mouth. He went to the side window and looked out at the town.

Coogan's Fuel Stop was perched atop an incline on Grover Street, the main thoroughfare, and the town was nestled below. New sunlight glared off some of the windows and Coogan could see a couple people ambling into the Lemurian Diner. It was named after the little people who supposedly lived inside Mount Shasta; the owner, Chelsea Darmont, a round little widow who'd read too many of those Tolkien books, had decorated the place with paintings of the little folks she claimed to have seen more than a few times. They were her own paintings, of course. She had a table at the crafts fair every spring, selling little Lemurian figurines made of clay and Lemurians painted on everything from velvet to tree bark. She'd sell a couple items with a good turnout, but usually didn't move much at all.

The sidewalk on that side of the street was still wooden. Back in seventy-nine, the town fathers had decided to replace the old wooden sidewalks with concrete, but after completing one side of the street, a lot of people began complaining that the new walk looked too modern for the old town, that they were tearing up the town's roots and should let it be. If tourists wanted to see concrete sidewalks, the citizens protested, they could stay in the city; they came to Grover to see old red-brick buildings—like the town hall and the Methodist church—and soda fountains with marble counters and the Swiss-style storefronts and, dammit-all *wooden sidewalks*. At a town council meeting, Wilma Jeeter, who was then Grover's oldest citizen—she turned ninety-four that year—had stood from her wheelchair in the middle of the sheriff's speech supporting the new sidewalks and, shaking a gnarled fist in the air, had shouted in a surprisingly strong voice, "Next thing you know, you'll wanna level the mountain and put in a goddamned *shopping* mall!" The roaring ovation that followed was the last sound Wilma ever heard; she plopped back into her wheelchair and promptly stopped breathing, fist still clenched.

The parking lot of the Mountain Motor Inn on the far side of town was full and a few travelers were loading suitcases and garment bags back into their cars. They would have breakfast at the diner, then come up to Coogan's to fill their tank before they started out for wherever they were going.

"And if you don't get the lead outta your ass, old man," Coogan muttered around his cigarette, jarring a long finger of ash from the tip, "you're gonna lose their business." He slipped his hands into the pockets of his robe and focused his eyes on his own hazy reflection in the windowpane.

His silver hair, yellowed on the tips from nicotine, was still full on the sides and in back and was tangled from a night's sleep, but only a thin tuft remained on top. A film of perspiration still glistened on his creased forehead. The ghost of the nightmare still lingered in his eyes; it stayed with him longer each morning as the weeks passed, even though it was little more than a fog in his memory. The details weren't there, but the *feeling* was . . . the feeling that something was wrong, that someone was in trouble, or would be soon.

He thought of his little granddaughter, Katie, as he had at that very moment the previous morning, and the morning before that, and Bill Coogan closed his eyes, plucked the cigarette from his lips and exhaled smoke.

"Oh, please, God," he breathed as he walked back through the store, "let me be senile. . . ."

The bell over the door was seldom silent that morning and Coogan had no time to pay attention to the brittle ache in his knuckles and wrists. A few regulars dropped in after breakfast—

Wally Schumacher, Amos Haas, Chuck "Flash" Gordon—and stood around the register drinking coffee from Styrofoam cups, smoking cigarettes, and talking about the upcoming Independence Day dance and spaghetti feed. Coogan nodded and said "uh-huh" at all the appropriate times, dividing his attention between the men, the customers, and the gas pumps, which he had to clear after each sale. But his mind was on none of it.

He was thinking about little Katie. He hadn't seen her in—what was it, a week, now? Two weeks? Paula used to come in nearly every day, usually for no more than a few minutes, but at least she'd come. Better yet, she'd bring Katie with her. She'd bring Jake, too—Katie's nine-year-old brother—but he wasn't too fond of his grandpa, not like little Katie; he was quiet, fidgeted a lot, and gave Coogan the feeling he couldn't wait to get away from this fat old man. It didn't bother Coogan, mostly because what Jake lacked in affection and respect, Katie made up for twice over. But he hadn't seen her in . . .

. . . *how* long?

That, he was almost certain—

—*Dead certain*, he thought, *you just don't want to admit it*—

—was the cause of his anxiety, perhaps even the root of his nightmares. But—and this irked him—he didn't know why.

Paula came in less often now, hardly ever, really; she was usually alone, sometimes with Jake, but never with Katie. Worse yet, she seemed to skirt any questions Coogan asked about his granddaughter.

A stunning young woman—blond, tanned, wearing short denim cut-offs and a T-shirt with the bottom half torn off—came in, bought a bag of Dorritos and a six-pack of Coors and left without saying a word or tossing so much as a glance at the three old men standing around the end of the counter sipping coffee and staring at her as if they hadn't seen a woman in years. As they watched her leave, Coogan noticed their eyes were locked onto the firm half-moons of flesh below the frayed edge of the cut-offs; even after she was out the glass door, they watched her.

A few moments after the bell had stopped jangling, Flash smacked his lips and said, "Used to date a girl when I was in school looked like that."

Wally, still watching her outside as she eased into a red Camaro, said, "Flash, you didn't stay in school long enough to date *nobody*," and, almost simultaneously, Amos, whose stained lower lip bulged with chew, mumbled, "You never said *hi* to a girl looked like that."

Smiling, Coogan leaned on the register and watched her himself as she pulled her long dark legs into the car. But his smile shrank when he saw Paula's blue Ford pick-up pull into the parking lot. He squinted to look through the dirty windshield; she was alone.

"Fellas," he said, "whatta you say I meet you all later for coffee and a roll at the diner after my boy comes in and takes over?"

They saw her, too, and exchanged nodding glances. Wally patted the counter and said, "Catch you in a while, Billy," and they filed out the door, their voices mingling as they all spoke at once, as they always did. As they went out, they passed a couple coming in, a man and woman, obviously tourists, probably from the city, judging by their dress.

But Coogan's eyes looked beyond them at his daughter as she got out of the pick-up.

She'd gotten her momma's build and face—tiny, thin, with a squarish jaw and big brown eyes—and she *used* to have her momma's odd mixture of gentleness and irreverent humor. Not anymore.

Paula looked determined as she slung her purse over her shoulder and pushed through the door. She wore a white camisole that exposed her midriff, a pea-green skirt that fell just below her knees, and sandals.

"Hi, Pop," she said, smiling. A small cylindrical crystal sparkled on a chain around her neck.

"Hey, baby." He tried to relax his eyes and loosen the knot in his gut, but could do neither successfully. "Where's the kids?"

"Home."

Home was no longer *home*—the little house she'd moved into with her ex-husband when they were married almost eight years ago—now she and the children lived in a cottage behind the Sleeping Woman. *She* called it a cottage, anyway. But visitors were not allowed back there, so Coogan had never seen it.

"How's business?" she asked.

"The Fourth pulls 'em in."

She put her purse on the counter, leaned over and pecked his cheek, her lips barely touching him. "Looked like you were having a rush when I passed by earlier."

"Yeah," he nodded. "You haven't left those kids alone all day, have you?"

"They're never alone there, I've told you that before."

"Yeah," he nodded again. "How's my little girl?"

"I'm fine, Pop. I need some aspirin."

Coogan chuckled. "You're not my little girl no more. Not dressed like that, you ain't. You're my little *woman*. Look mighty pretty today, Paula."

"Thanks."

"No, I meant Katie," he said, turning to the shelf of aspirin and cold medicine behind him, just in case his anxiousness showed in his face. "How's my little Katie?"

"Oh, she's fine, Pop, visiting friends."

"Friends?" He looked over his shoulder at her, his hand frozen inches from a bottle of generic aspirin. "What friends?"

"Just some friends, is all."

She's with some of them, he thought with a little anger. *Some of them damned crystal rubbing neo-hippies.* "Here?" he asked.

"Over in Weed."

"I thought you said she was home."

"Well, Jake's home. Katie's with friends."

"In Weed."

She nodded, then cocked her head and spread her arms. "What? She's with a *friend*, some little girl she knows. Okay?"

Coogan dropped his arm and faced her. "Some little girl? You don't even know who she's with?"

Paula sighed and pressed three fingertips to her temple for a moment, then laid her hand flat over the crystal on her chest and closed her eyes a moment.

"Look, I've got a little headache, Pop, so could you—"

" 'Course, honey, here." He tore the plastic from one of the aspirin bottles and handed it to her. "I'm . . . sorry, hon, I know you wouldn't let Katie run off with just anybody. I'm just . . . well—" He chuckled, trying to tell himself to lighten up. "—it's almost like I don't have a granddaughter anymore, y'know? Never see her. Lord, it's been, well . . . *weeks*. I . . . think about her."

"She's fine, Pop." Paula shook three pills into her palm, slapped them into her mouth and crunched them between her teeth.

"Good Lord, honey," Coogan growled, heading for the dairy

case, "drink some milk with that. You wanna tear up your stomach?"

"I'm fine, really. I had a late breakfast." She capped the bottle and stuffed it into her purse, then hitched the purse strap over her shoulder again.

Coming back to the counter, Coogan said, "Must be some headache."

She shook her head and dismissed it with a little wave of her hand. "Hey, Pop? I was wondering. You know that box of Mom's jewelry? The old stuff she left me? Where'd you pack that?"

No, he thought with a sinking feeling in his center, *no, not the jewelry. I won't allow it.*

"Well . . . you said you probably wouldn't wear it, so . . . I put it all away."

"Yeah, I know. I was just wondering where."

As he searched her face a moment, looking for the shame—there had to be at least a sliver of shame in her eyes, just a speck, perhaps, because he knew what she wanted to do with her dead momma's jewelry, he *knew*—his mouth curled up a bit at the ends, but it wasn't quite a smile; it was more of a twitch. "Change your mind?" he asked. "About the jewelry?"

"Change my—what do you mean?"

He shrugged. "Well, you didn't want to wear it before. You got a date, maybe? Want to impress some fella? That's some pretty fancy jewelry your momma had."

Paula rolled her eyes and smirked. "No, Pop, I don't have a date."

When Coogan spoke again, what little hope had been in his voice was gone. "Then . . . what do you want it for?"

"I'd just—I'd—I'd like to go through it, is all. Okay, Pop? Where is it? The shed?"

"The *shed*? You know I'd never put it in the—" He pressed his lips together abruptly, stood straight and ran his fingers through the tuft of hair atop his head. He lost his will to tread softly with his daughter; he knew there was no way to avoid a fight this time and the best he could do was keep his voice down. "Okay, Paula, what is it? What's going on?"

She hooked her thumb under the purse strap and slapped her other hand to her thigh. "Here we go. Just a simple question, and right away we've got to—"

"It's not a simple question," he hissed. "I wanna know why all of a sudden you're interested in your momma's jewelry."

"Look, she left it to *me*, okay?"

"No. Uh-uh. No, Paula, she left it to the daughter she had when she died."

"And what . . . is *that* supposed to mean."

"It means you'd better give me a damned good reason to see that jewelry or you *won't*, because I don't know you anymore, Paula. A few years ago—no problem! I'd be happy to know you *wanted* to see your momma's jewelry, but *now* . . . now I just don't know."

She pressed herself against the counter and dug her fingernails into its edge. "If you don't know me, it's only because you don't *want* to. You don't understand what I'm doing with my life—it's not what you had in *mind*, is it?—so instead of trying to understand, you just, you just brush it all off and say you don't know me anymore. Well, you know what, Poppa, you know *what*? I don't give a damn!" She slammed a fist on the countertop and jutted her face forward until they were an inch or so apart, Coogan and his daughter, and he had to fight the urge to shrink back in horror from what he saw in her eyes, the flash—like sheet lightning—of white-hot rage that came from nowhere and spread from her eyes to cover her whole face like a disease; it made him want to strike her for the first time in his life, made him want to swing his arm back as far as he could, double his fist and just let her have it, because nothing she could have said or done would have hurt him as much as that horrible look. He even clenched his stiff fingers into a fist at his side and dug the knuckles into his thigh, but he didn't do it because—

—she really wasn't his daughter. He'd spoken figuratively a moment ago, but he realized, as he stared into that furnace of a face, that she *wasn't* his daughter, he really *didn't* know her anymore. It made him sick with sadness for a moment, the thought that she'd finally slipped away from him. He'd always expected it, he supposed, because that was what happened, wasn't it? Sons and daughters grew from dependent children into mature individuals who had their own thoughts and made their own decisions. But it didn't leave her face, that rage, it didn't fade away or even diminish a little, and his sadness turned to fear. She hadn't *grown* into anything; the mask had just fallen off. And his fear was not for her, but for his grandchildren.

All of this rushed through his head in one great overwhelming wave and he leaned on the counter, his shoulders suddenly weak, as if his hands were bricks attached to his wrists.

There were whispers in the back of the store and Coogan remembered the couple who had walked in just ahead of Paula.

"Listen," he whispered, "I got customers, so you just calm yourself down, little lady. You wanna talk about this some more, we'll do it back there." He jerked his head toward the curtained doorway that led to his living room.

"I don't want to talk to you. About anything." She hurried around the corner and slapped at the curtain.

"Where you going?"

She turned to him. "To get what belongs to me."

"So you can *sell* it?" he growled.

Paula said nothing; her breasts rose and fell with angry breaths.

"Like you sold your car? And your stereo? And the boat your husband left behind? All for *them*?"

"That's none of your business."

"Like hell it's none of—"

She was gone, leaving behind only the fluttering drape.

Coogan cleared his throat and called, "Be right with you, folks," then followed her. "You're not gonna find it 'cause it's not here. It's in a safety-deposit box and that's where it stays."

She turned again. "You can't do this."

"Well, you'll have to be more convincing than that, 'cause I'm doin' it."

"She left that jewelry to *me*."

"Not to sell."

"How do you know I'm going to—"

"Because that's all you been doing, girl! They *own* you! If they told you to paint your face and go sell yourself on a street corner, I bet you'd—"

"God . . . damn you."

"What is it this time, Paula? You give 'em a thousand dollars and they get you a free ride on a flying saucer? Or maybe they're gonna let you talk to—who? what?—*Elvis*, maybe?"

"Dammit, *listen* to you. Listen to what you're doing. I never . . . not *once* did I ever make fun of your beliefs. When you and Momma used to go to church every week? I never said anything, I wouldn't *think* of it, because I knew it was important to you. But this . . . what *I* believe . . . it's different. It's not Sunday school and church picnics and *tithes* and *offerings*, so you make fun of it, you act like—''

"But it *is*, sweetheart, don't you see that? It's the same damned thing. Your momma and I, we went to church, but just 'cause it was something to do on Sundays. We saw people, we got outta the house. But we never gave 'em a penny, because I *knew* Reverend Chalmers and I never trusted him as far as I could fart, and because we always figured if God wanted our money, He'd come get it. But even if we *had*, it wouldn't have been this much and not for these reasons.''

"What reasons?''

"I don't *know* what reasons!'' he barked. "That's the problem. These people you're hanging around with—''

"Are people you'll never understand. Because you're ignorant. Like everyone out there. In the world. *Ignorant.* You're afraid of the truth, because it's too *big* for you. You'll never let go of your old ignorant ways. Right and wrong and good and evil and God and man.'' She spat the words from her mouth like rotten meat and that look of rage and hatred crawled back over her face as she spoke. "You'll never grow or ascend, you'll never reach *any* of the higher planes because you're so—you're so—'' She stopped.

Coogan heard a small crunching sound and realized Paula was grinding her teeth together.

"Ignorant," she hissed, then darted around him and through the curtain.

Before she could get away, he grabbed her elbow and spun her around and they faced one another behind the register.

"Look at you,'' he whispered, *"listen* to yourself, spouting that bullshit. What *is* that, anyway? Is that what they teach you, that stuff? Dear *God*, I'm afraid for you, Paula, I really am. Hell, I'm beginning to think you'd sell your own *children* if that woman told you to.''

Coogan regretted his words almost immediately and wanted to snatch them back, undo them, before they could do their damage. He was going to reach out, take her hand, pull her into his arms and embrace her, kiss her on the head like he used to when she was small and beg her forgiveness. He was going to do all of those things until—

—he saw her face.

He couldn't pin it down at first, the thing in her face that made him feel so cold. For a moment, he thought she was going to cry, but there was no sadness in her eyes, no hurt. There was . . . surprise. Yes, that was it, she was *surprised*. And maybe a little afraid. Coogan realized he'd seen that look before, back when—

—Paula was a little girl and he'd walked into her bedroom one evening to find her feeding some of her dinner to a stray cat she'd sneaked into the house that day. She wasn't supposed to have pets in the house and she knew it, because her mother was allergic; she'd been caught and she *looked* like she'd been caught: lips parted, eyes wide, cheeks pale with guilt. She'd looked at him that way many other times throughout her childhood and—

—she was looking at him that way again.

The look was there for only a single beat, then it was gone.

But it remained a visual echo in Coogan's eyes and he swayed where he stood, reached out and clutched the register for support, his hand crushing several of the keys. The cash drawer clattered open with a ring and startled Paula. She took a step back, then another, and he knew she was going to turn and leave, walk out of the store without saying anything more.

"Oh God," he said in a cracked, trembling voice. "Where are they?"

Paula took another backward step.

"Where's Katie and Jake?"

She turned and hurried for the door.

"What have you *done* to those *children*?" he shouted, but—

—she was gone, and the bell over the door was clanging cheerfully, and Coogan's heart protested with an icy shudder, making his chest feel swollen. He braced himself for what he feared was coming, for what his heart had threatened to do now and then in the recent past—he could almost hear its labored voice wheezing, *Okay, Coogie, this is it, I swear to God, I'm throwin' in the towel, buyin' the farm, cashin' in my chips, I am* outta *here!*—and he slapped his hand over his big chest and his fingers clawed at his brown and tan plaid shirt until the buttons were straining against their threads. Between two beats of his frantic heart, he broke into a cold sweat. But it all passed quickly.

"Oh boy . . . oh boy," he breathed, leaning against the cash register, weak with both relief and an overwhelming heaviness that rested on his back like some wretched, snot-nosed little fat boy stubbornly hanging on for a piggy-back ride.

"Are you going to be okay, friend?"

Coogan had forgotten about his customers again and was startled by the man's voice.

They stood at the counter, this couple, the man looking concerned, the woman looking . . . well, she looked kind of lost, like maybe she was torn between bursting into tearful sobs and screaming at the height of her voice.

Coogan pulled a handkerchief from the back pocket of his old brown corduroys and swept it over his moist forehead, then around his neck, taking a deep steadying breath.

"Yeah," he lied, taking a couple more big breaths. The sweating wouldn't stop and his shirt was beginning to cling to his damp skin. "Yeah, just . . . just a little . . . a little upset, is all. My daughter." He nodded toward the door. "Just a little . . . you know, a . . . family problem." His hands were trembling and he silently damned them as he dropped them behind the counter and smiled at his customers. "Now. What can I do for you folks?"

The woman stepped forward and her pretty face bunched into a frown. She reached up and touched the tips of her fingers to her shoulder-length red hair, a nervous gesture, empty and unconscious.

"You said something about a little girl?" she said quietly. "To your daughter, I mean. You were talking about—"

"Honey," the man interrupted, "it's none of our business."

"But maybe she—"

"Honey." He turned to Coogan again. "You sure you're going to be all right? Maybe you should . . . sit down, or something."

"Well . . . y'know, that might not be such a bad idea." He backed up and sat on the stool behind the register, his breath still a little short. Tiny speckles flickered in the periphery of his vision like silver gnats. His mouth was sticky with the foul aftertaste of bad coffee and he stood to get something to drink.

"Whoah, wait a second," the man said, stepping around the counter. "I think you should just stay there awhile. You need something? I'll get it for you."

"Well . . . I could use a bottle of apple juice. They're back there, by the soft drinks."

"You got it." The man whispered something into the woman's ear as he passed her on his way to the back of the store.

She moved toward him and spoke hesitantly: "Is there, um, anything else I can get you? Do you have some pills? Uh, for your, um . . ." She touched her fingertips to her chest and raised her eyebrows high.

"Oh, no, honey. Thank you, but no. Doc McCurdy wanted to put me on some, but . . . I figure when it goes, it goes. No use juicin' it up with pills. Nobody lives forever." He almost laughed at the ease with which he spoke those words, knowing that, five minutes ago, when his chest was filled with that deadly fluttering, he would have been happy to *beg* for a pill—or a shot or an operation—*anything* that would hold death off awhile longer.

The man returned with a round bottle of apple juice, uncapped it, and handed it to Coogan.

"Thank you much." Coogan tipped the bottle back and emptied it with a few big gulps.

"Lorne Cusack," the man said, offering his hand.

Coogan shook it, taking a moment to savor the taste of the apple juice and size up his visitors with a smile.

Lorne Cusack was somewhere in his thirties, probably new to them, with blown-dry hair the color of lightly browned meringue and a hairline that had already begun its backward journey over the top of his head. He wore wire-rim glasses and sported an even, well-tended tan, like the woman with him, and their clothes—with subdued colors on thin, summery materials—were the clothes of city folk at play, the kind of clothes purchased specifically for vacations and weekend getaways. Coogan suspected they'd driven up in a BMW, or maybe a Porsche.

"This is my wife, Bonnie," Cusack went on. "We're from Santa Barbara. We just got in, in fact."

"Well, that's quite a drive," Coogan said. "What brings you to our little town?"

"A break from the rat race, mostly."

"I hear the rats are winning."

"By a wide margin," Cusack laughed. "Actually, we've always wanted to see Mount Shasta, so we thought we'd come up, do a little hiking, and celebrate the Fourth here."

"You picked the right place for it. We put on one hell of a do here in Grover."

"So I've heard. Uh . . . are you feeling any better?"

"Yeah, sure am. Thank you." He stood. "I'm Bill Coogan, by the way. Didn't mean to be rude. You folks looking for anything in particular?"

"We stopped to get some gas, maybe some soft drinks."

"Soft drinks're right back there. What kind of gas you want?"

Cusack asked for premium and Coogan cleared the pump as the man and his wife went to the soft drink case in the back and got a six-pack of Diet Pepsi.

"So, what's there to see here in Grover?" Cusack asked, setting the six-pack on the counter.

"Well, let's see now. There's the old jailhouse. It's a museum now. Kids usually get a kick out of it. You got any kids?"

"No, not yet," Cusack replied quickly, glancing at his wife.

"Okay. Well, you'll want to do some hiking, of course, like you said. We got some good guides around here. And-uh . . ." Coogan tucked his lower lip beneath his big mustache, cocked his head back and squinted at the ceiling to give it a thought. "Well, our town is old and pretty, but not very exciting. 'Course, this weekend'll be a different story. There'll be a lot of parties and dances, the big spaghetti feed on Sunday, and there's always the—"

"And the New World Festival," Cusack interrupted.

"Uh . . . yeah." Coogan shifted his weight from foot to foot behind the counter. Cusack's mention of the festival revived the bitter confrontation he'd just had with his daughter, it sat up rigidly in his mind like a reanimated corpse on a mortuary slab. "Yeah, they're having some, I don't know, a confab of some kind this week. Today through Friday."

Cusack nodded. "Uh . . . excuse my nosiness, but . . . well, I couldn't help overhearing you and your daughter, and . . . well . . ."

"Yeah?" The word came out between closed teeth and Coogan tried to relax the suddenly tense muscles of his face; he didn't like eavesdroppers, but it *was* a small store and this fellow seemed well-meaning enough. "Yeah," he said again, but gently this time. "That's what we were talkin' about. The Alliance."

"I didn't know they were so controversial around here," Cusack said.

Coogan chuckled without humor, muttered, "You're reachin' into a bucket of worms there," then slapped a meaty hand on the six-pack of Pepsi. "This be all for you?"

"A bucket of worms? What do you mean by that?" Cusack wore a curious half-smile and leaned toward the counter with genuine interest. "*Is* there some sort of—" He shrugged. "—controversy? About the Alliance, I mean?"

Coogan smelled a rat. Actually, the smell more closely resembled that of a reporter, a profession with which Coogan, on the whole, had no quarrel—the last one he'd met had been a pleasant, straight-talking man who had, unfortunately, disappeared shortly after their meeting—but he disliked chicanery in *any* profession, and if this fellow was a reporter, he was a smoothly dishonest one.

"You a newsman, Mr. Cusack?"

He blinked, frowned, shook his head slowly and said, "No," then laughed. "No, of *course* not. I—my wife and I—we run a chain of video stores in southern California." He quickly removed a business card from his shirt pocket and handed it over. "Matinee Video, it's called. We have two stores in Santa Barbara, two in—well, that's not important. But no, I'm not a reporter. Why, do you get a lot of them?"

Coogan felt his cheeks warm as he looked at the card. He averted his eyes, pulled a cigarette from his pocket and lit up, shaking his head sheepishly.

"Sorry about that," he said. "I don't mind reporters so much, as long as they're up front about it. Don't like the ones who sneak around, though."

"Then . . . you *do* get a lot of them. I thought you said Grover wasn't very exciting."

"Well, it's not. We don't get a lot of them, but once in a while a writer'll wander up here tryin' to dig up a little dirt on the Alliance, or just to do a story on 'em. Or maybe that actress'll show up. Sheila Bennet? That's about the most exciting thing happens around here. She pals around with some of them Alliance folk, comes up here now and then for their to-do's. No doubt she'll be here for this one."

Cusack removed a twenty-dollar bill from his pants pocket and put it on the counter as Coogan rang up the purchase. "Do they find any dirt on the Alliance?" he asked, leaning his hip on the edge of the counter.

"Hmph. You ever *read* any dirt on the Alliance? Those that don't believe in it just laugh at it like it's a joke. Others talk about it like it's some kind of important new school of thought.

Like it's a fresh way of looking at life and the universe and all that jolly juice." He couldn't keep the contempt from his voice.

"And what do *you* think it is, Mr. Coogan?" Cusack asked.

Coogan's eyebrows crawled up his forehead like coarse, wiry caterpillars and he looked at Cusack questioningly, chin tucked downward. "You really want to know? Most people aren't interested in my opinion these days. Even when they *say* they are. My opinions aren't . . . what's the word? *Hip.*"

"I'm interested."

Coogan bagged the six-pack slowly, debating his words. He'd always tended to guard his words closely when speaking of the Alliance, but he was losing tolerance for the group. He could see no good in what it had done to his daughter and what it *might* do to his grandchildren, and his most recent confrontation with Paula reinforced that attitude. He decided to stop holding back.

"I think the Universal Enlightened Alliance is a godless, evil lie. And if you can show me when a lie—an *evil* one with no goodness or love in it, nevermind an innocent little *white* one— ever did anyone any good, I can show you where you're wrong."

Cusack frowned. "Well, I don't know a whole lot about the Alliance, but I've seen Hester Thorne on TV and read about her in magazines. All she ever seems to talk about is love and harmony and . . . well, things like that."

"She also says that each person is a god, and a god is a being who doesn't make mistakes. I know some good people, but I've never met *anybody* doesn't make mistakes. Far as I'm concerned, there's only one God, and turning your back on that fact so you can say *you're* a god, is not something I'd call wise."

"Are you a religious man?"

"I don't need religion to believe in God. But . . . that's just my opinion." Coogan smiled. "How much gas you want, Mr. Cusack."

"I'll go out and fill it up." He fished keys from his pocket and turned to leave.

Mrs. Cusack stepped forward and quietly said, "It's none of my business, Mr. Coogan, but you seemed concerned that something might have happened to your daughter's children. Do you think the Alliance has done something to—"

"Honey?" Cusack called over his shoulder suddenly. "You wanna come out and do the window while I fill up?"

Coogan saw something odd cross her face then. Her eyes closed and she pulled her lips between her teeth; her whole body seemed to lose some of its strength and her shoulders fell. Then she opened her eyes, tried to smile, but failed, and followed her husband.

Watching them as they left the store, Coogan sensed a tension between them as Cusack spoke without looking at her; they walked out of sight and, a moment later, a grey sedan—not what he'd expected—pulled up to the tanks with Cusack at the wheel. They both got out, Cusack filing the tank as his wife washed the window. Cusack came back in alone, smiling.

"Twelve bucks," he said.

"Hope my opinion didn't offend you," Coogan said, making change. "But you did ask for it."

"Not at all."

"Your wife seemed upset, and I thought—"

"No, we weren't offended. In fact, we'd like to see you again while we're here. Maybe have lunch? Our treat."

"Well, that'd be nice. You can always find me here or at the diner."

"Great. It's been a pleasure talking with you, Mr. Coogan. See you around."

As he watched Lorne Cusack leave, Coogan felt a pang of guilt for his suspicion, but it didn't last long. He tossed the apple-juice bottle into a wastebasket, smiled and muttered, "There's still some good ones out there, Lord. It's nice to know." But his smile was short-lived because an instant later, he thought of his grandchildren and once again began to feel afraid.

2.

"I told you to let me do the talking," he said, pulling out of the gas station parking lot.

"I'm sorry, okay? But you don't seem to understand that I'm—"

"*You* don't seem to understand that this is my *work* and you are here as a *favor*, not as an assistant. I don't *need* you to speak. If I do, I'll *tell* you when and what to say."

They rode in silence for a while and he didn't look at her as he drove the car over the hill toward the hotel. When he heard her sniffles and quiet sobs, he clutched the wheel tightly and sighed.

"I'm sorry," she whispered. "For crying. I'm sorry. But I'm . . . scared. I know he's here somewhere. I *know* it. And if something's happening to children, like that old man seems to think—"

"I apologize," he said. "All right? I shouldn't have snapped at you. But this is important. I don't want to spoil my cover."

When she spoke again, her voice was iced with sarcasm. "My *apologies*, Mr. Cross. In my emotional state, I inadvertently put my son's *safety* above your . . . fucking . . . *cover*." She found a tissue in the glove compartment and wiped away her tears.

Jordan shifted behind the wheel and ran a hand through his dyed hair, which still felt strange; he'd shaved it back in front and thinned the top to give the illusion of a receding hairline.

"Look, if you want us to find your son," he said, "you have to do it my way. All right? I don't want to sound callous, but—"

"Oh, you're not callous, Mr. Cross," she laughed humorlessly. "A callous person is one who has developed a hard shell to protect his feelings. You *have* no feelings."

You knew this would happen, Jordan thought. *You knew it.*

From the beginning, he'd had doubts about his decision to bring Lauren Schroeder with him. Deep in his gut, murmuring somewhere within the folds of his intestines, a small, quiet voice had warned, *You'lll . . . beee . . . sorrr-ryyyy.*

"Let's just forget it, okay?" he said, trying hard to sound congenial but with only marginal success.

She stared out the window silently.

The temperature inside the rented car seemed to drop several degrees.

"Please keep in mind," he went on, still trying, "that I'm not here specifically to find your son, I'm here to gather information for my client, who, by the way, is picking up the tab here. I *want* to find your son, and if he's here, there's a very good chance we will." Then, with emphasis, he added, "But only in the process of gathering my client's information, which means we have to do it *my* way."

"Then why don't you just let me do this my*self*, so I can get this damned coloring out of my hair and concentrate on finding Nathan.''

"You can't do that now because you've already been seen as Bonnie Cusack and you could damage my cover."

"Ah!" She rolled her eyes. "Your *cover* again."

Jordan's knuckles cracked as he clenched the wheel again. This was not the same woman—the desperate vulnerable woman—he'd met in the Sheraton several days ago.

"It would not be a good idea, Mrs. Schroeder, for you to look for your son on your own."

"Because of your cover?" she snapped. "You're afraid I'll—"

"No, *not* because of my cover."

Curiosity slowly broke through her angry mask then. "Why?"

Jordan had told her nothing of his reasons for coming to Grover and didn't want to, but now that he had involved her, he supposed he would have to tell her *something* to keep her in line with what he had to do.

"Earlier this year," he said, "someone came to Grover asking questions about the Alliance. Pretty innocent questions, as far as I can tell. But for some reason, this person disappeared and it's beginning to look like this person was kidnapped, possibly murdered. Does that answer your question, Mrs. Schroeder?"

She thought about that a moment, absorbed it, then turned toward him, cocking a knee up in the seat. There was fear in her voice when she spoke. "Then there is something going on here. Something bad."

"I don't know yet, but I'm—"

"And if Nathan is here, then I'm right—he might be in trouble." Her voice trembled and cracked when she leaned toward him and said, "He might even be *dead*."

Bad idea, Jordan thought. "No, I'm not saying that, Mrs. Schroeder, I'm just saying that if we're going to look into the Alliance—for my purposes *and* yours—we're going to have to do it very carefully, and since this is my *job*, I would like you to believe me when I say I know what I'm doing. All right?"

Her frightened eyes stared at her hands for a while as her fingers wrestled lightly with one another.

"All *right*?"

"I'm . . . sorry," she whispered, covering her forehead with a palm. "I'm . . . please understand that I'm just . . . scared."

"I understand that. But *you* have to understand that we've got a much better chance of finding your son if we do this my way."

She nodded and looked out the window again.

It had not been a hasty decision to bring Lauren Schroeder with him to Grover. He knew she would be very emotional and sometimes irrational under the circumstances, but he knew something else, too. He knew that a single man on his own was not half as trustworthy to the average person as a man accompanied by a woman identified as his wife. The chances of Lauren solidifying his cover—and perhaps even making the assignment less difficult and somewhat less time-consuming in the process— outweighed all of the drawbacks. Largely because the drawbacks were, for the most part, personal ones.

Jordan did not enjoy keeping company with women on his own time, not to mention *working* with one. But, for a million dollars—at *least*—Jordan could tolerate a lot.

Streaks of sunlight came through the branches of tall pines and spattered the car as Jordan drove through the gate of the Sleeping Woman Inn. Neither of them spoke as he maneuvered the car down the winding narrow road until he eased to a stop in front of the enormous white building.

"Now remember," he said. "Bonnie and Lorne Cusack. Please, try to smile. You're on vacation. You're seeing something you've never seen before and you're impressed. Okay?"

She nodded.

"And," he added, "when we get into the room, we keep this up, right? The names, the vacation, the whole thing. If you have to tell me something that's too revealing, write it down until I say it's safe to speak. Okay?"

Another silent nod, but the fear was leaving her eyes by slow small degrees.

As they got out of the car, Jordan kept his eye on her, worried that he would come to regret his decision.

It hurt Lauren to walk into the Sleeping Woman Inn; she felt an actual physical discomfort, a clutching in her chest as she entered the lobby with Jordan. It seemed that if she were to look to one side, Mark would be with her, and Nathan would be on the other, looking around with open-faced amazement at the extravagant lobby. She forced herself to smile as they went to the front desk, but inside, she felt ill.

Jordan paid for their room at the desk and a young blond man in a white suit carried their bags to the elevator. He let them into the room and just inside, Lauren stopped and stared at the bed with a sinking feeling in her gut. There was just one king-size bed. She glanced at Jordan as he fished a tip out of his pocket, then back at the bed again, wondering why this part of their "cover" had not occurred to her before.

"If you need anything at all," the young man said, "my name is Mitch."

"Thank you very much, Mitch." Jordan closed the door behind him and turned in time to see Lauren pointing to the bed and opening her mouth to protest. He quickly held up a hand and shook his head. "Beautiful, isn't it, honey?" he asked, his voice so natural and relaxed that it seemed to belong to someone else.

She nodded distractedly, then realized she was supposed to speak and said, "Yes . . . yes, it is," but what she *really* wanted to do was groan because she was suddenly overwhelmed by the certainty that this was all a big stupid mistake.

Jordan went to his suitcase on the bed and removed a small black box the size and shape of a pocket calculator with a switch, two dials, and a short antenna on one end. He plugged a tiny earphone into the box, put the plug in his ear, and flipped the switch.

"Whyn't you turn the TV on," he said. "I'm gonna unpack." But he didn't unpack; he walked around the room, slowly scanning the walls, furniture, and telephone with the antenna on the box pointed forward like a gun.

Lauren wanted to take her bag and leave without hesitation, just as she had taken Nathan and left Mark the last time she'd visited the hotel. But if Jordan was right and this *was* the best way to find her son, she'd go along with it. For now, anyway . . .

She crossed the room to the television, switched it on, and a powerful voice immediately filled the room.

"—godless system of belief with godless leaders and confused followers and chief among those leaders is a woman who would have you believe that you—not the Creator of the universe, not Jesus Christ, but *you*—are a *god*! *You* have all the answers you need and *you* can do no wrong—you can only do what's right for *you*. Now tell me, ladies and gentlemen: whatever you may think of my ministry or the Christian church in general, do you see any truth in that? The Universal Enlightened Alliance wants you to think it's the truth, but I'll *tell* you the truth: Hester Thorne, like the Devil himself, *wants . . . your . . . soouullll*!''

At first, Lauren blinked with surprise as the picture began to materialize on the screen; as she sat in a room in a hotel owned by Hester Thorne, someone on television was comparing her to the Devil. Then the face took form and she recognized Reverend Barry Hallway and chuckled quietly.

He was the most popular televangelist in the country; he had a strong influence on most of the country's political leaders, including the president—with whom he had lunch once a month—as well as most of the country's major corporations. Eight years ago, Hallway had formed the American Moral Allegiance (the AMA), of which there were millions of card-carrying members, all of whom were eager to boycott any store, magazine, company or corporation that Hallway felt was offending God. When Reverend Hallway spoke, the leaders of the country—both political and financial—listened.

Lauren, on the other hand, did not; she felt no different about him and his organization than she did about Hester Thorne and hers.

"What's funny?" Jordan asked.

"This guy." She sat on the end of the bed watching the screen.

"Oh, yeah. A riot. He's always reminded me a little of Mussolini, a *fat* Mussolini. Except this guy's smile is a little more sadistic, I think.''

She laughed again and turned to him; he was still sweeping the room with his black box, making his way to the television set.

"The Bible has warned us," Reverend Hallway went on, strutting on a stage in front of an enormous audience, "of false Christs who will come to fool even the very elite of God's people. They will come in many different disguises—rock stars, popular novelists, even *religious leaders*—people whom we admire and lavish with praise. But they will try to lead you away from the truth. They will try—and sometimes succeed—to make you believe a lie. *That*, ladies and gentlemen, is a false Christ. And Hester Thorne is a false Christ.''

Jordan flipped the switch on his black box again with a loud click and sighed, "Looks clean.''

"Clean? What does that mean?''

"It means there aren't any bugs in the room or taps on the phone."

"Did you think there would be?"

"Didn't know. That's why I did this." He removed the earphone and put the box back in the suitcase.

"Why would the room be bugged?"

"I don't know. I just had to find out."

"So you wouldn't blow your cover."

"That's right." He sat down on the bed beside her and smiled a cold, sarcastic smile. "You know how very important my cover is to me. My next step is to find a small animal and, after sunset, sacrifice it to the great god of private investigators so my cover won't be—"

"Okay," she said, standing and slapping her hands on her thighs, "I want you to know right now that I do *not* like being in this situation. I'm not sure yet, but I don't think I even like *you*. If you knew me, you would know that I usually like *everyone*, I'm a very easy-going person, but you are making this very difficult and you *know* that I'm under a lot of pressure here. I'm worried about my son's *life*. And, as if your grating personality weren't enough, there is something very wrong with this room. I wonder if you've noticed it yet?"

"The bed."

"The bed, yes. Now, I suppose this is my fault, but when I agreed to pose as your wife for the sake of your *cover*, it was not my intention to sleep with you. What do you suggest we do about this little inconvenience?"

"Well, Mrs. Schroeder—"

"There, *that's* what I'm talking about. I've already asked you to call me Lauren. I think this situation would be more tolerable if we could at least be on a first-name basis, but you won't do that! It's almost as if you don't *want* to make me comfortable. Frankly, Mr. Cr—*Jordan*—I don't think you're a very nice person."

He gave her that humorless smile again and said, "You're right, Mrs. Schroe—okay, okay . . . *Lauren*—I'm not. I'm sorry, but I'm not a very nice person. But I *do* want you to be comfortable. Believe it or not, that's important to me. Under the circumstances, *you* are important to me—"

—Because of your fucking cover, she thought—

"—and I want to make this easy for you. But I assure you

that I have no intention of seeking carnal knowledge of you. I intend to sleep in this bed. You're welcome to sleep in this bed, too, with my solemn oath not to lay a hand on you. Otherwise, there's a sofa right over there.''

She frowned and shook her head. ''What's wrong with you?''

''Nothing. Now, if I had the urge to jump your bones, yes, I would think there was something wrong with me. But that's not the case. Now.'' He stood and began removing clothes from his suitcase—which, like hers, was equipped with a tag that read PROPERTY OF LORNE AND BONNIE CUSACK, 1938 LARKSPUR, SANTA BARBARA, CA—and taking them to the closet. ''We are going to make ourselves familiar with this town. If you'd like to take a shower first, please do. If not, I'm going to change my clothes and we'll be off.''

She clenched her teeth as she watched him hang clothes in the closet, resisting the feeling of helplessness that washed over her and made her want to scream at him and cry like a child. Instead, she opened her suitcase, removed a change of clothing, and went into the bathroom, slamming the door behind her as Reverend Barry Hallway said ominously, ''Those who walk into the satanic trap set by Hester Thorne will surely . . . *surely* . . . be lost.''

3.

Mark sat at his small school desk in the seminar room, his notebook open before him, trying hard to listen closely as Hester lectured before the group that surrounded him. But listening wasn't easy. He was exhausted from lack of sleep.

''—but remember that, throughout the Bible,'' Hester went on, pacing in front of the group, ''the ultimate sin, the act that results in decadence, destruction and ultimately, death—what I like to call the three D's—is separation from God. But the lie that has been fed to you and others throughout time is that God is some great invisible omnipotent force and I'm telling you— and you've probably already realized this, or you wouldn't be here—that just doesn't make *sense*. We are now living among the three D's like we've never seen them before and *why*? Because we've lost sight of—we've been separated from—*ourselves*. We now focus on greed, possessions and pleasures. Some call this selfishness. I call it selflessness, because in doing all of this, we don't consider what it does to *us*. We have been separated from the one true God—we've been separated from ourselves. We all, each and every one of us, make up the Godbody, but right now, the Godbody is ill. And what we are trying to do in the Alliance is heal it. Before it's too late.''

Mark scribbled some notes—mostly to appear attentive— frowning at the pages before him, his thoughts elsewhere. He was surprised when he noticed everyone standing and filing out of the room. He quickly sat up, closed his notebook, and stood.

''Mark, wait.''

He turned to Hester, who started toward him, carrying a brief-case. ''What's wrong?''

''Oh, nothing,'' he smiled, ''I was just—''

''You weren't even in this room.'' When the door closed and they were alone in the room, she reached up and gently brushed aside a strand of hair on his forehead, then her fingertips trickled down his cheek like tears, brushed along the line of his jaw until her hand came to rest over his heart, palm first. ''What's wrong?'' she whispered.

Warmth spread from the touch of her hand and filled him like a drink of strong liquor.

''I'm sorry,'' he said, ''I'm just . . . I was thinking of Na-than.''

''I thought so. Are you worried?''

''Well, not worried, just . . .'' He shrugged and let the sen-tence dangle.

''You know what it does to me when I see you like this? It hurts me. It makes me think you don't trust me, that maybe you even suspect me of something—'' She chuckled. ''—something . . . sinister?''

''No, no, not at all. I've just never been separated from him for this long. I . . . think about him a lot. It would help if, you know, if I could just . . . see him for a minute or two. Talk to him.''

''Just to make sure he's all right?''

''Well . . .''

''So you think he might *not* be all right.''

He sighed, feeling defeated. He couldn't make her under-stand.

''I understand, Mark. I would probably feel the same way in

your position. But believe me, I'm doing what's best for both of you. See, you've both been misled, Nathan for five years, but you . . . you've been living outside the truth considerably longer. Now I know, Mark, that you would never knowingly mislead Nathan, but that's the *point*. If you were with him, you might *inadvertently* do or say something that would turn his eyes from the truth we are trying to ingrain in him in as little time as possible. Being your son, Nathan would naturally be more likely to follow *your* example than he would *ours*. Think of it this way: you're both in a hospital recovering from an illness. You're staying in the adult ward, Nathan is in pediatrics. It's temporary and, most of all, it's for the best."

Another sigh blew up from his chest, but this time it trembled, slightly weakened by her gentle touch.

"How would you like to go for a walk?" she asked.

"Sure."

In the hall outside the seminar room, Hester stopped one of the white-suited men, gave him her briefcase and said, "Take this to my office for me, please?"

"Certainly, Hester."

Everyone was on a first-name basis in the Alliance.

They left the complex—which was located behind the hotel—and followed a path up a small hill, holding hands, until Hester veered off the path and led him into the dense shade of a wooded area, cool from the lack of sun. The gurgle of a distant stream drifted through the darkness and above them, through the branches of the trees, the mountain watched as they walked in silence—

—until Hester spoke: "Is everything else okay? Aside from missing Nathan?"

"Yes, everything's fine."

"You're sure? Don't you . . . miss your wife, too?"

"Lauren. Well . . . I think of her."

"How do you think of her?"

"I wish she'd come here, too."

"You thing she might?"

"I . . . doubt it."

"Do you want my opinion? My experience?"

"Sure."

"She won't. She may come looking for you, but she won't come looking for the truth."

"You think she'll come looking for me?"

"Did you leave her anything?"

"I left her the house, the—"

"But no money."

"Well . . . no. I feel a little guilty about that. But you did say *everything*."

"And for a reason. If you leave something behind, you might be tempted to go back to it. I don't *need* your money. You're cared for very well here, and that, of course, is not free, so what you contribute goes toward that expense. But when Jesus told the rich man to give up all he had, he was trying to tell him how pointless it is to become so attached to his belongings. They won't be around forever. The truth, though, the *real* truth, is eternal."

Mark couldn't hide his smirk. "I thought you didn't like that stuff, all that stuff about Jesus. Christianity, I mean. You're always calling it a lie."

"Only what men have made of it. Jesus was actually the most well-known channel in history." She smirked, too.

After a silent moment, Mark said, "Sometimes I wonder how Lauren is doing, because I took all our money, I—"

"Don't worry about that. She'll get by. She's not helpless. Maybe I'm wrong, maybe she'll come here and investigate the truth that you've found. But it's never happened before."

"Should I . . . get a divorce?"

"That's up to you." She stopped walking and stepped in front of him, still holding his hand, moving her other hand to his face, stroking his cheek. "Do you ever get lonely?"

He started to respond, but did not; he wasn't sure if she meant lonely for companionship—because there was plenty of that, he was *surrounded* by people—or lonely for a woman.

"You can tell me. It's okay. Don't you get lonely . . . for a woman?"

It was something she did a lot: answer a question an instant after he'd asked it silently, in his mind. He smiled and asked quietly, "Do you read my mind, Hester?"

"No," she whispered, lightly brushing a fingertip over the lashes of his right eye, "I read your eyes."

After a moment, he said, "I get lonely sometimes. For . . . well, for quite a while, really. We haven't been very, um . . . intimate for a long time. Sexually. Lauren and I, that is."

She moved closer until her breasts were pressing against him and her breath was warm on his face.

"There's no need for you to be lonely," she said. "None at all." She lifted his hand to her shoulder and pressed it there, then lifted both hands to his face, leaning forward and giving him a light, gentle kiss on the mouth. "I'm here for you, Mark. I'm here for all of my people. But I especially want you to know that I'm here for *you*."

She was so close, so warm . . . he resisted the small temptation to step away from her and, instead, slid his arms around her and pulled her closer, gently at first, until he put his mouth over hers again, then he pulled her body hard against his, giving in to the warmth that came from her, not opening his mouth at first, for fear she wouldn't respond. But when her lips parted and he felt her tongue moving against him, he smiled, let her in, let her lick his lips, run her tongue over his teeth, let her draw his tongue into her mouth and suck on it like a penis, moving her mouth backward and forward on it, flicking her tongue over it, gently biting it, letting loose a throaty laugh as she pulled her mouth off of it and looked at him with promise in her eyes. He'd grown hard against her and was embarrassed for a moment, almost pulled away, but she quickly whispered, "No. No, don't. If this is what you need, I want you to have it. See . . . that's part of the truth, too. We need each other. We've lost that." She smiled so brightly, so happily. "Do you want me, Mark?"

He didn't answer.

"Do you want me?"

He *couldn't* answer, so he nodded, tightly closing his mind's eye to shadowy images of Lauren.

"Then I want *you*."

They kissed again and he moved his hands over her slowly, feeling her back, her shoulders, her hair, her breasts. . . .

There was a sound in the woods. At first, Mark thought it was the brook in the distance, chuckling over rocks and fallen branches, but—

—it was a laugh, a high, melodic laugh wafting through the dense gathering of trees.

Hester pulled away, still smiling, but looking around them.

"Ah," she whispered, "I forgot. We should go."

"What? You forgot what?"

The laugh came again and this time it was undeniably that of a child.

"I forgot the children are performing exercises today," she said.

"Exercises?" He backed away from her and looked around until he spotted two children. They were not *easy* to spot; they were dressed in clothes that blended perfectly with the woods around them, but he was unable to see their exact color because the children darted behind the fat trunk of a tree. "What exercises?"

"Educational exercises."

There were more of them farther away, darting from tree to tree, only these children were silent, quick, almost invisible.

Hester took his hand and began leading him back toward the path.

Mark asked, "But what kind of educational exercises would—"

He stopped speaking, froze in place and gaped at a space between two large trees where—

—Nathan ran beside another child, hunched low, dressed in the same camouflaged clothing and moving in perfect silence. At least . . . he *thought* it was Nathan.

"Nathan?" he called. *"Nathan?"*

"Mark," Hester said, her voice firm now, "we shouldn't interrupt them."

A small head peered around a tree trunk, face lost in shadow. "Daddy?"

It was Nathan's voice.

Mark let go of Hester's hand and moved toward the tree several yards away.

"Nathan! It's me!"

"Dad!" the boy hissed.

Mark blinked. There was no happiness in his son's voice, nothing to tell Mark that Nathan was playing, having a good time or glad to see him.

In fact, Nathan's voice was thin and high-pitched. He sounded terrified.

"Dad, you gotta *hide*!" Nathan rasped.

"What?"

"Come *on*, Mark, we're interrupting their exercises." Hester took his hand and tugged him toward the path.

"Nathan?"

"*Hide*, Dad! They'll kill you! They'll *eat* you!"

"What?" Mark shouted. He spun toward Hester. "What did he say?"

"Remember what I told you, Mark? Remember, I told you we're *educating* him? In the *truth*?"

"What did he mean, they'll—"

She stepped close to him again, but this time her face was dark, stern, and she clutched his elbow hard. "Mark, I will explain if you want me to, but you *still* won't understand. This is just an exercise, just a lesson. We're doing what we have to do to teach these children and—"

"C'mon, Dad, *hide*! Don't let them find you!"

Hester pulled hard on his arm and he went with her, only for an explanation.

"What the hell is he talking about, Hester?"

"It's a lesson, an *object* lesson, like a fairy tale with a moral at the end. It's just a *game*, Mark. But now that he's seen you, it might not work at *all*! Don't you understand that children have to be approached differently than adults? Can't you *see* that?"

They were on the path again, heading toward the complex, but behind them, Nathan's voice traveled on the slender breeze: "Dad! Hide! *Hide*, Dad!"

Hester clicked her tongue and looked perturbed. "He'll be marked down now. For coming out of hiding."

"Hiding from *what*?" Mark asked, looking back over his shoulder toward his son's voice.

"From *lies*. Well, he doesn't see it that way yet, but he will, afterward, when it's all been explained. It's just a game now. Didn't you ever do that when you were a child? Learn lessons from games? From *exercises*?"

They slowed their pace and Mark turned to her; he felt confused, uncertain. "I . . . guess so. I don't know."

"That's all they're doing, Mark. And it's my fault that we interrupted. I should have remembered they were doing exercises in the woods today. I'm sorry if you're upset. It's my fault."

He stopped on the path and looked back again, listening for Nathan's voice. It was gone.

Mark wanted to go back and find his son, take him away from whatever game he was playing and hold him, talk to him.

"You can't teach it to him, Mark," Hester said quietly, standing behind him. "The truth is new to you, too."

He faced her again.

"Let *us* do it. It won't take long. When it's over, you'll see him, Mark, I promise. You'll see him the *second* his education is finished. Please, Mark, tell me you trust me."

He searched her face for whatever it was he needed to see to give her his trust—to give her his *son*.

"Please, Mark."

A thought of Lauren rose up in his mind—the way she used to admonish him for exposing Nathan to the Alliance literature he used to keep around the house—but he pushed it away. Slowly, he nodded, his lips pursed tightly over his teeth. Then he relaxed—*tried* to relax—and started walking again, walking fast, trying to stop clenching his teeth.

"I'm sorry that happened, Mark, it was *my* fault. I should have remembered."

He nodded in response. He couldn't speak yet, because he was afraid of what he would say, of how he would speak to her. He told himself to trust her—

—*You* have *to trust her*, he thought, *you've left everything else behind, trusting her is all you've* got—

—and kept walking, barely aware of her at his side.

"Are you angry with me?" she asked.

After a moment, he forced himself to say, "No, I'm not. Really." It came out in a dry whisper.

She took his arm. "You are. But give it time. You'll come to understand, and your anger will go away."

They walked together silently as Mark thought, *Please, let it go away, let me understand. I have to. I need to. . . .*

4.

Before it got bloody, it had been a busy day for Joan Maher in the Lemurian Diner, a long parade of rude demanding customers, most of them irritable tourists who expected to be treated like dignitaries, endlessly pondering the two-page menu as if it were a fat Christmas catalog, then changing their orders after Joan had turned in the ticket. They were relieved only by the long-winded regulars who wandered in and talked politics and auto mechanics and made shameless, guffawing passes at Joan as they drank their coffee and chain-smoked at the coffee counter.

The part-time girl who usually came in for a few hours to help during the lunch rush—a voluptuous blond teenager preoccupied with her hair and figure—had called in sick that day, leaving Joan to face the summer tourists by herself. Chelsea, the owner, was in the kitchen working the grill because the cook—a broad-shouldered blond teenager preoccupied with his hair and muscles—had also called in sick. Either the flu was going around, or the cook and waitress were together in some secret place groping one another's sweaty preoccupations.

Joan rushed a Denver omelette and a chicken salad sandwich to a quiet aging couple at a corner table, then grabbed the coffeepot and went from one end of the counter to the other pouring for the men perched on the blue vinyl-covered stools.

"You pour coffee," Flash Gordon muttered through his little mouth, "*almost* as well as you pour yourself into them jeans," then squeezed out a long wheezing laugh.

Joan smirked and replied affably, "I don't *have* to pour the coffee as well, because it's only ninety-five cents a cup."

Amos Haas slapped a grease-stained hand on the counter and whopped, "Hoo! She gotcha, Flash!"

"Damn right she's got me, anytime she wants me."

"Show some respect," Wally grumbled as Joan poured his coffee. "Woman with tits like them deserves a little more *respect*."

"Tell ya what, honey," Flash said, beckoning Joan with a crooked finger, "Whyn't you c'mon over t'my place after work an' I'll take you up in my 'copter? You can join the Mile High Club," he laughed.

Joan tried to ignore him, but couldn't keep from smirking.

"You couldn' *get* that whirly-bird a-yours a mile off the ground," Shorty Mattocks grumbled, his words slopping out between toothless gums. "Just far enough t'scare the corny shit outta tourists."

Flash's smile disappeared and he frowned down the counter at Shorty. "Howda *you* know? You couldn't fly yourself a *kite*. Why, I bet you never even been *up* in anything."

Turning her back on them, Joan replaced the pot with a sigh and a slow shake of her head, running a hand through her short chestnut hair. This reaction to the behavior of the Lemurian's regulars was a vast improvement over her reaction during her first week on the job. Back then, it was only her desperate financial condition and need for gainful employment that kept her from splashing their faces with hot coffee, shattering the glass pot, and disfiguring them with the shards. But Joan had changed.

When asked what she did for a living, Joan replied with a smile, if caught in just the right mood, "I put up with bullshit." This was always said jokingly, but with a certain amount of sincerity, because it was true. But the bullshit she encountered at the Lemurian was far more palatable than the chickenshit she'd dealt with at Diamond-Barr, the monstrous insurance company she'd worked for in Los Angeles before coming to Grover. Bullshit was *always* better than chickenshit.

Bullshit, as Joan saw it, was big and lumpy and clearly visible so you could step around it when you saw it ahead of you; chickenshit, on the other hand, was tiny and messy and, once it oozed between your toes, was hard to shake off.

The men at the coffee counter were loud and vulgar, but their hearts were big. During her second week at the Lemurian, her car had broken down. She had no money for repairs at the time and had to get up at three o'clock every morning so she'd have time to walk to work from the boarding house where she was living between Grover and Weed. She asked no one for help because she knew no one she liked in the area and was planning to get out as soon as she could afford it. As she was walking to work one morning, Amos passed her in his battered old Chevy pick-up and pulled over to give her a ride. She was reluctant at first; knowing how he acted in the diner every day, she shuddered at the thought of being alone with him. But she was tired and cold and she climbed into the truck against her better judgment. It was the beginning of her love affair with Grover and its citizens because once he learned of her troubles, Amos, the town's star mechanic, had her Volkswagen towed to his garage and replaced the starter, the fuel pump, changed the oil and tuned the engine. And he charged her nothing.

"Worry about it when you can afford to worry about it," Amos said with a floppy wave of his hand.

The least she could do, she thought, was pay for his coffee in the diner, but he wouldn't let her do that, either. She still hadn't been able to pay him and Amos had never mentioned it once.

That was a whole world more than she could say about anyone she'd worked with at Diamond-Barr.

Bullshit washed off easily; chickenshit left a permanent stain.

The door of the diner rattled open and Joan turned to see a couple, obviously tourists, looking around at Chelsea's paintings of the little elf-like people with sinister slanted eyes that were hung all over the walls of the diner. When they saw her approaching them, they smiled; first the man—a big warm smile—then the woman—more tentative, but pleasant—and Joan was rather taken aback by the notion that there were actually some *friendly* people taking a vacation somewhere.

"Smoking or non?" she asked.

"Smoking," the man replied, still smiling, but still scanning the diner.

Joan led them to a table against the wall, gave them each a menu and, when they said they wanted coffee, went to get the pot. As she poured, she asked, "Are you visiting or just passing through?" She usually didn't strike up conversations with the customers, but it was such a relief to wait on nice people—people who were pleasant in spite of the summer heat—that she wanted to savor it.

"We're on vacation," the man said. "From Santa Barbara."

"Really? I spent a couple weeks there once with my ex-husband. I'm from L.A."

"Oh? Did you like it?"

"The beach was nice, but . . . well, no offense, but I thought the town looked a little too much like a giant Taco Bell."

He laughed. "I feel that way myself, sometimes."

The woman remained silent, studying the menu.

"Well," Joan said, "this is a good place to get away from it all. There's going to be a small carnival over in Weed this weekend, by the way. It comes every year. Do you have kids?"

The man said, "No."

"Oh. Too bad. The kids love it."

She tended the other customers, pouring coffee and refilling water glasses until she noticed that the couple from Santa Barbara had set aside their menus. Joan returned to their table, set down the pot and removed her order pad from the pocket of the small apron she wore over her jeans. "What'll you have?"

They ordered—a burger and fries for him, chef's salad for her—and she quickly turned in the ticket, then took the order of a man who'd just come in and seated himself by the window. When the couple's order was ready, she took it to their table.

"Did you come for the Fourth of July celebration?" she asked.

"Yes," the man said. "Heard it was the best in the state."

"That's probably true. It's a small town, but they know how to throw a party. Especially a patriotic one."

The woman smiled tentatively, but still said nothing. Joan figured they'd probably had a fight or were perhaps just a little tired of one another after the trip.

When Chelsea slapped the cheeseburger onto the deck of the pick-up window, Joan crossed the restaurant, swept it up and began winding her way around the tables toward the man at the window. He looked very involved in reading a newspaper.

"Here you go," she said, poising the plate over the table, waiting for him to move the paper.

He didn't seem to notice her, so she tried again, raising her voice just a little, but she never finished the sentence.

At first, she thought a bird had slammed against the window-pane in flight—it had happened several times before, startling whoever was sitting by the window, then landing stunned or dead on the sidewalk outside—so it took her a few seconds to realize that whatever had struck the window was still there, pressed to the glass. She stopped speaking and turned to it, mouth open, and when she saw it clearly and realized what it was—

—a bloody hand, slapping the glass, leaving a wet reddish-brown smear on the pane, fingers clawing, nails making a sickening screech—

—her fingers weakened and the plate tipped, dumping the cheeseburger and onion rings over the table, then dropped from her hand, landing on the coffee mug and splashing steaming black coffee onto the man, who jerked into a half-standing position behind the table, hissing, "Sshhit!" Then he turned to the window as a face slowly rose above the sill—

—a mangled, broken face, darkened with glistening blood that dribbled like tears down the swollen cheeks, curling around the puffed lips.

It was a man, but that fact was not readily apparent. His face was a mask of scraped and lacerated flesh and his eyes were swollen to razor-thin slits. And his head . . .

. . . it was misshapen . . . somehow *wrong* . . .

Joan slowly pulled in a breath to back the scream that was building in her chest, and as she inhaled, the man lifted his other hand and slapped it against the window, his sausage-like lips trembling to speak, but when he opened his mouth, the only thing that came out was a spray of blood, speckling the window and running down the glass like splashed paint.

She saw the sport coat he was wearing, tan corduroy beneath the dark blood stains, and the face suddenly came together in her mind, conjuring up a familiar name.

"Paul!" she screamed, backing away from the table and lifting her hands to her jaw, curling her fingers over the flesh of her own face, as if to reassure herself that it was still there, still unbroken and smooth. "Paul *Kragen!*"

There was a stir in the diner; voices rose and chairs scraped over the floor.

But Joan's attention was focused on the torn man in the window as he slid down the glass, one cheek pressed flat and trailing blood, until he disappeared beneath the sill.

A woman in the back of the diner screamed as Joan staggered toward the door, jerked it open, and rushed out to the sidewalk where Paul Kragen lay in a heap beneath the window, the sidewalk smeared with blood around him.

Joan's feet skittered over the cement as she jerked to a halt a few feet away from him, her body frozen, mind numb.

She had never seen so much blood.

"Good God!" barked a winded voice as heavy footsteps rushed up behind her. "What's happened?"

She vaguely recognized Bill Coogan's voice but couldn't turn to him, couldn't move at all, could only stare as Paul Kragen's head turned stiffly, something dark and gelatinous dribbling out of a small opening on the balding crown of his skull; he stared up at her with eyes that looked no different from the cuts that covered his face. The lips writhed again, like slugs caked with raw meat, and he inched his shattered right hand over the cement, trembling as he lifted it toward her.

Joan stumbled forward and knelt beside him, wincing suddenly; she'd always heard that blood had a very distinct scent, but she'd never actually encountered the smell before.

"Whuh-what, Paul?" she croaked through the coming tears that burned in her throat. "What ha-happened? How did this happen, Puh-Paul?"

He tried again, moving his lips, making small but labored sounds, until he managed, "Chuh." Something fell from his mouth and chittered over the sidewalk. Two teeth.

"What?" She leaned closer to hear.

"Don't move him," Coogan said, kneeling beside her out of breath. He pounded a knuckle on the window of the diner and shouted, "Somebody call an ambulance!"

Faces peered through the glass, eyes fastened to the bloody mess on the sidewalk; none of them moved.

"Lord, somebody sure . . ." Coogan raised his voice. "Paul. Who did this to you?"

"Chuh," Kragen said again. "Chil . . . dren."

"What?" Joan asked.

They began coming out of the diner now, gathering around. The couple from Santa Barbara stepped forward and the man hunkered down beside Coogan.

"Any idea what happened?" he asked.

Coogan shook his head, his face pulled into a tight wince.

"Who is he?"

"Reporter for the *Sentinel*." Coogan tossed the man a suspicious glance. "Why, Mr. Cusack?"

"Because somebody doesn't like him a whole lot. I was just wondering."

"Yeah," Coogan nodded slowly, "you wonder a lot, don't you? Okay," he barked, "everybody back off now, c'mon."

"Children," Kragen rasped.

"What?" Joan asked again.

"Cuh-cave . . . children in . . . the cave . . ."

"Something about children," someone muttered.

"Children?" The woman from Santa Barbara hunched beside Joan. "Did he say something about children?" she whispered. She sounded frightened; she looked it, too, as she clutched Joan's arm. "Did he?"

Feeling ill, Joan could only shake her head. "I'm . . . not sure."

"C'mon, honey." The man put his hands on his wife's shoulders and gently tugged her away, but she stayed.

Joan gulped and asked, "What . . . what did you say, Paul?"

In the pool of shadow cast by the small crowd around him, Paul Kragen's breathing degenerated from a rasp to a thick wet rattle.

"Sounds like he's got some broken ribs," a woman in the crowd said.

Coogan stood and waved them back. "C'mon, let's clear away, huh?"

"Caaaave . . ."

"Cave?" Joan asked. "Is that what you—"

"The chil . . . dren . . . in . . . the cuh-cave . . ."

Joan felt a hand on her shoulder and turned to see the man Coogan had called Cusack leaning forward, looking intently at Kragen.

"What children?" he asked.

"Sons . . . duh . . . daughters . . . in the woods . . . the cave . . ."

"Who did this to you?" Coogan asked in a throaty whisper. "Was this Alliance, Paul? Did they do this?"

"Mon . . . ster . . . horrible monster . . . big . . . stinking . . ." His breathing worsened still and he began gasping, dragging bloody breaths into his lungs, which sounded like tattered cellophane. His good fingers clawed the sidewalk, curled into fists, and his swollen eyes parted slightly, tried to widen, but failed. With mouth yawning, blood dribbling from his swollen lips, he began to thrash, desperately trying to breathe.

When the ambulance siren began wailing in the distance, Paul Kragen uttered a horrible wrenching cough that spewed blood over Coogan and Joan and the Cusacks. Then he died.

Coogan slapped his thigh and stood, clamping a hand over his mouth as he turned and walked away.

Joan moved much more slowly: stood, backed away, swallowing rapidly, her vision blurred by tears.

The ambulance arrived and the crowd dispersed, losing interest, some going back to their tables in the diner, others strolling on down the street.

"Did you know him?"

Joan wiped her eyes, sniffed, and looked at the Cusack woman. "Yes. We were . . . friends."

"Who could have done that?"

"I don't know," Joan lied. "He . . . he was a nice guy and everyone liked him. Everyone. I don't know . . . who would want to hurt him.'' She spoke haltingly, unable to look the woman in the eye, because she *did* know who would want to hurt him, but she was too upset to talk about it and didn't think it was any of this woman's business anyway.

She touched Joan's arm and asked, ''Is there anything I can—''

''Excuse me.'' Joan hurried into the diner and into the women's room, where she knelt over the toilet and vomited for several minutes.

5.

''Come on, Coogan. You mentioned the Alliance, I heard you.''

''What if I did?''

''You think they might have had something to do with that?''

''Doesn't matter what I think. That's up to the police.''

''Well, if you think you know something, maybe you should tell them. Did the Alliance have something against this guy?''

''You know, boy, you ask a lotta questions for a tourist. You ask even more for somebody who just owns a few video stores down south, which I'm having a harder time believing every minute. In fact, if you *do* own those stores, if they even *exist*, I will take my shoe off, salt my right foot and *eat* it, *that's* how much I believe your video-store story. In *fact*—'' He stepped forward and poked Jordan's chest with a meaty forefinger, his eyes narrowing. ''—I'm goin' home right now to call that number on your business card and if I get a barber shop or a bowling alley or one of those goddamned phone company robots tellin' me I've reached a number that's been disconnected, you'd better be outta town by the time I leave the house or I'll have you *kicked* out. We don't mind questions, but we want 'em asked up front by people who put their cards on the table and don't sneak around. We've got enough troubles in this town without people like you—whoever the hell you *are*—creepin' around diggin' up dirt. Now am I gonna have to—''

''You don't have to go home.'' Jordan removed another business card from his pocket and handed it over, then took out his wallet, flipped it open and removed his telephone credit card. ''Call from that pay phone over there and charge it to my card.''

Frowning as if disappointed that his speech had been interrupted, Coogan adjusted his glasses and looked at the credit card, then back at Jordan.

"I'll do just that, by God. I don't bluff easy." He walked to the phone booth on the corner and slammed the door behind him.

Jordan smiled slightly. He was a tough old guy, Coogan, and very intriguing. He clearly did not approve of the Alliance, and yet he seemed to defend it, in an indirect sort of way, by solidly refusing to talk about it in detail or ask any questions; he also seemed to be protecting it from sneaky investigative reporters. Then again, maybe he was protecting something—or some*one*—else.

There were two police officers wandering around, making notes, chuckling to one another coldly as cops sometimes do to ease the blow of a bloody situation and divert their attention from the gore.

Lauren stepped up beside Jordan and said, "I'm going inside to talk with the waitress, see if I can do anything. She seems pretty upset. Is that okay?"

"Yeah, sure." He didn't look at her; he was following the streaked trail of blood on the sidewalk that led around the corner of the diner and down a narrow shadowed alley. It ended at an open garbage dumpster against the diner's wall where a large bag of heavy dark plastic was snagged on the dumpster's corner, half in and half out; the bag was empty, torn open and glistening with blood. Something small and wet at Jordan's feet caught his eye and he hunched down to find a bloody tooth; a few inches away from it was a small but growing puddle of blood being fed by drops falling from the bottom of the dumpster. Blood had trickled from the ripped garbage bag down the side of the dumpster and was dripping slowly to the pavement.

Paul Kragen had crawled from the dumpster, where he had been left, beaten and bleeding, in the garbage bag.

Jordan scanned the pavement around him searching for something, *anything* that might help answer his two biggest questions—who and why?—until a voice behind him spoke firmly and just loudly enough to startle him.

"And what do you think you're doing, friend?"

Jordan spun to face one of the police officers, smiled and said, "Nothing, really. I just noticed this blood. It led back here, so . . ." He shrugged good-naturedly as the officer came closer, looking around with a creased brow until his eyes fell on the garbage bag.

Wrinkling his nose, the officer moved closer to the bag, joined his hands behind his back and leaned forward to inspect it closely, as if he were sniffing it.

"What a way to go, huh?" Jordan said, slipping his fingers into his back pocket.

"Did you see anything?"

"No. Just what everybody else saw. Less, really. I wasn't sitting by the window."

The officer called over his shoulder, "Hey, J.B.!"

The other cop ambled around the corner and down the alley, frowning as he made a note on his pad. They both inspected the dumpster, muttering to one another until the first one turned to Jordan and said, "Do you mind if we ask you a few questions? Nothing much, really, just routine. I doubt anything's gonna come of this. Probably some creeps coming through town, messed the guy up, robbed him." He averted his eyes. "Sure as hell nobody around here who'd do that." He twitched his shoulders, removed a notebook, smacked his lips three times and never again, through the entire exchange, met Jordan's eyes.

Jordan smiled and said, "Sure, I don't mind," knowing full well the officer was lying. . . .

"Listen, honey," Chelsea said into the telephone, standing behind the register with a fist on her hip, "I don't care if you've got gangrene in both legs and a migraine headache, we need you down here *now* and if you don't come, you'd better send somebody else who can waitress right away or you're out of a job."

Most of the customers had gone. Two couples on opposite sides of the diner were preparing to leave. The man at the window with the newspaper and the food on his clothes. A few older men—obviously regulars—were still hunched at the coffee counter, speaking in low tones.

Lauren watched Joan Maher lift her cup of tea, hand and lips trembling as she sipped. They'd introduced themselves and made small talk for a few minutes before Joan lapsed into a silent pause in which she seemed to forget she was not alone.

"Would you like me to go?" Lauren asked quietly.

Joan smiled weakly. "No, I'm sorry, I'm being rude. I appre-

ciate your concern. Most tourists . . . well, they wouldn't give
a damn. I know—I deal with them almost every day. Especially
during the skiing season. I think the suicide rate among wait-
resses skyrockets during the skiing season in Grover.''

"You seemed upset, so I thought you could use an ear.''

"Yeah.'' She nodded. "I am upset. I'm . . . pissed. Paul was
a good guy. We saw a lot of each other. We . . . well, I guess
you could say we were *dating*, for want of a better word. That
sounds so—'' She laughed sadly. "—so juvenile. But we spent
most of our spare time together. You know, I don't want to talk
down about the people in Grover, because they're great, they
really are. They're big-hearted and generous and accepting and,
most importantly, unpretentious. But . . . well, there aren't very
many people around here who share my interests. You know,
literature, old movies . . . pornography.'' She laughed again,
but this time it was genuine. "But Paul was different. He loved
Grover as much as I do, but—also like me—he didn't quite fit
in. And we sort of . . . *found* each other. And the thought of
those people doing that to him . . . hurting him like that . . .''
Tears rose in her eyes and she curled her lips into a small *O* and
exhaled hard. "I need a cigarette,'' she said, rising quickly and
going to the cigarette machine by the rest rooms in back, fishing
in the pocket of her apron for change.

Those people? Lauren thought. *What people?* She watched
Joan's trembling hands deposit the coins and push the glowing
button, and Lauren felt a chill. Out on the sidewalk, Joan had
said she had no idea who might have killed her friend, but just
now, she'd spoken the words *those people* as if she knew *exactly*
who had murdered him, or at least had suspicions. Lauren toyed
nervously with the ashtray on the table, frowning as she stared
at the woman fumbling with the stubborn cigarette machine.

Maybe Jordan's right, she thought. *Maybe we should handle
this carefully. Cautiously. Maybe this is more dangerous than I
thought.*

She'd tried to discount the nagging feeling that Nathan was in
some kind of danger, telling herself that it was just the shrieking
voice of her panic, that nothing would happen to him as long as
he was in Mark's care. But now she began to entertain the possibility that perhaps even *Mark* was in trouble and—although
she'd wanted to claw his eyes out lately—when it came right
down to it, that scared her, too.

Joan returned to the table and Chelsea—a pear-shaped woman with a face that looked in need of a good ironing—came to them with a coffeepot.

"Would you like some coffee, sweets?" she asked.

"No, no." Joan stood again and reached for the pot. "Let me do that, I'm fine, really, I'll just—"

"Sit yourself down and relax. Cindy's on her way in. She'd better be, anyway—" She turned up the coffee mugs on the table and poured. "—or she'll be livin' off of Mommy and Daddy again as of tomorrow. It's slowed down, anyway. Relax."

Joan sighed, "She's great," then sipped her coffee and lit a cigarette.

"That man out there," Lauren said, "the one who was with you—"

"Coogan?"

"—he said something about the Alliance. He seemed to think maybe . . . well, that maybe they had something to do with what happened to your friend." Without saying any more, she cocked a questioning brow.

Joan exhaled a burst of smoke and lowered her eyes to her coffee before sipping again, then shook her head. "Don't know anything about it."

Trying to remain casual, Lauren chuckled quietly and said, "I don't understand them. The Alliance, I mean. They're so . . . *big*. People seem to eat that stuff up. I've never been a religious person of any kind. You know, Catholic, Protestant, anything like that. But at least those religions seem to make a kind of . . . you know, sense. At least they have a sort of history, a *base*. All this stuff about crystals and ancient entities . . . I just don't get that. But I guess it takes all kinds, huh?" She added cream to her coffee and stirred slowly, hoping Joan would give her some kind of response.

She didn't.

"What do you people think about them? I mean, the people who live around here. Do you like them being in your town? Attracting so much attention here?"

"The local merchants don't seem to mind. It's good business."

"Yeah. I guess so. But . . . well, no offense, but this area has always been the center of some . . . you know, some pretty weird beliefs, hasn't it? UFOs, people living in the mountain . . ."

"Don't let Chelsea hear you say that. The little folks on the walls here are Lemurians—the people who live in the mountain—and she claims to have seen and talked with them. And she's serious, too." She shrugged. "Yeah, it's true, there's some pretty loopy people up here, but for the most part, it's a good town. And you don't have to worry about offending me. I haven't been here long, so it's not like I'm devoted to the place, or anything."

"What brought you here from L.A.?"

"Oh—" Another shrug, uncertain this time. "—just looking to get away from the city, I guess."

"Did you know someone here, or . . ." She let the sentence hover.

"Yeah. Yeah, I guess you could say that. I knew someone here."

"Oh, I'm . . . I'm sorry. Your friend?"

"No, it wasn't Paul. I met him later. After I moved into town."

"Oh. You lived outside of town for a while?"

Joan fidgeted in her seat, took two quick puffs on her cigarette and a long swallow of her cooling black coffee. "A boarding-house near Weed," she said after a moment.

"Ah." Lauren didn't want to push too hard, but she had the feeling she was onto something. She drank her coffee and looked around the diner and tried to come up with something innocuous. Finally: "What did you do in Los Angeles?"

"I worked for an insurance company. A big one. Diamond-Barr?"

"Oh, really? Yes, I've heard of it. In fact, I had a friend who—"

"Yes, everybody does, if they don't have it themselves. It was awful. So . . . big. And the people I worked with and for . . . God, they were vile. On top of that, I was in a marriage that was like . . . well, it was like the professional wrestling of marriages. And I had a little girl who . . . she really suffered from that marriage. So I got a divorce, and things went well for a while, until my daughter got sick. She . . . it turned out to be . . . it was a bone cancer." Her brow wrinkled and her eyes began to glisten. She looked everywhere in the diner except at Lauren, who began to feel very uncomfortable and guilty for prying. "Too advanced to stop. After she died, I started groping for something—*anything*—and left the city to . . . well, I needed something that . . . see, I was raised in a very strict Catholic home and that . . . well, it just didn't work for me. I mean, I don't harbor any hard feelings toward my parents because . . . they, you know, meant well and felt they were doing the right thing and . . . they're dead now. My brother, too. He died of cancer in eighty-nine. Then the divorce . . . well, that was nothing, a *relief*, but when my daughter died . . . I needed something to believe in.''

Joan paused for a while, but Lauren said nothing. Joan was upset enough already, but something within her had apparently opened up; Lauren decided Joan *needed* to talk to someone or she would have remained silent, so Lauren said nothing and let her continue.

''Catholicism hadn't worked and . . . well, Christianity in general seemed a joke to me, so . . .'' She finally looked at Lauren and smiled a weak, sad smile, her lashes spiked with tears. ''I joined the Alliance. I mean, I didn't just jump into it. I did some reading, some research. It had a little bit of everything. Eastern religions, a touch of Christianity, even some secular humanism. So I moved here, into the colony up behind the hotel. I was there for a year. It wasn't a bad year, but . . . well, it . . . didn't work. That's all. It just didn't work for me. Just like Catholicism. So I backed out. I *tried* to back out graciously. I had no money because I'd given them everything. I mean *everything*, every penny I had. They took good care of me while I was there, but when I decided to leave . . . they didn't want me to. I had nothing, so I had no way to leave. I got a job here in town, moved into the boardinghouse . . . and they . . . they . . .''

She stopped. Silence. Joan stared at the wall.

''They what, Joan?''

She shook her head. Shrugged. Smoked. Punched out her cigarette and lit another. After finishing her coffee, she took a long, deep drag on her cigarette and exhaled smoke with tightly closed eyes and a stiff posture. Then she relaxed, looked at Lauren, smiled gently and said, ''I finally had enough money to move to Grover. I'd really come to like this town, the people who live here, so . . . I stayed. I plan to stay. Paul was my best friend and I'm going to miss him, but . . . I'll get by.''

''What did they do, Joan? You were going to say something about them, about the Alliance.''

The cover came back; she frowned briefly, shrugged and said, "They just didn't want me to leave, that's all. Sort of like my husband." She laughed. "But that's okay. I did leave them. And I stayed in Grover anyway."

"Anyway? Did they try to chase you away?"

She thought about that a moment. Chewed her lip. Took a puff. "Yeah. They did. But I'm here to stay. I was angry that they wanted me to leave someplace I loved. They don't bother me now." A brief, flitting smile. "I've sort of become a fixture."

"What did they do?"

Joan looked at her differently, then. Suspiciously. "Why?"

"I'm just . . . curious." Lauren blinked, backed off, feeling guilty again. "I've heard some . . . well, some stories about them and I just wondered if they're true."

"What stories?" Before Lauren could respond, Joan said, rather firmly, "If you think they're so strange, why did you come to Grover in the first place? I mean, this is their headquarters."

"Oh, I didn't mean to say that I . . . I mean, well, I hope you're not offended. I didn't mean to insult your beliefs. After what you've been through, I can understand perfectly why you'd need something to turn to. My God, if anything ever happened to my son, I don't know what I'd—" She realized her mistake mid-sentence and froze as Joan leaned forward suddenly, narrowing her eyes.

"I thought you said you didn't *have* any children."

Lauren felt sick and wanted to leave the diner as quickly as possible.

"That's what you said, isn't it?"

Her mouth moved, but no words came out, only the clicking of her throat opening and closing, until finally, "Well, yes, yes, we . . . well, we don't actually have any. Children. But . . ."

Suspicion poured like syrup over Joan's face and she leaned so close, her breasts were mashed against the tabletop. "Who are you?" she whispered. "What do you want? Are you reporters?"

"No, no, of course we're . . . like my husband said, we're . . . on vacation." Lauren could feel her cheeks flushing, knew her guilt was brilliantly visible, and wanted to cry. Jordan would be furious. If he found out.

"Why did he say you don't have any children?"

Lauren thought of a couple explanations she could give—"I have a son by another marriage, but he's with his father," or "We adopted a little boy who's staying with my sister this week, but we don't have any children of our *own*"—but knew she'd never be able to give either of them convincingly, if she could at all without stuttering like a nervous schoolgirl during show and tell.

"Well?" Joan raised her voice slightly, impatient, indignant. "You *said* you don't *have* any *children*. You sit here asking me all these questions like—Jesus, I don't know—like you're *interviewing* me, or something, and now you say you have a son. So what's going on? Why did you say you don't have any children?"

"I'm . . . sorry. I'm sorry." Lauren lowered her eyes to the pack of Marlboro Lights on the table. She hadn't had a cigarette since they'd been taxed so much that one pack cost as much as a paperback novel, but she reached for Joan's now, her fingers quivering as she shook one out and lit it with Joan's butane lighter. She coughed lightly with the first drag but not at all with the second. "I have a son," she said quietly.

"So why did your husband say you—"

"He's not my husband," she whispered, then quickly added, "Please, please keep that to yourself, I don't know what he'll do if he finds out I told you, but—but—"

"Are you in trouble?" Joan's eyes were wide now, her suspicion replaced with concern.

"No, it's nothing like that. I'm . . . my son is—"

The door opened and Jordan's laughter accompanied Coogan's apologetic voice: "—let me buy you a cup of coffee."

"No, you don't have to do that. We just had some with lunch."

"Dessert, then. I insist. That's twice in one day I jump down your throat for no reason. Nothing wrong with being curious, for crying out loud. It's a free country. How about a piece of pie?"

"Well, if you insist."

Lauren turned to see a young blond girl follow them in and hurry behind the counter into the back of the diner.

Jordan and Coogan headed toward the table.

Lauren quickly looked at Joan and breathed, "Please don't say anything. We'll talk."

Joan nodded, stared at Lauren a moment with a tight, worried expression, then looked up at the men and smiled.

"How you doin', sweetheart?" Coogan asked her, gently putting a hand on her head.

"I'm okay, Coogan."

"Atta girl. He had family, didn't he?"

"A sister in Seattle. I should call her." She sighed heavily and closed her eyes, leaning her head on Coogan's ample belly.

"You want me to do it, Joanie?"

"Oh, no. I will. I just don't look forward to it."

Chelsea waddled out of the kitchen and stood beside Coogan. "Cindy's here, babe. You go home now, okay?"

"No, Chels, I think I'm going to do some shopping."

"Sounds like a plan. You need some cash?"

"No, but thanks." Joan stood and turned to Jordan. "You mind if I steal your wife away for a couple hours? I could use some company right now."

"Sure, no problem," Jordan said, then to Lauren: "You want to meet back at the hotel?"

She nodded, unable to look at him.

Joan dismissed herself to get her things in the back, and Coogan asked, "What kinda pie you like, Lorne? Apple? Banana cream? Peach?"

"Banana cream's fine."

When Coogan went to the counter, leaving them alone, Lauren stood and busied herself putting the cigarette out in the ashtray.

"You all right?" Jordan whispered.

She nodded, still not looking at him.

"Okay, listen. See what you can find out about Paul Kragen. Apparently she knew him, so see if he had anything to do with the Alliance, if he didn't like them, maybe. Okay?" When she didn't respond, he said it again, and Lauren nodded. "Try not to be too long."

Coogan returned to the table with two slices of pie and Joan came back out, apron gone, purse slung over her shoulder. Lauren was silent as Joan said goodbye to the others and they went out onto the sidewalk where—

—Paul Kragen's blood was drying to a rusty brown on the concrete.

Joan stumbled and made a quiet strangled sound in her throat before quickening her pace, eyes front, neck stiff. Two leftover tears rolled down her cheeks but were quickly swept away with a trembling knuckle.

"I'm gonna be okay," Joan said with a sniff. She seemed to be speaking to herself rather than to Lauren. "Now. I think you should talk to me, Bonnie."

"My name is Lauren."

Joan stopped, turned, and studied Lauren for a long moment, her puffy red eyes hard as they moved carefully over Lauren's face. Then she nodded, began walking again, and said, "Yeah, you should definitely talk to me."

Lauren did talk; she told Joan everything.

6.

Jordan spent nearly an hour in the Lemurian talking with the men at the coffee counter. Actually, he did more listening than talking because the dominant topic of discussion was Paul Kragen.

They talked about his generosity, his sense of humor, his sensitivity (although the Lemurian regulars saw this as more of a weakness than a strength—they could not quite understand a man who cried at sad movies and made no apologies—they all thought highly of him anyway); they praised his community spirit, his talents as a journalist and his reliability.

But no one spoke of his death.

Jordan waited, expecting someone to ask, *Who could do such a thing?* or to say, *When they find the son of a bitch who did this . . .*

But no one did.

In spite of their apparent admiration for Paul Kragen, the men at the coffee counter did not question his death; they did not express outrage or indignation. They seemed instead to accept it, perhaps even ignore it, and spoke only of what a good man Paul Kragen had been.

"What did he do at the newspaper exactly?" Jordan asked during a pause in the conversation. "Did he write a column or was he a reporter?"

"Both," Coogan said. "He wrote a column every week and did some reporting, too."

"Good writer," the man called Flash added.

"A little opinionated," Amos said.

"That's what made him so interesting," Coogan responded, lighting another Camel.

Then at the end of the counter in a quiet voice that barely rose above the others and the clamor from the kitchen, Wally mumbled into his coffee cup, "Guess he was a little *too* interesting."

Although this resulted in a few self-conscious harrumphs and loud sniffs at the counter, Jordan acted as if he hadn't heard the remark and fought his desire to pursue it. Instead, he stood, thanked Coogan for the pie, reminded him of their dinner date that night, and said goodbye to the others, telling them he wanted to take a walk through the town before going back to the hotel.

He indeed planned to walk through town—straight to the library, where he hoped to find a few samples of Paul Kragen's work. Jordan suspected he knew what Kragen's favorite topic was, but wanted to confirm his suspicion by reading a few of the columns himself.

Coogan left the diner, too. His shoes felt heavy as he walked to his pick-up truck parked around the corner and it was only with effort that he did not hang his head and stare at the ground. Coogan himself felt heavier than usual and seemed to sink deep into the patched and taped seat of his truck. He tried not to drive too fast, but wanted to get to his bed as quickly as possible. The short trip seemed much longer than it actually was because he felt some bad shakes coming on; he was surprised they hadn't come much earlier because he'd felt their subtle beginnings, but now that they'd started—deep in his bones where they always started, too deep to be seen yet—they weren't wasting any time in coming to the surface.

After parking at the top of the hill, he walked through his store—which was being tended by eighteen-year-old Teddy Caulder—through his living room, and straight to his bed, slamming the door of his bedroom behind him. His legs weakened halfway across the room and he reached out for something to lean on, but only fell forward, slamming onto the mattress heavily with a deep and miserable groan. He clumsily propped himself up on one elbow and hugged his pillow to his big chest to hold back the tremors that began to roll through his body, but it did no good. His arms quaked, then his legs; his head rocked on his neck and his shoulders hunched uncontrollably. It hadn't happened with such force since his wife died; it hadn't bothered him so much then because it was expected, it seemed a natural reaction to such a great loss. But this was different. It frightened him . . . because it told him he was more scared than he'd allowed himself to admit and Paul Kragen's bloody death had jarred that fear loose, allowing it to rise up, like something bloated and rotten and clotted with moss rising from the bottom of a dirty river.

Coogan groaned again, hugging the pillow even harder as he shook.

He looked at a picture of his daughter and two grandchildren on his dresser across the room. They were all wearing the kind of smiles he'd not seen on their faces in far too long.

Coogan did something else he hadn't done in a long time. Moving unsteadily off the bed, he knelt beside it and silently prayed for them.

In the library's dense silence, the dry rustling of newspaper pages being turned sounded like great trees being mowed down *en masse* in the forest.

Jordan could feel the librarian's eyes on his back like two needle-thin laser beams. She was a skeleton with nicotine-stained skin—like yellowed parchment—so tautly stretched over her bones it seemed ready to rip and crumple around her at any moment. He was a stranger in a small tourist town that was not accustomed to strangers using the library, and he'd expected such scrutiny, so that, in itself, did not bother him. But in light of what he'd been reading, he began to wonder if he shouldn't be bothered by *everything*.

For thirty minutes, he'd been thumbing through back editions of the Grover *Sentinel* looking for Paul Kragen's columns and articles. There was no shortage of them; Kragen had apparently been the *Sentinel*'s primary contributor. His column, *Kragen's Korner*, was well written, usually humorous with serious undertones and always concerned with his community. But more than half of the columns Jordan read involved, in one way or another, and *always* negatively, the Alliance. It was obvious that Paul Kragen had not been pleased with the Alliance's decision to set up headquarters in Grover.

After apparently researching the group at length, Kragen had come to the conclusion that the Alliance—unlike many of the other small and unusual religious and spiritual groups that had made Grover their home—was in pursuit of more than just enlightenment, peace and harmony; he concluded that they would eventually seek out publicity, national acceptance, and of course, money, and that they would by no means remain small. Compared with other similar groups at the time, the Alliance had been a reasonably large group already when it made Grover its home base, but for some time Kragen had been predicting that it would become larger and more powerful—financially and politically—and this bothered him, mostly because he feared the group's power would begin in Grover. He was afraid the group would quickly set deep roots in the town and have a strong effect on its people. On *his* people.

In later columns, after his predictions began to come true, he used quotes from Hester Thorne's many interviews on television and in national publications to make his point, and his point was this: the Alliance was an organization whose message was not only vaguely broad but so "wishy-washy and interchangeable" that it could, if properly manipulated, please just about anyone looking for something to believe in, and lacked the firm conviction of sincere principles and teachings that usually accompanied a belief system that simply wanted to convey a heartfelt message. Kragen maintained that, if carefully scrutinized, the group's core message was morally and ethically questionable, but was so hidden in sweetened double-talk that most people couldn't *find* it, let alone understand it. In short, Paul Kragen believed the Alliance was up to something. Without coming off as a paranoid crank ranting about global conspiracies, Kragen eloquently expressed his fear that the Alliance had greater (and far more sinister) aspirations than it was admitting to and this disturbed him for, apparently, one reason only: it was reaching for its secret goals from the town he loved, using the people he loved as a sort of innocuous front for whatever those goals might be. Although he never actually said so, Kragen was clearly determined to learn *exactly* what those goals were and to expose them to the people of Grover, to whom he was so obviously, strongly—and touchingly—devoted.

Maybe he found it, Jordan thought, closing the last paper of the stack. *Maybe that's why he's dead. Just like Harvey Bolton.* After a moment of silently staring at the stack of papers, fingering a corner of the top one and chewing his lip, Jordan thought, *Of course that's why he's dead, you idiot. But why doesn't everyone else realize that, or even mention it? And if that's the case, why did Kragen's killers dump him half-alive in the middle of town while Bolton disappeared entirely? Did they think he was dead, maybe? Or was it a message—a warning—to the whole town?*

Then again, maybe the Alliance had nothing at all to do with Kragen's death, perhaps not even with Bolton's disappearance.

But Jordan doubted that; he doubted it strongly.

"Is something wrong?"

He jerked in his chair and looked up at the cadaverous librarian, who stood beside him with hands locked behind her back, eyes somehow gently curious and stern at the same time. Her voice sounded like something thick and wet being sucked down a drain.

"No," he said with a smile, "no, just thinking. That's all."

She nodded stiffly and returned to her desk.

Jordan returned the stack of papers to the proper shelf and left the library with his hands in his pockets.

By the time Lauren was finished talking, she and Joan were seated on a bench at the edge of a grassy square in the center of town; picnic tables, a swing set and jungle gym were arranged on the grass in the shade of several tall oak trees that leaned protectively over the small park.

Lauren could say little of Jordan's reasons for coming to Grover, but she'd talked for nearly half an hour of her own. She hoped for some sympathy, perhaps even some advice considering Joan's former involvement with the Alliance.

But Joan said nothing, didn't even look at Lauren; she stared, instead, at an old clock set into the Alpine-style false front of a building across the street. The clock's face was cracked and the hands were frozen at eleven fifty-nine.

"I don't know why I've told you this," Lauren said, deciding to stare at the clock, too. She suddenly felt foolish for telling her secret to a total stranger. She also felt guilty. What if Jordan found out? She wondered if she had put them in some sort of danger; Joan didn't seem to be a threat, but Lauren didn't *know* her and had no reason to trust her. "This was stupid. I'm sorry.

Really.'' She turned to Joan to say, *Forget about it, okay?* Instead, she just frowned.

Joan Maher had a pleasant face, almost pixieish, but Lauren had thought from the moment they'd met that it was a *flexible* face; it could probably look very mysterious and sexy if Joan wanted it to and, if she became angry, probably very cruel. Now it looked deeply troubled. Her small nose was slightly wrinkled, eyes narrowed, lips pressed hard together as if a string behind the bridge of her nose were being pulled, tightening the features of her face.

''Why?'' Joan asked finally.

''I'm sorry?''

''Why did you tell me?''

''I . . . don't know. I needed to tell someone, I guess. Jordan and I . . . we don't seem to get along well. I don't think he wants me here. But I'm desperate. I want my son and he said he'd try to help me get him back. And *you* said you were with the Alliance once, so I thought . . . I guess I don't know what I thought.''

''You want me to help you? Is that it?''

Lauren leaned closer to her. ''*Can* you?''

After a moment, Joan shook her head, still staring at the clock, then she blinked, as if coming from a trance, and looked at Lauren. ''You want some advice?''

''Please.''

''Go home and hire someone to kidnap your son. Don't try to get him yourself.''

''Hi . . . hire someone to . . . *kidnap* Nathan? *I can't afford that!*'' she hissed. ''I told you, my husband took *all* of our money! I wouldn't know how to hire a kidnapper anyway. I doubt they're listed in the Yellow Pages!''

''You can find someone in the back of *Soldier of Fortune* magazine. They're expensive, but . . . you want your son back? Borrow the money. Steal it if you have to.'' She spoke quietly and calmly, as if she were telling Lauren how to write a résumé. ''Because if you try to get him back on your own, you know what's going to happen? They'll call the police the minute they know you're on the grounds and you and your friend will be hauled off to jail. And you know what else? They'll have the law on their side. They've broken no laws and you'll be trespassing and disturbing the peace and God knows what else. They'll press charges as hard and as far as they can and you'll waste a lot of time with police and bail bondsmen and lawyers. And you won't get your son back.''

Joan's words were like a slicingly chilly draft on the back of Lauren's neck. "This has happened before, hasn't it? *Hasn't it?*''

Joan turned to the clock again.

"Has . . . has it happened to *you*? Is that why you're not answering?''

Joan's face did not change; she stared at the clock.

"Is he in trouble?'' Lauren whispered. "Is my son in danger?''

"Just do what I told you. Leave here. Okay? It'll be a lot easier and a lot more effective. And a lot safer.'' Looking at her again, Joan asked firmly, "Okay?''

"I . . . I don't know if I can.''

Joan stood abruptly. "Then we shouldn't be seen together. They don't like me as it is.''

Frightened, Lauren stood, too, but on weakened legs. She spoke rapidly and without thinking: "What did your friend mean? About the children and caves? Did they do that? Did they kill him? Coogan thought so. Didn't he?'' When Joan didn't look at her, Lauren clutched her elbow with a trembling hand. *"Did they kill him?''*

"Here comes your friend,'' Joan said quietly.

Jordan was crossing the street toward them, smiling.

"Please—'' Lauren began, but Joan turned to her and said, "Don't worry, I won't say anything. Call me if you need to. I'm listed.'' Then, patting Lauren's shoulder, she said, "Good luck. You'll need it.'' She waved at Jordan and smiled half-heartedly, then headed back to the diner.

As Jordan approached and Joan went away, Lauren felt coldly alone, abandoned and trapped. She wanted to back away from Jordan and go—

—where?

He was all she had.

He came to her side, gave her a husbandly peck on the cheek and took her hand as they began to walk. "So, did you learn anything?''

Lauren was afraid that if she spoke, her voice would reveal

her growing panic and her betrayal of their secrecy, but not responding would only be worse. "No. Nothing."

"Oh? Well, either she doesn't know anything or she's not talking, because I learned plenty."

She glanced at him and was disturbed by the contrast between the pleasant, calm expression on his face and his dark tone of voice.

"For one thing," he said, chuckling as if he were telling her about something amusing he'd seen earlier, "apparently these Alliance folks are *not* nice people."

7.

"Is it necessary for you to be so *affectionate*?" Lauren asked testily, speaking the last word through clenched teeth. They were back in their hotel room, but earlier, outside, Jordan had spent a lot of time with his arm around her, holding her hand, stroking her hair and kissing her now and then on the head or cheek. She hadn't liked it.

"As a matter of fact, it *is*." Jordan removed another shirt and some jeans from the closet, then turned to her. "A man who knows he's being followed is likely to be preoccupied and anxious, not relaxed and affectionate with his wife. And a man whose wife has just watched someone die is likely to be very attentive and comforting. O-kay? We're trying to be convincing, remember?" He went into the bathroom to change.

Lauren sat on the edge of the bed and sighed. He was right. Again.

"Okay," she said apologetically. "What now?"

From the bathroom: "Now we take a romantic twilight tour of the hotel grounds. Guided if possible. Lots of smiling and nodding and admiring comments. And, you'll be sorry to hear, more hand-holding." He came out in jeans and a sport shirt. "We pay close attention to everything the guide shows us. Especially the places we're *not* supposed to go."

"Why?"

"So that later—" He smiled. "—I can go there."

* * *

Their guide's name was Demi—early twenties, blond, wearing an Alliance emblem on the lapel of her blue blazer—and throughout the thirty-minute tour, she did not stop smiling once.

"You picked the *perfect* time of day," Demi chirped, clapping her small hands together once. She led them out of the lobby, saying, "As the sun sets, the lights come up and the grounds are *so* beautiful."

They're all so happy, Jordan thought. And they were, *all* of them; not a single employee could be seen wearing less than a broad, white-toothed smile on his or her face and there wasn't a hint of the rudeness, weariness or even indifference so often found in—and to be expected of—people who dealt constantly with the demanding, often cruel public.

But why? he wondered. *Why?*

With practiced patter and hand gestures that bordered on mechanical, she showed them the vast green behind the hotel—actually, it was a small park—scattered with bright patches of flowers and animal-shaped hedges—lions and bears, elephants and giraffes—a few trees, some benches, and a few tables and chairs beneath bright white umbrellas; in the middle of it all was a small pond with ducks floating lazily on the water. A few people strolled over the impeccable lawn or sat restfully at the tables with drinks.

"And over there—" Demi gestured to the right. "—is our restaurant, the Crystal Unicorn, where we offer the finest dining in the area from four P.M. to midnight. The restaurant also provides twenty-four-hour room service for our guests, and that includes breakfast, lunch and dinner, as well as snacks and desserts."

She was a walking, talking brochure.

The restaurant, castle-like in appearance with large rectangular windows through which Jordan could see diners huddling over candlelit tables, was connected to the hotel with a covered walkway. In front of the restaurant, rearing up on its hind legs, was an enormous, sparkling crystal unicorn. Adjoining the restaurant was a gift shop, its windows displaying shelves of crystal figurines of all shapes and sizes.

Turning, gesturing, Demi said, "And to your left is our recreation and fitness center, available twenty-four hours a day to all of our guests. There's an outdoor pool for summer and one indoors for winter, as well as a steam room, three Jacuzzies, a variety of Nautilus equipment and a handball court. And just beyond the building are four tennis courts.''

This isn't a hotel, Jordan thought, smiling and holding Lauren's hand. *It's a country club.*

Demi faced them, joined her hands before her and cocked her head abruptly, chirping, ''Tell me, Mr. and Mrs. Cusack. Do you enjoy art?''

They glanced at one another, Jordan shrugged and said, ''Yeah, sure.''

She began leading them across the green, around the flowers and hedges, tables and benches, to a red-brick building on the other side. It resembled an old schoolhouse, except it wasn't old and it was too big.

As they went up the front steps, Demi said, ''This is the Sleeping Lady Art Gallery, featuring the works of Ms. Thorne's followers, all of whom live beyond this building in a colony nestled at the foot of Mount Shasta surrounded by untouched wooded land.''

As they went inside the gallery, Jordan wondered if the tour would include the colony. He seriously doubted it.

Inside, they roamed up and down rows of artwork, some quite beautiful, but most nothing more than what Jordan considered New Age bullshit: paintings of mystical landscapes with castles and unicorns and dragons, that sort of thing. There were mostly paintings, but also a number of sculptures and some pottery and ceramics.

There was something odd about the work, though, the paintings in particular. It took a while for Jordan to pinpoint it, but after they'd been in the gallery for a while, it occurred to him.

None of the paintings were signed.

They strolled the aisles between the displays until they came to a section of small framed drawings, crude drawings, some watercolors, others in crayons, still more in pen or pencil. They were the works of children.

Jordan saw trouble coming, knew it was a bad idea to linger on this section, and tried to quicken his pace when Lauren clutched his hand tightly and gave a stifled gasp.

''C'mon,'' he whispered. ''Look at this over here, honey,'' he said, leading her to a sculpture of an egg cracking open to reveal the planet Earth inside. But he knew it was too late.

Something had set her off. Her hand still clutched his tightly and she seemed stiff, fighting back whatever had disturbed her so.

They got through the rest of the gallery quickly, but without appearing in a rush, and Demi led them back outside.

"Any questions?" Demi asked on the front steps.

Jordan asked, "Is it okay if we take a walk through the woods back there?"

Demi's smile stumbled just a bit, but quickly recovered. "I'm afraid we don't allow that. As I said, the woods are untouched, so there are no trails and it's very easy to get lost. But there are plenty of woods to see in the area. And we provide trips to the mountain twice daily, where Ms. Thorne gives a full body channel."

"I see," Jordan said, thinking, *Figured as much.*

"Well, if you have no further questions," Demi said, clapping her hands again, "I'll leave you two alone. Feel free to roam the grounds and take advantage of the facilities. And I recommend dinner at the Crystal Unicorn. The food is fabulous." She gave them a finger-waggling wave, turned, and headed back across the grounds.

As Jordan led Lauren down the steps, he asked, "What's wrong?"

Her voice was a harsh, pinched breath. "He's here."

"What?"

"Nathan. Huh-he's here. I know it n-now."

"How?"

"Two of those pictures in there. A crayon and a watercolor. I know it, I'm *sure*, I'm *positive*. They're his. . . ."

"How can you *tell*?"

"Because I know. I've seen his work before."

"They all look pretty much the same to—"

"And do you have children? No. You notice things like that, you . . . I don't know, you become familiar with the way your child does things and . . . *and two of those pictures were his.*"

"Calm down until we get back to the room, okay?"

"But I'm—"

He squeezed her hand and she stopped as he turned back to the gallery. It was flanked by dark woods, tall green trees that towered above its red-brick walls. But there was something else, something he hadn't noticed before.

Just beyond the trees, easy to miss if one weren't looking for it, was a concrete wall. It was about eight or nine feet tall, and although it was hard to tell because of the cover of the trees, it appeared to go all the way around the grounds.

He'd found it.

That was where they didn't want him to go. . . .

═══ THREE ═══

MARVIN

1.

Driving his black Thunderbird onto the grounds of the Napa State Hospital, Marvin tried not to stare at the pathetic figures shuffling around on the grass. Some looked fine, while others chattered to no one and others picked at their clothes and hair and faces, while still others—the worst of the lot—limped and thrashed and jerked spastically as they walked through the shafts of morning sunlight shining down through the lush trees.

Saddest of all was the speed and blindness with which life passed them by; the cars and motorcycles and trucks and buses that sped by in front of the hospital, the airliners and small planes and helicopters that flew by overhead, all oblivious of the men and women on the hospital grounds, living out their days locked inside their own minds, some twisted, others bent beyond the point of breaking, most heavily medicated and many simply gone, lost, living in worlds familiar to no one else, beyond anyone's reach.

He felt sorrow for them, but couldn't stop the shudder that passed through him, the knowledge that it could happen so easily to anyone, to *him;* one false move by some infinitesimal, mutinous part of his brain and it was over, he was a goner, slobbering and picking or twitching and chattering. . . .

He shuddered again as he parked the car.

On his way into the hospital, a woman walked by, middle-aged, wearing a thin, smock-like dress; she was thin and a little hunched as she shuffled by him, glancing at him suspiciously and waving him away.

"No, no," she murmured, "don't get him near me, don't

wanna see him, he'll run all over me, mess up my dress, take him away, take it away, take it. . . . ''

And then she was gone, heading for the grass to join the others.

He went to the front desk and smiled at the officious-looking woman seated there.

"I'm here to see Michael Lumley," he said.

"Lumley." She glanced at something on her desk. "Oh, yes. You're the uncle, correct?"

"That's right."

"Mm. Doesn't get many visitors," she said, looking him over.

"No, I'm afraid not. Most of the family . . . well, you know how it is."

She nodded curtly, then gave him directions to another desk down a grey corridor where he could find someone to take him to Michael.

At the second desk he met a hefty fellow dressed in white with short sleeves and a name tag on his shirt that read TED McCOY. Marvin introduced himself.

"Oh, yeah, the uncle," Ted said, checking a clipboard. "Kinda surprising, since he doesn't get many visitors. Hell, *no* visitors. This way."

Marvin followed him down the grey corridor that smelled vaguely of urine and disinfectant. Through open doors, he heard the cold emotionless sounds of bureaucracy: telephones chirping, papers shuffling, computer printers burping up streams of paper.

Around a corner, through a couple sets of swinging doors, the odor became stronger, the office sounds faded and Marvin found himself walking past more of the same people he'd seen outside. A young woman leaning against the wall stabbed an accusing finger at Marvin as he passed, her face twisted in anger, mouth working furiously but silently; an aging man smiled at him and said, "Hey, Phil, how're the horses doin'?"; an old woman stooped down to pet an invisible animal, making dry kissing sounds with her lips.

Ted spoke up: "You probably already know this, but Mike doesn't say a whole lot these days. In fact, you'll be lucky to get anything out of him. He may not even *know* you."

"I expected that."

Ted nodded toward a closed door, pushed it open and went

in ahead of Marvin saying, "You've got a visitor, Mike. How about *that*, huh?"

Marvin entered and saw Mike Lumley seated at his window.

He was slouched in a worn green vinyl chair and wore standard hospital pajamas; his dark hair was uncombed but his beard and mustache were trimmed. He looked overly thin, with tendons taut in his neck, head bowed slightly but eyes open beneath bushy brows, staring through the barred window at the morning outside.

Ted leaned down and scooted Mike's chair to face Marvin. "See, Mike? It's your uncle. He's come to see you. Whatta you think of that, huh?" Ted's voice rose slightly, as if he were talking to someone who was hard of hearing. When Mike gave no response—simply stared at nothing, unblinking—Ted turned to Marvin and shrugged. "See? Well, maybe you'll have better luck with him. I'll leave you two alone."

On his way out, he kicked the doorstop down, propping the door open, but Marvin immediately kicked it back up and said apologetically, "If you don't mind, I'd like some privacy. It's been a long time, you know."

"Yeah, sure thing."

Marvin closed the door, then watched Mike for a long moment, wondering how to start. Reaching into the inside breast pocket of his suit coat, he switched on the microcassette recorder; his tie tack was a microphone. He pulled a chair away from the wall and seated himself in front of Mike, leaned forward with elbows on knees and folded his hands.

"Hello, Mike," he said gently, smiling. "My name is Marvin Ackroyd. I'm, uh, I'm not—" He chuckled. "—I'm not your uncle, of course. Well, *you* know that. I just said that to get in here without having to answer a lot of questions."

Still no response. Mike's eyes did not shift, not a single muscle in his face—his whole *body*—moved in the slightest.

Marvin took a deep breath.

"I need your help, Mike. You can help me by answering some questions. Just . . . just a few questions, that's all. If you . . . if you would?"

Nothing.

"I need to ask you some questions about your wife." A pause, looking for something, *anything*. "Your wife, Hester. Hester Thorne?"

A long, *long* silent moment, then—

—a tremble in the corner of his mouth, almost as if his lips were about to curl into a sneer, then—

—a twitch in his right eyebrow and—

—his eyes, for less than a heartbeat, met Marvin's.

Marvin leaned forward, expecting him to speak, but he only turned his head to the window slowly, *very* slowly.

Doped up, Marvin thought, knowing that wouldn't make things any easier. Now that he'd gotten *some* response, he spoke more seriously. "You see, Mike, I need to find out a few things about your wife. There's not much out there, you know. In the news, I mean . . . the magazines, the papers, TV. I need to find out some of the things that *aren't* covered by the media. And I thought that, since you were married to her and you'd—"

"Who sent you?"

His voice was flat and quiet and thick, perhaps with fatigue or medication or even disuse, and it so startled Marvin that he jerked upright in his chair.

"Wuh-well, um . . . well . . ." He was about to say, *I'm not at liberty to divulge that information*, the standard confidentiality response, but paused, thinking.

How seriously did the staff at Napa State take Mike Lumley? When—and *if*—he spoke, how closely did they listen? What did they believe? After all, this man, according to the police records and newspapers Marvin and Jordan had trudged through before Jordan had left, had stabbed his mother several times, nearly killing her, apparently intending to kill his own *wife*, and had been a basket case ever since, going from the Vacaville Mental Facility to this hospital, where he had apparently taken to staring out the window and speaking to no one, showing no emotion, no response to anyone or anything.

If he told Mike something that got as close to the truth as he could safely get, Marvin might have a better chance of getting information from him; and if Mike told anyone about it, who would believe him?

"Well, Mike," he said, "I can't name any names, I'm not allowed to do that, but I will tell you this. I'm working for someone very, very important who is interested in finding out as much as possible about your wife and her, um, her . . . organization?" he asked uncertainly.

"The Alliance," Mike said without looking away from the window.

"That's right."

"Why?"

"I'm sorry?"

"What . . . is this person . . . lookin' for?"

"Well, more specifically, *who* is this person looking for. It seems someone very close to my client disappeared while seeking information about the Alliance. This person disappeared on a visit to Grover. And my client is anxious to find out where this person is and whether or not this person has been harmed."

Mike stared out the window awhile. His thick eyebrows huddled together over the bridge of his nose. "They're dead."

Marvin blinked several times. "Um, do you know this for a fact?"

After a moment, a small, almost indistinguishable shake of his head.

"Then why do you say that?"

"Because . . . I know my wife."

Marvin stumbled a moment, not sure how to react to that one. "Wuh-well, um, what-uh, what do you know about your wife that makes you say that?"

A long silence, then: "You're a reporter."

"Oh no, no, I'm not—"

"They still come sometimes. A lot, at first. Now just once in a while. They come askin' . . . questions. About her. I don't talk. No sense talkin'. They . . . they won't find nothin'."

"Find what?"

"What they're lookin' for."

"And what is that, Mike?"

"Somethin' . . ." A slight shake of his head. "Somethin' bad."

"Is there something bad for them to find?"

Mike's head turned slowly, his dark, deep-set eyes burrowing into Marvin's, and the left side of his mouth curled into a cold, mocking smirk as his eyes narrowed suspiciously. Then he turned back to the window.

"Look, I'm *not* a reporter. I sell surveillance equipment. See here?" He removed his wallet and took his driver's license, business card, business license and held them out to Mike.

He gave them no more than a cursory glance.

"Right now," Marvin said, "I'm working with a friend of mine, a private investigator."

Mike had apparently retreated once again to his staring silence.

Marvin whispered, "Listen, Mike, two people have disappeared. A reporter and a little boy. Both have been connected to the Alliance and certain people have reason to believe the Alliance is somehow involved in their disappearances. Now, if you can tell me something—*anything*—about your wife, her work, her background, her church, you might help us *find* these people, and if there's something illegal or—"

"That's no church."

Marvin stopped, waited.

"Churches are supposed to do good. Supposed to help people. Comfort 'em." Another slight shake of his head. "That's no church."

"What is it, Mike?"

Nothing.

"Remember, Mike, you might be able to help these two people, this reporter and this little boy, you might be able to . . . " He saw that was getting nowhere and stopped. Scooting his chair closer to Mike, Marvin put his hand on Mike's arm cautiously; when nothing happened, he gave the arm a squeeze. "Tell me, Mike. Why did you try to kill your wife?"

"No one believes me."

"I'll believe you."

"You'll print it."

"I'll tell no one but my associate."

"I can't talk about it."

"Why not?"

"Because I . . . it makes me . . . I get . . . " The emotionless mask began to twitch. He frowned so deeply that his forehead, suddenly lined with deep razor-cut lines, seemed to age ten years. He shook his head, hard this time, as if shaking off a fly. His hands trembled. "They give me medicine. Pills. Sometimes shots. But they . . . they don't ever help. Not really. Not enough. After all these years, it's . . . still there, still in me, like it's still happenin', like I'm still seein' it, and . . . and I . . . "

"Still seeing what, Mike?"

"No. I can't." Firmly, clenching his teeth now.

"Please."

He was silent awhile, staring out the window as unfallen tears began to glisten in his eyes and his lips pressed tightly together, so tight they became white-rimmed. "I . . . I loved her . . . so much," he breathed. "When we met, she was . . . she seemed . . . *perfect*. So pretty. Funny. And smart, smarter than me, 'cause I never finished high school. But she . . . she wasn't what I thought. Not at all.

"I pray every day, every day of my life, for God to forgive me for what I done to my momma. Don't blame her for never comin' to see me. None of 'em do. Never have. And that's okay, because I don't deserve it. But—" He looked at Marvin, his face more alert now, burning with pain, but more alive. "—I ain't never asked God to forgive me for what I *tried* to do, for tryin' to kill *her*. All I ever ask is why He didn't let me do it . . . why he didn't let me kill her like I *meant* to."

"But what made you want to kill her? What had she done?"

"It's not what she done. It's what she *is*. She's so, so—" He stopped to wipe a thin sheen of sweat from his forehead. "—she's so evil and so . . . so *powerful* . . . that there ain't enough medication in the world to make me stop bein' afraid of what she might do. To *all* of us . . ."

Mike made a great effort to regain his composure. He took a deep breath, exhaled slowly and closed his eyes for a long time, clutching his knees tightly until his white knuckles began to get their color back. His movements were sluggish but his face was suddenly alive with nervous tics.

"My dad was a contractor and I worked for him," he began quietly, unsteadily. "She was goin' to Shasta College and worked in a restaurant where Dad and me and some of the guys had lunch sometimes. I finally got the guts to ask her out and . . . well, a while after that we were married and . . ." A shake of his head. ". . . boy were we happy. We lived in a house my dad had built just down the street from my parents. Took our honeymoon in Grover, up near Mount Shasta. My parents got us a room in a real fancy hotel. Room service and everything."

"The same hotel Hester owns now?"

He nodded.

So far, everything Mike said jibed with everything Marvin and Jordan had read and heard about Hester Thorne after poring over magazines, newspapers and books and watching all of her videotapes.

"Our first night there, we, uh—" A dry chuckle. "—we didn't get much sleep, so I slept in the next morning. When I woke up, Hester was gone. She came back a couple hours later, said she went for a walk. She did the same thing the next morning. Then she asked if we could stay a few more days 'cause she was enjoying herself so much. So we did. And she went for a walk every morning before I woke up.

"Then . . . then she, um . . ." Mike's face screwed up for just a moment as if he were about to cry or scream, then he stared at his lap. "A few weeks later, she told me she was pregnant. We'd decided if it was a boy we'd name him Benjamin. But it was . . . it wasn't . . . it-it . . ."

Marvin could hear Mike's teeth grinding.

"I was in the delivery room with her," he breathed. "When it was comin' out, I was holdin' her hand, tryin' to comfort her and everything, and . . . and I was waitin' to hear it . . . y'know, waitin' for it to cry. But there was nothin'. Just all them, y'know, sticky wet noises. I looked down at the doctor and . . . and it was all *over*. He was just starin' at us like, like he felt real bad for us, or somethin', and I *still* didn't hear no cryin', there was *nothin'*, not a *sound*, and I started *screamin'* at him, 'Why isn't it cryin'? Why isn't it *cryin'*?' But he just shook his head a little and the nurse took it . . . took the baby away and . . . then they took *her* away and . . . then the doctor took me to a little room and sat me down and told me."

Mike was very agitated now. His fingers toyed with one another and his feet jittered as he squirmed in his chair and his facial expression changed rapidly from fear to disgust to grief to confusion and back again; as he spoke, his breaths came sharp and fast and his eyes darted around the room as if looking for something—or someone—hiding in a corner or behind the bathroom door or under the bed.

"He gave me a cup of coffee and told me he had bad news," Mike continued. "Said the baby was a boy, b-but it was d-d-deformed. Deformed real bad. Said it was the worst he'd ever seen. Asked if my wife'd been X-rayed during her pregnancy, or if she'd been exposed to radiation of any kind. I said no. He said it'd be best if we gave it up, had it institutionalized, because it was gonna need lotsa care, special treatment all the time, and it'd cost a lot of money and . . . and he said it'd be best if we just gave it up and had another one later. Said before I talked to

Hes . . . to, um, my wife and we made our decision, he thought I should have a look at it myself.

"I couldn't for a while. Went to a bar down the street and got drunk first, then went and . . . and looked at it, and-and . . ."

He lifted his arms, fingers curled into hooks and, for a moment, Marvin thought he was going to claw his own eyes out, but the hands only trembled for a while as Mike ground his teeth together, looking around the room frantically.

"I couldn't even tell what it *was*!" he hissed as a tear dropped from his eye. "It was just this *thing* layin' there flappin' like a, like a-a-a twisted up *fish*, and I-I couldn't—I just—I wanted to-to . . ."

He shuddered so hard, the chair's legs chattered against the tile floor and Marvin reached over and squeezed his arm again. He was afraid Mike would get *too* upset and then the whitecoats would come in and kick him out before Mike had told his whole story.

"Can I get you some water, Mike? Anything?"

A violent sweep of arm, a burst of breath through his nose as he pressed his lips together.

"Well," Marvin said, "you can take your time. Take it easy. I'm in no hurry."

After a while, a little calmer now: "I tried to talk to her, talk some sense into her about the . . . the, uh . . . baby. About giving it away. Trying again. Having others. She wouldn't. Didn't even wanna talk about it. And the thing that always bothered me was . . . when I told her, and even when she *saw* it, she never got upset. She could always coo at it, hold it, rock it, just like any other baby. Never bothered her at all, even the first time she *looked* at it."

"So you kept the baby."

Mike nodded. "We kept it. The doctor—hell, every doctor in the *hospital*—couldn't believe we were keepin' it. They all thought we were crazy. So did I. But . . . but, y'know . . . it wasn't like I thought it'd be. At first, he repulsed me, but . . . other than the way he looked, there was really nothin' wrong with him. He . . . smelled. But he wasn't so hard to take care of. In fact—" A slight smile. "—I could make him laugh. He seemed to like being with me. When he got a little older, we played. He talked to me . . . as much as he could, anyway. We had fun. 'Cept when *she* was around."

"What do you mean, Mike?"

His face was darker now and he took a long, deep breath, let it out slowly and said, "When she was around, he changed. We'd be playing—maybe catch, say, with a Nerf ball—and she'd walk in the room. Benjamin would drop the ball and walk over. Like a dog that'd been called. He'd push himself right up next to her, real close. Stand there starin' at me like I was a stranger. When she was around, he wouldn't have anything to do with me. And he'd get this sorta . . . flat, dead look in his eyes. Sometimes he'd scare me when he did that, 'cause he was gettin so . . . *big*.

"As he got older, it got worse. He spent more and more time with her. Alone. They'd go down into the basement—I'd made it into a playroom—and stay there for hours. He started talkin'—justa word or two now and then—but he'd only talk to *her*. Never to me. Just shuffled around the house, slobberin' and makin' snorin' noises. 'Cept once . . . just once in a while . . . when we were alone together, he'd give me the best smile he could with that poor face of his. Or he'd reach out and squeeze my hand as he passed. But she never let that happen much.

"Then some weird things started happenin'. I woke up one night and Hester wasn't in bed. I looked around the house and found her in the laundry room standin' in front of the washer-dryer—y'know, the stacked kind, with the dryer on top—just standin' there talkin' to it. Talkin' to the dryer, real soft so I couldn't understand her, like it was a secret and stoppin' every once in a while like the dryer was talkin' right back at her. I just watched her for a little while, then said something, and she turned to me real fast, blinkin' and stutterin', confused, y'know? Then she kinda smiled and said, 'Have I been sleepwalkin'? I haven't done that since I was a kid.' Then she yawned and went back to bed and never said a thing about it again.

"Week or so later, I woke up and found her in the kitchen talkin' to the 'fridge. Only it was more like she was *listenin'* to it. Noddin' her head and whisperin' things like, 'Yes, I know,' and, 'I understand,' and, 'Yes, anything you say.'

"Next day, I told her maybe she should see the doctor 'cause she'd been sleepwalkin' again, but she just said it was probably somethin' she'd ate or stress or somethin'.

"But it kept happenin'. I even came home from work once—middle of the day, remember—and found her whisperin' to a lamp in the hallway, whisperin' a sort of, I don't know, like a *chant* or somethin'. But *this* time—'' He frowned now, his troubled eyes crinkling to slits, and there was a fearful tremble in his voice. ''—Benjamin was standin' right next to her, holdin' her hand, breathin' through that flat snotty nose and lickin' his big lips with that fat tongue and-and he tuh-turned and looked at me with them eyes . . . looked at me like I'd better back off or he'd rip my throat out and I got so *scared* then—I wasn't sure why, I just knew somethin' really *wrong* was goin' on—I got so scared I just turned and left, went out and got drunk. We never talked about it or nothin', but from then on . . . I don't know, I felt different about Hester. We wasn't as close anymore. We didn't talk much. Almost never . . . y'know, had . . . had intercourse, and when we *did*, she didn't seem to enjoy it much, sorta seemed to be somewhere else. It was almost like maybe she was seein' somebody, but I knew that wasn't true. Somehow I knew it was somethin' else . . . some-somethin' *worse*.

''Then she started goin' on them walks. Them *walks*.''

Mike stood and walked around the chair, leaning on the windowsill with both hands staring through the glass, shaking his head. He wasn't very tall but seemed almost diminutive because of his posture: somewhat hunched, slouched, as if he were trying to curl up and disappear. He kept shaking his head and breathing, ''Them walks, them . . . I don't know, them . . . them *walks* . . .''

After a long wait, Marvin asked softly, ''What about the walks, Mike?''

''She . . . she'd leave once in a while on the weekends. She'd take Benjamin on a drive, say they were going up to see the dam or go into the mountains and walk around, look at the trees and stuff. I believed her at first, didn't have no reason *not* to, but . . . then it was *every* weekend. And they'd be gone for hours, all *day*, they'd leave in the mornin' and come back at *night*, and when I asked where they'd been she'd just say they'd went for a drive, they went to the mountains or up to the dam or the river or the lake or . . . *whatever*. But pretty soon, I didn't believe it anymore. Every weekend? From eight in the mornin' till eight or nine at night?'' Staring out the window, he shook his head. ''No, I knew they were doin' somethin' else. Somethin' . . . somethin' bad. So one weekend, I borrowed Dad's truck and—'' He turned to Marvin and paced slowly. "—and I followed 'em." As he paced, he twisted the hem of his pajama top with trembling hands.

"They went to the mountains, all right. They went up to Grover. Stopped for breakfast in a little diner. I parked and watched, then followed 'em when they left. Followed 'em to the north side of Grover toward Mount Shasta. They drove down a dirt road, real twisty and narrow, then parked and walked. They walked a long way through woods, really dense woods. Like . . . like they knew exactly where they were going. They *did* know."

Mike stopped pacing, put his head in his hands, ran fingers through his hair, pulled lightly on his cheeks for a moment then ran a finger over and over one eyebrow, his face looking lost, sweaty and frightened.

"They went to a cave. Huge. A big, big cave, dark and, and . . . with those—whatta you call those? Stalam . . . stalat . . ."

"Stalactites and stalagmites?" Marvin prompted.

"Yeah, yeah, yeah, those things, and . . . she had a flashlight with her, but . . . I got the feelin' she, like, didn't really *need* it, y'know? Like she would've been able to find her way through all that dark, and they went, they went . . . *deep* into this cave—" Gesturing frantically with his hands now, very animated as he glanced around the room, as if he were being watched. "—real deep they went, and I followed a ways behind and watched and watched and they didn't say nothin', just walked and walked and they went deeper and deeper and I felt creeper and creeper and darker and—no, no, I—no, wait a minute, I'm—" He shook his head hard and held up his palms in a *stop*! gesture. "—I'm, I went, I followed and pretty soon I started hearing things and smelling things, dirty things, thirty things, thirty dirty things—" Walking in circles now, his voice dry and breaking as his words spilled out and ran together. "—and there were flapping sounds, like-like wings, like big wings and pretty soon I saw them up ahead, three of them, flying around this hole, this-this *thing* in the rock, like a-a-a *cunt*, a big giant slit that was—it was—I *saw* it, it had these, like these *lips*, and there was like this light coming out of it, a light from deep inside, a bad light, sick, like a, like a-a, I don't know, like *radiation*, or something, and these things were flying around it, these big things with big wings, things and wings, wings and things, and—" A little laugh now, a quiet, high-pitched machine-gun laugh. "—and they all flew down to see her and they-they *bowed*, these things, they *bowed down* in front of her, but not before I saw what they had, what they had between their legs, these-these big huge wet . . . *dicks*, and then I knew, I *knew!*'' He spun around and faced Mike, grinning around yellowed teeth. "I knew Benjamin wasn't human, he *wasn't*, and I knew . . . he wasn't . . . my son."

Martin was afraid. He'd been growing more and more anxious as Mike's behavior deteriorated rapidly, but now he was genuinely *afraid* because he saw nothing sane in Mike Lumley's eyes, nothing safe or familiar, nothing he could identify with . . . only something to fear.

Mike rushed toward him suddenly and Marvin stiffened, terrified, as Mike clutched the arms of the chair, pressed his face so close to Marvin's that he could smell Mike's fetid breath, and spittle sprayed Marvin's face as Mike screamed at the top of his lungs, *"I knew she'd FUCKED one-a them THINGS, one-a them THINGS with giant DICKS and WINGS and then she'd had that fucking MONSTER and made me think it came from ME and she was EVIL I knew she was EVIL as SATAN and I had to KILL HER!"*

Footsteps scuffled outside the room and the door shot open and three men—Ted among them—burst into the room and pulled Mike away from Marvin. Mike struggled, flailing his arms uselessly as they held him back.

"But she KNEW I was gonna kill her so she made my MOMMA come over she MADE her come over so I'd STAB her stab my own MOMMA instead of her SHE done it SHE made me stab my MOMMA—"

He screamed on and on, fighting the men as a nurse rushed in with a hypodermic on a small rectangular tray and Ted shouted above it all, "You'd better go, Mister. Sorry, but—" Then he went back to holding Mike, dragging him to the bed with the other two men, trying to avoid Mike's attempts to bite them and scratch them.

"She's EVIL she FUCKED them THINGS and she's EVIL and she's gonna take 'em ALL she's gonna take all them PEOPLE straight to HELL she's EVIL and SHE'S GONNA TAKE ALL THEM PEOPLE TO HELLLL!"

Marvin hurried from the room and fought the urge to run down the hall. He stayed close to the wall, occasionally running his hand over it for balance as he rushed out of the hospital, his heart pounding like a quiet drumroll.

2.

Marvin felt clammy as he drove away from the hospital and switched on the air conditioner, then reached into his coat pocket, rewound the tape a bit and hit the PLAY button. Mike Lumley's pinched voice screamed from the recorder:

"—I *knew*! I knew Benjamin wasn't human, he *wasn't*, and I knew . . . he wasn't . . . my son. *I knew she'd FUCKED one-a them THINGS, one-a them—*"

Marvin turned it off, wincing at the sound of Lumley's tortured voice, seeing again the man's mad saucered eyes.

He was sorry Lumley had snapped so soon, before he could find out what had *really* happened to Benjamin. All the articles on Hester Thorne had said the boy had died years ago of complications brought on by his deformities. None of them had specified what the complications had been or where and when the boy had died, just that Ms. Thorne became "very emotional and quiet" or that she "paused tearfully and asked that the interviewer proceed to the next topic." Cross and Marvin both suspected that the details surrounding Benjamin Lumley were probably more interesting and, perhaps, more unusual than Hester Thorne wanted anyone to believe. Marvin had been certain he'd learn something, or at least get a lead, from Mike Lumley, but he, of course, hadn't expected Lumley's outburst.

After what he'd just seen, it was pretty obvious to Marvin why Lumley was residing at the state hospital, but then again . . .

Before his story had become so frantic and disjointed, Marvin had seen more fear than frenzy in Lumley's behavior. His reluctance to tell his story had been obvious, but once he'd started, he seemed lucid enough. At least, until the story had become so . . . fantastic, so unbelievable. As unbelievable as it had been, though, Marvin couldn't ignore its vividness. The picture Lumley had painted—great bat-like beasts with glistening erections flying around a vaginal opening in a deep, dark cave—was undeniably chilling . . . chilling enough to make Marvin work hard to forget it.

He left Napa and went east on Interstate 80, heading for his next stop.

3.

Corben and Ida Thorne lived on a farm just east of Wheatland, a tiny town surrounded by flat fields yellowed by the summer sun. Houses and barns speckled the fields and cows roamed lazily within the expansive confines of barbed-wire fences. Occasionally, a tractor could be seen moving at a crawl in the distance, leaving behind a misty cloud of dust that would hover in the still, hot air, taking its sweet time to disperse. Most people who had never been to California—and even people *native* to many parts of California—thought the state was made up entirely of beaches and movie stars and golden gates; places like Wheatland, they assumed, existed only in the Midwest. They were mistaken.

Marvin despised such flat rural areas, and although he hadn't quite reached the town yet, the slight downward curl of his lips showed his disdain as he headed southeast on Highway 65, looking through the tinted glass at the bleak surroundings. Small towns and old houses and miles of fences and power lines disappearing on the horizon always reminded him of those grainy B horror movies in which tourists got butchered and served up as sausage or barbecued ribs at a roadside diner or were simply chopped up and fed to grinning old Farmer Brown's pigs. They looked too innocent and quiet for his comfort and he didn't trust them. Stupid and paranoid, maybe, but having been a city man all his life, he couldn't shake the association.

Marvin had the Thornes' address written in the notebook on the seat beside him but knew that a few numbers and the name of a road would be no help; he would need directions. He needed gas anyway, so he pulled into the first gas station he saw: Lahey's Fill-n-Grill, about ten or twelve miles east of town.

It was little more than a run-down shack—it actually seemed to sit at an angle, as if it were about to fall over—with a garage attached to one end and a half dozen or so cars scattered around in various states of repair. A dirty old-fashioned soda cooler sat on the wooden porch beneath the crooked eave that appeared on the verge of collapse. A handwritten sign hung in the grimy window:

**HOMMADE BBQ RIBS
TO GO**

Marvin's stomach tightened as bloody, low-budget movie images flashed through his mind in faded living color.

A man who resembled a dirty, over-ripe fig in grease stained overalls and wearing a dirty cap that bore the slogan BEAVER HUNTER emerged from the darkness of the garage wiping his blackened hands on a filthy red rag, smiling as he chewed something sloppily, making his fleshy, wrinkled, sun-browned jowls jiggle. Considering the wisdom of it, Marvin rolled down his window, getting a blast of hot dusty air.

"Do for ya?" the man barked, showing tobacco-stained teeth through his smile.

"Premium. Fill it up."

The man went about his business and Marvin tried to ignore his surroundings. As the gas pumped, the man began cleaning the windshield.

Marvin leaned his head out the window and asked, "Can you tell me how to get to Emmet Road?"

"Goin' out t'the Thorne place, haw?"

"Yeah, as a matter of fact." He tried to sound amiable, harmless, and at ease.

"I c'n tell ya. Won't talk t'ya, though."

"Beg pardon?"

"Them Thornes. Won't talk t'ya. Don't like you reporters."

"I'm not a reporter."

He laughed. "S'what they all say."

"All? You get a lot of reporters out here?"

"Oh, ever once in a while. Comin' out lookin' for Ida n' Corben. Askin' 'bout the daughter." He shook his head and snorted. "Crazy bitch n' her crystals. New Age phil-*los*-phee." He snorted, speaking the last three words as if they were in a foreign tongue, then craned his head back and spat tobacco over his shoulder.

"Well, I'm not a reporter. I've come to see them about some business matters," Marvin lied. "A small inheritance."

"No shit?" The man stopped and grinned through the windshield, cocking the bill of his cap back. "Yeah, I c'n tell ya how t'get there. But they prob'ly won't see ya nohow. Don't see nobody, let alone strangers."

"Well, I guess I'll just have to see, won't I."

"Yeah, you'll see. Check unner th' hood?"

"No, thanks. But you can answer one more question if you don't mind."

"Answer it if I can."

"Do you know of a woman named Elizabeth Murphy?"

The man's face brightened. "Lessee, Elizabeth Murphy. Hmm. Oh, you mean *Lizzie*. Lizzie Dayton. Murphy's her married name. Husband kicked off. Hell, yeah, I 'member her. Crazy bitch n'her Bible. Sal-*vay*-shun!" He laughed, a pig-like sound.

"Does she still live around here?"

"Oh, no, not Lizzie. No, Lizzie went south, far as I know. Last I heard she was somewhere 'round Irving, or thereabouts, runnin' some kinda church or shelter or somethin'."

"A shelter?"

"Yeah, y'know, one-a them places for homeless drunks n' such."

"Any idea how to find this place?"

"From what I heard, it's right on Interstate 5."

"Near Irving."

"Thereabouts." He sent another missile of chewing tobacco to the ground.

"Thanks, I appreciate it. Now, how do I get to the Thornes' place?"

The man leaned his arm on the door and gave Marvin detailed directions in what amounted to broken English and Marvin jotted some notes, trying to avoid the man's spoiled-fruit-and-garlic breath.

"They ain't gone see ya, though," the man said when he was finished reciting the directions. He returned the nozzle to the pump when the car was full, spat again, and said, "Twenny-one forty."

Marvin gave him cash.

As he made change: "Got mighty fine ribs. To go. M'wife made 'em herself."

"No, thanks."

"Hot n' juicy. Been travelin'—" He nodded toward the garment bag hanging behind Marvin. "—prob'ly hungry."

Marvin's stomach began to rebel against his fleeting but morbid thoughts of nubile teenage travelers and chainsaws and meat cleavers. "No thanks. Just ate awhile back."

He shrugged and clucked his tongue wetly. "Well, you take care. Tell the Thornes hey for me. They ain't gone see ya, though. Prob'ly chase y'off with a garden hose. Or their dog. Strange folk, them Thornes. Ain't sociable types 'tall."

Marvin attempted a smile. "We'll see." He drove away from Lahey's Fill-n-Grill with great relief and a little shame for entertaining such ludicrous fantasies.

The Beaver Hunter's directions led Marvin through the small town, then down a narrow pot-holed road that wandered through the fields beyond. He came to the silo the old man had mentioned, then the crooked mailbox with no name or box number. Just beyond that was Emmet Road, which was little more than an unmarked dirt trail.

"Terrific," he muttered, stopping the car to look down the road with a scowl. It led to a house that looked tiny in the distance and, beyond that, a barn and, further still, more structures made indistinguishable by motionless clouds of dust.

Marvin was not pleased. If there was any truth to the old man's claim that the Thornes were strange folks, they'd be waiting for him when he arrived; the Thunderbird would kick up a trail of dust visible for miles over the flat terrain.

"You owe me *big*-time, Jordan," he growled under his breath as he turned onto the road and drove slowly through the cloud of dry, gritty dust that rose around him. The car would definitely need a wash after this stop.

The wooden fences along the road had not been tended; the white paint had long since peeled and some of the slats—between which cows stared blankly—had rotted.

As the distance closed, the house grew larger and more distinct and Marvin saw the remains of an old swing set, rusted and collapsed, in the shade of a huge oak tree in the front yard. A battered old pickup truck was parked between the house and a squat building that was apparently some kind of shop or storage shed. A rustic aged station wagon was up on blocks and beside it was parked a well-worn Ford sedan from the late eighties. Even the house itself looked neglected. Paint was peeling, the roof was in need of some repair and the roomy wooden porch was cluttered with boxes and bags, some chairs and a crooked end table with several dried-up potted plants on it. Dark tendrils of ivy crawled up a corner support post, over the porch's roof, and up a side of the house, creeping around the corner eagerly.

As Marvin stopped the car at the edge of the yard, he saw some faded pink curtains fluttering in an open front window. An old pale face with eyes lost deep in oval shadows appeared in the darkness beyond, but only for a moment.

Marvin didn't like it one bit and reaching under his coat to touch the loaded .38 strapped to his side reassured him only slightly. He killed the engine and reached between the front seats for a clipboard. On the clipboard were three sheets of paper, each of which contained a number of questions written by Jordan and Marvin and printed out on Marvin's computer. He got out of the car and tucked the clipboard under his arm, trying to look professional.

The dusty heat made his body prickle with sweat immediately. His glasses began to slide down his nose and he straightened them, then reached into his pocket and turned on the recorder as he started toward the house.

Jagged cracks separated chunks of the walk leading to the house and bits of the concrete crunched beneath Marvin's feet as he approached the porch. He was halfway up the sagging wooden steps when the front door opened a crack and one squinting eye peered out at him.

"What can I do for you?" It was a woman's voice, thin and more than a little suspicious.

Marvin gave her his best smile and said, "Good afternoon, ma'am. Are you the lady of the house?"

"Who're you?"

He was on the porch and tilted his head in an old-fashioned, gentlemanly way as he said, "My name is Marvin Ackroyd and I—"

"Whatta you want?"

"Well, I'd like to speak to the lady or the man of the house, if it wouldn't be any—"

"I mean *why*? Whatta you want with 'em? You a reporter?"

Sure are a lot of people worried about reporters today. Marvin thought. "No, I'm not." Still smiling: "I'm conducting a poll."

"A *what*?"

"A poll. A, uh, survey. It's a CNN poll concerning—"

"A *what* poll?"

"CNN? The Cable News Network?"

"We don't have tee-vee."

"Ah. I see. Well, that's very interesting." He plucked a pen from his pocket and scribbled on the clipboard as if making a note. "Well, then, let me explain. Occasionally the Cable News Network conducts polls on various topics to determine the American public's opinions and habits. Sometimes these polls are conducted by telephone, sometimes—"

"You'd better go now," the woman said solemnly, her voice dropping almost to a whisper.

"This won't take long, I promise. I'd just like to ask you a few questions about—"

"No you wouldn't."

"I'm sorry?"

"You're lying."

"No, I assure you I'm conducting a legitimate—"

"You wanna ask questions about *her*!" she hissed.

Marvin stopped midsentence, not quite sure how to react to that one; he hadn't expected it but didn't want to look surprised. Jordan was much better at this sort of thing than he.

"I'm sorry, I don't know what you're—"

"You gotta go now," the woman whispered urgently, closing the door a little, narrowing the crack even more. "My husband's gonna come."

That didn't sound encouraging. "But I'd like to speak to both of you, if you'll—"

"He'll know, too. He'll know why you're here and he won't like it. You don't wanna be here then."

He knew the wise thing to do was to take her advice, get in the car and make a clean exit, but he had a job to do and he was determined to give it his best shot. But before he could continue:

"I mean it, mister. You better get outta here *while* you *can*."

Something about that—either what she said or the way she said it, he wasn't sure—gave Marvin a bad feeling standing there in the heat with sweat trickling down his back and temples, a sinking feeling in his gut that gradually got worse, so bad that he took a step back from the door without even thinking about it and was about to turn around and head down the steps, just go while he could, because there was something wrong here, something he couldn't do anything about and the wisest move would be to *go*, but before he could do that—

—gravel crunched under heavy feet and Marvin jerked to his left to see a tall thin aging man standing at the end of the house. He stood with the knuckles of his left fist resting on his blue-jeaned hip and his right hand hanging loose at his side. Just beneath his right hand, a dog stood still and silent, its glistening eyes locked on Marvin. It was a squat solid pit bull the color of old bones and it didn't move a muscle, didn't even pant as most dogs would in such heat, just stood there with its mouth closed and stared.

"Can I do for ya?" the man asked in a low, gravelly voice. His narrow head was tilted forward and he stared up at Marvin through wiry grey brows. A lock of thin silver hair fell on the creased sun-browned skin of his forehead.

Too late, Marvin thought, his chest tightening. *I waited too long and now it's too damned late and what the hell are you gonna do now?* he asked himself as he stared open-mouthed at the man.

"I *told* you!" the woman hissed and the door slammed shut.

Marvin licked his gummy lips and tried to smile. "Well, sir, I'm conducting a, uh, a survey. For, uh, CNN."

The man stared at him coldly.

So did the dog.

"Uh, you know, the Cable News Network?"

"We don't have tee-vee."

The lie wasn't working.

"Well, sir, that's okay, I think I'll just—"

"I don't think you're doin' no survey," the man said, finally tilting his head up, exposing his long craggy face. His eyes were so narrow, Marvin couldn't see what color they were.

"Uh, well . . . uh, if that's how you feel, I—"

"I think you're here to poke your nose where it don't belong."

Marvin chuckled as if the man were telling a good-natured joke. He took a sideways step toward the porch steps, then another and another, until one foot was on the second step down.

"I think you're here to ask questions about things that're none a your bidness."

Another step down.

"Just like all them others come sniffin' 'round here lookin' for information 'bout her. Wantin' things to write. To print. Wantin' to ask 'bout things they shouldn't know. Things nobody should know."

Another step.

The pit bull never took its black glistening eyes from him.

"That why you're here, *Mister Sur*-vey? *Mister Cable* News?"

Still smiling at the man, but terrified and trembling, Marvin walked sideways down the rest of the steps and was just starting down the walk, glancing over his shoulder, when the man slapped his right hand to his thigh and made a sound like, *"Hee-yup!"* and the pit bull shot away from the man like a bullet, its stout legs pumping, muscles working beneath thick skin as it charged across the gravel, kicking up dust and baring its yellow fangs as a thunderous growl rose slowly from deep inside and—

—Marvin broke into a run, dropping the clipboard as he made for the car with the sound of his heart pounding in his ears almost as loud as that of the dog behind him kicking up gravel and snarling wetly now, sounding not at all winded and—

—he approached the passenger side of the car, dodged around the front of it and ripped the door open so hard he hurt his arm, diving in as—

—the pit bull jumped onto the hood, rocking the car with its weight as Marvin slammed the door and started the engine with fumbling fingers, and the dog remained on the hood, clawing at the windshield and snapping its jaws at Marvin, splattering the glass with spittle and—

—Marvin put the car in reverse and slammed his foot on the accelerator and the tires scattered gravel as the car shot backward and the pit bull slid off the hood to the ground as Marvin backed quickly away from the house.

The dog landed on all fours.

Then it chased him. Its jaws continued to snap and spittle continued to fly as its legs pumped and its eyes remained locked on the car. Corben Thorne had not moved; he stood by the house, watching.

The dog grew smaller with distance, lost in the cloud of dust kicked up by the car.

Marvin reached the paved road and the tires screeched as he shifted into drive and headed back toward town, wheezing and shaking.

He knew he wouldn't be able to get away from Wheatland fast enough.

4.

Marvin was back on the freeway, still shaken but calmer, looking for a roadside stop that looked safe and clean when the car phone chirped. He knew it was Jordan and jerked the receiver to his ear shouting, "You son of a *bitch*!"

"What the hell's wrong with you?"

"I'm gonna rip your head off and shit down your neck!"

"What's the *matter*?"

"I'm gonna kick your ass in directions that'll defy the laws of physics! I just left the Thornes' and I nearly got myself killed! Your *stupid* CNN poll story wasn't worth *shit*!"

"What did they do?"

"Did you see *Cujo*? *Cujo* is what they did, only it was a pit bull and it chased my fucking car down the *driveway*!"

"They weren't too friendly, huh?"

"They were the Texas fucking *chainsaw* massacre!"

"You didn't find out anything?"

Marvin nearly drove the car off the road. He said nothing for a moment, then shouted into the phone, "Are you *listening* to me? If that damned thing had caught me, they would've buried my pieces out by the toolshed and you'd never *see* me again!"

Jordan was silent a few moments and Marvin knew Jordan was giving him time to calm down. Then:

"You think they're afraid of something, Marvin?"

"Definitely. Reporters, for one thing. Scared to death somebody's going to ask them about their daughter. I got it all on tape. Lumley, too. Wait'll you hear *his* story."

"Mm. Where you headed now?"

"Lunch. Then south to find Elizabeth Murphy. That may take a while."

"Well, I have faith in you, Marvin. Sorry about the dog."

He was calm now and smiled. "Hey, it comes with the territory. But the poll-taking shit? From now on, that's *your* job. You're the actor. How are things there?"

"Crowded. People have really been pouring in since we got here. The lady herself is across the street from me right now, surrounded by cameras and microphones. You might want to catch the news today, see what they say. Any idea how much longer you'll be?"

"Not really. All I can say is, I'll get there as soon as I can."

"And you'll bring your toys?"

"I'll bring my toys."

After he hung up, Marvin turned on the radio and searched the dial for a news station as he kept an eye open for a place to have lunch.

5.

He'd had to look hard, had even driven by it a couple of times, but by mid-afternoon, Marvin found the Freeway Chapel and Shelter.

It wasn't much to look at, but it was surprisingly big. It looked like a barn that had been built on extensively. The barn-red paint was peeling in a few places, but it seemed in good enough shape. There was only one sign in front that was readable from the freeway. A Bible and cross were in the top right corner and below that:

THE

FREEWAY CHAPEL

AND

SHELTER

A REST FOR TRAVELERS ON THE ROCKY ROAD

There were only four cars parked in the front lot, but when Marvin went inside, there were more people than he'd expected. The entrance led into a dining room where about a dozen people were seated at long tables eating. Half of them looked like transients.

The clattering, clanging sounds of a kitchen echoed through the large room. In the back, behind a long empty coffee counter, a rectangular window opened onto the kitchen and he saw people hurrying back and forth busily. One of them—a grey-haired little woman with thick, owlish glasses—spotted him, smiled and waved, calling, "Just a sec!"

Marvin went to the counter, took a seat on one of the stools and waited.

The woman came out in a couple of minutes, her movements quick and bird-like as she wiped her hands on a towel.

"And how are you today?" she asked, slightly winded.

"Just fine, ma'am, and yourself?"

"Great. Can I get you something?"

"Actually, I'd like to see Elizabeth Dayton, if she's available."

"You wanna see Lizzie? Well, she's around here somewheres. Can I tell her who's askin'?"

"My name is Marvin Aykroyd, but she won't know me."

"Be right back."

She disappeared and never came back. Instead, a few minutes later, a tall woman came through the swinging doors behind the counter. She was large but appeared solid, not flabby. In fact, she was almost imposing except for her face, which was soft with warm, generous eyes and a profoundly sincere smile. Her hair was brown with silver streaks and pulled back into a bun. She wore a stained white smock over a simple blue dress. She went to a rack behind the counter, removed a white coffee mug, got the steaming pot and poured, then set the coffee before Marvin and grinned, leaning on the counter.

"You're here about Hester Thorne, aren't you?" she asked.

Marvin flinched with surprise. "Well, uh . . . yes, I am. How, uh, did you know?"

"I've been expecting you." She stood straight again, still smiling. "I can be ready in about half an hour or so. I've had some stuff packed and waiting for quite a while. I even made arrangements for somebody to take over for me while I'm gone."

"While you're g-guh-gone?" Marvin was confused.

"Yes. I'm going with you."

"B-but I-I didn't—I didn't come to-to—you can't—"

"Look, Mr. Ackroyd, there's a lot to be done and not much time to do it in and I have a feeling that some very bad things are going to start happening soon. And I know more about Hester Thorne than anybody you'll find. You need me. And we *all* need God. So—" She slapped a hand on the counter and laughed girlishly. "—whatta you say I bring Him, too? Be right back." Then she was gone.

Marvin sat at the counter with his mouth hanging open. He didn't even bother to stammer.

FOUR

GROVER

1.

While Marvin was having lunch at a roadside coffee shop, Jordan and Lauren were licking ice-cream cones as they stood across from Penny Park, where Hester Thorne was holding an impromptu press conference.

There was standing room only on the lawn and there wasn't a single vacant parking space in all of Grover. A lot of people had been coming into town when Jordan and Lauren arrived the day before, but there seemed to be *twice* as many by morning. They were everywhere: single people, small groups that had gathered to travel great distances, married couples who had packed the kids into their station wagons and Broncos to attend the Alliance gathering in the mountains, and television, radio and newspaper reporters looking for a light, bizarre human-interest story to tack onto the end of a broadcast or a quirky article for the Living section of the paper.

Jordan wondered if any of them knew how close they were to a top story. *He* knew . . . he just didn't know what that story was yet.

"Well," he said with a smile, taking Lauren's hand, "shall we go see what's going on?"

She shrugged and they started across the street.

Jordan noticed that Lauren didn't seem to stiffen when he touched her as she had the day before. Maybe after last night, she'd finally realized that he really *wasn't* after her body. He'd read over the notes and articles he kept in a locked briefcase, all pertaining to Hester Thorne and the Alliance, until he'd been unable to keep his eyes open.

"You're serious about us sleeping together, aren't you?" Lauren had asked as he got ready for bed.

He came close to a sarcastic reply, but swallowed it. She was still shaken after their trip to the art gallery and he knew it wouldn't help things to make her feel any worse. Yes, she was a pain in the ass, but she was also afraid and anxious to find her little boy; it was in Jordan's best interest to reassure her—especially if he wanted her to cooperate in maintaining their cover—so he took a deep breath and turned to her.

"Look," he said softly, trying hard not to sound annoyed, "I know how it looks to you and I understand. But what if some maid walks in here in the morning to change the sheets and towels and one of us is on the floor? We're supposed to be married, right? Well, we're gonna have to act like it."

She was reluctant, but she'd gone along with it, lying stiffly at first, practically on the edge of the bed, as far from him as she could get.

"This isn't very comfortable for me, either," he whispered in the dark. "I'm used to sleeping alone."

He dozed off in a few minutes, but was awakened each time she moved, startled by the presence of someone else in his bed. The last time he was disturbed, though, was not by her movement; Lauren was crying softly into her pillow, her stifled sobs gently shaking the bed.

Shit, Jordan thought, sighing. "What's wrong?" he whispered.

After a moment, she croaked, "I'm suh-sorry."

"That's okay. What's the matter?"

"Nothing. Never mind."

He said nothing more for a while, just listened to her sobs.

He knew she was probably upset about her son; that was natural, wasn't it? Maybe she was upset about her husband, too. From what she'd told Jordan and Marvin, their marriage was over as far as she was concerned. But Jordan knew it wasn't that simple. No matter how unhealthy or painful a marriage might be, Jordan knew that *ending* it hurt just as much. He thought of Teri, of their plans to have children, and of how he might have felt if they'd had them and the same thing had happened to him that had happened to Lauren. He thought about that a long time, frowning up at the darkness. Finally, he slid his arm over the mattress and gave her shoulder a gentle squeeze. He felt her muscles tense as she started to pull away but, before she could, he whispered, "I know you're worried about your boy. But believe me, I'm sure he's not in any danger. And . . . well, we're doing our best to find him."

After a moment of sniffling and throat clearing, she said hoarsely, "How could he do such a thing? Take everything like that? Even *Nathan*. How could he do that to me?"

Jordan realized she was speaking more to herself than to him and he said nothing.

"I'm . . . I'm sorry, really, I shouldn't . . . I mean, I promise I won't let this happen again."

"It's okay," he whispered, squeezing her shoulder again. "Don't worry about it." He pulled his hand away and prepared to go back to sleep, when he realized he could hear nothing from her, not even breathing. She was completely silent and motionless for a while, then a great sob lurched from her, shaking the entire bed, and she clutched her pillow.

"I-I-I'm juh-just so sc-*scared*," she hissed.

Jordan had scooted over a little closer and rubbed her tense neck and shoulders, murmuring reassurances to her, until she'd finally quieted down and, slowly, her tense muscles relaxed. He'd continued massaging her until her breathing was slow and rhythmic and she lay motionless and relaxed beneath the covers, finally asleep.

That morning, neither of them had mentioned their late-night conversation and now things were pretty much as they'd been before, with one small difference: they were more relaxed with one another.

"A press conference," Jordan muttered to Lauren as they stepped up on the opposite sidewalk.

Hester Thorne was standing in the gazebo in the center of the park, holding court with a crowd of reporters and, behind them, a parkful of followers and curious onlookers. Television cameras whirred, photographers snapped pictures and reporters took turns asking questions, which Hester Thorne answered politely and thoughtfully as she leaned on the gazebo's white railing, leaning toward the tangle of microphones before her; her words became clearer as Jordan and Lauren got closer to the gazebo, shouldering their way through the crowd.

"—as an exercise in unity. I saw this as a chance to bring together people from all over the country who are looking for new answers, new solutions to their problems. I wanted it to be in a relaxing, tranquil location so that the people who came would perhaps be more willing to open their minds to ideas they might otherwise reject wholesale. I hoped to achieve something similar in spirit to the Harmonic Convergence of 1987, which took place in several key locations around the globe, but I wanted to centralize it, bring it together in one single place.''

When it was clear she'd finished, the reporters spoke all at once in an explosion of chattering questions, until the sharp voice of a middle aged red-headed woman with a tape recorder slung over her shoulder rose above the others.

''Ms. Thorne, is there any significance to the fact that you're beginning your gathering on the Fourth of July?'' she asked, one hand raised.

''Not especially. I just thought it would be appropriate to hold such a gathering on the birthday of our nation. I love America with all my heart, although at the moment it seems to be in poor health. But I truly believe that the philosophy of the Universal Enlightened Alliance can breathe new life back into the faltering lungs of this great nation of ours. I believe it's not too late to revive this country and restore it to the position of respect and dignity it once held. But I believe we must act now . . . because it *will* be too late very soon.''

''Hey, kids,'' Coogan whispered as he sidled up to Jordan. ''What's doin'?''

''Just watching the show,'' Jordan smiled.

A rotund, mustachioed reporter waved a hand and shouted, ''Does that mean you'll be involving yourself in politics, Ms. Thorne?''

She laughed and shook her head. ''I'm not a politician.''

Another reporter started to shout a question but was interrupted by a stir that passed through the crowd in ripples until everyone was facing south and chattering with anticipation.

Jordan got up on tiptoes to see over the heads. A sleek black limousine with tinted windows was parked at the curb on the far side of the park.

''A limo,'' Jordan said, glancing at Coogan, who looked vastly uninterested.

''The actress,'' he muttered.

''What?''

''Sheila Bennet. She's always making dramatic entrances like this whenever they have their little get-togethers.''

''This get-together isn't so little.''

''All the more reason for her to make a dramatic entrance.''

Reporters rushed across the grass toward the limousine as the driver got out and opened the door for Sheila Bennet, who stepped out with a flourish, wearing a flowing tan and white silk suit that fluttered in the breeze as she lifted a hand to wave at the approaching reporters. As Sheila climbed the gazebo steps, Hester Thorne said, ''Ladies and gentlemen, Miss Sheila Bennet!''

The crowd cheered.

The actress approached the bank of microphones smiling and waving, said a few words about how happy she was to be there, how much she valued her friendship with Hester and the ''awareness'' that Hester had given her, and how happy she was that her night-time soap opera, *Empire*, had been renewed for another season. Then, gently passing on the reporters' questions, she stepped aside and let Hester take center stage again.

''Sheila will be here for a few days,'' Hester said to the reporters in front, ''so you'll have a chance to ask her some questions—*if* it's all right with her,'' she added, glancing over at Sheila, who shrugged noncommittally.

''Are we going to have an opportunity to hear from Orrin?'' a black woman asked, holding a microphone toward the gazebo.

Hester looked out at them for a long moment, her eyes anxious and uncertain. ''I've been getting some uncharacteristic messages from Orrin lately.''

''What does that mean?'' a reporter asked with a smirk in his voice.

''Well, some of the things Orrin has said lately have not been terribly, um . . . positive. I'm not sure that it would be a good idea to—''

Murmurs began to rise from the crowd, some of disappointment, but others of annoyance and a kind of snide satisfaction, as if some people were saying, *I figured she wouldn't do it for free*.

She frowned then, her eyes scanning the crowd, and said, ''Okay, okay. But I won't promise you'll like what you hear. It might not be very positive.''

There was a loud, enthusiastic response from the reporters as well as the onlooking crowd.

"All right, all right. Um, let's see . . ." She moved away from the microphones and started down the gazebo's stairs. "I'll have to ask all of you to move back and, um . . . Jerry, could I get you to bring two of those cushions over here for me?"

One of her young male assistants wearing the standard Alliance ice-cream suit hurried to her side carrying two large, cream-colored cushions. The reporters backed away and the cushions were placed on the grass before the gazebo as some of the news personnel hurriedly moved their microphones in front of the cushions, where Hester Thorne lowered herself gracefully, sitting Indian style. She wore her usual: baggy pants and blouse, both of white silk.

The chattering voices in the crowd hushed and restless movement ceased. An almost reverent silence descended on Penny Park.

Hester Thorne held the gaze of every eye around her.

For the next few minutes, she went through the same series of deep breaths and jerking motions she'd gone through at her seminar in San Francisco. As he watched, Jordan popped the last bite of his sugar cone into his mouth and put an arm around Lauren, muttering, "This ought to be fun." Her shoulders were tense, and when he looked at her, Jordan saw that she was clenching her teeth; the rest of her ice cream began to melt as she neglected it, staring hatefully at Hester Thorne. "Try to loosen up a little," he whispered in her ear. "Your fangs are showing." To show her he meant well, he squeezed her shoulder.

"Greetings, sweet souls!" Hester Thorne shouted in the same deep, almost male voice Jordan had heard her use in San Francisco.

The crowd responded with a mixture of amusement and respect.

She went on in Orrin's voice, spouting a lot of wordy gibberish about the spirit of their gathering. "I sense much love here, much unity. I sense a positive spirit that holds much hope for the future, as it shall be." There was a long pause, then Hester Thorne's face darkened so suddenly that Jordan flinched. "Your hopes are well and good, but they are not enough and will soon be shattered by the oncoming darkness that will envelope this world . . . *if* you do not unite beneath the shelter of truth and light that are my words, *if* you do not rally 'round this vessel called Hester Thorne!''

Dead, heavy silence in the park.

Jordan looked around at the mass of faces frozen in shock at the harsh tone of Hester Thorne's voice, at the coldness in her eyes.

Her head dropped forward and her eyes rolled back in their sockets, showing only their icy whites, and when she spoke again, her voice was so much deeper, throatier, and more masculine that several surprised gasps shot up from the crowd.

"Already the darkness is descending. Already those who have slandered this vessel Hester Thorne and the truths that I speak through her are standing in its shadow. Their time is short and yet they continue to shun the light I have offered. The darkness falls even today . . . and standing beneath it now is the Reverend Barry Hallway.''

Jordan and Lauren exchanged a glance.

Something was wrong with this, Jordan could feel it. Until he'd seen her on stage in San Francisco, he'd heard only innocuous things about Hester Thorne and her invisible entity. But in San Francisco, and again here in Grover, there was nothing innocuous about the things she said to her audience.

"Are you saying that Reverend Hallway is going to *die*?''

"Even as I speak,'' the deep voice continued, "the reverend's re-embodiment approaches. Only if he recants, only if he withdraws his hateful words and false accusations, will he be spared.''

A prickly chill skittered over the back of Jordan's neck.

"And there will be others after him, those who have rejected the truth and led others from the light it sheds. See to it that you are not among them. Heed my words, join the Godbody and follow the example of this vessel Hester Thorne and all will be well, you will come through the time of darkness and walk safely into a New Age of peace and harmony, as it is and forever shall be.''

And then Hester Thorne collapsed on the cushions and two of her aides rushed to her side.

There was an explosion of activity among the reporters as they rushed away from the gazebo with their tape recorders and notebooks and cameras and hurried across the street to the pay phones, hurried to their cars and vans, anxious to share their tidbit of information with their editors.

One of the aides stood and politely dismissed everyone, saying that Ms. Thorne would be unable to continue but promising that they would see more of her during the coming days.

"What the hell was that all about?" Coogan asked.

"Some kind of prediction," Jordan said.

"That Barry Hallway is going to die?"

"Something like that."

Jordan looked at him. The old man frowned and sucked on his lower lip, deep in thought; he obviously didn't like what he'd heard, but chose not to comment. Jordan was disturbed, too; there was something very unsettling about Hester Thorne/Orrin's comments about Reverend Barry Hallway.

"Something wrong?" Jordan asked.

"Mmm." He shook his head, still frowning, and turned around, staring out at the street with his hands tucked in the back pockets of his pants. "Never seen the place this crowded. Can't say I like it."

Jordan took Lauren's hand and they headed out of the park, Coogan walking with them. Lauren tossed the remains of her ice-cream cone into a garbage can and they crossed the street.

The sidewalks were crowded with pedestrians who walked slowly by shop windows; parked cars and recreational vehicles lined the streets.

"It's not even this crowded during the skiing season," Coogan said softly, looking around.

Jordan and Coogan made small talk as they walked aimlessly down the sidewalk, dodging other pedestrians, but Jordan paid little attention to the conversation. Hester Thorne's words weighed heavily on him. He was sure that Lauren, so wrapped up in her son's situation, had dismissed the channel's predictions, but Jordan could not. From what he knew of her, it seemed unlikely Hester Thorne to make such a risky prediction.

Unless, he thought, *she has a good reason.*

But what would that be?

He considered discussing it with Coogan, but decided to keep his thoughts to himself. He had a plan for that night—the very thought of which, especially in light of everything he'd learned and seen, made him nervous—and hoped that perhaps he would learn something then.

2.

Mark Schroeder missed reading the newspaper. He even missed watching television once in a while. But there was no outside reading material, televisions or radios allowed in the complex. It didn't really matter, though, because he only missed those things when he had time to think about them, and that was seldom.

Right now, for instance.

He was seated at the desk in his small square room with four white walls, bare except for the painting of the Alliance emblem over his desk and the PA/intercom speaker over his bed, studying one of the many books that made up the list of reading materials required of new seekers. He wasn't sure what time it was—there were no clocks in any of the rooms in the dorm-like structure and watches were not allowed because Hester said they had to learn to rely on their "inner timepieces"; the time was announced over the speakers on the hour—he only knew that it was time to study. Later, it would be time to sleep—for a while, at least—but that time wouldn't come soon enough for Mark. His head was drooped over the desk and his heavy-lidded eyes burned from the light of his small desk lamp. Sometimes his eyes would close and he would sway forward slowly, then jerk awake, sitting upright with eyes open wide, and go back to his studying . . . until his head began to bow again and his eyes began to close.

He didn't think of Nathan as much as he had when he'd first come to Grover, which had been . . . how long ago? He wasn't quite sure, but it didn't matter much. He didn't think of Lauren, either, except to pity her because she was missing out on so much. In fact, the person he thought about most was Hester Thorne.

Since his arrival, he'd learned a great deal; he and Hester had become very close and she'd made him feel he was an integral part of the Alliance's movement. Being a part of the Alliance, though, involved a great deal of work and very little of it was easy. Each morning, a young woman brought to his room a gallon of salt water which he was required to drink as quickly as possible so he would vomit and cleanse his body of stomach mucus. He was assigned a number of chores, some of which were apparently senseless—like moving rocks or wood from point A to point B and then back again—to strengthen his powers of concentration and teach him humility. His diet was entirely vegetarian with emphasis on sprouts, carrot juice, asparagus broth and lots of garlic to cleanse the liver. Every three days he received a colonic containing something called Bentonite and he was required to inspect his stool afterward, looking for the black speckles in his feces that would prove to him that, before joining the Alliance, his body was riddled with vile impurities. Mark's least favorite part of the program was the bodywork session that he endured every day. He was told that his muscles retained all of the psychological traumas of his life, and in order to restore the "physical peace" necessary for him to retain truth and enlightenment, it was necessary for a bodywork technician to grind knuckles, knees and elbows into the major muscle groups of his body for one hour each day, which, needless to say, was excruciatingly painful. The bodywork sessions were held in a pyramid-shaped building called Physical Peace Plaza and, walking by, one could hear the screams and cries of those receiving their treatment; it sounded like a torture chamber. The studying, meditating, "ascension therapy" and other requirements of the program were easy in comparison, but they were still—although he would never say so aloud—tedious. In spite of it all, Mark was thrilled to be there because—

—he knew that great events were coming that were to usher in the New Age, events that would be at once wonderful and horrible because of the resistance of those who did not believe. The certainty that he would be actively involved in those events excited him and made every sacrifice and inconvenience worthwhile.

A burst of static sounded and Mark jerked, backing away from the single puddle of light in the dark room to turn toward the speaker over his bed.

The familiar female voice said, "The time is eight p.m. The *time* . . . is *eight* p.m."

The static crackled for a moment longer, then stopped abruptly.

Sometimes Mark wished the voice would give the day and date, too; he often lost track. But that was okay. Hester had told him once that when the New Age finally began, which would be soon, things such as hours and minutes and days and dates would become relics of a past best not remembered.

There was a quiet knock at his door and Mark called weakly, "Come in."

As if his thought had summoned her, Hester entered the room smiling. She wore a flowing silk duster over a blouse and slacks, but in the poor light, her clothes—as well as her hair and skin—lost their color and took on a sickly greyish hue. "Good evening, Mark. Studying?"

He stood, nodding as he returned her smile. Although he'd spent a good deal of time with her and felt closer to her than he had when they'd first started meeting, he was still overcome with a boyish clumsiness whenever she was near. It was silly and embarrassing . . . and yet at the same time it felt rather nice.

"And what's next?"

"A rest."

"Ah, that's nice. Are you sleeping well? Are you comfortable?"

"Oh, yes, fine."

Actually, he hadn't slept well when he'd first arrived. The seekers were allowed only three hours of sleep at a time—Hester said there was far too much to accomplish to spend more than the absolute minimum amount of time sleeping—and at the top of every hour, the time was announced over the speaker loudly enough to frighten Mark out of his sleep.

"What are you scheduled to do after your rest?" she asked, taking a couple steps toward him.

It was going to happen again, just as it almost always did whenever they were alone. Mark tensed with anticipation. "Chanting and meditation," he replied. "At eleven-ten."

"Well." She moved closer and ran her fingertips lightly up and down his left arm. "As long as you promise to make up your chanting and meditation period—and as soon as possible, because that's *very* important—I'd like to borrow you for a little while." She lifted her other hand and her gentle strokes became more intense as she met his gaze with a slight smile.

"Oh? Borrow me for what?" His voice broke only slightly, as it always did when she touched him. He fought to resist becoming aroused in order to avoid the frustration it would bring, because her advances never went any further than touching and kissing. He often wondered if she treated any of the other seekers that way, but always decided he didn't want to know.

"In your studies, you've come across references to the Inner Circle, haven't you, Mark?"

"Of course. We've even talked about it."

"That's right. But you still aren't quite sure what it is, are you?"

"Well . . . no."

Her voice a whisper now, a sweet-smelling breath: "I'd like to give you your first Inner Circle experience."

Mark felt a rush of excitement. It sounded important, this Inner Circle experience, even though he didn't know what it was. He was thrilled to be involved in the Alliance at all, but to be taken into the Inner Circle . . . *that* was more than he'd ever imagined.

"Would you like that?" she breathed, her lips touching his, her arms encircling his neck.

He tried to respond, to tell her that *yes* he would like that, of *course* he would like that, but her tongue began to tease his lips and he slid his hands tentatively over her back and enjoyed the kiss, until she finally pulled away, smiled, and stroked his face.

"I'll see you at eleven," she said, then left his room.

Mark stood there for a long moment, reliving the kiss and wondering what might lie ahead of him. Then he undressed and got into bed, doubting that he would sleep now that he had something to look forward to.

He did sleep, though, and he dreamed of Hester. She stood just a few feet in front of him in a very dark, cold place. An icy breeze blew her shiny blond hair, she was smiling seductively with her arms open to him, beckoning, and she was naked; her nipples looked like hardened dabs of chocolate against her pale skin and light from an invisible source glistened on the small triangle of wheat golden hair below her naval. He moved toward her, wanting to touch her skin, taste it, hold her body to his, but—

—as he moved forward, she moved backward, not walking— Mark couldn't even see her feet—but . . . *gliding*, like a ghost, beckoning him to her but moving away from him, taunting, teasing, as Mark noticed that—

—something was looming behind her, a shape in the darkness, a huge mass that was even *blacker* than the darkness around it, and from the shape a reddish-orange glow began to appear, growing brighter as Hester continued to float away from him in slow motion, arms open, breasts swaying a bit, moving like honey, and then—

—there was a sound and Hester's mouth opened as if to speak and the darkness filled with a horrible hissing sound, a garbled electronic sound, and—

—the familiar female voice blared over the speaker, "The time is nine p.m. The time is nine p.m." and—

—Mark sat up with a gasp, his fingers digging into his thin mattress.

The static stopped.

The room was silent.

He lay back down with a sign and, eventually, drifted back to sleep.

And the dream continued. . . .

3.

When Jordan stepped out of the bathroom, he was pleased to hear Lauren's gasp of disbelief.

"So what do you think?" he asked.

"It's incredible." She moved closer, squinting at his face, looking for flaws, for some hint that it was makeup. "Absolutely incredible."

Jordan turned to the mirror over the dressing table. He was somewhere in his seventies with a ruddy prune-like face, stringy white hair and a large bald patch on top. He wore dark clothes that weren't likely to be seen in the woods at night, and he would cover the white hair with a cap.

"Okay," he said, taking a small AM/FM radio from his nightstand, "here's the plan. I'm gonna leave this radio playing in the bathroom. Anybody comes, you tell them your husband's taking a bath. It might be a good idea if you put on your nightgown and a robe, too. Make it look like we're getting ready for bed. Okay?"

She nodded.

He found some music on the radio and put it beside the sink in the bathroom, then he slipped on a slightly tattered tweed sport coat, a small wool cap and found a small flashlight. From his suitcase, he removed a pint of vodka, unscrewed the cap and took a couple of wincing swallows, then exhaled with a groan.

"What's that for?" Lauren asked.

"In case I get caught." He recapped the bottle and put it in his coat pocket. "I'll just be a drunk old man lost in the woods. Um, let's see." He went to the closet and took out the cane he'd brought with him, then began to pace back and forth, perfecting his aged walk and posture—stooping a little, limping a bit, giving his head and left hand a slight tremble. Then he made some harsh grumbling noises in his throat until his voice became hoarse and he recited "Mary Had a Little Lamb" in an old, shaky, gravelly drawl, then turned to Lauren and smiled.

"Fun, huh?" he said.

Her smile was sincere, but not very enthusiastic. In fact, Jordan thought it was rather sad.

"Well, I'm off. Wish me luck."

"Are you sure you know what you're doing?"

"No, not at all. I didn't say that, did I?"

"Well . . . no."

"Oh. Good. No, I don't know what I'm doing, but I don't know what *else* to do. They've blocked off a large area out there; I suspect it's for a reason. And after what that Paul Kragen fellow said about a cave just before he died yesterday—"

"A cave with *children* in it," Lauren added urgently.

He nodded. "—and after what everybody else in town *didn't* say, I think there's a good chance I might come across something."

"If you say so." She looked away from him, either terribly disappointed or suddenly preoccupied.

"Don't look so sad," he said. "I might find something that'll lead us to your son."

She closed her eyes and breathed, "I hope so. I hope so."

He nodded toward the door, and as they'd planned earlier, Lauren opened it, took a look up and down the corridor and said, "It's clear."

As Jordan started out of the room, Lauren placed her hand on his back and whispered, "Good luck. And be careful."

He winked over his shoulder and, in his flawless old man's voice, said, "Why, thank you much, young lady." Then he hobbled down the corridor.

4.

A bright full moon glowed over Hester Thorne's Camelot.

The rubber tip of Jordan's cane thumped on the concrete path behind the hotel as he walked at a leisurely pace, looking around as if he were admiring his surroundings. Old-fashioned street lamps—the kind that reminded him of black-and-white Sherlock Holmes movies starring Basil Rathbone—surrounded the green, casting circles of light onto the grass and Jordan walked under them casually, just an old man, unable to sleep, strolling the grounds with nothing to hide.

A couple of the young Alliance men saw him walking through the lobby; he'd nodded at them and they'd smiled without raising a brow. A young woman wearing a waitress uniform paused on her way from the restaurant to the hotel to give him a perky, "Good evening, sir," and Jordan had replied, "Hello there, hello," with an unsteady wave.

In the dark, the hedge animals took on an ominous appearance, looking as if they were about to attack the first thing to come along. Live ducks lazed on and around the pond. Moths darted around the lamps, casting enormous shadows that flitted over the grass and trees.

As he neared the edge of the woods, Jordan carefully looked around and made sure no one was paying him any attention. He spotted people here and there, alone or in pairs, but all seemed on their way to someplace, probably to turn in for the night, and Jordan hobbled on until he reached the trees that flanked the gallery.

There were four bright lights positioned at each corner of the rectangular plot of land behind the hotel. Jordan avoided them. He went, instead, to a patch of blackness that lay beneath a few of the tall pines, walking carefully until he found the wall. Standing beneath it and looking up, it seemed unsurmountable, but he tried not to think that way. Instead, he tossed his cane up and over the wall, heard it land in the brush on the other side, then turned to the closest tree, an enormous pine that stood about four feet from the wall. He looked behind him, took a deep breath, and trying hard to recall the tree-climbing days of his childhood, hugged the prickly trunk and began his laborious ascent, crunching the chip-like bark beneath him as he dragged himself upward slowly, grunting and grinding his teeth, further and further up, gummy pitch sticking to his palms, until he was high enough to get a hold on the first branch and pull himself up to another, and another, until, exhausted and out of breath—

—he turned to his right and saw the top of the wall.

About four feet away.

Grumbling softly under his breath, he climbed a bit higher, until he was looking down on the top edge of the wall. Testing the strength of a branch with his foot, he finally decided it was heavy enough to hold him and carefully moved around the trunk until he was standing on the branch facing the wall, and then, bracing himself for the inevitable pain of the impact—

—he jumped from the tree, pushing himself outward, and hooked his arms over the top of the wall when he hit it. His breath exploded from his lungs as his chest slammed into the wall, but his arms remained firm on the edge, holding him up. Gasping for air, he tried to recover fast, shaking the fog from his head as he lifted his right leg until he was able to hook his foot over the top of the wall and pull himself up. He sat on the wall as if it were a horse and looked around, his eyes now well adjusted to the darkness, until he spotted another tree on the other side just a few feet ahead of him, even closer to the wall than the one he'd just climbed. Crawling along the top of the wall, he reached the tree, launched himself over the small gap easily enough, endured another bone-rattling slam as he hugged the tree, slipped down a few feet, nearly screaming aloud from his fear of falling, then shimmied the rest of the way down, noticing for the first time just how good the ground felt beneath his feet.

He took out his flashlight, found his cane, then stood staring into the deep, black woods.

At that same instant, two things were happening that, in a short while, would directly affect Jordan: Hester Thorne was knocking on Mark Schroeder's door, knocking hard enough to wake him because it was not yet eleven o'clock; and thirteen children holding lanterns and wearing white robes were forming a circle in a small clearing about twenty feet from the yawning black mouth of a cave.

As Jordan trudged through the woods, trying not to make *too* much noise as he pushed branches and bushes aside with his cane, heading straight for the circle of children and the white-robed woman who stood in the center, Mark walked down the corridor away from his room, groggy with sleep, and Hester took his hand and said, "Others will join us there. Everything is being prepared. You're in for quite an experience." Thinking of his bed and craving more sleep like a trembling, dry-mouthed alcoholic craving liquor, Mark looked at her with heavy-lidded eyes, and a little while later—

—Jordan heard voices and slowed his pace, switching off his flashlight and hunkering down into a thick patch of ferns.

The voices grew closer—a man and woman—and with them came footsteps hissing through the weeds and snapping brittle twigs. Jordan froze and listened to the voices.

They were polite, soft, discreet, almost . . . reverent, but the words were unintelligible.

A couple of young Alliance members out for a forbidden late-night tryst beneath the pines? Maybe a couple of visitors who, like Jordan, were sneaking around after hours to see what they could see?

No.

The woman's voice—the one doing the most talking—sounded familiar as it grew closer.

"—that will prepare you for your destiny," Hester Thorne said. "The Universal Enlightened Alliance, and Orrin him*self*, need you *very* much. We want you to know how important you are to our movement, Mark."

Mark? Jordan wondered. *Schroeder? Maybe . . .*

They passed directly in front of him wearing white hooded robes, one of them carrying a lantern. Jordan cocked his head slightly, listening.

"The only people brought into the Inner Circle," she went on, "are those who will, at one point or another, be able to do great work for the Alliance and who can, if they choose, *directly* aid us in ushering in the New Age that Orrin has spoken of. You'll see things you won't understand tonight, but that understanding will come later as you . . ."

Her voice faded into the night and, a few seconds later, so did their footsteps.

Still hunkering in the bushes, Jordan frowned. They were on their way to something, but what? What was the Inner Circle? And what "great work" could Mark Schroeder do for the Alliance? He filed the questions away in his memory and stood very slowly, with no more than a hushed sound of movement, but—

—he dropped back down when he heard more footsteps coming from the same direction the others had, moving toward him. More people this time. Muted voices, some talking over one another, one chuckling. Closer . . . closer . . . until—

—they passed by rather rapidly, five of them, all carrying lanterns and dressed in the same flowing white robes, three with the hoods pulled up over their heads, two without, speaking so quietly he could understand nothing they said. Watching their backs as they moved away from him, he noticed how bright the light of the moon and lanterns made their robes and how it glinted off the golden stitching around the collars, hems and cuffs.

What the hell is going on? he thought as they disappeared into the woods.

After waiting for a few minutes to make sure no one else was coming, he came out of hiding and headed in the direction of the white robes. He quickly became extra cautious and tried to avoid open spaces because it didn't take him long to realize that the woods were alive with the presence of others.

Voices filtered through the darkness from all directions and the surrounding crackle of footsteps jerked his attention from left to right, from front to back. The sounds faded slightly as they moved beyond him, then seemed to merge some distance ahead to be joined by other voices that sounded quite different. They were higher in pitch and seemed to be chanting something in a gentle tone.

Children . . . they were the voices of *children*.

The realization reminded Jordan of Paul Kragen's dying words and a chill crept over his body like an army of tiny ants. He went deeper into the woods, even more careful to be silent than he'd been before, heading in the direction of the chanting voices. And as Jordan pressed on—

—Nathan Schroeder stood in the circle, holding hands with the children who flanked him—just as all the others were—concentrating hard on his request as he chanted—which, of course, was the same request that all the other chanting children were making of the Ascended Masters: to be chosen on this night for the Translation.

Mount Shasta loomed over them and the moon gave a sheen to their robes, but Nathan noticed nothing, not even the others around him or the tall figure who stood in the center of the circle or the robed adults who passed by to gather at the mouth of the cave beneath the mountain; he was even unaware of the hands that he held, of the meaning of his chant and of the length of time that he chanted before—

—the woman that stood in the center clapped her hands hard a single time and the chanting stopped instantly, the children opened their eyes and looked at her. Nathan looked into the oval of blackness in her hood where her face was hidden by darkness.

Standing in one spot, the woman began to turn slowly, like a figurine on a music box, as she spoke.

"And now we must concentrate on strength," she said, as—

—Jordan huddled down behind a patch of manzanita and listened.

"We must ask the Ascended Masters to send to the Chosen One the strength needed for the important task at hand."

She lifted a hand and the children closed their eyes again and continued to chant, but now Nathan's thoughts were focused on the strength needed by whoever was chosen for the Translation. He held the hands and chanted the chant and the world fell away quickly as Nathan became lost in his concentration and—

—Jordan watched, fascinated, as the children chanted what sounded like a series of names—one of which was Orrin, if he wasn't mistaken—and swayed ever so slightly with the rhythm of their words. The woman in the center continued to turn slowly, her cauled head bowed slightly so she could look at each child as she moved.

Beyond the circle of children, Jordan saw a group of robed figures milling about before the cave he'd hoped to find; others came from the woods and joined them.

Watching the children, Jordan wondered what the hell they were doing, what the "important task at hand" was, who the Chosen One was and if Nathan Schroeder was among them. He couldn't find out now. For the moment, he was more interested in finding out what the people outside the cave were doing and saying, so, staying behind bushes and trees, Jordan crept around the circle of children toward the cave as—

—the woman in the circle stopped the chanting with a clap of her hands and removed from the deep folds of her white robe a small dark box. Removing the lid, she walked from one child to the next, proffering the box. Each child reached in, removed a round plastic coin-like object and held it in a fist. When the woman was finished, she returned to the center and—

—Jordan stopped and listened, not wanting to miss whatever was going on as—

—the woman said, "You may look."

The children held their plastic coins to the lantern.

Nathan was disappointed to see that his was blank; he'd hoped to be chosen. But someone in the circle had received the coin bearing the Alliance emblem and the small shrouded heads began to lift and look around, until—

—a hand rose slowly and the quiet voice of a little girl said, "I have it."

Beckoned by the woman, the little girl stepped into the circle, leaving a gap that was quickly closed. The girl stood in front of the woman with the woman's hands on her small shoulders.

"Now," the woman said, "we must ask once again for the strength of the Ascended Masters so that our Chosen One, Katie Coogan, may properly fulfill her destiny and rejoice in her re-embodiment." The children began their chant as—

—Jordan thought, *Re-embodiment? What the hell is that?*

There was something very familiar about that name, Katie Coogan. A relative of Bill Coogan's, maybe? Then he remembered Coogan's daughter and how upset Coogan had been with her on the day Jordan and Lauren had first met him.

Katie was Coogan's granddaughter.

Jordan was certain then that he had found something in those woods that was bigger and more important than he'd expected—or even *intended*—to find. Turning his attention from the children and their haunting, almost hypnotic chant, Jordan headed toward the cave, positioning himself behind a large rock jutting from the earth and surrounded by manzanita just a few feet from the growing crowd, where he heard Hester Thorne saying quietly—

—"Mark Schroeder and he's joining us for the first time. So this is a very important, exciting night for him." She turned to him, smiling. "Isn't it, Mark?"

He was so tired that it was difficult to speak, but he managed a feeble smile and a weak but affirmative response. It *was* important, he *was* excited . . . he was just too tired to show it. His muscles ached, his head was filled with a thick, murky fog and his eyes burned so from weariness that they were not to be trusted. But he fought to show his enthusiasm and met the other eyes with his own, smiling and nodding.

Hester took his hand and said, "I'm taking him inside to get him familiar with the territory. I'll be back out in a moment."

She led him into the cave and as they passed through the low opening, Mark heard someone say happily, "They found the Chosen One! It's a little girl!"

He wondered what that meant as Hester sidled up to him, snaking her arm around his waist.

"What's the Chosen One?" he asked, his words sliding together lazily.

"Hmm. I think that's information best left for the future, Mark. But . . .'' She stopped, faced him and placed a hand on his neck, stroking his skin. The lantern swung on its U-shaped handle and a circle of light danced around them as the rest of the cave remained dark. ". . . the very *near* future, I promise. We *need* you, Mark. *Orrin* needs you. That's why I've brought you here so early on in your education. We have to speed up your enlightenment so you'll be ready to meet—and to *understand*—your destiny. We can't wait for you, Mark. You're too important."

"What is my destiny?" he asked.

She grinned, ran her fingers through his hair and said, "You'll see."

Then they continued walking deeper into the cave, deeper into the damp chilly darkness, where Mark got the gnawing, clinging sensation that they were being watched, as—

—Jordan bristled with excitement at having heard Hester Thorne mention Mark Schroeder. Could he have possibly gotten so lucky so soon? If he could somehow contact Schroeder, let him know that Lauren was with Jordan, maybe he could get some information from him, learn some things about the Alliance, about Hester Thorne . . . and about what happened to Harvey Bolton. He wiped away the beads of sweat that were prickling on his forehead, then followed them quietly, keeping a safe distance and staying behind bushes and trees as—

—Hester Thorne squeezed Mark's hand and began to walk

faster, saying with breathless anticipation, "Come on, let's hurry. We don't have much time."

"For what?"

"There's something I want to show you before everyone else comes in."

They continued in silence. Hester obviously knew her way around the cave—she never hesitated or missed a step, even though she was walking so quickly—but Mark was uncomfortable. He would be uncomfortable in *any* cave, but this one was especially disturbing. The darkness that blanketed them seemed to be concealing something; Mark not only had the unshakable feeling that they were being watched, but he sensed they were being watched from all directions—from above and the sides, from ahead and behind—and if he listened closely as they walked, he could *almost* hear sounds . . . small, moist sounds of movement so faint that they could just as easily be aural hallucinations brought on by his fatigue.

He forgot about them almost completely when he saw light up ahead. It was faint, blue and seemed to pulsate.

"Remember what I said, Mark? That you would see things tonight that you wouldn't understand?"

He nodded, frowning.

"Well, you're about to see one of them. It will all be explained to you in the coming days, but I promise you that, when you see it, you will experience a sudden understanding, of sorts. A gut-level *knowing*. This is knowledge already possessed by every human being on earth. But it's been lost over the centuries. Abandoned by humanity in favor of conventional science or antiquated religion or drugs or liquor. And it's right here, Mark, right here with you. You'll see it, touch it, bask in it."

They were nearing an elbow-like curve in the subterranean path they'd been following and it was from around this curve that the light came.

"And," she went on, "you'll know that it has *always* been here. Just waiting."

As they rounded the corner, Mark felt the hair on his arms and neck stand up, heard a ringing in his ears and gasped as a fist clenched in his chest. He stopped, took a step back and stared at the pulsating blue light. For a moment, he wanted only to tear himself away from Hester, turn and get out of that cave as quickly as possible. His stomach roiled for a moment and a sickening hum began to fill his head, as if his teeth were vibrating rapidly in their sockets.

"It's okay, Mark," Hester cooed, putting an arm around him and leading him on around the corner. "It always feels like this the first time. It's very powerful, and unfortunately, it's a power that we've been separated from for so long that being near it again is . . . well, a bit overwhelming. But you're going to be all right, you're going to be just fine."

She kept talking quietly, never pausing as they went around that seemingly endless curve until—

—Mark could see part of it, just one side, and he automatically started to squint against the light, but found he didn't need to because, bright as the light was, it was gentle, actually rather soothing, and as he continued around the corner, as it came into full view, static crackled softly through his hair and his knees trembled unsteadily, but he wasn't afraid. Instead, he—just as Hester had promised he would—basked in the blue light.

It came from an enormous, narrow, almost teardrop-shaped vertical crevice in the cave wall several yards away. The crevice was about fifteen feet tall and along each side of it were folds of smooth, glistening, fleshy stone. All around it, stalactites and stalagmites came from the ceiling and floor of the cave like fangs in a gigantic mouth. Above and around it, on the curved and lumpy walls, Mark saw something else, something that almost diverted his attention from that wonderful light.

Like granite gargoyles perched on the ledge of an old European cathedral, murky figures were straddling, squatting and standing on natural stone platforms jutting from the cave's walls. Mark couldn't see them in any detail, so wasn't sure if they were carvings or real people—or *things*—watching him from above, but it hardly mattered, because—

—all Mark could think of was that light, that glorious, loving, healing light that filled him with a sense of euphoria that brought tears to his eyes, splitting the light into millions of glinting shards that seemed to shoot out, surround and embrace him, and a quiet sob escaped his chest as he put a weak hand over his mouth.

"Isn't it wonderful, Mark?" Hester breathed.

"Wuh-won . . . wonderful. What . . . what is it?"

"The Center of the Vortex."

Mark couldn't take his eyes from it. Hester turned off her

lantern and set it down, but Mark didn't notice; the lantern's light had been completely obliterated by the blue glow.

Even the crevice itself looked inviting, as if it were warm and comfortable inside, and somehow Mark knew that if he were to crawl inside and curl up, he would never have another worry or problem, not the slightest discomfort whatsoever, ever again. His muscles burned to move him forward, to walk him right into that blue light, through the teardrop opening of that crevice to whatever wonderful thing lay on the other side. He almost did it. In fact, he took the first step but got no further because—

—Hester's arms were around his waist, holding him tightly, her hands sliding over his back and she was moving in front of him, brushing her lips across his, her hands moving down his sides now, over his hips and around to the front where her right hand moved up and down.

"I've been holding off for this," she whispered, her breath hot on his face. "I wanted to do it here. We have time, Mark. It'll be a while before everyone's here and they're ready to begin. Here, Mark. In the light. In front of the Center of the Vortex. Now."

She lifted his robe. He felt her hands on his bare legs underneath.

"Feel that light, Mark? Do you feel what's in it? It's full of love. Energy and love, Mark. Right here. Now."

They were kneeling on the smooth stone floor and Mark was moving his hands over her, kissing her, tasting her, and in the glow of the light each sensation was magnified, each time his fingertips touched her skin he felt connected to some powerful electrical current that shot through his body, rejuvenating him, cleansing all impurities, wiping away all flaws, and as they made love in the pulsating blue glow and under the gaze of the figures in the dark overhead, Mark began to cry out joyfully as—

—Jordan watched and listened and waited. The crowd outside the cave grew and the people talked among themselves in hushed voices. He heard a few things—something about a vortex, more mentions of Katie Coogan and the Translation, even something about Reverend Barry Hallway—but nothing helpful, so he turned his attention to the children.

Their chanting had become more intense. Jordan had never heard such raw passion in such young voices. The chanting went on for several minutes, but to Jordan it seemed like mere seconds; it was so easy to become swept up by the hypnotic cadence of the chanting that he'd lost track of time and even, for a few moments, of *place*. When the children stopped, Jordan blinked several times and shook his head hard, then watched the woman who stood in the center of the circle.

She turned the little girl around to face her and said, "On this night, Katie Coogan, you will meet your destiny. You will pass through the Center of the Vortex and into your next incarnation, whatever it may be."

Next incarnation? Jordan thought. *But I didn't think that happened until . . . until—*

Until you died, he almost thought, but couldn't bring himself to form the words in his mind. Surely that was not what this was all about. Surely they weren't into *that*.

"Take with you," the woman continued, "the courage, energy and peace we have called down from the Ascended Masters and know that, in undergoing this early translation, you are helping to hasten the arrival of the New Age of Enlightenment."

The woman bent down and embraced Katie Coogan, holding her tightly for a moment as the circle began to break up. The children formed a line behind the woman, and when she moved away, the first child stepped forward, set down the lantern, embraced the girl, retrieved the lantern, then moved aside to make room for the next child . . . and the next . . . and the next.

They've done this before, Jordan thought as a bad feeling settled into his stomach. *This is a ritual they've all gone through before and they'll go through it again.*

When they were done, they all headed toward the cave, single file, leaving Katie behind with the woman. The muted chatter among the adults stopped immediately and those with their hoods down pulled them up over their heads as they all stepped aside to let the children pass into the cave. Once they were all inside and the glow of their lanterns was swallowed up by the darkness, the adults followed.

Jordan waited, listening as their footsteps faded, until there was only the silence of the woods: the chirping of crickets, the croaking of frogs, the hoot of an owl in the dark distance. Once he was certain that no one had stayed behind to keep watch, Jordan made his way slowly through the bushes, around the rock and toward the cave. At the cave's mouth, he stopped and listened for movement in the darkness. When he heard none—

—How far in there have they gone? he wondered—
—he went inside, as—

—Mark watched the crowd gather, watched everyone setting aside their lanterns as they entered. His mind was still reeling from what he'd just experienced: the act of making love with Hester in the light from the Center of the Vortex. It had been the most invigorating and energizing experience of his life. No, no . . . those were inadequate words; it had been life-changing. Now he was certain, beyond the shadow of a doubt, that he had made the right choice in bringing Nathan here to Grover. He knew now that he had been *called* here, there was a *reason;* the light from the Center of the Vortex made him realize—gave him the *assurance*—that his presence here had *purpose*. He could not have taken the smile from his face if he *had* to; his happiness was almost palpable, he could almost *taste* it in his mouth. It was the most beautiful feeling he'd ever had and somehow he knew that nothing could ever take it away.

The children filed in first, forming a half circle around the crevice; Mark joined the adults in forming another wider half circle behind the children. Hester stood in front of them with her back to the crevice, her body silhouetted by the shimmering, pulsating blue light that came from the crevice just a few feet behind her.

"We have come together here," she began, smiling, "in a spirit of celebration to witness a Translation that will aid us in expediting the New Age of Enlightenment, which Orrin has assured us is in our reach *right now*, but which is being held back by the disbelief of those less informed—less *enlightened*—than you and I. We have come here to rejoice in the knowledge that this New Age is being ushered in by young and old alike, by people of all colors and backgrounds, and that *we* are lucky enough to be a *part* of it."

Mark's chest swelled, his grin felt uncontrollable, as if it might damage his face. He lifted his head with pride as—

—Jordan made his careful way through the darkness of the cave, flicking on his flashlight now and then to make sure he wasn't about to run into any stone walls, shielding the narrow beam with his fingers, hoping not to reveal himself to anyone, except he didn't *see* anyone, there was no one coming toward him out of the darkness, no one hiding behind rocks, until, until—

—he heard a voice, Hester Thorne's voice, rising and falling up ahead in the distance, delivering what sounded like some kind of speech that was sometimes buried by the hammering of his heart sounding in his ears. In a few moments, Hester's voice stopped and, after a brief pause, a chorus of voices began to chant deep within the cave, adults and children.

He pressed on, wondering exactly how far in those people had gone, wondering what they were doing and, most importantly, if he *really* wanted to know.

As the chanting grew louder, Jordan noticed that a faint blue glow was infusing the darkness; the farther he went, the brighter the soft, throbbing blue glow became until his flashlight was no longer necessary. He stopped to slip the light into his coat pocket and was about to continue when he noticed it, just a vague feeling of anxiety deep in his gut at first. But it increased. His palms became moist and clammy, his mouth became dry, and he suddenly felt vulnerable, as if he were about to be attacked from all sides. He walked on. The blue light became brighter and the feeling inside him grew worse. It was more than simple anxiety now, more than just a discomfort. It was now a raw, sickening fear and his steps became uneven, he swayed a bit from side to side, closed his eyes a moment and—

—his mind exploded with hideous, vivid images—a mangled body lying in the rain as its blood rushed down a muddy gutter, an infant being thrown hard against a rock wall, burned flesh, gouged eyes, torn lips—and he opened his eyes as wide as he could to escape them and took a deep breath as sweat poured down his back, and beneath all his makeup, his skin began to prickle with perspiration, but he couldn't worry about his makeup at the moment because something was terribly, *terribly* wrong here and the feeling he was having—the sense of *badness*, of naked, throbbing *evil*—was beginning to nauseate him and he felt like he would vomit soon.

He staggered to his left and leaned against a fat pillar of stone, lifting a hand to shield his eyes from the light. But even when he wasn't looking at it, he could *feel* it all around him, could feel it inside his bones like a silent, impossibly deep thrum, and closing his eyes to the light only brought back the frightening images that pierced his mind like shards of glass. Leaning heavily on the stone, he looked ahead.

The light was brighter up there, unbelievably bright, and yet it didn't hurt his eyes, didn't even make him squint, although he squinted anyway because there was something wrong with that blue glow, something very wrong. It's source was just around a bend that lay up ahead.

That's where they are, he thought. *Just around that corner.*

Contradicting his better judgment and the small voice inside him that kept saying, *Turn around now, get out, get away from this cave, this town, these people, get out getout GETOUT!* Jordan pushed away from the pillar and, using the cane for *real* instead of just show, headed toward the bend up ahead. As he neared it, the light grew brighter and the deeply invasive sensation it gave him increased; the chanting became more distinct until he recognized it as the same chant he'd heard outside earlier: apparently a series of odd, exotic names, one of them being "Orrin."

He lurched toward the bend and, moving very carefully, climbed up over a large formation of rocks that resembled a head of cauliflower until he was against the lumpy wall of the cave. He was so close to them now, he could discern individual voices in the crowd of chanters, could hear each word they said . . . even if he didn't understand them.

The blue light pulsed from around the corner, shafts of it seeming to seek him out like the tentacles of an octopus. He edged around the curved wall, his feet searching for purchase on the uneven knobs of rock until he was almost able to peer around the corner, almost, *almost,* but—

—his fear was worse now, a solid lump in his gut rising steadily to his throat, and the sweat was stinging under his makeup and making his shirt cling to him, his breath was coming fast and his head was throbbing dully, but when he closed his eyes, even for an instant, he saw—

—mountains of naked decaying corpses and human body parts scattered over a vast barren landscape where buzzards feasted on red-black entrails, so—

—he kept his eyes open and tried to calm his breathing as he leaned forward carefully, so very carefully, until he could see them.

He was standing slightly above them and looked down on the

two hand-holding half circles of children and adults. But they kept his attention for a brief moment. Instead of watching them, he stared in open-mouthed awe at the enormous crevice through which the blue light glowed. He wanted to look away but couldn't. Whatever the source of that light, it was something unnatural, he was certain, something *wrong* . . . but it was also mesmerizing. It held his attention so firmly that, when he finally managed to turn away, it was only with great physical effort. Pressing his back against the wall and grinding his teeth, Jordan listened to the chanting until he heard another sound . . . a sound like—

—wings flapping over Mark's head.

He was so lost in the chant that it took him a while to realize he was hearing something besides the other voices, but when the sound finally registered, Mark allowed himself the small infraction of opening his eyes during the chant and looking up.

There were four of them. They glowed with a white light—*A heavenly light*, Mark thought—that made them stand out in the blue glow. They flew in graceful circles over the chanters, their wings flowing up and down fluidly, arms moving in gestures of approval, as if they were giving a sort of blessing, and—

—Jordan stopped breathing when he saw them flying around over the chanters, the blue light glistening off the sheen of slime that covered their grey flesh . . . if it could be *called* flesh. Their bat-like wings looked frayed as moth-eaten fabric but moved with frightening power. Something viscous dribbled from their snouts, but because of the shadows playing over them, Jordan couldn't see their faces in any detail, and for that he was thankful.

They were—

—naked, Mark noticed. Their creamy bodies were sexless, hairless and perfectly smooth, their head oval-shaped with delicate, almost perfectly round eyes that reminded Mark of Little Orphan Annie's eyes, except instead of being empty, they sparkled with love, with joy. They—

—flew around the chanters like vultures circling carrion and Jordan felt tears on his cheeks before he realized he was crying silently. He was crying because what was happening before him completely shattered his worldview, utterly destroyed with one sweep the years he'd spent trying to exorcise from his mind the God-and-Jesus-versus-Satan-and-the-demons upbringing he'd so despised, the care he'd taken to reject anything supernatural, to scoff at the idea of heaven and hell, of good and evil, and cling only to those things that were visible, tangible and could be scientifically proven, but this, *this* was happening right in *front* of him, he was watching winged, man-sized lizards flying around in a blue light and he felt as if someone had taken the top of his skull off, dipped the two aluminum beaters of an electric mixer into his brain and flipped the switch.

He stared at the flying creatures, trembling.

They were—

—*Angels,* Mark thought, *they're angels*—

—feverish nightmares, they were, to Jordan, pictures from the thick yellowed pages of some ancient, hellish book never meant to be read to children, they were—

—*The salvation of Man,* Mark thought, *our only hope. They've come to lead us by the hand like children into the New Age, they're*—

—evil. It had taken Jordan years to convince himself it didn't exist, but only seconds to convince him that it not only existed but was visible, tangible and very hard at work.

As he watched, the winged creatures dispersed and settled into nooks high in the cave wall that were deeply shadowed; they crouched and huddled on stone shelves that jutted from the wall . . . watching.

The chanting stopped.

Hester stepped before the robed figures, looked to her left, held her hand in that direction and said, "Bring the Chosen One."

Jordan followed her gaze to an enormous rock. The little girl appeared from behind it, walking between two people, one of whom carried what appeared to be a blanket or mat rolled up beneath one arm. A gap opened briefly in each of the half circles so the three people could pass through. They went to Hester's side and one of them said, "She has been bathed and cleansed," then rolled out the mat on the rocky floor.

Hester smiled, nodded, and said, "Thank you."

The two escorts turned and joined the half circle of adults.

Hester put a hand on each side of the little girl's face and grinned down at her. "You understand what you are about to do, Katie Coogan?" she asked.

Katie nodded.

"You are fully willing to enter your next incarnation? You *want* to do this?"

Another nod.

"Then—" Hester stood straight and faced her audience. "—we're ready." She reached behind Katie's head, unsnapped something, and the small white robe fell away. The girl was naked underneath. Hester waved toward the mat and Katie lay down on her back with her feet just inches from the glowing crevice.

Hester turned to her right and reached out a hand. One of the adults broke away from the half circle, came to her side and handed her something, then returned. It was a crystal. A sparkling crystal, about eighteen inches long, that came to a fine, needle-like point. The crystal took in the blue light and glowed as if with a light all its own. Hester wrapped the fingers of both hands around its thick, heavy end with the sharp point aiming downward and knelt at Katie's side.

Jordan felt sick again, but this time it wasn't because of the light.

"No," he breathed, "no, God, no . . ."

Hester began to chant a series of words that were nonsense to Jordan as she lifted the crystal high above her head.

"No, Jesus, please, no," Jordan breathed, clutching his cane so hard that his knuckles whitened and ached as—

—Mark watched the vague, sparkling trail of energy left behind by the crystal as Hester lifted it above her head, watched the energy settle over the girl, watched it sprinkle down on her like a spring rain and cover her with a fine, not quite invisible light as she lay motionless at the opening of the Center of the Vortex. Hester swayed back and forth and more of it fell down on the girl, fluttering lightly through the air like glitter, and

when the girl was in what appeared to be a faint cocoon of
light—

—Hester plunged the crystal down fast and Jordan's throat
closed on his cry as the point entered the girl's chest and the
small body jerked once, twice, then—

—she was still, and Mark smiled because he knew that her
spirit—like *all* spirits, as he'd been taught, as Orrin himself had
told him—had gone, had moved on to its next vehicle, its next
destiny, and the girl's body was empty now, husk around which
the sparkling light faded now, until—

—Jordan slapped a trembling hand over his mouth as he
watched two of the adults step forward, flank Katie's body, bend
down, lift her up and slide her through the glowing crevice.
She was gone.
An instant later, the light brightened.
Blinding shafts of it shot from the crevice.
Hester stood and lifted her arms and those gathered around
her raised their clasped hands above their heads and began to
drone a low "Aaahhh" that rose in pitch, louder and louder,
until—

—Mark was singing his note of praise with the others, basking
in the light, absorbing the energy that came from the Center of
the Vortex. Their combined voices reverberated in the cave and
the light brightened until it was almost too overwhelming to look
at, but Mark couldn't close his eyes, couldn't turn away from it,
he just stood there and bathed in it, let it wash over him, as—

—Jordan clambered to get back on his feet, head spinning and
heart thundering, his voice rising as he murmured, "No no no,
please, Jesus Christ, no," and the more he fought to stand, the
farther down he fell until he was lying facedown, his cane rattling against the moist lumps of stone as his voice rose even
higher—"please please God no please no God no"—and as he
lifted himself up, his mind replaying Katie Coogan's death again
and again, he looked down at the people who had begun to chant
again and heard their voices echoing through the cave as the
intense blue glow began to diminish.

Jordan turned and, using the cane to maintain his balance, started down the rock formation. Once he was back on the path, he headed away from the ceremony—

—*Sacrifice!* he thought. *It was a human sacrifice!*—

—and away from the blue light and the slobbering winged creatures. He staggered for a while, but the farther he got from the glow, the more certain his steps became; he stopped sweating and his trembling and sickness gradually went away. He took the flashlight from his pocket as the darkness closed in to replace the blue glow. The darkness was an immense relief; he began to feel better—although having seen what he'd just seen, he couldn't possibly feel *good*—and safer.

Until he caught the smell.

He slowed his pace a bit. He hadn't smelled it on the way in and that seemed odd because it was the kind of smell that took a long time to develop. It was a bit like the stench of a dead animal in the process of decaying, but with something else to it, something like . . . like *body odor*? He continued walking, but cautiously now, flashlight off, using his cane the way a blind man would.

A sound.

Jordan froze. It had come from behind him.

He heard it again. A heavy sound. A footstep.

Another.

The smell became worse suddenly, became so overpowering that his throat closed, making him gag, then cough, and he spun around, sensed something just inches from him in the impenetrable darkness and flicked on the flashlight and—

—Jordan screamed.

The mountainous creature lifted a thick arm and swept it through the air, striking the side of Jordan's head and sending him spawling over the path. He clutched the cane and flashlight tightly as he fell and rolled, the inside of his skull exploding. He slammed against a row of stalagmites that lined a section of the path like a fence and lifted his head in time to see that—

—the creature was lifting a huge booted foot over him, about to stomp on his stomach and—

—Jordan rolled to his left, got to his knees and was standing when he turned to see the creature bounding toward him. Dizzy from the blow and nauseated from the stench, Jordan swung the cane in an arc, landing it hard on the creature's misshapen head.

The twisted mouth opened to show a few broken, yellowed teeth and the beast staggered back a step, releasing a wet, guttural sound of pain. Jordan struck the creature's head again, then quickly a third time.

The creature twisted away, slapping both gnarled hands over its bleeding forehead and staggered back into the darkness.

Jordan ran. He didn't bother covering the flashlight beam anymore and did his best to ignore the ringing in his ears and throbbing in his head. He just ran hard, using his terror as fuel, until he passed through the mouth of the cave and into the woods, through bushes and over rocks and logs, darting around trees, the flashlight beam bouncing wildly through the darkness until it fell on the wall and Jordan tossed his cane over, pocketed the light and climbed the tree closest to the wall faster than he'd ever climbed a tree as a boy.

Once on the other side, he found his cane and hunkered in the dark, panting for a long time, trying to calm down, willing his heartbeat to slow and his head to stop pounding, willing the fear to go away . . . but it wouldn't.

As he hobbled back to the hotel, the trembling in his hands and legs was real and he felt decades older than he had ninety minutes ago.

5.

While Jordan was gone, Lauren lay on the bed with the television playing. She'd been lying there for what seemed like hours, paying no attention to the images that passed across the screen, although she stared at it as if she were deeply involved.

She'd been thinking about Nathan. She could think of nothing else, except when a bilious anger rose inside her and she tensed from head to foot; that was when she thought of Mark.

Adding to her anger and loss was the overwhelming sense of loneliness that came down on her at such times like a lead weight; although she knew Nathan was near by, being in an unfamiliar place with a stranger made her feel like the last person on earth.

The news was on, and when Lauren pulled herself out of the mire of her thoughts, she heard the announcer talking about Reverend Barry Hallway.

"The reverend was accompanied by Matthew Ridgely, a personal aide, and the plane's pilot, Simon Ketter,'' he said as pictures of the three men appeared. The youngest was Ketter, the pilot, a handsome blond man in his twenties. ''No official cause has been given for the crash yet, but the speculation is that a malfunction in the plane's autopilot system was at fault. The plane was a Mitsubishi, a make which has had a series of problems with autopilot systems.'' A picture of the wreckage appeared; the plane had plunged several feet into the ground and pieces were scattered over the area.

The announcer returned. ''Reverend Hallway was best known for founding the American Moral Alleigance back in the eighties, but more recently he had become one of the most outspoken opponents of the Universal Enlightened Alliance, headed by Hester Thorne, a self-proclaimed channel. What makes this odd is the fact that, just a little over two weeks ago at a seminar in San Francisco, Miss Thorne warned, in non-specific terms, of Reverend Hallway's death. Or rather, Orrin, the entity Miss Thorne claims to channel, gave the warning.'' The man allowed a vague smirk to creep over his lips as he continued the story, but Lauren stopped listening and sat up on the bed, burying her face in her hands.

What did *that* mean? Was there any truth to Hester Thorne's abilities, or was it just a huge coincidence? And what would happen if Hester Thorne really was what she claimed to be?

No matter what questions she asked herself, they always brought her back to her son: what would become of Nathan?

Once again, the television was forgotten and she was lost in her thoughts, crying, softly at first, then so loudly that she pressed a hand over her mouth. She cried until her chest ached from sobbing, then forced herself to stop.

If Jordan were someone she could talk to, it might not be quite so bad. But she had no one . . . not even Mark anymore.

Then Lauren remembered Joan Maher's invitation to give her a call if she needed someone. It was late and Joan was probably asleep, but she *had* offered. She thought about it awhile, wondering how much longer Jordan would be gone, then decided to risk it and found the telephone book.

After several rings, there was an answer and Lauren could tell she'd awakened Joan by the unintelligible sounds Joan made.

''Joan? I'm really sorry, but I . . . I, um, needed someone to talk to, and you said to call . . . remember?''

"Hoozis?"

"Lauren Schroeder? We met yesterday when—"

"Oh, yeah-yeah." There were waking-up sounds then: throat clearing and soft groaning and rustles of movement. "So, uh, wha's up?"

Lauren said nothing for a moment. Suddenly, calling Joan seemed like a stupid thing to do; this was *her* problem, not Joan's, so why was Lauren waking her up in the middle of the night.

"Oh, jeez," Lauren said, "I'm, look, I'm really sorry, I shouldn't've called you, this is really not your problem and—"

"Are you alone?" Joan asked, sounding more awake now.

"Yes."

"Where's your friend?"

"He's . . . out."

"Poking around the Alliance, is he?"

"Well . . . that's why he's here." The tone of Joan's voice made her nervous; it was stiff, cold, the same way it had sounded after Lauren had told her about Nathan and when Joan had advised her to hire someone to go in and get him.

After a pause, Joan spoke again, but now there was something new in her voice: tension. "What's he looking for this late? I mean, is he sneaking around the grounds, or something?"

"Yes. Well, um . . . the grounds? I'm not sure what that is. All I know is that he's gone into the woods behind the hotel. But that's not what I called to—"

"My God, he went into those woods tonight? He's there *now*?" Joan snapped.

Lauren's tongue stumbled nervously until she finally blurted, "Yes, yes, tonight, right *now*, what's *wrong*, Joan, what's the *matter*?"

Joan began to breathe rapidly and swallowed a few times as if to calm herself. "Listen to me, if he comes—*when* he comes back, and I want you to listen to me *very* carefully, do you hear, and do *exactly* as I say—when he comes back, I want you to promise me that you will pack up and get—no, no, *scratch* that. Don't wait for him. Right now, do you hear me, *right now* I want you to call a cab, pack your bags and come here to my place and I'll see to it you get the hell out of this town *tonight*. You've done the same thing—don't you see?—the *same thing* that I almost did, but *I* knew they'd *kill* me, so I just bucked up and went on with my life. And that's what you're going to have to do, Lauren, you're going to have to walk away from it.''

Lauren sat on the edge of the bed, rigid with horror, perspiration breaking out on her brow. "Whuh-what're you talking about? I-I duh-don't understand, walk away from *what*? What're you *saying*?"

"This problem, Lauren, you're going to have to walk away from this problem."

Lauren suddenly felt ill. "My *son*? You want me to walk away from my *son*? Why, do . . . do you *know* something? Tell me, do you know what's happened to Nathan? *Tell me!*" she hissed. "Tell me what they're doing to my son in there, tell me, tell—"

At that moment, she lifted her head to see Jordan standing just inside the door.

——— FIVE ———
THE GATHERING

1.

Night.
The road hummed beneath the car punctuated by the cracks
in the pavement that made small *ka-bop* sounds against the tires.
But Marvin didn't hear them or the music playing at low volume
on the radio because he was too involved in his conversation
with Lizzie Murphy.

At first, he'd thought she was just another one of *them*, one
of those smiling have-a-nice-day televangelist-watching fanatical
fundamentalist Christians who were always cheerfully defensive
under any circumstances and who pleasantly informed everyone
else that *they* were going straight to hell. He didn't like fanatics
of any kind—and he certainly didn't think the Christians had any
corner on the market—because they were impossible to reason
with and if they did not have their beliefs to cling to, they'd be
under the same roof as the likes of Mike Lumley.

But in the case of Lizzie Murphy, he was terribly mistaken.

2.

After leaving him at the coffee counter for a while, Lizzie had
returned with a heavy suitcase, just as she'd promised, and set
them down behind him.

"Let me get my purse," she said, turning.

"No, wait."

She didn't wait.

"Wait!" he barked, standing.

She stopped, turned to him.

"Mrs. Murphy, I did not—"

"Oh, please call me Lizzie."

Marvin closed his eyes a moment, summoned patience, then smiled and said, "I really didn't come here to *get* you, just to talk. If you don't mind, of course."

She shrugged. "Sure. If you want to do that first, I don't mind. But I think we'd save time if we started driving first."

Marvin was thoroughly confused. He frowned and rubbed the back of his neck. "What do you mean we'd save time?"

"Oh . . . I thought you would have figured all that out by now."

"Figured all *what* out? By *when*?" He was sounding irritated now, unable to hide his impatience.

"I see. Well . . . maybe we *should* sit down and talk." She went behind the counter, got a diet cola, said, "Come with me," and led Marvin down a corridor to what appeared to be a sort of lounge. Chairs were scattered around a round table in the center. Coffee brewed on a counter beneath a window with packets of creamer, sugar and artificial sweetener gathered in little containers beside it.

They sat at the table facing one another and Lizzie popped open her cola, sipped a few times and swallowed slowly, so there was a long silence in the room.

Marvin cleared his throat. "Mrs. Mur-uh . . . Lizzie, no offense, but so far I haven't understood anything you've said. Did someone *tell* you I was coming, is *that* how you knew?"

"Well, I didn't exactly know *you* were coming, you specifically. I just knew *someone* would be coming to ask questions about Hester Thorne. I guess *know* is the wrong word; I suspected . . . I had a feeling."

"How? Why?"

"I've known Hester for a long time, Marvin. You don't mind if I call you Marvin, do you? Anyway, we went to school together, and ever since the fifth grade, I've known that, sooner or later, something would bring us back together again . . ." Her voice softened a bit and she frowned thoughtfully as she looked down at her drink. ". . . that something would . . . I don't know, put us face to face . . . again."

"You say 'again.' "

She nodded.

"So you've had a confrontation with her before?"

"Oh-ho yes," she said with a cold and heavy laugh, as if he'd made an understatement.

Marvin said, "I read an article that mentioned you recently, and it said—"

"Oh, that," she sighed, rolling her eyes.

"Did they misquote you?"

"No."

"Then why the reaction?"

"That article just . . . well, it stirred up some trouble for me. That's all."

"What kind of trouble."

"With the Alliance. They didn't like what I said, needless to say, and Hester sent a few of her drones out to see me. It wasn't a social visit, either."

"They came here?"

"No, I didn't have this place then. I was back in Wheatland trying to figure out what to do with my life. The reporters came, asked me what I thought of Hester Thorne and the Alliance, so I told them. I said I thought the New Age in general, and the Alliance in particular, were among Satan's slickest and most attractive deceptions and being lured in by them was like being romanced and finally seduced by someone who is actually a bloodsucking vampire, except that the Alliance doesn't suck blood, it sucks souls. Something like that. Anyway, Hester wasn't flattered, and a few days after the magazine came out, three guys showed up at my house and broke a few things to show me just how *much* she wasn't flattered."

"You mean they damaged your property?" Marvin was appalled and, at the same time, pleased because this information was a real find.

Lizzie looked troubled; she fidgeted in her chair and ran her tongue around in her cheek. "Yes. They . . . damaged some furniture, broke a few, um, knick-knacks and, um . . . they, um . . . killed my dog."

"I'm . . . terribly sorry to hear that," Marvin said. He was stunned; these people were clearly not afraid of getting into trouble, not if they didn't hesitate to put on such an ugly show. "How long ago was this?"

"Five . . . maybe six years."

"And nothing was done?"

"What was to be done? Surely you know enough about the Alliance to know it would have been useless to tell the police."

"It would?"

"Sure."

"You're saying all the police are involved?" His voice sounded heavy with disappointment; it looked like Lizzie Dayton was another nut after all.

"Of *course* not. I'm saying the Alliance covers its behind better than anybody since the U.S. government."

"Ah, I see," he nodded, feeling a tad better.

"They would've made me look like a fool. No one would've believed me. If I'd done that, I wouldn't have been able to get an *insurance salesman* to talk to me after the Alliance was done running me through a ringer."

"So what did you do?"

"I came here and went about my business. Never forgot it, though. Somehow, I knew it would come up again, would be important. Like right now. Just like I knew I would confront Hester sooner or later. I've had so many dreams about those men and . . . my poor little dog. About Hester and the vision she—uh, well, I haven't gotten to that yet. But I never *dwelled* on those things. The chapel keeps me busy. And happy." She was quiet a long time, thoughtful, then: "Why don't I back up and start at the beginning."

"Fine."

"You promise you're not going to laugh at me or give me that look you probably give people you think are insane?"

He shrugged, smiled. "I don't want to promise anything until I've heard what you have to say."

"*Good* for you," she said, patting the table for emphasis. "That way you won't make a liar of yourself. The only reason I ask is, um . . . some of this is going to sound a little crazy. But you *do* want to hear everything I can tell you about Hester Thorne, right?"

"That's right."

"Okay, then . . ."

After a few swallows of her cola, Lizzie began, speaking carefully, self-consciously at first, and being very choosy with her words as she told Marvin what it had been like to go to school with Hester Thorne. She told him of Hester's blind popularity among students and faculty alike, of her smiling cruelty and the way it seemed to spread like contagion among her little follow-ers. She told him of Hester's hurtful pranks, of the things Hester had said and done to Lizzie and the horrible things she'd seen Hester do to small animals. And then Lizzie recounted for Mar-vin that day on the school playground when her anger got the best of her and she pushed Hester from the swing and Hester showed Lizzie a vision that had been vividly branded on her memory ever since.

As she described what she'd seen in detail, Marvin felt him-self tense up and realized his palms were slick with perspiration. Although he wanted very much to dismiss her account as some sort of religious delusion inspired by the apocalyptic book of Revelations—no matter how hard he *tried* to dismiss it—he could not. She spoke with eloquence—not the eloquence that came with rehearsal, but that came with the vivid memory of a trau-matic event. Rather than telling Marvin of the experience, she was reliving it for him in her mind and pulling Marvin into the experience with her words.

Her story gave him a heavy, ominous feeling; he found him-self thinking of Jordan and Lauren in Grover, hoping they were okay.

When Lizzie was done, Marvin cleared his throat again and asked, "Why do you think that happened, Lizzie?"

She shrugged. "There are several possible reasons. To frighten me. To make me feel hopelessly insignificant. To show me what was coming and make me feel helpless. Or maybe it knew we would meet again and it wanted to plant in my mind early on the seed of failure, to convince me decades in advance that I would be defeated in any conflict."

"It? What do you mean, *it*? Are you referring to Orrin? You think she's been involved with Orrin since she was a child?"

"Of course. That was what spoke to me through her on that playground."

"Orrin."

"If you want to call it that."

The next question stuck in his throat because he was pretty sure what her answer would be: "And what, uh . . . what would *you* . . . call it?"

She smiled. "Satan."

He looked at her smile for a long time, sipped his coffee and tried not to show his disappointment as he muttered, "Mmmm.

Satan, huh? Is that the part you thought would make me look at you like you're insane?''

"Oh, no. I figured the vision would do that. But you obviously don't believe in Satan."

"I'm not a very religious person, Lizzie. No, I don't really believe in Satan."

"That's okay. Satan, as they say, believes in you."

He chuckled. "Correct me if I'm wrong, but I believe Satan is strictly a Christian belief. What connection would he have to a non-Christian belief like the Alliance?''

"Do you agree that the Alliance can be categorized as spiritualism?''

"Sure."

"Well, they borrow extensively from everything—Christianity, Buddhism, Judaism, Hinduism, just about every religion. Even *Satanism*, believe it or not; the idea that the only judge you have to answer to is yourself is big with Anton LeVey. So it appeals to everyone. It claims that you can worship God and Christ and *still* communicate with aliens and dead people. Of course, that idea has no biblical backing whatsoever. And it's certainly not new. Spiritualism has always been around. King Solomon consulted a medium, according to the Bible. Others did the same.

"And, as far as I can tell, the American spiritualist movement goes back to 1848 in Hydesville, New York. The family of a peppermint farmer, the Foxes, began hearing strange poundings and knockings on their walls at night. After several nights, the youngest of the two daughters, Kate, communicated with the source of the knocking by snapping her fingers and asking it to answer. It did. The family worked out a code—silence meant no and one knock meant yes—and found that the source was—or *claimed* to be—a salesman who had been killed in the house years before. Everyone in town came to talk with this spirit. They asked it questions about the afterlife, about the future, about their own problems and desires.

"Someone wrote a little book about it. News of the Hydesville Rappings, as they were known, spread fast and finally reached Leah Fox Fish, one of the Foxes' older daughters whose husband had left her and her little girl. Leah saw dollar signs and rushed to Hydesville to her parents' house and asked her little sisters, Kate and Maggie, exactly how they were making the sounds because she didn't believe the dead salesman story for a second. They told her they'd tied an apple to a string that led to their bed and pulled on it at night, knocking the apple against the wall. It was intended as a joke, is all, but it got out of hand, and when people started coming around *talking* to the ghost, they had to devise more sophisticated methods. And their methods worked because the folks were lining up to talk with this spirit. Well, Leah knew a good scam when she saw one and ended up taking her little sisters all over the country to give lectures, conduct séances and communicate with the dead. *Everybody* wanted to talk with spirits, ask for advice, learn from their wisdom. The Fox sisters met their need as they traveled. They also made a lot of money.''

"Okay, but I don't see what this has to do with Satan," Marvin said. "They were fakes."

"Yes, they were fakes, but five years after the Hydesville Rappings, do you know how many professional and amateur mediums there were in America? About thirty thousand. The movement literally exploded. People all over the place were consulting the dead, seeking their advice. They've been doing it ever since. Human beings seem to crave magic, mysticism and, of course, answers. So, obtaining *answers* in a *mystical* way from *spirits* has always been very popular. Like I said, there's really nothing *new* about the so called New Age."

"Fakes. They're all fakes. You're talking about a con man's playground. I don't see the connection to your Satan."

"First of all, he's not mine. Secondly, if *you* were Satan, Marvin, if *you* wanted to foil God, your archenemy, if you wanted to confuse His children and turn them away from Him, how would you do it?"

"Please, Lizzie, I really don't have a lot of time and I just wanted to ask you a few—"

"No, please, give me a second. What would you do? Would you possess little girls and make them curse and growl, make their heads spin around and send pea soup shooting out of their mouths? You think that would win anybody over? Or would you appear in a gentler way? As something like, say, a spirit? How's this sound: a spirit that has nothing but good news about the afterlife and reassures people that their dead loved ones are happy . . . when actually the Bible says, in Ecclesiastes 9:5, that 'the dead *know not any thing*.' A spirit that tells people they've lived

before and will live again and again in other bodies . . . when
the Bible says the dead *sleep* . . . a spirit that tells people they
are completely self-contained, when God said, 'Thou shalt have
no other gods before me' . . . a spirit that tells people what they
want to hear, that makes them happy, makes them feel good . . .
isn't that what you'd do?''

"Yeah, I-I . . . yeah, I suppose something like that would
work.''

"It does work. He's the greatest con man in the universe.
Always has been. Coming off as a monster, like he does in the
movies, would defeat his purpose. He uses beauty and twists the
truth and people line up around the world.''

"But you're assuming I believe in the Bible, which I don't.
Well, not anymore . . . I was raised in a Christian family, but
that was a long time ago. And you're assuming these mediums
are all *real* when you just told me yourself about this apple on
a string trick. I may not like frauds like the Fox sisters and
Hester Thorne, but I certainly don't think they're *satanic*. They're
just making a buck off of the gullible and are, for the most part,
harmless.''

"Ah, but if you were Satan, isn't that what you'd *want* some
people to think? If the ones who are on the look-out for you
think you're a fraud, then they won't take you seriously and you
can go about the business of sucking up all the people who *do*.''

He sighed, rubbed his eyes beneath his glasses. "What are
you getting at?''

"Just because a few of them are frauds doesn't mean they *all*
are. Look at my *own* belief. It's riddled with frauds. Look at all
the televangelists who've been caught with their pants down or
their hands in the offering plate. But does that mean *all* Christian
ministers should be dismissed as crooks? No, not any more than
a few cleverly deceptive mediums and channels mean that *all* of
them should be dismissed as frauds. Hester Thorne is *not* a fraud.
I knew that long before I ever found out exactly what she *is*. I
believe her to be completely genuine *and* evil, but I'm apparently the only one who combines the two. Those who believe
she's *not* genuine think she's harmless and those who think she
is genuine think she holds the wisdom of the ages and will be a
savior to all mankind. So that leaves me looking rather silly.
Except I'm right. I *know* I'm right.''

As she spoke, Marvin thought of the Alliance seminar he and

Jordan had gone to just a few weeks before. The bad feeling he'd had then began to come back. He remembered the look on Hester Thorne's face, the lights that shattered and sent sparks raining down, and the icy wind that had swept through the room.

"Are you okay?" Lizzie asked.

Marvin blinked, pulling himself from his thoughts. "Hm?"

"You looked troubled."

"Oh. I was, uh . . . just remembering something."

"Want to talk about it?"

He decided against it at first, then, with a what-the-hell shrug, he told her about what he and Jordan had witnessed at the seminar.

Lizzie's face darkened. "And you *still* think she's a fraud?" she asked quietly, almost as if her feelings were hurt. "After seeing *that*? What did you think, she had a wind machine hidden under her dress?"

"Everything happened very quickly. It started, then it was over and we were out of there. I was never really quite sure what I saw and I'm still not. I just told you what I *think* I saw."

"Who was this woman who burst into the place?"

"Uh, sort of a client of ours."

"A client of you and your friend. You're private investigators?"

"Sort of."

"What's that mean?"

"He's a private investigator, I'm in another part of that business, and sometimes we work together. We've been hired to look into the Alliance, that's all."

"This woman who was shouting about her husband . . . she's hired you to find him?"

"I'm not at liberty to give out that information."

"I see. Have you discovered anything interesting about Hester?"

"Just doing research, really. I tried to talk with the Thornes earlier today, but . . . I was, um, unsuccessful."

"I can believe that."

"My friend is in Grover. I don't know what he's learned."

"Why don't we go see." She stood.

"Wait a second. Like I said before, I didn't come here to get you. I'm working now, I can't just pick people up and—"

"I can tell you the rest of my story in the car, and if you'd like, we can stop by Wheatland on our way and you can talk with the Thornes. I know them.''

He stopped and thought about that a moment; it was tempting. Then: ''I don't think it would be a good idea for you to come to Grover and get involved in—''

''Look, I'm coming whether I'm with you or not. If you leave here without me, I'll be right behind you. I *told* you I've been prepared for this for a while now. Marvin, you need me.''

That made him a little angry and he stood. ''What do you mean, I *need* you? Why the hell do I—''

''Because you're getting involved with something you don't even believe in. It's something very big and very dangerous. And I not only believe in it . . . I know how to *fight* it.''

3.

As they headed north on Interstate 5, Marvin still could not believe he'd allowed Lizzie to talk him into it and still wasn't sure how she'd managed. Jordan probably wasn't going to like it; they'd already taken on one extra person and when he learned they'd taken on another, he wouldn't be pleased.

It had taken them a little while to get away from the chapel, because on their way out, Lizzie had been approached by a stick-thin little man with an oversized head and no teeth. He was bald on top with long dark hair all around, had no eyebrows and grinned at her ceaselessly. His dirty, tattered clothes possessed an odor that was impossible to ignore, but Lizzie didn't seem to notice. She met him with a grin.

''Well, Teddy, you're back,'' she said very loudly, leaning toward his right ear. ''How's it going?''

''The thame, Lithie, the thame.'' He nearly shouted his words.

She opened her arms and gave him a hug. ''I think it's time to wash those clothes of yours, Teddy. Why don't you go in the back and talk to Bev.''

''Yeah? Okay, okay. You gotta plathe for me to thtay, Lithie?''

''We've *always* got a place for you, you know that.''

They talked for a while, then a round old woman approached and struck up a conversation with Lizzie. Then a younger woman dressed in filthy rags and flanked by two small children. Lizzie accepted each of them unflinchingly and spoke to them no differently than she'd spoken to Marvin.

At first, Marvin was annoyed that they were being delayed, but after watching Lizzie for a while with the weary travelers and the transients, he was touched.

Once they were on the road, Lizzie talked about the Thornes.

"They kept to themselves," she said. "No one in town knew much about them. I knew them from church. They showed up every week. They weren't rich, of course, and I think that made them very self-conscious. They struggled financially but seemed to provide well for Hester. Everyone seemed to think that Hester was their pride and joy, to the point of being spoiled. But I always wondered about that. Sometimes I got the impression they didn't spoil her so much as they *appeased* her. I told you what a temper she had. I'm sure the playground wasn't the only place that came out. And after the experience *I* had with her, I wondered how much her parents knew about her. Maybe they were *afraid* of her. I know if I had a little girl like that . . . who could do what she did to me . . . *I'd* be afraid of doing the wrong thing, making her angry, setting her off. Yes, I have a feeling there was very little discipline handed out in that house."

"So what do you have in mind?" Marvin asked. "Are you planning on asking the Thornes about Hester's . . . I don't know what to call it . . . her *powers*?"

"Not right away. I'd just like to talk with them about her, watch their reactions, see how they behave."

"What do you think made Hester that way?"

Lizzie was quiet awhile, thinking, then she shrugged. "Who knows."

The sky was smeared with purple and orange from the setting sun by the time Marvin stopped the car just short of pulling into the Thornes' long driveway.

He turned to Lizzie and asked, "Now, you're sure these people will be glad to see you."

"I didn't say that."

"What?"

"I said they *knew* me, I didn't say they'd be glad to see me."

Marvin closed his eyes, put his elbows on the steering wheel and his face in his hands. It was going to continue like this, he just knew it, with Lizzie testing his patience and Jordan's, and Jordan finally making him take her all the way back to Irving.

She *did* know a great deal about Hester Thorne and she *was* very interesting, but she was a big mistake.

"Do you know," Marvin said deliberately, "what these people do to visitors they're not glad to see? They feed them to the *dog*, is what they do."

"They have a dog?"

"No, no. They have a genetic experiment gone *awry*, is what they have. A pit bull that looks like something out of a Japanese monster movie. It tried to eat my car this morning."

She smiled. "I'm not too worried. Let's go."

"Well, you're the only *one* in here who's not too worried." He put the car into gear and turned onto the dusty road. "What do you plan on saying to these folks? Providing you get to speak before that mutant with a collar rips your throat out." He got no response. When he glanced at her, Lizzie was wearing a relaxed expression and her eyes were closed. "Hello? Hey. *Hey!*"

Her eyes opened slowly. "Does my praying bother you?" she asked with a slight smile.

Marvin felt as if he were about to blush, like a little boy who'd just stepped in on his mother undressing. "Uh . . . oh. I see. I'm, uh, sorry."

"You ought to try it sometime," she said as they continued down the bumpy road. "It's very comforting and anyone who tells you it doesn't work hasn't done it enough."

"What did you ask for . . . if, uh, you don't mind my asking."

"No, I don't mind. I asked for help."

"Ah. I see. Well . . . I'm not sure I believe in God, myself."

"Oh, really?" She thought about that a moment, then turned to him and smiled. "You know, a planeful of athiests are likely to start praying if the plane's going down."

He laughed and said, "You think so?"

"Don't *you* think so?"

Marvin didn't say so, but he *did* think so.

He parked in the same place he'd parked earlier that day. In fact, his clipboard was still lying on the ground untouched. When they got out of the car, it was only with great effort that he managed to make his legs work. His eyes were not still for a second as he watched for any sign of the dog, knowing he wouldn't hear it when it came.

Lizzie, on the other hand, walked with confidence, head held high as she went up the front steps to the porch, tan clutch purse tucked under her left arm. She gave four sharp knocks then took a step back.

Marvin stood behind her, watching nervously for the pit bull as he reached inside his coat to turn on the recorder.

There was movement inside, but no answer.

Lizzie stepped forward and knocked again, then waited.

When there was still no answer, Marvin moved up to her side and said quietly, "Look, there's really no point in this. It's not necessary. Why don't we just—"

A bare yellow light bulb above the door came on and the door opened a crack. Marvin saw the same woman peering out that he'd seen that morning.

"*You* again," she hissed. "You oughtn'ta come back here. My husband's goin' out the back door and you know what *that* means, don'tcha? He's gonna be comin' 'round here with—"

"Mrs. Thorne?" Lizzie said, smiling. "I'm Lizzie Dayton. Remember me?"

The woman squinted at her, looked her up and down, then said. "Oohh, yeah. I 'member you." She opened the door a little more, her face softening with a cautious smile. "How you been?"

"I've been just fine, Mrs. Thorne. And how about you and your husband?"

"Oh, we been—" She stopped and her smile fell away as she glanced past them and scanned the front yard quickly. Then: "What're you doin' with *him*?"

"This man is a friend of mine. He means no harm and he's not trying to trick you into anything. He just needs very *much* to talk with you, and I thought that, since I haven't seen you in so long, I'd come along and catch up on things."

"Oh. Well, um . . . ." She reached up and tugged on her lower lip, frowning. "Corben's not gonna like it, but . . ." She seemed torn, even a little afraid, and was about to speak again when—

—Marvin heard familiar footsteps on the gravel and spun to see a dark figure standing in the twilight. And hunkering beside it was the dog.

"Oh, God," Marvin breathed.

"Corben!" Mrs. Thorne called, opening the door and stepping out. She was tiny with a slight hunch to her back and her brown-streaked silver hair was so thin that her pink scalp was visible in patches. "It's Lizzie. 'Member Lizzie Dayton? She's come to—"

"I don't care 'bout her," the man said in his deep, quiet voice. "All I know is that this fella don't know when he ain't wanted. *Do* ya, mister?"

Marvin's mouth worked but nothing came out at first, until: "I—I was juh-just wondering if m-maybe I could speak with—"

Before Marvin could finish, Mr. Thorne made that sound again and the rock-solid dog shot forward and around the corner of the front porch toward the steps and—

—Marvin stumbled backward, mumbling, "Oh my God oh my God" and he swung his arm up, pushing Lizzie away from the steps and toward the door where—

—Mrs. Thorne backed into the house and closed the door on them and—

—Marvin slammed his back against the door as the dog's deep growl became louder and its paws made chittering sounds coming up the porch steps and—

—Lizzie stepped forward, almost casually, until she was standing at the top of the steps and Marvin shouted, "No no get away from—" but he didn't finish because—

—the dog stopped just two steps down from her.

Lizzie stood motionless, her head bowed to stare down at the dog. She didn't move a muscle.

Neither did the dog. It froze on the steps, staring up at her, its lip quivering ever so slightly, its growl continuing like the idle of a distant engine.

Mr. Thorne came away from the corner of the house and stood at the bottom of the steps. "What the *hell's* a-matter with you, dammit! *Hee-yup!* C'mon, dog, *hee-yup!*"

But the dog did not move. It didn't even react to the man's voice. It simply stared at Lizzie, its growl slowly diminishing until it was making no sound at all, its head lowering gradually but its eyes staying on Lizzie, until—

—the pit bull made a soft whimpering sound and turned its eyes away, looking shamed as it turned and started back down the steps. Marvin noticed something astonishing: the dog's tail was tucked between its hind legs.

Mr. Thorne stared up at Lizzie, his jaw slack. The dog returned to his side.

"You really should put that dog on a leash, Mr. Thorne," Lizzie said. "He might hurt somebody."

He stared at her a moment longer, then kicked the pit bull and shouted, "*Git* outta here! *Go* on! Damned coward, *git!*"

The dog kicked up gravel as it ran yelping around the corner of the house. Mr. Thorne followed, grumbling to himself.

"How the hell did you do that?" Marvin hissed when Lizzie turned.

She smiled. "I *told* you I asked for help, didn't I?"

Coffee brewed as Marvin, Lizzie and Mrs. Thorne sat at a table in the bright, spotless kitchen. Mr. Thorne said nothing to them and stayed in another part of the house.

The house was old-fashioned with lots of old wooden furniture and handmade afghans on the two sofas and the chairs in the large living room and several braided rugs positioned here and there on the hardwood floor. There were no family pictures on the walls, tables or fireplace mantel. In fact, there were no photographs at all in the house. Instead, the walls were decorated with paintings and drawings of Christ, some framed, some not, and crosses of wood and plastic, some with small figures of Christ hanging on them. There were needlepoint samplers that quoted scripture. One in particular had caught Marvin's attention in the hall between the living room and kitchen. It read:

> SATAN HIMSELF
> MASQUERADES AS
> AN ANGEL OF LIGHT
> *II CORINTHIANS 11:14*

"You know, I suspect you and Hester didn't get on so well," Mrs. Thorne said to Lizzie, smiling crookedly as her fingers fidgeted with one another.

"No, I'm afraid we didn't."

"Didn't think so. Hester didn't get on well with certain people."

"How did she get on with you?" Lizzie asked.

Mrs. Thorne pulled her thin, papery lips between her teeth and bowed her head as she shook it slightly. "We tried, but . . . well, she just never seemed to take to us either." She lifted her head. "I don't understand. If you ain't gonna write a book or a article, how come you're askin' all this stuff?"

Lizzie said, "Some people went up to Grover where Hester's group is and they never came back. Mr. Ackroyd is trying to help find them. We thought you might be able to tell us something that would be helpful."

She turned to Marvin and studied him for a while. "You think maybe Hester's done something bad?"

"I-I don't know, Mrs. Thorne, I just thought maybe you'd—"

"If you don't know, then you don't know anything about the Alliance."

"Why do you say that?" Lizzie asked.

"You were born in the faith, Lizzie. Your momma took you to church every week. You've accepted Christ and you know the Bible. Ain't nothin' good about what Hester's doin' now and you know it. She's still my daughter and I love her with all my heart and always will, but . . . I'll never know how she came to believe what she believes now. She didn't get it from this house."

Marvin asked, "Does she know how you feel about her beliefs."

"Oh, I suspect she does. But Hester's had nothin' to do with us for . . . oh, a lotta years. I just about lost track, I think. Breaks my heart, too. Her daddy lost patience with her a *long* time ago and don't even want to hear her name, but I know it hurts him, too. Deep inside." She scowled. "Letting that . . . that *thing* she calls *Orrr*-in talk through her."

"What do you think Orrin is, Mrs. Thorne?"

She stared at her hands a moment and watched her restless fingers, then said, "I don't know," as she pushed her chair away from the table abruptly, stood and went to the coffee maker. "Who wants java?"

They both said they'd like some and told her how they took it. As she poured their coffee, Lizzie said, "Surely you have some opinion about Orrin. It seems everyone else in the free world does. Not all of them are good, I'm sure you know." She waited for a response, but none came; Mrs. Thorne simply busied herself at the counter. "When did you first find out about Orrin?"

The old woman dropped a spoon and it clattered into the sink as she leaned against the counter, shoulders rising and falling with slow breaths.

"Mrs. Thorne? Are you all right?"

"Oh, sure, Lizzie, I'm fine." She brought their coffee and

returned to her seat, but she looked preoccupied and shaken, as if she were thinking thoughts she did not want to think.

"So," Lizzie said. "What *do* you think of Orrin?"

Mrs. Thorne's eyes met neither Lizzie nor Marvin's. She stared at her coffee, looking uncomfortable. Her eyebrows rose, then fell, rose, then fell, and her lips squirmed, quivered, opened, closed. The tears came slowly and she blinked rapidly to hold them back. When they finally trickled down her pale, wrinkled cheeks, Lizzie reached over and put her hand on Mrs. Thorne's.

"I try to come up with somethin' else," Mrs. Thorne whispered, voice trembling. "I try and try, but . . . I always come to the same conclusion. When I read her books and listen to her tapes . . . when I hear about her on the radio and read about her in the newspapers . . . I always come to the same conclusion. There's . . . some . . . *demon* in my little girl. Some horrible *monster* come to twist her soul into a weapon against God. Heaven knows we did our best to teach her right when she was growing up, but still, there were times . . . like once when we was arguing about church. When she was a little girl, Hester seemed to like church fine and went every week. Then, when she got older, she didn't like it so much, wanted to stay home or go over to a friend's house to watch the tee-vee. Then she just stopped. Refused to go. I talked to her about it one day and she threw a tizzy. Started breakin' things in her room, callin' me names—awful names, the most *horrible* names, words I didn't know she *knew*—and for a second there, just for a little second, so quick I wasn't even sure for a while if I heard it, she spoke in this . . . *voice*. T'wasn't Hester's voice. And I knew—I still know today—that she couldn't've *possibly* changed her voice *that* much. It was a man. A deep, cold man's voice."

"What did it say, Mrs. Thorne?" Lizzie asked urgently.

"Oh, I won't repeat such things, I won't pass such words over my lips. It was just a second of profanity . . . all aimed at me. Couldn't've shocked me or scared me more if she'd punched me in the mouth. Couldn't've hurt me more, either."

"Did it ever happen again?"

"Twice. Both the same. During arguments. Plus she . . . changed as she got older. Became angrier, meaner. Couldn't have any pets. She did horrible things to 'em. Don't know why, but she did. We were never sure, but we suspected her of hurtin' some of the cattle, too. She just got worse until she finally graduated from high school. And then one day she just . . . left. It seemed so sudden, like. Just left. Never hear from her. Never see her. You don't know how much I'd love to see her again, in spite of all this Orrin stuff. I think I'd burst with joy to see my baby. He'd never admit it, but I suspect Corben would, too. He's gotta tough skin, but . . . but . . .''

Until that moment, her tears were accompanied only by the slightest quiver in her voice, but she suddenly quaked with sobs that came out as mere whimpers from behind her tightly closed lips. Her body grew limp and she leaned forward, elbows on the table, hands covering her face. Lizzie stood and went to her side, putting an arm around her hitching shoulders. "How could it happen?" Mrs. Thorne asked, her voice a harsh, ragged whisper. "What'd we do wrong, huh Lizzie?" she sobbed. "Whatta you suppose brought this on? D'you suppose it happened when she was born? I never told nobody 'bout her birth.''

"What about her birth, Mrs. Thorne?" Lizzie asked.

"Hester was born dead. She was stillborn.''

Marvin and Lizzie exchanged a glance.

"She was born right here in this house. We had a midwife. She cried out when she realized the baby wasn't breathin' and then started snifflin' like a little girl. Corben saw what was wrong and started prayin' right beside me, prayin' like I never heard him pray before. Then pretty soon we heard the cry. A loud wail. We knew our baby was alive. The midwife just stared at it, pale as a ghost. And then . . . then . . . later . . .'' She turned her teary eyes upward to Lizzie. "Why? Was it a punishment for Corben and me? Did God allow the devil to enter our baby when she was born?''

Lizzie pulled her chair to Mrs. Thorne's side and sat down, taking her hand. "You can't blame yourself for this, Mrs. Thorne. It has nothing to do with you. God wouldn't want you to hurt yourself like that. Keep in mind that we're not sure *what's* happened to Hester. We'll never know how many proddings the Lord's given her, how many times He's tapped on her shoulder. We all have a *choice* as to whom we serve, Mrs. Thorne. Hester's made hers. All we can do is pray she'll change her mind.''

Marvin could tell by the look on Lizzie's face that she didn't think that would ever happen.

4.

They'd driven in silence for a while after leaving the Thornes, but once they'd started talking, they hadn't stopped, and were still at it even now as Marvin drove through the night.

"Well, maybe the Universal Enlightened Alliance is *right*," Marvin was saying, playing the devil's advocate . . . quite literally, in this case. "Maybe they're harmless and their teachings have a lot of truth to them. Maybe Satan has nothing to do with them at all. And even if he does, Lucifer, if I'm not mistaken, means 'bringer of light.' "

"You're right, Lucifer does mean 'bringer of light.' But the *Enola Gay* was a bringer of light, too, and I don't think you'll find any Japanese people to agree that it was harmless."

"Yeah, but that was a war."

"And this isn't?"

They talked a little about one another. Marvin told her how he got into the electronic surveillance business and Lizzie told him about her brief marriage.

"He was in Wheatland visiting relatives. We met in church. A nice man, ten years older than myself but such a charming gentleman. He was quite wealthy, too, but that had nothing to do with my attraction to him. I didn't even *know* that then. We hit it off immediately and he came back to Wheatland to see me on weekends. That was shortly after my mother had died. After she was gone, I really had nothing holding me there in Wheatland, so when Neville asked me to marry him, I didn't hesitate to say yes."

"What about your father?"

"He was killed before I was born. Then, less than two years after we were married, Neville died. He was perfectly healthy, except he had brain cancer and we didn't know it until it was too late."

"I'm sorry."

"Oh, so was I, but I'm glad we had that time together. Anyway, after Neville died, I went back to Wheatland for a while—I'd been living in Napa, but didn't really feel comfortable there without him—until I finally decided to take the money he'd left me and start the chapel. I've been there ever since."

They chatted on as Marvin turned on the radio and searched

the dial until he found the news. An officious-sounding female voice giving the latest details of the president's planned movement of troops into the Vatican. The Russian government was playing it safe and had said nothing so far; the British prime minister, however, strongly supported the president's attempts to root out terrorists and reminded everyone that this could bring a halt to the incredible rise of terrorist activity throughout the world.

When that story was over, the voice said, "A private plane owned by Reverend Barry Hallway's Truth and Light Ministries went down this afternoon over a densely wooded area in Colorado. Passengers included Reverend Hallway himself, five members of his staff and a crew of three. There were no survivors."

She continued speaking, but her voice was a distant hum to Marvin. He stared open-mouthed into the night, a sudden chill blanketing his back and shoulders as he remembered the prediction made by Hester/Orrin at the San Francisco seminar.

"Jesus Christ," he whispered. Then, a moment later, he turned to Lizzie and muttered, "Sorry."

"Oh, you don't have to apologize to me," she said. "It wasn't my name you used."

Marvin turned to her, a smile coming on slowly, then a quiet chuckle, the shock of the news momentarily forgotten. "You're okay," he said. "For a Jesus freak."

She laughed. "And you're okay for someone who doesn't believe in anything."

"Hey, I didn't say I don't believe in *anything*."

"Well, you didn't say you *did* believe in anything. What *do* you believe in, Mr. Ackroyd?"

"Uh, well . . ." He thought awhile, scratching his chin. "I believe in, um . . . I believe . . ."

After a long pause, Lizzie said, "That's an awfully long pause." Marvin chuckled. "It's not good to go through life with no firm spiritual beliefs, Marvin. Marriages dissolve and careers end and the body falls apart and governments crumble. But no one can *ever* take away your faith, no matter how hard they try."

Music played on the radio and they said nothing as Marvin thought about how rare it was to have something that no one could take away.

5.

"Talk to you later," Lauren whispered to Joan, then hung up without taking her eyes from Jordan.

His makeup was torn from one cheek and part of his forehead and he was bleeding. He dropped his cane and tossed his cap and coat onto the bed, then began to pace the room frantically, running his fingers down his face like claws and ripping away his makeup. He was winded and trembling and his voice cracked and wavered as he asked, "Who were you talking to?"

"Nobody," she said quickly . . . *too* quickly.

"Don't tell me that." He stopped in front of her and threw the globs of makeup at her feet angrily, leaning forward onto the bed, his arms flanking her as he spat his words through clenched teeth. "Don't *tell* me *that*, dammit, *who* were you *talking* to?"

Lauren shrank away from him. "Juh-Joan Maher."

"*Who?*"

"Joan, th-the woman we muh-met yesterday. At the diner."

"And you were talking to her? Just *now?*"

She nodded timidly, suddenly afraid he was going to hit her. He looked monstrous with his makeup dangling from his face like tattered skin.

"What did you tell her? How much does she know?"

"I-I was juh-just telling her about N-Nathan. Th-that's all."

"So she knows you have a son. And that we're not married. Does she know why we're here?"

Lauren closed her eyes, sick with dread. She nodded.

"Son of a *bitch!*" Jordan barked, pushing himself away from the bed with clenched fists. He rushed to the door and threw the bolt, then faced her. "You wanna get us *killed?* Huh? What good will we do your son then, huh?"

Her fear of Jordan suddenly forgotten, she stood and asked, "What did you see?"

He turned from her and began pacing and removing his makeup again, tossing it carelessly to the floor.

"Tell me what you saw!"

"Not . . . yet. I think I should wait until we're all together."

"Who?"

"Marvin. Maybe Coogan, because we're gonna need all the help we can get." He turned to her angrily. "And since you filled your friend in on everything, we might as well bring *her* into it, too. Unless, of course, you just spilled your guts to a friend of the Alliance's.''

Lauren sank back onto the bed, whispering, ''I'm sorry.''

''Little late now.''

Her fists clenched slowly. ''I just needed someone to *talk* to. I'm scared.''

''That's why I didn't want you to come.''

''Oh, well *you* don't look very courageous at the moment. You're shaking like a leaf.''

''I . . . am?'' He stopped, looked at his hands, then backed up and plopped into a chair. ''Yuh-yes,'' he breathed, ''I'm scared, too.''

''What did you *see* tonight, Jordan?''

He closed his eyes, shook his head. ''I don't want to go into it right now. But . . . I will tell you I saw something awful. What's going on here is more than just some goofball religion. This is . . . I don't know, this is—'' He winced when he said the word. ''—evil.''

''What were they doing that was so bad? Please tell me, I *can't* wait.''

''No, no, it wasn't just what they were doing. There was something going on back there, something evil . . . a supernatural evil.''

She felt chilled. ''No. That can't be. It's just a cult. Evil, maybe, but only because of what it takes from people and does to them and their families.''

He shook his head and smirked, but it wasn't a sarcastic smirk; it was one of pity. ''You're wrong. It's *not* just that. There is a cave, just like Paul Kragen said. And they do take children there. They sacrifice them to something. They sacrificed a little girl tonight and fed her to some bright, sickening blue light that was coming from a crevice in the cave wall. And I think your husband was there.''

Lauren stared at him for a long time, then rushed to the bathroom to vomit.

Jordan sat in the chair as Lauren retched over the toilet. He tried to think of nothing, tried to clear his mind, but he could not. The telephone rang, giving him a start. He'd been expecting Marvin's call, but the fact that Lauren had told Joan Maher about them worried him and he wondered if someone *else* could be calling.

It was Marvin.

"Where are you?" Jordan asked.

"The motel in Weed. What's wrong, you sound like hell."

"Tell you later. Do you think you're up to an all-nighter?"

"Well . . . *I* am, but there's something I think you—"

"There's a guy I need to call and drag out of bed. It's risky to bring anybody in on this, I know, but in this case, I think it's necessary. He might be able to help us. How about if we all meet at your motel room?"

"Sure. We don't mind."

"We? We *who*?"

"Myself and Elizabeth Dayton."

"You *brought* her?"

"Hey, you just told me yourself that sometimes it's necessary."

"Yeah, but not *her*. The last thing we need around here is some Bible-beating Christian."

"Uh, she's not like that, Jordan. I think you'll be surprised. She knows some things about Hester Thorne that are, um . . . pretty scary."

"Yeah? Well, so do I." He sighed, exasperated. "This damned thing is turning into a circus."

"Okay. Hey, did you hear about Hallway?"

"As in Reverend?"

"Uh-huh. His private plane went down today. He's dead."

Jordan could say nothing; he had no voice and his throat felt thick.

"Blew me away, too," Marvin said. "You think it was a coincidence?"

"No. Not anymore. Maybe a couple hours ago, but not anymore."

"Me either."

"Marvin, did you ever eat a bowl of cereal as a kid and then, halfway through it, discover that the cereal was full of bugs?"

Marvin made a disgusted sound, then said, "Plenty of times."

"That's how I feel about this case."

After he hung up, Jordan sat on the bed digesting the news about Reverend Hallway. Everything was going wrong; when he'd taken the case, he'd expected the possibility of a little danger—in dealing with cults, that was much wiser—but he hadn't expected *this*. Hester Thorne had also predicted Everett Fiske's death; in the morning, Jordan would call and warn him.

Lauren came from the bathroom, walking unsteadily, and seated herself in the chair facing him. She looked pale and washed out. "There's something I should tell you," she said, her voice weak.

Jordan listened as she told him what Joan had said, both yesterday in town and that night on the telephone; she quoted some of it word for word.

"So she knew I was in danger," Jordan said.

"I think so."

After a few silent moments Jordan said, "Call her back."

6.

The Evergreen Motor Inn was a modestly priced motel, no different from any other in its class; it offered no luxuries and its rooms were meant to be nothing more than brief resting places for weary travelers. They were *not* meant to be used as meeting places for groups of six. But that is what Room 9 became that night.

There were only two chairs positioned at a round table, a small footstool and the bed to serve as seats, but they were sufficient. Lauren and Lizzie were given the chairs while Joan sat on the bed with Coogan and Marvin.

Joan held Coogan's hand; he was visibly upset. When Jordan called, he'd been angry at first, complaining about the hour and returning to his accusations that Jordan was a reporter. He'd become much more receptive, however, the moment Jordan said he knew something about Coogan's granddaughter Katie. He'd finally agreed to meet at the Evergreen and to bring as much hot coffee as he could carry.

He'd brought it in two containers, which stood on the table between Lauren and Lizzie; he'd also brought several large-size Styrofoam cups and each person in the room had one filled with steaming coffee.

The air in the room was thick with discomfort; Joan and Lauren fidgeted and smoked along with Coogan, whose Camel trembled between his fingers and Lizzie scratched a fingernail back and forth along the edge of the table. Jordan paced rapidly about the room as he spoke, stopping occasionally to perch a foot on the stool and rest an arm on his knee as his fingers twitched. Marvin was the calmest of the lot.

Jordan began by explaining everyone's presence there.

Coogan interrupted: "Why the hell didn't you tell me all this in the first place? I would've kept quiet and given you all the help I could."

"I didn't know that," Jordan said. "I had to play it safe."

"Yeah. Guess so."

Then Jordan told them what he'd seen that night.

The silence that followed was stifling and it lasted for a couple of minutes. When the implications of Jordan's story sunk in, Lizzie gasped quietly, reached over and took Lauren's hand and said, "Sweetie, you must be sick to death with worry."

Lauren's lips were trembling; she looked away and concentrated only on not crying.

Jordan turned to Marvin and said, "That thing, that monster that knocked me around tonight . . . I think that explains the Bigfoot headline and the underlined references to Hester Thorne's son, because I think that thing *is* her son."

"It fits Lumley's description. He says the kid was always way too big for his age and smelled to high heaven."

"But this thing . . . it looked only vaguely human. It was *hideous*." An involuntary shiver passed through Jordan as he remembered. "I've been, uh . . . well, I've been thinking. Lumley said that Hester went for walks every morning on their honeymoon. Well, let's say, um . . . let's say she got pregnant on the first night. Let's say she was carrying Benjamin when she went on those walks and, um . . . and she *found that light*. I'm telling you, that light is . . . it's *sick*, it's *bad*. If she stood in that light while she was pregnant . . . well, if X-rays can deform a child while it's in the womb, why couldn't that light?"

"But why would she be hiding him?" Marvin asked.

"Maybe to use him. Remember the phone call from Bolton? He made references to a *monster*. Maybe Hester Thorne's deformed son is a sort of hit man, an intimidator."

Coogan had begun to smoke his cigarette rapidly since Jordan had told of the sacrifice. Now he leaned forward, one knee bobbing nervously, and asked, "Mr. Cross, when you called, you,

you said th-that you knew something about Katie. Is that true? I mean . . . whuh-what do you know?''

Jordan sat on the edge of the dressing table, running fingers through his hair as he frowned. He looked indecisive, pained, and it was a while before he replied.

"There's no good way to put this," he said quietly. "The child they sacrificed was a little girl named Katie Coogan."

Coogan stared at him through thick glasses for a long time, then let his head hang as his shoulders began to jerk up and down. "What'd she do?" he sobbed. "What'd she do with them babies? *Why?*" He took his glasses off and scrubbed his face.

Joan put an arm around his shoulders and hugged him, tossing an icy accusatory glance at Jordan.

"I'm very sorry," Jordan said.

"You shouldn't have come," Joan said, barely keeping her voice level. "You should've stayed home and kept your nose *out* of this." Then, in a heated whisper: "Look what you've *done!*"

Jordan got off the dressing table and walked over to her. "What *I've* done? I just told him about it is all. He would've found out sooner or later."

"No he—" She stopped suddenly and turned away from him.

"I think now would be a good time for you to tell us what you know, Miss Maher."

"I don't know what you're talking about."

"I mean, tell us what you know about the Alliance. About your experience with them."

"I don't know *anything.*"

"You used to be a member."

Joan turned her icy glare to Lauren.

"Please," Lauren said. "Please help us. My little boy is in there. You had a daughter, you must have *some* idea how I feel."

Coogan fought to regain composure; he sat up, wiped his red eyes and sniffed, then put his glasses back on and turned to Joan. "You know something about this?"

She didn't reply.

"You've gotta talk about it, honey. You've *got* to. If they're . . . if they're doing things like *that*—" His voice cracked. "—to them *kids* . . . oh dear Jesus, I'm . . . I . . .'' He stood, staggered toward the bathroom and fell heavily against the wall.

"Coogan!" Joan shouted, rushing to his side.

"No, no. I'm okay. Just going to the bathroom. You talk to

those folks, okay, honey? For me?'' He pushed away from the wall, went into the bathroom and began washing his face.

"Okay," she said, her back to the others. She sat on the bed, got one of Coogan's Camels and lit up. "Okay. I've been telling people for a long time that my little girl died of cancer. That's not true. In fact, I've been telling people a *lot* of things that aren't true, mostly because I don't think they'll understand the way I've handled the truth. They'll say I'm cold and unfeeling, a monster. But I'm not. I'm really not.''

The others exchanged glances during the long silence that followed until Lauren whispered, ''What really happened to your daughter?''

"Well, after my divorce, Lisa and I—that's my daughter's name—were both a mess. We'd been through a lot of abuse. Then we got another kind of abuse from my family because my husband had put up such a good front, no one realized how cruel he was to us and when I left him they thought I had no good reason, and that's something a good young Catholic woman just doesn't do. So, over time, I got involved in the Alliance.''

"How?" Lizzie asked.

"The same way a lot of people do, I suppose. I needed *something*, and a friend of mine knew someone whose brother . . . something like that. I read the literature, went to the seminars, listened to the tapes, and finally quit my job, came to Grover and gave them everything I had . . . which wasn't much. Over time, they squeeze more from you if they think you've got it, but I didn't.''

"That's what they've been doing to my daughter," Coogan said, coming out of the bathroom scrubbing his neck with a towel.

"I went through the whole program," Joan said, "which I now realize is nothing more than a sort of brainwashing process. I wasn't allowed to see Lisa. I didn't know where she was or *how* she was, but they kept promising me I'd see her as soon as her training was finished. That time never came, though, and it bothered me. Ever since I was a kid, I've never handled authority well, especially when it tells me to do something I don't *want* to do. So, in little ways at first, I began to rebel. I didn't follow the program exactly. I slept more than I was supposed to. And I did the one thing I was specifically told *not* to do: I sneaked around places when I wasn't supposed to be there. I eavesdropped on conversations. I finally met a woman, by accident, who was sort of doing the same thing I was, and for the same reason. Her name was Betty Kravitz. She had a little girl there, too. Between the two of us, we learned of something called the Inner Circle. They met frequently, but never regularly. There was no pattern to the meetings. A group of adults and a group of children would go to a cave deep in the woods. I never found out what they did in there.''

"I did," Jordan said.

"Betty disappeared shortly after that. I never saw her again. I'm sure she's dead, maybe at the bottom of a lake somewhere. I went to the people in charge, told them I'd decided to leave and I wanted my daughter. They took me to her.'' Joan's face had been without expression up to now; it began to twitch, to wilt. "She said she didn't want to go. Said she'd . . . never leave. Said she was . . . was waiting to be . . . the Chosen One . . . that she wanted to fight falsehoods like a good soldier of truth. I didn't know what the Chosen One was then, but . . . I guess I do n-now. Anyway, I left and went to the police and they talked to Hester Thorne, who said that Lisa had left with me. It was in their records. She said no one, especially a child, would ever be held by the Alliance. She told them to search the place, and they did. They didn't find her.

"Of course, I realized later that the police in Grover are taken care of very well by Hester and her people. I suspect a lot of money changes hands. That's why they didn't find Lisa, and that's why they never contradicted my story about her dying of cancer, because they knew that I knew that they knew that I . . . well, you know what I mean.

"Anyway, I was sure she was hidden, so I talked to private detectives, all of whom told me to hire someone who specialized in removing cult members. But they were *way* too . . . ex-*pen*-sive," she hissed through clenched teeth. She finally lost her hold and seemed to collapse upon herself; her shoulders sagged forward, she dropped her cigarette into the ashtray and her hands fell limply between her knees as she bowed her head and sobbed. "Cuh-can you im-imagine *that*? They were too ex-*pen*-sive? That sounds so *horrible* now, that I couldn't pay somebody to find my baby, that I couldn't find the money, I, I . . . I should've *stolen* it, I *should* have!''

Lauren went to her side and put an arm around her. Coogan lowered himself on one knee before her and held her hand tightly.

Joan pressed a fist to her face and sobbed silently for a moment, then released a low, quavering wail. The others waited silently until she had calmed and was able to continue. "I tried to kill myself," she said, her voice thick and hoarse, "but . . . I wasn't able to do that right, either. So I stayed in Grover, just to be close to where she is . . . or, um, I mean, *was*. The Alliance people tried to scare me away, but it didn't work. I wouldn't *let* it work. Whenever someone asked me about my background, I told them the truth . . . except I told them my daughter died of cancer. And . . . here I am."

Coogan sat down beside her and put his arm around her shoulders as she'd done to him earlier. "I guess we're all learning a little more about each other tonight, huh?" he asked soberly as he squeezed her to him.

After a moment, Jordan said, "Okay, now we're kind of short on time tonight, so—" He stopped when he saw the cold stares he was getting from the others; then they all turned back to Joan, who was pressing her face to Coogan's shoulder, crying softly.

Jordan pulled the footstool away from Lizzie's chair and sat on it with a sigh. "I'm sorry," he said. "I don't mean to be insensitive. Really. I'm very sorry about what happened to your daughter, Joan. After what I saw tonight, I'm sorry for *anyone* who gets involved with those people. But what I'm concerned with right now is the fact that there's something really horrible going on here, and maybe we can *do* something about it. I came here to do a specific job, but now . . . well, I mean, after what I saw . . . now I'm thinking, um . . . Well, see, I came here a confirmed agnostic, I didn't believe in *anything* supernatural, but I . . . Well, now I'm thinking that . . ." He leaned forward, sighed, and put his head in his hands.

" 'By beholding, you become changed,' " Lizzie said pleasantly.

"Hey, don't *start* with the Bible verses, okay? That doesn't *work* with me."

"Oh, I'm sorry. I thought you were saying your beliefs had changed."

"Well, yeah, maybe, but that doesn't mean I believe in *that*."

"Why not? You can't very well have forces of evil without

forces of goodness, can you? The way you were *taught* to believe is not necessarily the *only* way, remember that.''

Jordan turned to Marvin. ''What've you been telling her?''

''We discussed your background on the way here. Briefly.''

Jordan stood up angrily and paced, trying to hold back his anger.

''I think it would be a good idea,'' Marvin said, ''if Lizzie told us what she knows.''

''Fine,'' Jordan said curtly, still pacing.

Lizzie told them everything she'd told Marvin as well as what they'd learned from Hester's mother and they listened closely. Coogan seemed to be affected most; he stared at her with an expression of fear, nodding as she solidified a nebulous belief he'd always held but had never been able to articulate. Lauren was interested, but looked cautious. Joan listened closely as she continued to cry silently; her puffy eyes were intense and rejected nothing. Jordan continued to pace.

Coogan said, ''So, you're saying Hester Thorne is . . . possessed?''

''I'm not saying anything, really,'' Lizzie replied. ''Just telling you what I know. But if you want my opinion . . . I certainly wouldn't rule out that possibility. In fact, it might even top my list of priorities.''

''Well, we're not going by your list,'' Jordan snapped quietly.

Marvin said, ''C'mon, Jordy. Ease up on her, okay. She wants to help and I think she can. You agree that we've got something really weird on our hands here, right?''

Jordan stopped pacing, leaned against the wall and folded his arms across his chest. After a long moment, he nodded.

''Okay, then. I think we ought to start from there. How are we going to handle it?''

''Wait a second,'' Joan said, holding up a hand. ''I just wanna get this straight. We're going on the assumption that Hester Thorne is possessed by the devil? Because if we are, I think I'll just back out of—''

''No,'' Jordan said, ''we're not assuming that. That is just Mrs. Murphy's belief. But those things I saw flying around in that cave . . . the light that was coming from that crevice . . . Those things are not natural. So the only alternative is that they're *super*natural. You know from experience how those Alliance people are. A normal religious organization wouldn't behave that way. They're hiding something. And part of what they're hiding is what's in that cave and what they do to the children they take there. We might need your help with this and I hope you'll give it to us.''

She nodded after a while, then said, ''Yeah, okay. If I can help . . .''

Marvin stood and went to the table for a refill of coffee. In a low voice, he said, ''I think we ought to start by getting some phones tapped. Right away. Tonight.'' He turned, his eyes locked with Jordan and they stared at one another for a moment, looking very serious, very tense.

They had come, of course, with the knowledge that they would more than likely be tapping telephones, but with the hope that they would not have to. Marvin was good at it, but no one was flawless. There was always the chance they would get caught. If that happened, they had no defense. It was a felony. No matter what their reasons for tapping the lines, *they* would be the criminals if they were caught. They had done it before, and if they got away with it this time, they would probably do it again. But they hated it every time.

''Sounds good,'' Jordan said, trying unsuccessfully to sound casual about it. ''You've got everything?''

''Everything.''

''We've also got a stack of material here that I think you should all look at.'' Marvin left his coffee on the table and went to the closet to remove a brown leather satchel. He put it on the bed, opened it and removed a stack of papers, news clippings, folders and notebooks. ''This is information that's been collected about Hester Thorne and the Alliance. We'd appreciate it if each of you could look it over for anything that's significant to you, anything that you might be able to explain and anything . . . at all, I guess.''

The others gathered around the stack and began going through it as Jordan and Marvin sat at the table to talk. They leaned toward one another and spoke in low voices.

''You look pretty shaken,'' Marvin said.

''I am. I'm telling you, Marvin, that was the most terrifying experience of my life. Made me want to get the hell away from this town and tell Fiske to hire somebody else.''

''But . . .''

''Well, if we did that, the Alliance would just keep growing, maybe even get involved in politics and start having meetings with the president like the late great Reverend Hallway, how's *that* for a nightmare. Oh, and speaking of Reverend Hallway, Hester gave a similar warning yesterday about Edmond Fiske."

"Have you talked to him about it yet?"

"Not yet. I'm gonna call him in the morning."

"Okay. So. What do we do first?"

"I think we ought to get taps on the phones right away. Tonight. I know where the Alliance headquarters building is."

"Is there a basement?"

"I have no idea, that's the problem. Joan might be able to help us with that. She's probably been in there."

"When do you want to do it?"

"Right after—"

"I know this name," Lauren said.

"What name?" Marvin asked.

"This one. On this computer printout. Simon Ketter."

Jordan and Marvin joined the others around the bed. Lauren pointed to the circled name on the sheet.

"I heard this name on the news tonight, not very long ago."

"What was he doing on the news?" Jordan asked.

"He was the pilot of Reverend Hallway's plane. He died in the crash."

"Holy shit," Jordan said.

"Son of a bitch," Marvin said. Then, as an afterthought, he turned to Lizzie and said, "Excuse us."

A single bark of laughter escaped her and she shook her head, murmuring, "What do you think, I'm made of *porcelain*?"

"Maybe it's a different Simon Ketter," Marvin said.

"Maybe not," Jordan said. "It might explain the differences we noticed in this entry compared to all the others. No background, no financial history. Everyone else was covered that way, even the other withdrawals."

"That's another thing. He was a withdrawal. He left the organization."

"According to the records," Marvin said. "Maybe he left the organization by request . . . but remained faithful to it."

"And got a job with Reverend Hallway, maybe?" Coogan asked.

Marvin nodded.

"So you guys think Hester Thorne had Hallway killed to make her own prediction come true?" Coogan asked.

Jordan said, "It's beginning to look that way."

"Uh-uh," Joan said, shaking her head. "That's ridiculous. He was Hallway's *pilot*. You think he'd intentionally crash a plane that he was *in*? Just for Hester Thorne? Who in their right mind would do that?"

"Who said we were talking about someone in his right mind?" Jordan asked. "*You're* the one who used the word *brainwashing*. If this is really what happened, then he died for his beliefs. He was a martyr. That's not uncommon. Terrorists do it all the time. Earlier this year one in Washington and one in New York jumped from buildings into the street and exploded when they hit the ground. Human bombs. All for the cause. Why wouldn't one of these people do it?"

She frowned, but she couldn't argue; he was right.

Jordan led Marvin over to the bathroom doorway, out of ear-shot, and said quietly, "I'd better call Fiske right now, no matter how late it is. You talk to Joan, see what you can find out about the headquarters building." And to the others: "The rest of you just go on looking through that stack."

He went to the telephone, sat on the bed and dialed the number Fiske had given him. He reached an answering service. "Hello, I need to speak to Mr. Fiske immediately. My name is Sam Spade." He felt silly using the pseudonym, but Fiske didn't want him to use his real name and had told him to use the fictional detective's name on the telephone.

"I'm sorry," the woman said, "but Mr. Fiske is taking no calls until tomorrow. If you'll leave a message, I can have him get back to you."

"No, no, you see, he told me I could always reach him at this number."

"That's true. All messages are promptly forward to Mr. Fiske."

"So you could have him call me back tonight. Right away."

"I'm sorry, but that would be impossible. Mr. Fiske is un-available. As I said, he's taking no calls until tomorrow."

"So that means he'll be taking no messages, either."

"Mr. Spade, when Mr. Fiske is unavailable, that means *we* can't even reach him. You will *have* to wait until tomorrow. Do you have a message for Mr. Fiske?"

"Uhh, well . . ." He searched for something to say that would convey a sense of urgency to Fiske without telling the operator too much. "Yes, uh, tell Mr. Fiske that new developments have arisen that directly involve him and it's very important we talk as soon as possible. I'll call him first thing tomorrow morning." He was frustrated and slammed the receiver into its cradle.

Marvin sat down beside him and said, "No luck?"

"Uh-uh."

"Well, Joan gave me a pretty good run-down of that building. What do you say we go over there and bug some phones?"

"Sounds good. Get your stuff." Jordan stood and turned to the others, who were still looking through the stack of material collected by Harvey Bolton. "Marvin and I are going to have to go. With any luck, we won't be long. I hope you'll keep looking through that stack and I hope you'll all be here when we get back. Of course, it's up to you, but . . . well. It's up to you."

Coogan glanced at the others around him, then gave Jordan the best smile he could muster under the circumstances. "I think we're all gonna be here, Mr. Cross. You be careful."

That made Jordan feel a little better as he left.

7.

The others waited in the motel room while Jordan and Marvin went to Grover, parked a short distance from the hotel and walked the rest of the way.

Marvin had a leather satchel hanging by his shoulder from a strap and hooked to his belt was a small leather pouch that held a number of picks. Once they'd crept around the hotel and made sure no one was watching, he used two of the picks to open a side door.

They followed Joan's directions to an unmarked door at the end of the corridor; it led to the basement staircase and was kept locked. Marvin fished a couple more picks from his leather pouch as Jordan held his small flashlight on the doorknob. They were through in less than a minute, but Marvin had to use his picks again because the door to the basement was locked, too.

It was cool in the basement and even darker than the rest of the building with no windows to let in even a sliver of moonlight. HVAC ducts ran along the low ceiling surrounded by webs of pipes. The furnace took up a corner and fat, black sewer pipes snaked upward into the ceiling. Power meters hummed and clicked diligently and one wall was covered with shelves of banker's boxes, most likely filled with bookkeeping records. And on the far wall they found the telephone junction box.

"Doesn't look easy," Jordan whispered, eyeing the countless wires connected to the box, which was spotted with grime and corrosion.

"It's not. But it's not hard, either. Just give me a few minutes and I'll see if I can—" Something beside the box caught Marvin's eye. "What the hell is this?" he asked, nodding to a smaller, cleaner box. "They've got a separate line. Completely separate from the others. And it hasn't been here long. Looks kinda sophisticated, too."

"What do you think?"

"No idea," he said, shaking his head. "We'll just have to wait and see what we pick up on it. I'm gonna have to cut into each of these lines, so it's gonna take a little while. And I can't guarantee how long they'll last. These guys might do a sweep every so often . . . maybe more often than *that*."

"We'll cross that bridge when we come to it. Do your stuff."

While Jordan and Marvin whispered in the darkness of the basement, other voices whispered to Hester Thorne in dreams of vast flat and barren landscapes that she would only vaguely remember in the morning . . .

. . . Mark Schroeder sat in a small room with eleven other people and, in the flickering glow of candles, chanted softly and meditated on the coming New Age of Enlightenment. Somewhere in the complex, another group was doing the exact same thing. The groups changed every hour, but the chanting and meditating never stopped for more than a minute. Hester said that the energy it generated would help to speed the coming of the New Age and would help to "center" the participants in their purpose. It worked for Mark because, as he chanted, focusing completely on the New Age, he thought of nothing else . . .

. . . not even of Nathan, who was in the woods once again with several other children, in the middle of another of what Hester called "drills." Hester taught them that before the New Age began, there would be a time of great upheaval, which would very likely include a war in which the United States would be the target of an invasion, perhaps even a nuclear attack. Food and weapons—knives and spears that would not be dependent on ammunition, would kill silently and had been left at the foot of the crevice to bask in its blue glow for twenty-four hours and "absorb purity," Hester said—had been hidden in the woods and shelters had been prepared for the children. They were taught to fight and kill in classes held twice daily. Hester told them the responsibility of preserving and upholding the truths taught by Orrin could one day fall on their shoulders and they had to be prepared. In the event of an invasion, they would have to fight and kill the enemy, but if there were a nuclear attack, it would be even worse; people they normally trusted would become desperate for food, so desperate that once there was no more food, those poeple would try to kill and eat *them*. Such thoughts terrified Nathan. He'd never *heard* of such things, not from his parents or books or even television. If that might happen, then of course he wanted to be ready, but he'd always thought it was *adults* who fought and killed, not children. But if Orrin told Hester and Hester told them, it *must* be true.

Grover was quiet and insects hovered in small clouds around the few streetlights.

And deep in the cave behind the Sleeping Woman Inn, blue light pulsed from the crevice as Benjamin Thorne hunched on a rock in a dark nook within the cave wall where the light could not reach him. It frightened him sometimes, made him see bad things in his head, and he avoided it whenever he could.

Benjamin sat in the dark, waiting for someone to come give him something to do. Just waiting.

8.

By the time Jordan and Marvin returned to the Evergreen Motel, it was almost two a.m. and the others were getting tired. Joan had already dozed off on the bed, drained by the experience of telling her story—her *true* story—for the first time in years. Coogan would sit in one of the chairs until he began to nod off, then get up and pace, agitated and perspiring, until he finally sat down again, only to repeat the process. Lauren and Lizzie talked endlessly, Lauren mostly to ease the tension brought about by her frayed nerves, Lizzie to calm her.

"Okay, think you got it?" Marvin asked Jordan as they walked into the room.

"Yeah."

"And remember, as soon as you know or have a good guess as to which phone in the building a line goes to, jot down the number on the dial and some ID for the phone, whether it's the phone in accounting, or the mailroom, or whatever."

"I've got it," Jordan said, closing the door and turning to the others. "So, have *you* folks got anything?"

Joan awoke with a start and Coogan leaned forward taking a deep breath, trying to act as though he hadn't been nodding off.

"Well," Lizzie said, standing, "none of us have been able to find anything in this stack of any significance, *but*—" She picked up the computer printout. "—we're all pretty intrigued by this. Do you have any idea how old it is?"

"It's from last year, probably late in the year," Jordan said.

"Would it be possible to get a more recent one? Maybe one that's more complete?"

Marvin shrugged. "I brought my computer. I can give it a try. But we'd need a copy of Hester Thorne's book *Masters Among Us*, because the password is always—"

"Yes," Lizzie said, going to one of her suitcases across the room and removing a paperback book. "I brought a few of Hester's books from my collection. I thought I might get her to sign them," she added with a smirk.

"See, Jordy?" Marvin said. "I *told* you she'd be able to help us."

Jordan rolled his eyes.

Marvin got his laptop computer, printer and modem from the closet and put them on the bed. Lizzie opened the book to the appendix titled "Index of Masters."

"Would you like me to read these to you?" she asked.

Once he'd turned on the computer, called the number, placed the receiver in the modem and run his fingers over the keyboard a few times as he watched the screen, he said, "Okay, go ahead."

She read the names one at a time—names like Ishtar and St. Germain and Love-and-Peace, Joseph and Paul and Lazaris— and he typed them in, nodding for her to go on when a name was rejected, until she read Ramtha.

"Bingo!" Marvin said. Once his fingers had chattered over the keys again, the list of members appeared on the screen and the printer began to make busy chirping sounds.

They waited.

By the time the printer stopped, Marvin's hands were already poised over the keyboard to terminate the connection with the Alliance computer. Then he tore the stream of paper away from the printer and said, "Let's see what we got."

They went over the list from top to bottom, taking turns reading the names and information aloud in tired voices.

Simon Ketter was no longer listed but there was one entry exactly like his. Walter Oland was listed simply as a withdrawal with no further information or withdrawal date given.

"What do you think?" Marvin asked Jordan.

"I don't know. It could be lots of things. Ketter left the Alliance sometime last year, probably because they knew it would take a while for him to wiggle his way into Hallway's camp and get a job as his private pilot."

"*If* it's even the same Simon Ketter."

"Yeah. Anyway, we don't know *when* Walter Oland was withdrawn. He *could* have been a withdrawal when that other printout was made, but we don't have all of it. He could also be out there giving a hand to Hester Thorne's prediction about Edmond Fiske."

"Or," Joan said, "maybe he just pissed them off and they killed him."

"He *could* be a real withdrawal, you know," Lizzie suggested.

"Maybe," Jordan said. "But I've got a feeling I'm right."

They continued down the list with Lauren reading the entries aloud until—

—her voice broke suddenly and she gasped, "Oh, my God."

The others leaned forward to see for themselves what had startled her, but she read it aloud anyway, her voice trembling.

"Schroeder, Mark. Withdrawal. Schroeder, Nathan. Withdrawal."

"But he was *there*!" Jordan said. "He was there *tonight*. I heard Hester introduce him to the others. Why would he and Nathan be listed as withdrawals?"

Lauren backed away from them and plopped into a chair, a hand pressed over her mouth. "They've killed him," she murmured into her palm. "My God, they've killed my little boy."

"Now, you don't know that," Lizzie said, going to her side.

"B-but then, why does it say—"

"We don't know why yet, but we don't know that they've *killed* him, either. For all we know, that means he's leaving here. Maybe tomorrow. Wouldn't that be a good thing?"

The others watched silently as Lauren simply stared at her hands in her lap.

9.

Jordan was still awake when early daylight began to ooze across the sky. Lauren slept deeply beside him, her breaths coming in small whispery snores. He'd bought a bottle of over-the-counter sleeping pills at the drugstore the day before and she'd taken one before going to bed.

They had broken up just half an hour after discovering Mark and Nathan Schroeder on the computer printout. They'd agreed to meet in Grover in the morning, then Lizzie had accepted Coogan's invitation to stay in his spare bedroom and Joan had gone home.

Jordan hoped they were all sleeping better than he.

Birds were chattering outside the window and daylight had arrived. Jordan crept out of bed and put on his robe. He looked out the window, paced around the room awhile, then opened the case that contained telephone surveillance equipment.

He knew it was too early for it but, just out of curiosity, he put on the headphones, took Marvin's small notebook and pencil from the case, flipped a couple of switches on the machine and listened. When he heard nothing, he turned the dial from 1 to 2, then from 2 to 3. He found only silence on every line. There was nothing. He'd been right; it was too early. He doubted anybody was in the building at this hour, and he'd probably—

—a sound.

Jordan froze, listened.

It was a soft electronic warbling, the familiar sound of another telephone ringing at the other end. Someone in the headquarters building was making a call, and judging from the quiet hiss on the line, it was a long-distance call.

In the middle of the third ring, a male voice said, "Hello?"

"Hello." It was Hester; that velvety voice was unmistakable.

It sounded to Jordan as if she were *trying* to sound sexy, seductive.

Then, very respectfully. "Oh . . . *hello*."

"It's time," she said.

After a long pause: "All right."

The connection was cut.

They'd hung up.

SIX

CONFRONTATIONS

1.

It was a cloudless day and the early-morning chill wore off quickly in the bright heat of the sun.

The Lemurian Diner was packed by eight o'clock and people had to stand just inside the doorway and wait for tables. The Garden Terrace, the diner at the other end of town, was doing identical business. Even Pancho's Cantina, a Mexican restaurant that normally opened at eleven, was serving huevos rancheros and chili omelettes to a full house.

But by the time Coogan and Lizzie walked down the hill into town, they'd already had breakfast. Coogan had assumed he would be up long before Lizzie—he was used to rising early to open the store and turn on the pumps—but he'd awakened to the smell of eggs cooking and coffee brewing.

They'd eaten breakfast together, Coogan feeling oddly comfortable with this stranger. She told him about the chapel she ran and they talked about their religious beliefs, and finally, the topic of Coogan's daughter came up. But he avoided it; it was too early in the morning after a restless night to stir up *that* pain.

Coogan called Bobby in early and walked Lizzie down the hill toward Penny Park.

"We have the same spiritual beliefs, Mr. Coogan," Lizzie began after a long pause between them as they walked, but he didn't let her go on.

"Oh, please, call me Coogan. *Every*body does. Sometimes I forget I have a first name and sign my checks that way, but everybody takes them anyway."

"Okay, Coogan. We're both Christians, so you don't have to feel funny talking about your beliefs with me. So. What do you *really* think is going on here in Grover? What do you *really* think of the Alliance?''

He considered the question for a while, stuffed his hands into his pockets. ''I can't really put my finger on it, Lizzie. I may be a Christian, but I'm not a biblical scholar, so I'm not sure how it all fits in, but . . . I think it's evil. There's something wrong with it, but it's so deep . . . it's almost impossible to see it.''

She nodded. ''Jesus once said that when Satan lies, it's perfectly natural because he is the Father of Lies. Not the brother of lies or the best friend. The *father*. He invented them, he's got the *patent*. So of *course* it's almost impossible to see what's wrong with the Alliance.''

''Well . . . what *is* it?''

''In everything your daughter has been taught, what are the two things that come up again and again? You don't die, you *re-embody*, you come back as someone *else*. And in all of those lives you get to live, you never have to worry about answering to some invisible, judgmental god because *you* are your *own* god and *you* judge your*self*.''

''Yep,'' Coogan said firmly. ''That business has bugged me from the beginning.''

''It's the firstborn son of the Father of Lies. He used it to get Eve to eat the fruit in the garden. He told her 'ye shall not surely die,' and 'ye shall be as gods, knowing good and evil.' You won't really die and you'll be able to be your own judge, your own *god*, so you won't need any other.''

Coogan slowed his pace as he was struck by a deep chill and his skin suddenly felt too tight on his body. Why hadn't he seen it before? He'd learned about the original lie in Sunday school when he was a tiny boy; why hadn't he made the connection?

He stopped on the sidewalk and faced her. ''Then . . . then we're really sticking our fist into a hornet's nest. I mean, I knew something was wrong with it, I knew it was bad, but . . . but this . . . what with human sacrifice and . . . well, *this* is . . .''

''You look afraid, Coogan. Don't do that. We have to have faith. God's not going to abandon us. Somewhere out there, He's cheering this conversation on. But, of course, it won't be easy. Our friends might think we're a little crazy. Marvin and Mr. Cross and the ladies. But we can't just sit back and shut up because we're afraid of a little criticism, can we?'' She put an arm around him good-naturedly and they continued walking. "We need them and they need us. And with prayers and patience, we'll get along. I've been looking forward to this for some time. Hester Thorne probably hasn't thought about me once since she was a little girl. But I've been thinking about her a lot over the years. In fact—" She nodded toward the park up ahead, which was filled with people right out to the edge of the curbs. "—she might be over there right now. Shall we? This should be fun."

Applause broke out in the crowd now and then, and as they got closer, they could hear a woman's voice speaking through a sound system. It wasn't Hester.

"Sounds like the actress," Coogan said.

"Ah, yes. Sheila I'm-a-star-therefore-I'm-right-Bennet."

Coogan was right. Sheila Bennet stood in the gazebo and had the microphones to herself and she was fielding questions from the press. The reporters were gathered at her feet with microphones held out and cameras aimed. Behind them and all through the park stood fans and onlookers. Seated in a chair behind the actress, wearing her usual flowing white silk suit, Hester Thorne listened to her friend respond to the reporters' questions and smiled gently at the surrounding crowd.

Once they'd shouldered their way through the crowd until they were standing just behind the reporters, Coogan glanced at Lizzie. She was staring up at Hester with a smile very similar to the one on Hester's face. After a few minutes had passed, Hester began to squirm in her chair and turned her eyes from Sheila Bennet to the people directly in front of the gazebo. She glanced over the heads of the reporters until her eyes met Lizzie's.

Coogan felt that chill again when he saw some of the gentleness crumble away from Hester's face. Her eyebrows curled downward and her eyes narrowed briefly to slits.

Lizzie's expression remained the same: gentle, relaxed and smiling.

Hester's eyes seemed to hold as much confusion as suspicion. *It's been a long time,* Coogan thought. *She doesn't recognize her yet.*

The sounds around him—Sheila Bennet's voice and the questioning reporters competing to be heard—faded away as Coogan watched the two women stare at one another, their eyes locked in a silent confrontation that went unnoticed by the crowd, and then—

—applause broke out suddenly and Coogan flinched as his surroundings rushed in on him. Sheila Bennet backed away from the microphone, smiling and bowing slightly and Hester Thorne stepped in her place as the applause died down.

"I hope you'll all join us," she said, "at the Sleeping Woman Inn, where we're having a pancake breakfast. We'll be passing out programs listing all the activities taking place in the next few days and there will be a few words from Orrin. It's going on right now, it's absolutely free and I hope you'll *all* come! Thank you."

The crowd began to disperse immediately. Hester leaned toward Sheila Bennet, said something in her ear and left the gazebo, smiling as she headed toward them with two of her white-suited men not far behind.

Hester dodged reporters and cameramen as they gathered their equipment. She moved at a casual pace, smiling as she shouldered her way through and around small groups of people talking and laughing; she nodded to those who greeted her, but never took her eyes from the tall heavyset woman in the yellow cotton sundress.

She was accustomed to seeing familiar faces in an audience and they never bothered her, not even the ones whose names she couldn't remember. But there was something about this woman . . . about the way she stared at Hester . . . the odd smile she wore . . . something familiar. She had no idea of what importance the woman could possibly be—she looked like someone who went to garage sales every weekend—but something about her was important enough for Hester's inner voice to speak up and tell her to go see the woman . . . but with caution.

Like everyone else, Hester had a small voice in her mind, the voice that chided, argued, cajoled, mocked and cautioned. It was her conscience, her *own* voice and it was with her always. But *un*like everyone else, she had another inner voice. It was softer, it was male, and it was the voice she listened to and followed, even if it disagreed with her own . . . but that almost never happened anymore. The voice was Orrin's.

"Excuse me," she said pleasantly as she approached the

woman, glancing briefly at the familiar old man who stood beside her, "but don't I know you?"

Hester resisted the urge to recoil when the woman's smile grew, although she wasn't sure *why* she felt that way.

"It's been a long time, Hester," the woman said as she offered her hand to shake. "I'm Lizzie. Lizzie Dayton? From school?"

Hester tilted her head back slowly, lips parted in their cautious smile, as she eyed Lizzie. Yes, the name was vaguely familiar, but—

She is an agent of the enemy, the voice inside her whispered. *She has the smile and the confidence of the Great Lie and she has come to defame you and do damage to the truth.*

Hester didn't move; she continued to smile at Lizzie but listened intently to Orrin. His tone always became furious whenever he spoke of the Great Lie—monotheistic beliefs—but now there was a new urgency in his words, a tone that was almost manic.

Be wary of her and believe nothing *she says.*

Hester broke away from the spell of Orrin's voice in her head and saw that Lizzie's hand was still waiting to be shaken. Hester leaned forward, took Lizzie's hand and—

—something exploded silently in her head, something that gave off the light of a thousand atomic bombs and a fear like she'd never known spread through her body, dragging rusty fish hooks beneath her skin and her knees began to melt and she felt something overhead, something enormous, *vast,* bigger than her, bigger than the whole *planet,* and she was in its shadow which was growing fast as the thing plummeted straight down directly above her and she wanted to look up but the fear was so thick in her chest that she couldn't breathe and she knew that, in seconds, she would be lying in a heap on the ground screaming for mercy, *begging* for it, and she gave Lizzie's hand a curt pump then dropped it and—

—it was gone.

Hester didn't know if she still had a voice, but she tried: "Yes. Yes, it *has* been a long time, Lizzie. What brings you here?"

"I came to see you, of course."

"Well, we have a *lot* of catching up to do."

Get away from her. Quickly. Do something about her.

"Are you coming to the breakfast?" Hester asked.

"I've eaten. But I'll be there."

"Then we'll get together. It's *so* good to see you, Lizzie." She reached out to squeeze Lizzie's shoulder affectionately to authenticate the facade, but—

—*No! Don't touch her, she is a lie, a vile and dangerous lie and she is the* enemy!—

—instead, she simply said, "I'll see you at the hotel, then," as she backed away, and the voice continued—

—*vile, she is* vile *and you must take measures to protect the truth from her, hold her back, render her useless until I come.*

Hester turned and walked away, heading for the sidewalk with the two men close behind. She tossed a couple of glances over her shoulder, then walked briskly down the sidewalk. The men moved forward and walked on either side of her. Hester jerked a thumb toward the man on her left and said, "I want at least two people on that woman at all times. Until further notice, I want to know where she is and what she's doing every *second* of this festival. And I want to know as much as you can possibly find out about her, right down to what kind of *toothpaste* she uses, and I want to know *fast*, do you understand?"

"Yes, Ms. Thorne."

She jerked a thumb toward the man on her right. "The man with her is Bill Coogan. He runs a gas station here in town. I want someone to keep an eye on him, too. Find out what he's doing with *her*. His daughter, Paula, is a member. I want her in my office in five minutes, do you understand?" She held out a hand with all fingers splayed stiffly. *"Five minutes."*

"Yes, Ms. Thorne."

She headed for the car.

"Seemed friendly enough," Coogan said without conviction.

Lizzie watched her hurry down the sidewalk. "You didn't believe it, did you?"

"Nope, afraid not. Didn't seem to enjoy shaking hands."

"I noticed. And did you see the expression on her face when I told her my name?"

"Yeah. Kinda weird. Her eyes looked funny, sort of unfocused, like . . . well, like maybe she was listening to something far away."

"She was, Coogan. I'm sure she was."

2.

Hester eased into the chair behind her enormous oak desk with a sigh, willing herself to relax. Meditation would help, she knew, but there was no time for that right now. Orrin's voice was too insistent, too urgent to ignore, even for a moment. But she needed to relax so badly. . . .

What happened *out there*? She asked herself again and again.

She had felt something foreign to her, something to which she'd *thought* she was immune, something that she had not felt in a very long time: fear. Fear scared her. It was a weakness, anathema to a leader, particularly a leader such as Hester Thorne, who held the absolute truth in her hands and would change the world, a leader who had *nothing* to fear.

So how could someone as monumentally insignificant as Lizzie Dayton cause her fear?

To that question, Orrin had no answer. He remained silent.

So what had brought Lizzie Dayton here? Why would she suddenly pop up after all these years? And what did she have in mind?

She is an agent of the Great Lie, the familiar voice inside her said.

"An agent," Hester whispered, sitting forward and putting her elbows on the desktop, her face in her hands. "You said the Great Lie was just . . . a lie," she muttered into her palms. "So Lizzie Dayton is an agent of *nothing*."

Forces . . . the Great Lie has great forces and you must always be wary of them. I have told you that, as it is and always shall be.

She leaned back in the chair again and closed her eyes, whispering, "You're right. As always. I'm sorry for questioning you."

There was a cautious tap at the door.

"Yes?"

Her secretary, Roy, entered the office and said, "Paula Coogan is here. Would you like her to come in?"

Hester nodded and Roy led the woman in, then left and closed the door.

Paula Coogan stood just inside the door, hands clasped at her waist, her weight shifting nervously from one foot to the other.

In spite of her pale, drawn face, she looked rather girlish in her sleeveless yellow shirt and tan shorts.

Hester displayed her most generous smile. "Come in, Paula. Don't be shy." She stood, walked around to the front of the desk and leaned her hips on its edge, crossing her ankles. She nodded at the large leather-upholstered chair in front of her and said, "Please take a seat. I hope I didn't take you away from anything important."

"Oh no, no, of course not, Ms. Thorne."

Paula was frightened, that was obvious; with her wide eyes and tense lips, she reminded Hester of a small, frightened animal paralyzed in the headlights of an oncoming semi. She probably thought she was about to be disciplined for something, about to have some privileges revoked or be moved to less savory quarters.

"We haven't spoken in some time, have we, Paula?"

"Uh, no, ma'am. It's b-been a little while." She fidgeted in the chair, making the leather creak.

"That's too bad. We should get together more often."

A nervous smile flitted across her face. "Oh, I-I'd like that, Ms. Thorne."

"Tell you what, Paula. Why don't you call me Hester. I think we'd both be more comfortable."

"Okay. Um, sure."

"Good. So tell me, Paula, how is your dad?"

Bitterness darkened her eyes for a moment and she shrugged. "Still the same. He's . . . stubborn. He doesn't approve of, um . . ."

"Of your beliefs?"

Paula nodded.

"That's a pity. But you're not alone. Many of our members have the same problem. It tests one's patience sometimes, but it's to be expected. There will always be those who refuse to even *look* at the truth, let alone accept it. We just have to continue to love them and not hold their blindness against them. Bitterness and resentment only fill up places inside us better left open for more important things." She said nothing for some time, stroking her lower lip with a thumb, giving Paula a long thoughtful pause. Then: "Of course, people like that *can* stand in the way of the truth, keep it from spreading and reaching others. Sometimes." Hester left it at that, giving Paula something to think about.

Paula nodded slowly.

The Inner Circle, Orrin murmured. *She craves entrance to the Inner Circle.*

"You've shown some interest in the Inner Circle, haven't you, Paula?"

Her face brightened then and she sat up straighter. "Yes, Ms.—um, Hester. Yes, I have."

"You would like to join?"

She leaned forward. "Oh, *yes,* I've tried, I've tried so *hard,* but—" A pathetic smile. "—I just haven't been . . . valuable enough."

"Oh, you shouldn't think of it *that* way, Paula. You see, we—"

"If you give me another week—just a week, is all—I'm *sure* I can get my mother's jewels. They're really old and there's a big box *full* of them that are—"

"No, no, Paula, no. You've misunderstood the requirements." As she spoke, she walked slowly around the chair until she was standing behind Paula. "You can't *buy* your way into the Inner Circle. You must be able to serve us—serve *Orrin*—in some way, some *special* way. You must be of some specific value to Orrin and the Alliance. And Paula . . ." She reached over the back of the chair, put her hands on Paula's shoulders and massaged them lightly. ". . . I think you can be of far more value to us than *any* box of jewels. . . ."

3.

The parking lot at the Sleeping Woman Inn was overfull and cars were parked at the curbs up and down the long paved driveway. White-suited attendants directed cars through the lot to large patches of grassy land beyond and a white van bearing the Alliance emblem picked up those who had chosen to park on the road outside the gates and drove them to the hotel.

Once Marvin had parked his car outside the entrance, everyone agreed to forego the ride and walk up the long drive.

"So, did you talk to Fiske?" Marvin asked. Coogan, Lauren and Lizzie walked a few feet ahead of them, talking amongst themselves.

"No," Jordan replied. "I called twice and talked to the answering service, but the best I could do was leave a message. He won't be available until later today."

"Well, you did your best."

"I also caught something interesting on the tap." He told Marvin about the brief conversation he'd heard between Hester and the unidentified male voice.

"Did you get it on tape?"

"No, but I turned the recorders on when I left. They'll pick up any calls that take place while we're gone."

"Well, like I said. You've done your best."

"I don't know. This whole thing's starting to worry me. It started with just you and me, but now . . . ." He nodded toward the others. "And we're not exactly inconspicuous; I've got a big lump on my head and a pretty good scratch on my face, and Lauren and Coogan are pretty shaken up, walking around like zombies. And *now* we're going to this pancake thing with Lizzie, who's already introduced herself to Hester, so we're gonna stick out like nuns in a whorehouse."

"I don't know, Jordy, this might be interesting. And if not, at least we get a free breakfast. I'm starving."

The crowd was gathered behind the hotel where the pond in the center of the green was flanked by long buffet tables; people stood in lines that ran the length of the tables and all the way back to the hotel, moving at a steady pace as plates were filled. Behind each table were long grills where cooks flipped pancakes with a flourish and filled the air with the aroma of eggs, bacon and sausage.

While Jordan and Marvin got in line, Lauren waited by one of the trees with Lizzie and Coogan; she had no appetite. They spoke little, but when they did, it was about trivial things, silly things that would not normally come up in their conversations, things that kept their minds off their situation.

Lizzie could see the fear and pain in their eyes and ached to do or say something that would ease their minds, but there was nothing she could do, and since they chose to remain silent, she decided to say nothing. Instead, she gave a silent prayer for them and participated in their small talk.

"Miss Dayton?"

Lizzie started and spun around to see one of the white-suited young men smiling at her and holding a round silver tray with a fluted champagne glass of orange juice on it. She returned his smile and said, "Well, that's my maiden name, yes."

"Ms. Thorne would like you to have this mimosa with her compliments."

Lizzie stared at the drink for a moment, thinking how good it would taste, how good it would *feel*. It was even free. But to her surprise, there was no struggle involved this time; she simply did not need it.

"Tell Hester I said I appreciate it very much, but I don't drink."

"Oh. All right." He walked away, still smiling.

Lizzie turned back to two pairs of raised eyebrows.

"What was *that* all about?" Coogan asked.

Lizzie shrugged. "Maybe a little poke in the ribs. I'm an alcoholic, see, and maybe Hester knows that somehow and wanted to play a cruel little joke. It's something she would do."

"Good for you," Lauren said a bit timidly. "For not taking the drink, I mean."

"It's not easy, and the urge never really goes away. It does one good thing, though: teaches you to pray like a pro."

Coogan smiled and gave her a friendly wink, but Lauren turned away, watching the breakfast lines move.

"Last night, you mentioned your husband was addicted to cocaine, didn't you Lauren?" Lizzie asked. "How did he beat it?"

"Therapy."

"I see." Then, hesitantly: "Your family had no spiritual beliefs to turn to?"

Lauren nodded toward the two busy tables and the people surrounding them and spat quietly, "Not until Mark found *this*."

Lizzie moved a little closer to her. "I'm sure that, under normal circumstances, he would have rejected whatever attraction the Alliance held for him."

"Maybe so, but that doesn't get my son back. For all I know—" Her voice wavered. "—he's already dead."

Lizzie started to lift her hand to place it on Lauren's back as a show of support and sympathy, but stopped; she opened her mouth and took in a breath to say something comforting, but didn't. She was searching for something to say—*praying* for something to say—when a hand touched her shoulder and Hester said, "Don't you like mimosas, Lizzie?"

Lizzie turned. "I don't drink."

"Oh, no?"

"Not anymore."

"Ah, I see. Well, what do you say we take a little walk and chat a while?" To Lauren and Coogan. "Do you mind if I borrow her? We're old friends."

Lauren turned away abruptly, her lips pressed together; Coogan forced a smile and nodded once.

They walked away from the crowd and around the side of the hotel to the front where, as they spoke, Hester led Lizzie to a winding path that branched off of the parking lot and into the woods.

"Who are your friends?" Hester asked.

"Oh, just some people I met."

"I see. So what do you think, Lizzie?"

"Of your hotel? Your place here? I think it's beautiful. You picked a lovely spot. It must've been terribly expensive."

"It was. It *is*. But it doesn't belong to me alone, you know. It's shared by all of us. Each Alliance member who chooses to come live with us shared in its acquisition and they share in its upkeep."

Lizzie held back the smirk she felt coming to her lips; Hester was quoting, almost verbatim, one of her own pamphlets. "Then would it be fair to call this a commune?"

"I suppose. Technically. But I prefer community. The word *commune* conjures images of loose sex, no bathing, men with food in their beards and women with thick patches of hair under their arms, know what I mean?" she laughed. "This isn't that kind of place."

The path wound into a tunnel of tall pines that blocked the sun; the air cooled and Lizzie could hear small animals skittering through the woods around her.

"What are you doing with yourself these days, Lizzie?"

"Oh, I'm busy. I'm running a chapel and shelter center off Interstate 5 just outside of Irving."

"Really? That sounds interesting." There was no interest in her voice.

"Well, it's never boring."

"But how do you live? I mean, it doesn't sound very lucrative."

"Is *this*?" Lizzie asked, spreading her arms expansively to include her surroundings. She knew it was a stupid question—it was obviously *very* lucrative—but she wanted to hear Hester's response.

"Yes. Very lucrative. We adjust our fees according to how much each person or family can afford, but it's not free. I provide a great service here, lives are *changed* here."

There's no doubt about that, Lizzie thought.

"The truth," Hester said, "is never free."

"Oh? You don't think so?"

"No, I don't."

"Then the truth can only be obtained by those who can afford it."

"As I said, we adjust our fees."

"A good portion of the people I deal with have no money. None. In the world. We provide food, a place to stay and the truth. The same truth that was handed down by God and, later, Jesus Christ. They didn't charge a cent; neither do we."

"That must explain why evangelists drive huge cars and own private jets and why television preachers and their wives wear expensive jewels and live in mansions."

"Some of the people who say they're doing God's work are mistaken. Others are simply lying."

Hester stopped and faced Lizzie. She looked uncomfortable, tense. "Is that why you came here, Lizzie? To *convert* me, or something?"

"Certainly not. I was just answering your questions. What I do is not lucrative, not in a monetary sense, but our financial needs are met by people who support what we do and can afford to help out with donations."

"Well. That's awfully Samaritan-like." She folded her arms over her breasts. "I suppose that, in light of what *you* do, all this looks rather *business*-like. Rather worldly and selfish, hm?"

"Did I say that?"

"You didn't have to."

"It's not what I meant."

"Then what *did* you mean? Why *did* you come? I can't think of a single reason in the world for you to be here."

The conversation, the tone of Hester's voice, the whole situation stirred in Lizzie old and painful memories. She felt as if she were reliving that day on the playground when she pushed Hester in the swing. She could almost feel the lump of hatred and anger and pain that had grown in her chest that day, and on countless other days when she'd encountered Hester . . . but only *almost*. Now she felt confident, felt that she was in the right place at the right time; and toward Hester, she felt a little pity. The woman was actually trembling from either anger or fear or both. "Like I said, Hester, I came to see you. I see you on television, in newspapers and magazines. You're famous. Local girl makes good. I knew about the festival and thought I'd come see the show."

"Show? *Show?* That's all you think this *is*? A *show*?"

"Poor choice of words. I meant—"

"No, no, I think you said *exactly* what you *meant*. What *do* you think of the Universal Enlightened Alliance? Honestly. What's your opinion?"

"I don't really have to tell you that, do I, Hester? You know I'm a Christian. You know what *my* beliefs are, and I know what you think of them. Surely you must know how I feel about yours. Our beliefs are simply not compatible."

Hester's head tilted back and she began to walk slowly around Lizzie. "And why is that, Lizzie?"

"I don't have to tell you that. Besides, you know better than to talk about things like religion and politics. They make for poor conversations." She was fighting that smirk again.

"Isn't that why you came?"

"Did I say that?"

"You know, I was raised a Christian, too," Hester said, still circling Lizzie slowly, smiling.

"I know."

"Even later, as an adult, I studied Christianity myself. I've studied *all* religions. But I've found that so *many* religions claim, in one way or another, that we are somehow unworthy of existing, that we are filthy or sinful and must be cleansed by some god. That doesn't ring true for me. It seems so . . . *degrading*. But Orrin taught me that we are all perfect creatures and *we* judge our actions. I have finally found peace with what I believe today."

You will not die and you will be as gods, Lizzie thought. She said, "You know where my belief comes from. Where does yours come from, Hester?"

"From Orrin."

"Yes, but where does Orrin come from? Where *is* he?"

"He's everywhere. He's with me all the time. Every minute

of my life. His voice is in my mind, guiding me, encouraging me."

"He's been there all your life?"

She stopped in front of Lizzie and nodded. "Yes, I think so. I just didn't realize it until I was an adult."

"Why is he in you?"

"Because he *chose* me."

"Didn't any of that seem odd to you, Hester?"

"Well, at first, maybe it seemed a little—"

"No, no. I mean, considering your upbringing, what did you *think* of that voice at first?"

"At first, I thought I might be crazy. Then he began telling me things I couldn't possibly know, like things that were going to happen . . . and they happened. That sort of thing."

"And that didn't scare you a little? It didn't remind you of certain things you'd been taught?"

Hester's smile disappeared. "I know exactly what little corner you're trying to back me into and it's not going to work. I was *raised* a Christian, but I'd *rejected* the belief, so there was no reason for me to consider its teachings in my decision as to whether or not to accept Orrin."

Lizzie shrugged and cocked her head. "Oh well."

Hester didn't like that. She took a few steps forward until her face was just a couple inches from Lizzie's. Her eyes narrowed and her lips pursed into a pinched mask of anger and hatred.

"I want you to leave Grover, Lizzie. Today. I want you to say good-bye to your friends, pack your bags and leave."

"Why?"

Hester leaned even closer and when she spoke, another voice came from her mouth; it was the deep, rumbling, male voice Lizzie had heard on the playground so many years ago.

"Because you have no business here," the voice said, and Hester lifted her arms, hands flat and ready to slap onto each side of Lizzie's head as they had before, but—

—Lizzie grabbed Hester's wrists quickly and resisted with all her strength, thinking, *Oh, God, I'm gonna need some help here so, please, in the name of Jesus, give me a hand.* Then, in a loud and firm voice that, Lizzie was surprised to hear, did not tremble, she said, "*God* has business here!"

Hester's lips pulled back further than it seemed possible, exposing teeth and gums and saliva dribbled from her lower lip as she continued to struggle with Lizzie. They stood as one large *A*, locked arms over their heads, Lizzie's hands wrapped around Hester's wrists, each standing with one knee bent.

Spitting on her as it spoke, the unearthly voice said, "You've come to spread the Great Lie, but the power is on my side, the *people* are on *my* side . . . even those who have passed on . . . like your *husband*."

Lizzie felt a churning in her stomach.

"He buggers little boys in *hell*, you know."

Rage flared inside her, but she thought, *No, no, he* wants *you to get angry.*

"He's mine now. And so is the woman. I told you before, leave her—"

Somewhat winded from the struggle, Lizzie hissed, "In the name of Jesus Christ, get *away* from me!"

For just an instant, the blink of an eye, Hester's face became a hideous yellowed mask with inhuman eyes and rotted teeth and lips and, as if Lizzie had slammed a baseball bat into her stomach, Hester shot away from her butt-first, arms and legs outstretched before her as she released a furious and painful sound that was not of the earth. When she landed on the path a few yards away, her body began to convulse; her legs kicked and her arms flapped, hands slapping the path. Saliva spewed up from her mouth and the sound continued. It was the sound of a cage of animals burning alive, of metal crunching and an elephant vomiting, the sound of a spoiled child's tantrum magnified a hundred times.

Lizzie stood there watching and trying to catch her breath, but she didn't stay long. She backed away slowly at first, watching Hester continue to convulse, then stopped to look around and see if anyone was watching. No one. Just like on the playground, no one had noticed.

She turned and hurried back down the path. She didn't run, just in case someone saw her, but she walked very fast.

Once she was back in the parking lot, she slowed her pace. But she couldn't slow her pounding heart.

"Thanks, Lord," she muttered under her breath.

As she rounded the corner of the hotel, the hellish cry rose from the woods again and Lizzie was so startled by it that she tripped over her own feet and stumbled forward wildly until she regained her footing. Others walking around the hotel stopped chatting, some even stopped walking, and looked with concern in the direction of the cry. Lizzie moved on as if she'd heard nothing.

She saw the others standing by the same tree; Jordan and Marvin had gotten their breakfasts and were eating hungrily. When she got there, they all stared at her as if she were wearing a duck suit.

"What's wrong?" Marvin asked.

Lizzie realized she was trembling all over and her shoulders were rising and falling with her rapid breaths. "I'm fine," she said in a hoarse voice.

"Fine?" Coogan asked, stepping forward. "You're white as flour. What happened?"

"I, uh . . . had a little cuh-confrontation with Hester and it was j-just a b-bit unpuh-unpleasant. That's all."

Jordan perked up then. "What did she say?"

"Well, it's not so much what *she* said . . ." She caught her breath and, when he offered, she took a few swallows of Marvin's orange juice. "It was almost exactly like the playground all over again."

"Orrin spoke to you?" Jordan asked.

"You can call him whatever you want, but now I'm *dead* certain who he is, and his name's not Orrin."

"Well, what did he—"

"I'm so glad I found you!" Joan gasped, running up to them. "I figured you'd be here, but it's not easy to find anybody in this mess. I don't have long because I'm on break, but I thought you'd want to know this. It was just on the radio at the diner." She stopped to get her breath.

Lizzie was suddenly forgotten; everyone was staring at Joan, waiting . . . waiting. . . .

Then she said it: "Edmond Fiske is dead."

4.

Half an hour later, the large garbage cans at the ends of the tables were overflowing with paper plates and cups and napkins. The tables were cleaned off and cleared away and two large speakers were set up at the back end of the green. The press was there, too, of course, setting up equipment of their own.

The crowd began to gather before the speakers, sitting on the ground until the rectangle of grass was completely covered and surrounded by even more people who stood in the surrounding gravel, with everyone facing front.

They were seated in the center of it all, silent, waiting. Lizzie still had not quite recovered from her experience with Hester and the others had not quite recovered from Joan's news. Another of Orrin's "warnings" had come true.

"You think it's got anything to do with that phone call?" Marvin asked Jordan quietly shortly after Joan left.

"I'd bet money on it."

They decided to talk about it later when there was less chance of being overheard.

When Hester appeared, the hum of voices in the crowd was buried by applause. She looked fresh and lively in her shimmering white silks and waved with both hands at the audience. She tapped a finger on her lapel mike to test it, then said, "Good morning, sweet souls!"

Everyone in the audience responded loudly, as always. Everyone, that is, except for five people in the center.

Once the noise died down, Hester talked for a few minutes about the New World Festival and its purpose. "Your belief, your *energy*, is what will usher in this New Age of Enlightenment, and that New Age will unite this planet in a New World Order. We will be a planet of oneness. One leader, one government, one set of laws, one spiritual belief. There will be no wars, no churches, no disagreements."

In spite of the smiles and nods of affirmation and agreement she saw around her, Lizzie thought she could imagine nothing more frighteningly wrong.

"This festival," Hester continued, "is designed to bring on all of that more quickly. And if all goes well, I hope to have an announcement to make by the end of this festival. An announcement that will change your lives and mine, the lives of everyone on earth."

She talked about the various events that would take place at the festival—the channelings, crystal healings, aura massage training, hikes up the mountain for meditations, and more—and told everyone to be sure and pick up a program on the way out.

Hester showed no sign of the confrontation that had taken

place earlier. She looked unshaken, even refreshed. Lizzie watched her every move, waiting for a sign of uncertainty.

"Now that we've covered the festival," she said, "I think it's time for some words from Orrin. As many of you know, Orrin has been sharing with us some rather dark, but entirely necessary, things lately because, as I've said before, the New Age will be preceded by a time of turmoil and unrest. We are in that time right now, ladies and gentlemen, and Orrin is simply reminding us of that fact. He wants us to have courage and come through this time clean and untouched and in possession of the one and only truth. He wants the Godbody to be whole and healthy. Now, if you'll just give me a few moments . . ."

She lowered herself onto the grass and began the familiar procedure of opening the channel that would allow Orrin to speak through her. The crowd waited patiently and silently. The only sounds were birds and the rustling breeze, until—

—"Greeeetings, sweet souls!"

"Greetings!" the audience replied as one.

Hester stood and began to pace back and forth as Orrin said all the usual introductory things about unity and godness and the Godbody.

Jordan noticed something about his thought processes at that moment: as he absorbed the words coming from Hester Thorne and looked them over inside his head, he no longer thought of them as Hester Thorne's words as he had at the Sheraton in San Francisco. They were *Orrin's* words. Orrin was taking on a sort of personality in Jordan's mind, he was becoming a very real entity. Jordan didn't like that; it frightened him because it meant that things were being rearranged in the neat and tidy little room he'd set up within the walls of his skull, almost without him even *realizing* it. It had been happening a lot within the last twenty-four hours.

First, Orrin's warning about Reverend Hallway came true, and now the one about Edmond Fiske; he'd been killed when his private elevator dropped forty-eight stories because of a broken cable. Then there was Lizzie Murphy.

As far as Jordan was concerned, the fact that she was a Christian automatically made her suspect. But she didn't act like the Christians *he* had known. She condemned no one, she laughed and had a good sense of humor and didn't behave in a holier-than-thou manner. Yes, she quoted scripture now and then, but always good-naturedly. So she was an *amiable* Christian; that didn't change the way Jordan felt about the belief in which he'd been raised. And it didn't change her story. Had Hester Thorne manifested an Orrin-like phenomenon as a child? And how had Hester known that Lizzie was married *and* the name of her late husband? Lizzie had claimed there was no way Hester *could* have known, unless she'd kept tabs on Lizzie all her life, and Lizzie suspected the chances of that were microscopic. Then, of course, there was the biggie, the granddaddy of mind-benders: everything Jordan had seen in that cave.

All of those things had been stomping through Jordan's mind, leaving deep tracks that were impossible to ignore, and the impressions they'd made had completely changed the way he viewed Hester's channeling.

He broke through the surface of his thoughts and listened.

"—darkness descending upon the destroyers of the earth, upon those who continue to knowingly and willing escalate the decay and destruction of the planet that is not theirs to destroy, as it is now and shall always be. They refuse to participate in the few attempts made to stop this destruction and correct the damage. They refuse even to acknowledge what they are doing and make an attempt—however small—to change, although they profess to be doing all they can. They *lie*, so be it. The darkness of change falls upon them.

"And this is the most painful turmoil of all, for it shall claim the lives of innocents. Along with the destroyers of the earth it shall take those within range of its terrible light. But they shall be re-embodied and walk among us again. The light itself, however—the searing glow of nuclear power—shall be extinguished, for from this, others will learn and will go about making the necessary changes, as it is and always shall be."

"Oh, my God," Lauren hissed, startling Marvin, who sat beside her. "Oh, my God, the plant. The plant, the *plant*," she gasped, clutching Marvin's arm and shaking him.

"Sh-sshhh." He took her hand. "What's that?"

"The Diego Nuclear Power Plant," she breathed. "Mark used to work there. See? She's . . . oh, Lord, she's gonna use Mark the same way she used Simon Ketter to kill Reverend Hallway and the same way she might've used that *other* guy to kill Edmond Fiske."

Without taking his eyes from Lauren, Marvin reached around and beckoned Jordan, who sat on the other side of him.

"He was one of their engineers, he knows that plant inside and out and everybody there likes him. He could do it. If he really wanted to, he could *do* it."

"What?" Jordan whispered.

"You heard what Hester just said," Marvin replied. "Well, remember where Mark worked?"

It took a second, maybe less; Jordan's face seemed to age within that second. "Oh, shit. Holy shit."

"I think it's a mistake to discuss it right now," Marvin whispered. "This isn't exactly private."

"You're right," Jordan said. "As soon as this is over, we go someplace where we can talk. Jeez, unless—"

"Unless he's already *gone*," Lauren finished for him. "He could be on his way there right now."

"Maybe, maybe," Jordan said. "But I saw him just last night. Late last night. At the ceremony. Look, there's *nothing* we can do *now*. Let's just get the hell out of *here* as soon as we can."

Lauren tried to hold back her tears, but failed. Jordan and Marvin showed their anxiety in small ways as they feigned interest in what Orrin had to say; Jordan rocked slightly back and forth and Marvin picked at his socks furiously. The three of them didn't hear a word Orrin said.

When Hester was finished channeling—sitting on the grass again and hunched forward, exhausted—one of the white-suited fellows stepped forward, grinned and told everyone that they could pick up program sheets in front of the hotel and reminded them that Alliance literature and souvenirs were on sale in the gift shop.

Jordan stood and said, "C'mon, let's get out of here fast."

They stayed close together and tried not to look hurried. Lizzie and Coogan hadn't heard the brief conversation earlier, so they didn't know what the hurry was, but they could tell something urgent had come up.

As they were rounding a corner and starting along the side of the hotel toward the parking lot, a woman's voice called out behind them: "Daddy? Wait a second! *Dad!*"

Coogan turned toward the direction of his daughter's voice and saw her running toward them, cutting a wavery path through the gravel on legs that seemed bonier than usual.

"Hey, Dad," she said, smiling as she hooked her arm in Coogan's. "How's it goin'?"

When he looked at her, it was nearly impossible not to see Katie and he wasn't sure if he could speak to his daughter in a civil manner. He glanced at Lizzie—she raised her brows high as if to say, *Well? Go ahead.*—then glanced at Jordan—he gave a slight nod of encouragement—and Coogan turned back to his daughter. "Uh . . . fine, honey. How's by you?"

"Oh, I'm fine." She squeezed his arm.

He didn't *believe* she was fine, but had to dig deep inside himself to see if he cared. He looked at Jordan again and got another encouraging nod. "Uh, look, honey, we've gotta talk," he said quietly.

"Yeah, I know, Dad, that's why—"

"C'mere," he said, turning her away from the others and putting some distance between them. "I mean we've gotta talk *soon*, Paula. You and me. We've gotta sit down and do some talking."

"Yeah, I know. I'm . . . y'know, I'm sorry for the way I behaved the other day. I-yum . . . I didn't mean to say the things I said."

Coogan sucked his lips between his teeth for a moment to hold back what he *wanted* to say, then said, "Why don't you come over tonight."

"Sure. That would be great."

"And, uh . . ." He thought about it for a long time, staring at her with his mouth open. ". . . why don't you bring the kids. Give their ol' gramps a chance to spend some time with 'em."

"Well . . . I don't know, see, um, they're, uh . . ." She looked over his shoulder and her mouth opened in a big grin as she danced around him back to the others, asking, "Who're your friends, Daddy?"

Clenching his fists, he turned and followed her, clutching her shoulder to turn her away from them and saying, "Paula, why can't you bring Katie and Jake?"

She wouldn't look at him directly, but never stopped smiling. She turned to the others again. "Why don't you introduce me to your friends, Daddy?"

He looked at Jordan again. Another nod. He opened his mouth to introduce them, but couldn't. He turned to his daughter and said, "Paula, what . . . why can't you . . ." The next time he looked at Jordan, he got a *Not now* shake of the head and said, "Paula, this is Jordan Cross and Marvin Ackroyd, and this is Lizzie Murphy and—" He stopped involuntarily when he saw the looks Jordan and Marvin were giving him. He stopped and stared at them with a slack jaw, wondering what was wrong; they looked horrified, especially Jordan, who seemed to have paled. He continued. "—a-and this is, um, this is Lauren, uh, Lauren Schroeder." Jordan made a sound in his throat as if he were choking and Coogan noticed that his fists were clenched at his sides and his face was turning red.

"Well, I'm Paula," she said, her head bobbing. "Nice to meet all of you." Then she turned to Coogan and said quietly, "I'll be at your place tonight. Around six or so, 'kay?"

He looked at the others and saw only tension, hostility, and he didn't know why; it confused him and he turned away from *all* of them, standing still and silent for a long time, taking deep, quiet breaths. Then he turned to Paula and said, "I'll see you then."

She hurried away.

Jordan began walking so fast that his feet kicked up gravel. The others, one at a time, began to follow him. Except for Lizzie. She took his hand.

"You are about to get yelled at," she said quietly as they followed the others.

"Why? What did I do? I didn't think I was—I mean, I was just—"

"Don't bust a blood vessel over it. It's really not going to matter in the end. But see, you introduced Marvin and Jordan by their real names. Remember what Jordan told us about all that fake-name business?"

"Oh, Lord," he gasped, slapping a hand to his cheek. "Oh, no, no, how could I *do* such a thing? I was, y'see, I was so thrown by seeing Paula, I didn't—"

"I know, Coogan, I *know*. You're gonna get yelled at pretty quick, but just remember that I'm on your side."

They walked for a while, then he muttered, "Shit," and Lizzie let go his hand, put her arm around him and patted his back.

When they got into the car—Jordan and Marvin in front, Lauren, Lizzie and Coogan in back—Marvin slipped the key into the ignition but Jordan grabbed his arm before he could start the engine. Jordan turned in the seat until he was facing Coogan.

"You stupid son of a bitch!" he shouted, digging his fingers into the back of the seat. "Do you know what you've just *done*? Huh? *Do* you?"

Coogan's hands were trembling uncontrollably and his lips soon joined them as he looked down at his lap like a scolded child. The news about Katie had been weighing heavily on him since the night before, had been eating at him like a rat, and it had taken a tremendous effort to hold onto his composure. When Jordan shouted at him, Coogan felt himself losing that composure. He felt himself begin to cry and for that he hated himself.

"I'm sorry," he muttered, fighting the tears. "I-it was a muh-mistake."

"A *mistake*?" Jordan shouted. "Well, I don't know what the *hell* you were thinking, but—"

"*Stop!*"

Lizzie's voice startled Jordan. She was staring at him with fiery eyes.

"Don't you think Coogan's been through enough?" she asked quietly. "Don't you think he's entitled to a mistake or two?"

"Yeah, sure, I know, but do you know what that could cost me? We're trying to maintain a cover here. I have a job to carry out and I can't do it if—"

"Mr. Cross, you no longer have an employer. Are you *sure* you have a job to carry out?"

Jordan stopped. She was right. With Fiske dead, he and Marvin did *not* have a job. Fiske had given him a cash advance and told him to give a call whenever they needed anything at all; it would be provided immediately. The cash advance was running out rapidly and there would be no more money coming in. In fact, there was a good chance that Fiske's estate would deny any connection between Edmond Fiske and Jordan Cross. So what was he to do?

He looked at Coogan. The old man was on the verge of sobbing.

"I'm, uh . . . I'm sorry," Jordan said. "I'm kind of under some pressure and, uh . . . ."

Coogan slapped a hand on Jordan's shoulder and squeezed, nodding. His voice seemed to squeeze tightly through a swollen throat. "S'okay. I understand. Y'know . . . there's a chance she won't even remember your name. She's not as sharp as she used to be. Doesn't look too well these days. Anyway, she'll be coming to my place tonight. Around six.''

They sat in the car for a long time, saying nothing. There had been too many surprises, too much news, almost too much to absorb.

''Well,'' Marvin said, his voice hushed as if he were at a funeral, ''we've got a lot to talk about. What do you say we get out of here and decide what to do next?''

They agreed.

Hester stood in front of the hotel with Paula Coogan and the same two men who'd followed her out of Penny Park earlier.

''That woman is obviously Mark Schroeder's wife, Lauren,'' she said, watching them disappear down the long driveway. ''She seems to be sticking pretty close to that balding fellow.''

Paula said, ''His name is, um—'' She rolled her eyes upward to think a moment. ''—Jordan Cross.''

''And the other man?''

''Marvin Ackroyd.''

''We'll have to find out everything we can about them. But don't follow them for now,'' she said to the man on her left. ''They won't go far, I'm sure.'' A smile. ''And they'll be back.''

5.

Instead of going to the motel, they went to Coogan's where there was plenty of coffee and aspirin. Inside, Coogan settled everyone in the living room, then made sure things were going well in the store. He brought the pot of hot coffee in from the store, took it to the kitchen and poured cups for everyone. Coogan took his with a splash of whiskey. He seldom drank, and when he did, it was usually well after sundown. But there was nothing usual about this morning.

When Marvin wandered by the kitchen doorway and spotted Coogan's brandy, he stepped into the room wearing a lopsided smile and said softly, ''Medicate mine, too, willya?''

In the living room, Jordan was standing in front of the small brick fireplace leaning on the mantel, when Lizzie tapped his shoulder and whispered, ''Could I speak with you?''

''Well, yeah. Sure.'' He didn't sound too enthusiastic.

She led him halfway down a short hall, away from the others.

"Look, Mr. Cross," she whispered, "when I snapped at you in the car, I hope you didn't take it too personally. I'm sorry if you did. I just thought you were being too hard on Coogan."

Without ever meeting her eyes, he stuffed his fingers in his back pockets, nodded and said, "Yeah, I know. Don't worry about it. I *was* being too hard on him."

"I was also afraid I might have said the wrong thing when I reminded you that you no longer have a job here in Grover."

He looked her in the eye then. "What's wrong with that? It's true."

"Yes, but, in light of Mr. Fiske's death, surely you must be considering your options now. And one of those options is to simply walk away from all of this. It would certainly make sense, no doubt about that. No client, no money. And having no money can be rather paralyzing in your business, I would think."

His face hardened and his voice was coldly defensive. "So you're telling me to leave? So you can, what, take center stage, or something? Is that what you want?"

"I'm asking you to please stay."

He flinched, started to reply, but just blinked silently instead.

"We need you, Mr. Cross," she whispered. "You're clearly very good at what you do and you have a solid grip on this situation. We need some sort of leadership and you're providing it very well. And aside from all that, think carefully about what you'd be walking away *from*. Not only from people who need you, but from a very powerful, malignant woman whose forces will only continue to grow until someday they may affect you no matter how far away you go."

There was silence as Jordan considered what to say. He was going to say that he was planning to stay, but he simply could not resist . . .

"I don't know why you need me when you have your god," he said.

"My God hasn't stepped onto the stage and performed one of His spectacular production numbers in a very long time, as far as I know. Of course, He's perfectly capable of changing that, but I suspect He's taken to working through people these days. And He's done a wonderful job through you. I just hope you'll allow Him to continue." She smiled. "That's all I wanted to say, Mr. Cross." She turned to go.

Jordan wanted to kick something. He wanted to *break* something. Her smugness was a knife between his ribs. Her attitude of unquestionable *rightness* made him want to roar and pound his fist into something. She was just like his parents and all of their friends had been; she walked around acting as if she were superhuman, perfect, able to walk on *water*.

"Oh, one more thing."

He looked up to see her coming back.

"I, uh . . . I got started on the wrong foot with you and I want to apologize. Heaven only knows what you must think of me, and I don't blame you. I've said some things that pushed your buttons, I know. Some have been mistakes, but others, I admit, were intentional. I wanted to make you think, I guess. But I did a lousy job and I'm sorry. Like Marvin said, he explained your background to me briefly. You have every reason to feel the way you do. I'm sorry if I gave you *more* reasons. Tell you the truth, I'm not exactly myself." She laughed nervously. "I've been kind of tense ever since I left Irving. I don't get out much, really. The people at the chapel, they're all pretty needy. They need me to take care of them and that's what I do best. For the most part, they share my beliefs, so I'm not used to being around people who don't. And I'm not used to being this close to Hester. She . . . well, I guess my faith is weak, but I must admit—" Her voice trembled a bit. "—she frightens me. And on top of all that, I've been fighting the urge to drink for months now, and . . . this situation doesn't help any. I actually—" Another nervous laugh. "—I actually dreamed of vodka on the rocks last night, and that drink Hester sent to me this morning looked good. It looked *so* good," she whispered. "Anyway, I just hope you'll forgive me. For my sharp tongue, I mean, and for . . . anything else I've done to make you angry. I'd like us to be friends, Mr. Cross."

He sighed, his anger deflated, and after a moment said, "Forget about it, okay?"

She gave him a big smile.

"And call me Jordan."

"Thank you, Jordan."

She returned to the living room.

His nerves were raw, and although he didn't feel tired, his lack of sleep made his bones ache and his head buzz. Before returning to the living room, he stopped by the kitchen and saw

Coogan and Marvin, a tray of cups filled with coffee and a bottle of whiskey.

"Hi, guys," he said with a weary smile. "Can I have a shot?"

A few minutes later, everyone was seated in the living room but Jordan, who stood by the fireplace in front of them. He was a little more relaxed since the drink, but not much.

The first thing they agreed upon was the importance of stopping Mark Schroeder before he left for the Diego Nuclear Power Plant . . . if he hadn't already. The only problem was *finding* him. Perhaps Paula Coogan could help with that. Once they had him, though, they agreed that they had to use him, *somehow*, to expose Hester Thorne and the Alliance. Beyond that, they were still in the dark.

"Well," Jordan sighed, walking away from the fireplace and pacing the room slowly, "I guess there's nothing more we can do for now except wait for Paula to come this evening."

"You're all welcome to stay here for the day," Coogan said.

"May I make a suggestion?" Lizzie said.

Everyone turned to her.

"You said earlier, Jordan, that your cover was blown." She turned to Coogan and smiled. "Accidentally, of course. Anyway, I think you're right. It *is* blown. And I think it would be wise for you and Lauren to get out of that hotel as soon as possible. Especially if there are things in your room you don't want to be discovered."

Jordan felt his knees weaken. She was right. They might have searched the room by now. If they had, they'd found the phone-tapping equipment. If that were the case, they were finished. In tapping Hester's phones, they had commited a felony, and if they were caught in the act, Hester would have them out of her way in no time.

He turned to Lauren and said, "Let's get the hell over there *now*."

Marvin drove them to the hotel and dropped them off. Jordan and Lauren went in holding hands, giving one another an encouraging squeeze now and then as they tried not to rush up to their room. They were both afraid of what they might find, afraid they might somehow draw attention to themselves.

No one seemed to find them worth a second look. A few people smiled at them in the lobby, but that was all.

In the car, Jordan had told Lauren to say nothing in the room, so once they were inside and the door was closed, they began to pack in silence. Marvin gathered up the equipment, put it in its case, then filled his suitcases.

It seemed to take forever, but they were actually done in minutes and went straight to the elevator. In the lobby, they stopped at the desk. He assured the young woman at the desk that they were perfectly satisfied with the hotel's service, but a family emergency had come up and it was necessary for them to leave. Then he handed her the credit card Fiske had provided for him. It was in the name of Lorne Cusack. The card was what worried him most. Now that Fiske was dead, he didn't know if it would be accepted.

He wondered if he looked frightened, if the woman could hear his heart beating as she ran the card. She smiled at him, imprinted the card and handed him the transmittal. He sighed as he signed it, relieved. When the woman was finished, she wished them well and they picked up their bags and headed out the door.

They didn't see the young blond man who stepped out of the rest room that was across from the front desk near a bank of pay phones. His name was James. He was one of Hester Thorne's constant companions. He was on a break at the moment and had intended to change clothes, take a walk and get a bite to eat. Until, that is, he saw the man and woman leaving the hotel with their luggage. James rushed to the desk.

"Jessie!" he hissed.

"Oh, hi, Jimmy. How's it—"

"Jessie, who were those people?"

"What? Who was who? What people?"

"Those people who just checked out. The man and woman."

"Oh, those were the Cusacks. They're from, uh—" She checked the slip before her. "—Santa Barbara."

"Oh, no they're not," he muttered, reaching over the counter. "Give me the phone."

"Huh? What's the matter? They were nice pe—"

"Just give me the phone!"

She lifted it onto the counter and he quickly punched three numbers. "This is James. I need to speak to Ms. Thorne, please. It's urgent."

Jessie frowned, concerned now. She leaned her elbows on the

counter and, while he waited on the line, whispered, "What's going on?"

He turned away from her, waited a moment longer, then: "Ms. Thorne? There's something I think you should know. . . . "

6.

They spent the the first part of the afternoon listening to the telephone conversations that had been recorded by Marvin's tapping equipment. Most of them were innocuous business calls or queries from people interested in the Alliance. There were two, however, that were not innocuous at all.

The first was between Hester and an unfamiliar male voice that remained unidentified.

"I just wanted you to know that he'll be leaving tonight," Hester said.

"When tonight?"

"He'll leave here sometime between nine and ten o'clock. He'll board the plane at the airfield and go from there to Hollis Airpark just outside of Los Gatos. You pick him up there and take him to the plant. During the ride, I want you to keep reminding him of his purpose. Pump him up. When you drop him off, wait and make sure he's allowed through the gate, then leave, it's up to him from there. If he's *not* allowed through, he'll come back to the car and that will be that."

"And if he gets caught? If somebody stops him?"

"We've prepared for that. He'll be armed. If he's caught, he's to re-embody himself immediately. We will release a statement denouncing his actions as those of a disturbed man who, according to our records, withdrew from our program shortly after joining, and we will remind everyone that the Alliance condemns violence in all forms, no matter what the purpose. In any case, he's to re-embody himself after he's done his job. Don't worry, everything's covered."

"So this . . . this is really it? I mean, after this, it all happens? It all begins?"

"That's right. It all begins. Return here as soon as you're finished."

The connection was broken.

"My God," Lauren breathed, "that was Mark they were talking about, wasn't it?"

"Sounds like it," Jordan said.

"Who else would be going to a plant?" Marvin pointed out.

"We're going to have to be ready between nine and ten o'clock."

"Where?" Marvin asked.

"I know where the airfield is," Coogan said. "Just a few minutes from here."

Jordan massaged his forehead for a moment, took in a deep breath and said, "We should get to him before he gets there. Maybe we can get some ideas from Paula."

Lauren opened her mouth to ask, *But what about Nathan?* But she stopped herself because she knew that none of them could answer that question. Maybe Paula could tell them something about Nathan, maybe just about Mark. If they could get hold of Mark, maybe *then* they could learn something about Nathan. She tried to console herself with these thoughts.

"Why can't we just call the plant and warn them?" Lizzie asked. "Tell them a saboteur is on the way and—"

"It would never work," Lauren said. "During the years Mark has worked there they've gotten so many threatening calls—*countless* calls—they just don't take them very seriously. They have very tight security, steps they go through to keep the place safe. Every time they get one of those phone calls, they run through those steps smoothly and see that nothing's wrong. Nothing ever is. The calls are always cranks. And, of course, they would never suspect Mark of anything like that, even if someone told them they should. They all know him too well. They wouldn't hesitate to let him in if he showed up."

Marvin pushed the button and the tape continued to play.

They listened to seven more useless conversations before they came to the second notable exchange. Once again, Hester spoke to a male voice that remained unidentified. But the voice did not *need* identification. It was one of the most familiar voices in the world.

Everyone in the room exchanged slack-jawed glances, then stared at the cassette player as they listened.

It began after two simple, quiet hellos. Then:

"I'm sorry I can't be there," the president said, "but I'm sure you understand."

"Oh, of course I do," Hester said reassuringly. "I've been keeping track of your activities on the news."

"Well, as that guy in New York used to say, how'm I doin'?"

"Very well, *very* well. More importantly, Orrin is pleased. But it hasn't been easy, has it?"

"Oh, no. Not at all. You've heard, I'm sure, about all the flak I'm getting. Your suggestion for the Supreme Court opening has not exactly been met with open arms."

"I realize that. But their reactions are perfectly natural. Most people tend to reject the truth. So, in a sense, you've been complimented. Just keep pushing and see what happens."

"Yes, yes, I plan on doing that, but I . . . well, there are times when . . . uh, times when I have, uh . . .''

"Doubts?"

He sighed. "Yes. That's why I'm calling, even though I'm sure you're very busy."

"That's perfectly all right. Your doubts are natural. They are to be expected . . . but they are not healthy."

"I realize that, but . . . well, there are a lot of people who are very angry at me right now. If I could just tell them *why* I've done this, if I could give them the *real* reason, tell them the *truth* and—"

"Not yet. They aren't ready. You're doing this *because* they aren't ready." She paused, thought a moment, then sighed. "I wasn't going to tell you this yet, but I think it's necessary. Before the New World Festival is over this week—unless there is some horrible unexpected surprise, either on your end or mine—Orrin will materialize here in Grover . . . if there is enough belief in him."

"Enough belief? Is that the reason for Orrin's predictions? Like the death of Reverend Hallway and Edmond Fiske?"

"Orrin doesn't make *predictions*. He gives warnings. When enough belief has been generated and he *does* materialize, there will be a lot of very angry people. This is going to lay waste to the doctrine of their religions and they will be *very* angry. The religions of the world will be in a furor because this will contradict their every belief and they will fight like animals to condemn, denounce and prove false Orrin and his teachings. You *know* that your actions are needed to prepare for that, and you are the only one who *needs* to know. The religious leaders of the world will not be so quick to fight Orrin's purpose here—

which is to usher in the New Age—if they know he is backed by the most powerful nation on earth, and if some of that nation's power is gathered on their doorstep.''

"I don't understand why the churches of the world would react so negatively to something like this. Orrin isn't coming to harm anyone. He's coming to bring what most people would see as heaven on earth.''

"Think back. How did the world react to Jesus Christ. Like Orrin, he was another Ascended Master, a bringer of truth who was so misinterpreted and misunderstood by everyone around him that they finally ended up killing him. We want to make sure that doesn't happen. We want to make sure that Orrin has far more power on his side than Jesus Christ. We want to make sure he actually *accomplishes* something.''

A long pause, then: "I see what you mean.'' After another period of silence, the president said, "Is it really going to happen this week? There in Grover?''

"If there is enough belief.''

"*Will* there be enough?''

"I'm working on that. I am working very *hard* on that.''

After a few moments of effusive good-byes, Marvin hit the button.

"She certainly *is* working on that,'' Lizzie said. But she got no response. The room was so silent with shock that they could hear one another breathing.

Finally: "She's been talking to the president,'' Jordan whispered hoarsely.

"I wonder for how long?'' Marvin replied, sounding much the same.

"Does it matter?'' Lizzie asked. "She's gained entrance.''

Every head in the room, each bearing shocked expressions, nodded in agreement.

"It seems to me,'' Lizzie said, "that puts considerably more weight on what we're doing.''

"What did all that stuff mean?'' Coogan asked. "That business about there being enough belief?''

No one said anything. Then Lizzie asked quietly, "May I make a suggestion?'' She glanced cautiously in Jordan's direction.

"Sure,'' he said, "go ahead.''

She thought a moment, choosing her words carefully. "Hester

has obviously convinced the president that if enough people believe in Orrin, in his power, Orrin will materialize. She says she is working on this, apparently by making predictions—or as she calls them, warnings—in Orrin's name, then *making* them come true, like the deaths of Hallway and Fiske.''

"Well, if he's so powerful," Lauren said, "why doesn't *Orrin* do those things?"

"I can't answer that question definitely," Lizzie said, "but I think I can make a pretty good guess. Hester believes that, in order for Orrin to become that powerful in this world, there must be a great deal more belief in him than there has been. But because Orrin isn't powerful enough to stir up that belief himself, she must help him.''

"But why do so many people have to die?" Coogan asked. "Do you know how many people would die if there were a meltdown at Diego?"

"I don't think she's making the decisions here," Lizzie replied. "I don't think it was her idea to kill Hallway or Fiske or to do what she's going to do with your husband, Lauren. I think she's following instructions.''

Jordan took a deep breath and said, "Okay, I think we've heard enough of—"

"No, no, wait a minute," Marvin said. "What kind of instructions? What good would all those deaths do?"

"Hester believes she's helping to create belief in Orrin because Orrin is *telling* her this. She's doing it to enable him to materialize, as she says . . . but *he's* telling her to do it for his *own* reasons.''

"What reasons?" Jordan asked.

"I don't think there's anyone in this room who believes Orrin's intentions to be good, or who believes Orrin's very *nature* to be good. Am I right?"

Affirmative nods.

"Then you won't have to stretch your imaginations to accept this. Those who worship Satan claim that, in order to summon him, to make him *materialize*, a sacrifice is required. The sacrifice of a child is always preferable, and Lord only knows how many children have been sacrificed *here* in the name of Orrin. Those who practice such things believe sacrificial death cannot only summon Satan himself but bring power to *them*, bring them riches and success, just as Hester believes that what she's doing is for an ultimate *good*. And I think that the beliefs of Satan worshipers and the teachings of the Alliance all come from the same source."

With eye-rolling annoyance in his voice, Jordan said, "So you think the Alliance is really nothing but a bunch of Satan worshipers disguised as New Age believers?"

"No. They would deny that accusation because they don't believe it. They don't even believe in Satan. But then, when you eat a bowl of Chex cereal, it doesn't occur to you that you're eating a bowl of something made by Ralston-Purina, the people who make dog- and cat-food, does it? It kind of works the same way. Satan is the father of deception and nobody does it better."

"That still doesn't answer the question about all these deaths," Jordan pressed. "What good are they? I mean, even if it *is* Satan who's behind it, what purpose do all these killings—"

"That's your answer right there. Satan. Honey, his arrogance moved him to rebel against God long before mankind existed, and he's been having a tantrum ever since."

After a long silence, Lauren said, "It would be so much easier . . . to believe that Hester Thorne is just insane and . . . and that she's sucked all those people into her insanity. It would be so much . . . so much less frightening."

7.

Paula arrived at ten minutes after six that evening and came through the back door into the kitchen. Coogan, who had been watching the news with the others, went in to meet her.

"Hi, Daddy," she said cheerfully, flopping her black leather purse onto the counter. "How are you?"

She looked so happy in spite of her pallor and thinness. Could she possibly not know? Coogan didn't think so; he remembered the look of guilt on her face when he'd asked her about the kids a couple of days ago. He had to fight the urge to grab her by the shoulders, shake her like a rag doll and scream, *What the hell is wrong with you girl? You can smile at me when you know your own daughter was slaughtered?* But he simply stood at the kitchen doorway and looked at her, feeling as if he would be unable to support the weight of his leaden bones.

"I'm just fine, honey," he lied. "How 'bout you?"

"Oh, I'm okay. You got anything to eat?" she asked, heading for the refrigerator.

"Why don't you come on into the living room. I'll pour you some coffee and make a sandwich if you want. I've got some roast beef. Some turkey." He found himself wandering around the kitchen lost, as if he were a stranger in his own house.

She smiled. "Yeah, sure. That sounds good. I hear the TV," she said on her way into the living room. "Whatcha watching?"

Coogan watched her go through the doorway, stop and look around at the others, glance back at him, then say nervously, "Oh . . . hi. How are you?"

He poured a cup of coffee, took it to Paula and said, "Sit down." He took her elbow and led her to the sofa. She looked up at him, her face tight with discomfort.

"I didn't know you were going to have company," she said with a quivering smile.

Coogan slid the hassock over to the end of the sofa and sat on it, facing her. "Paula, we want to talk to you."

She looked from her father to the others sitting around the room; they were all staring at her expectantly, as if they were waiting for her to do or say something.

"We'd like to ask you a few questions," Coogan went on, his voice tense. "About the Alliance."

"Who are these people, Daddy?"

"You saw them this morning. They're friends of mine who have, in one way or another, been affected by the Alliance. Now they want a few questions answered. That's all."

"Well," Paula said, "I'm sorry, but if you have a gripe with the Alliance, you'll have to take it up with Hester Thorne or somebody who works for her. I just mind my own business and—"

"What can you tell us about the Inner Circle, Paula?" Jordan asked.

"What do you know about—how can you—" She turned to Coogan and whispered, "Why are you doing this?"

"Why am *I* doing this?"

"Trapping me here like this. With these people. Who *are* they, reporters? Is that why you're letting them grill me like this?"

"Never thought I'd say this, but I wish we *did* have a reporter or two here right now. Big ones. So people would find out what's going on up here." His voice was shaky and he felt himself on the verge of growling at his daughter.

"What are you talking about? There's *nothing* going on up here." She set her cup of coffee on the floor, stood and glared down at Coogan. "I think I should leave. I sure didn't come here so you could—"

"Where's Katie?"

She stopped, took a deep breath. "Katie is fine. She's back at the—"

"She's dead," Coogan rasped.

Paula flinched. She stood perfectly still for a long moment, then asked, "What are you talking about?"

Coogan stood, pushing his face close to his daughter's, and roared, "She's *dead*, Paula, Katie is *dead*! She was killed by your guru and—" He pointed at Jordan. "—*he saw it happen!* Now, I don't know how much you know about all this, but you're gonna sit your little ass *down* until we find *out*, and you're not going *anywhere* until I *say* so!"

Paula was shocked by her father's outburst and lowered herself slowly to the sofa again.

"They're gonna ask you questions," Coogan said, his voice quieter but no less firm, "and you're gonna answer them until they're through, you understand?"

"But I'm expected back in a couple—"

"So you'll disappoint whoever's expecting you." He turned to the others. "You go ahead."

Paula reached up and took Coogan's hand. "Is that true? What you said about Katie?"

Jordan said, "She was taken to a cave and sacrificed in some sort of, uh . . . I don't know, a ritual. It was something called the Inner Circle. We'd like to know if killing children is a regular function of the Inner Circle."

"Nobody kills children in the Alliance," she snapped defensively. "Besides, there's no such thing as death. People are just re-embodied. They return to human form and—"

"Hester Thorne stabbed your little girl with a long sharp crystal, then shoved her into a crevice in the cave wall, a crevice that glowed with light. You can call it what you like. I say she was killed."

She stared at Jordan for a long time. "Katie?" she whispered. "How do you know it was Katie?"

"They said her name. She was the Chosen One."

She closed her eyes, shook her head. "No, it wasn't a *sacrifice*. You're just trying to confuse me. You haven't been trained, you haven't been *taught*. You don't know what you're talking about. You're like him." She nodded toward Coogan. "Completely ignorant. Blind. You can ask all the questions you want, but even if I know the answers, you won't understand them. It won't do you any good."

Jordan said, "We'll ask anyway."

And they did. They grilled Paula for nearly two hours, most of which was frustrating because she was stubborn. Occasionally, she would interrupt the questions angrily, standing to pace as she told them how blind they were, how they would not stand long in their ignorance because Orrin would come soon and either cure their blindness or re-embody them. She broke into sobs once and cried for several minutes, muttering gibberish into her palms.

They learned from Paula that the Inner Circle was a seldom talked about faction of the Alliance made up only of people capable of making extraordinary contributions to the organization, whether in the form of money or of work to further the cause. Only those in the Inner Circle knew for sure what went on there, but Paula knew it had something to do with speeding the coming of Orrin and the New Age of Enlightenment.

When asked about Mark Schroeder, she looked at Lauren and said, "Ms. Thorne knows you're his wife. That's all I know. He's another member, that's all."

"He's a member of the Inner Circle," Jordan said.

"Good for him. I will be, too, you know. Soon. Ms. Thorne says I'm valuable because—" She grinned maliciously at Coogan. "—I'm your daughter. And because I can find out about all of you. Who you are. What you're doing here. And I'm going to tell her all about this. I *am*. You can't hold me here very long, you know. It's illegal. It's like . . . like kidnapping, or something."

"Do you know anything about Nathan Schroeder?" Lauren asked hopefully.

"Who's he?"

"My son."

"He'd be with the children then. The adults and children are kept apart. I don't know anything about him."

Jordan asked, "When someone leaves the compound you have behind the hotel, how do they get out?"

"There's an unpaved road that leads to Greenbend Road. It's pretty hard to see from Greenbend. I don't think anyone outside knows about it. Except, now, you. But I don't know what good you think it's going to do you. It's all private property. You'll be kicked out. Arrested." She went on that way for a little while—condemning them, laughing at them with a spoiled-little-girl laugh—until Jordan stopped her.

"That's enough," he said. "We know what you think of us, we don't need to hear anymore."

"Can I go then?"

"No, you may not." Jordan stood and turned to Coogan. "Marvin and I are going to have to leave pretty soon. Why don't you keep your daughter entertained until we get back." Then he headed for the kitchen, motioning for Marvin to follow. He did. A moment later, so did Lauren.

"We don't have much time," Jordan whispered. "We've got to decide how we're going to handle this. What do you think?"

"I don't know. It'd probably be a good idea to catch him before he gets too far. He's gonna have somebody with him, maybe *more* somebodies, and I'm sure everybody'll be armed."

"Including us. But I'd like to avoid gunfire."

"Who wouldn't."

"Excuse me," Lauren said tentatively.

They hadn't realized she was in the room and her voice startled them.

"No," Jordan said firmly, holding up a hand. "You're *not* going with us. Not this time. We'll get him—if we *can*—and bring him back here."

"No," Lauren said. "I think you're going to need me. . . ."

8.

Surrounded by dense woods, Mark lay down on a soft mound of earth, inhaled the evening air scented with the sweet smell of the grass beneath and around him and felt himself sliding almost instantly into slumber, felt all his cares, aches, and most of all, the tremendous responsibility he had been given, fading away. But she wouldn't let him.

"No, no, Mark," she purred as she lay down beside him. "You can't sleep. Not yet. Not until you've done your job."

"But that won't be sleep," he said. His voice was becoming ragged from fatigue. He hadn't slept in . . . he couldn't *remember* the last time he'd slept.

"Re-embodiment is *like* sleep. Like a very refreshing sleep. A brief respite from your earthly cares, and then a fresh start. A new life in a world unified by enlightenment and living under the guidance of a single being of pure light and knowledge."

"Orrin." He whispered the name respectfully, once again caught up in the picture Hester painted in his imagination. This was the second time she'd told him of this future since . . . how long had it been? Sometimes it seemed no time at all had passed since Hester had told him what he had to do and why, told him of his *destiny;* at other times, it seemed an eternity. But that wasn't important. What she told him sounded so right, so *true.* "It's really . . . going to be like that." It wasn't quite a question.

"Oh, yes, Mark. By the time you re-embody, the New Age will have begun. And all because of what you will have done tonight. Do you see why you're so important to me?" She stroked his cheek with her fingertips. "So special," she whispered, her lips touching his ear lightly. "And not only to me, to the whole *movement* . . . even though the others involved may never know it. This is what you were born to do, Mark. Every moment of your life has led you to this place, and you must let nothing stand in your way. Do you understand?"

He nodded as she kissed his eyebrow, brushed her lips over his lashes, ran her fingers through his hair. He felt a vague tingling of arousal, but he was so tired . . . *so* tired. . . .

Hester slid her hand over his chest and abdomen and began to stroke his thighs. "I have some disturbing news for you, Mark. Lauren is here in Grover."

He opened his eyes. "What?"

"Your wife. She's here."

"Lauren? Why? What's she doing here?"

"She's come to stop you. To keep you from meeting your destiny."

He thought about that a long time, frowning, as Hester continued to stroke his thighs. Then: "Can I see her? Before I go?"

"I don't think that would be a good idea, Mark. You must have only your purpose in mind. You must forget your past life.

Put it out of your mind. It was simply the vehicle that brought you here and now you have no further use for it. Do you understand?''

"But what about Nathan? Shouldn't I see him buh-before I leave?''

"He's a part of the past, Mark. Don't worry about him. He's in good hands. He'll be waiting for you in the New Age . . . in one form or another. That's simply the way it has to be, Mark. Understand?''

After a while, he gave her a preoccupied nod.

"But Lauren may come to see *you*. She may try her best to stop you. You *can't* let that happen, Mark, you *have* to be strong. If that happens, I want you to think of Orrin and of what you're doing for him. For the *world*. And think of me.'' She kissed his throat as she slid a leg over his hips and straddled him.

As Hester began to unbutton his shirt, Mark shook his head and muttered, "I-I really don't think I can right nuh-now. I'm . . . very tired.''

"Don't worry.'' She kissed his lips . . . "Later, I'll give you some pills to keep you wide awake.'' . . . his chin . . . "But right now, I want to make you feel better my*self*.'' . . . his throat . . . "I want to make sure you're thinking of me on your trip.'' . . . opened his unbuttoned shirt and kissed his chest . . . "I want nothing or no one else on your mind.'' . . . his belly . . . "Not Lauren . . . not Nathan . . . only the memory of what we do here today, Mark.'' . . . then she began to unbutton his belt.

In spite of his exhaustion, he felt himself growing erect. He lifted his head to see Hester smiling up at him as she unbuttoned his pants and slid her hand beneath them.

"Mark,'' she whispered, "you're going to change the world. . . .''

9.

A razor-cut line of golden sunlight outlined the peaks of the western mountains beneath a sky just beginning to sparkle with stars. That faint sliver of sunlight would be gone in minutes and the stars would grow brighter.

Mark found the sky especially beautiful this evening because he knew this would be his last evening beneath it. The sky was so much clearer here than back home, the moon and stars so much brighter. He was sorry he couldn't re-embody here under *this* sky, where the deep-blue blackness was made of velvet and the stars were diamonds hung from invisible threads.

"You look troubled," Hester said, holding his hand as they walked through the woods.

He was staring up through the trees and lowered his head to look at her. "Just thinking," he said.

"About?"

He looked up again. "It's so beautiful here. So clear and . . . *close*."

"Just think how much clearer it will be after you've re-embodied, Mark. It'll be clearer than this. *Everywhere*. Remember what Orrin has written through me?"

He recited it slowly and softly: "When the New Age arrives and the Godbody has become whole and healthy, that which is called by you the earth will be cared for jealously. It will be the first priority and anything or anyone that brings it harm or mars the beauty of it shall be, by the Godbody, abolished. So be it."

"*That'll* be some sky, won't it, Mark?"

"Yes. It will." He realized suddenly that they had stopped walking—although he wasn't sure for how long—and looked at her with a puzzled expression.

"Well, Mark? Are you ready?" She nodded toward something ahead of them and he turned to see the dark grey, nondescript car parked at the side of the dirt road just a few yards away from them. He couldn't tell if it was an Oldsmobile or a Chrysler and he didn't really care. All that mattered was that it was time.

"The man in the car is named Dave," Hester said. "He has everything you'll need, including more pills like the ones I gave you a little while ago. Speaking of which—how do you feel? Still tired?"

He thought about it. "Better. I feel a little better." He was surprised by the realization. He *did* feel better, more alert.

"That's good. Well. You're all set, then."

Mark thought this situation was beginning to sound suspiciously like his mother sending him off on his first day of school. But it wasn't. He told himself it was much more important than that.

Hester placed a hand on his chest and kissed his lips gently. "Go on. Get in the car."

He walked around the car to the passenger side and stared at the door. For just a moment, he was overwhelmed by a fear that dug its talons deep into his bones. He looked over at Hester. She smiled, nodded encouragingly. Mark got into the car.

The driver started the engine, smiled at Mark and said, "Hi. My name's Dave. How are ya?" He was wiry with a rough-skinned face and a bushy black mustache and he wore black leather gloves.

"I'm . . . fine."

"That's good."

The car began to move slowly over the dirt road. When Mark looked back to see Hester one last time, she was gone.

Dave said, "Everything you'll need is in the glovebox."

Mark opened it.

"A small packet of pills, in case you get tired again. And of course, the gun. Hester said you know when to use it and how, so I guess we don't have to talk about that."

Mark slipped the pills into the side pocket of his sport coat, but held the gun before him for a moment, at a loss.

"Oh, yeah, that's right," Dave said. "There's a shoulder holster in the backseat. Almost forgot to tell you."

Mark reached into the backseat, got the shoulder holster, then removed his sport coat, and with just a little difficulty, figured out how to put it on. With the gun tucked away beneath his coat, he tried to relax, hoping Dave would not be talkative. He wanted to think. He wouldn't be thinking again in a while, not like this. He would have to go through it all again: infancy, childhood, adolescence.

But he *couldn't* think. No matter how hard he tried, he couldn't clear the mist from his mind. Thinking hurt. But he could call up images in his mind and the first one to appear was that of Lauren.

How was she? Was she really here in Grover? Did she hate him?

He couldn't actually articulate the questions in his mind, but he *felt* them. They were too disturbing, too painful and he pushed them away, closing his eyes, leaning his head back and making himself aware only of the dirt road's bumps and potholes. He couldn't sleep—the two pills Hester had given him were now sending an electric hum through his bones—but he was no less exhausted.

"What the hell?" Dave muttered, slowing the car.

Mark lifted his head and saw Greenbend Road just a few yards ahead. But someone was standing in the way of the car. A woman. She stood motionless, arms at her sides, and the car crept closer and closer. She lifted her arms and waved them.

Dave brought the car to a stop and said, "I don't like this."

The woman stepped forward, into the headlights, and Mark gasped.

"What?" Dave snapped. "What's wrong? Who is she?"

"My wife." Mark reached for the door handle to get out.

"Uh-uh, no way," Dave said, clutching Mark's left arm.

"I won't be more than a minute. I just want to have a word with her."

"*No*, you *can't*, we have to *go*, you've got to be at the—"

In one quick movement, Mark jerked his arm away, opened the door, slid out of the car and slammed the door behind him, saying, "Lauren?"

She moved toward him cautiously, but said nothing.

Dave got out of the car.

Mark asked, "Lauren, why are you here?"

Still, she said nothing.

Mark felt gooseflesh rise on his shoulders. Something was wrong here. She just stood there and said nothing.

"Get back in the car, Mark," Dave barked. "Right now!"

Without taking his eyes from Lauren, Mark held up a hand in Dave's direction to shut him up. "What's going on here, Lauren? Why are you—"

There was a burst of movement behind Mark and another behind Dave, and before he could spin around, two strong arms hugged Mark's chest from behind and—

—Mark saw a man dash from the bushes behind Dave with his arm raised and a large rock in his hand, which he swung down hard and the rock struck the back of Dave's head and—

—Dave slammed into the side of the car, but instead of going down, he started to push himself away from the car and face his attacker as—

—the man holding Mark slipped his hand under Mark's coat, slid his gun from the holster and jabbed Mark in the ribs with the barrel and—

—Lauren held up her hands, palms out, and said rapidly, "Listen, Mark, don't move, okay? Just don't do *anything*," and—

—Dave started to shout but gulped down his voice as the rock hit his head again with a wet crack and he dropped heavily to the ground as—

—Lauren said, "You're gonna come with us now, Mark, you're gonna come with us and you're not gonna try *anything*, do you understand?" and—

—Mark felt something in his mind kick in and begin to work and he thought, *This isn't right, no, this is all wrong, this isn't supposed to happen I have things to do important things world-changing things that have to be done and I have to do them so this can't happen I can't let this happen*, and as the man holding him began to push him forward, Mark kicked his right foot back hard and the heel of his shoe dug into the man's shin and the man hissed, "Shit!" as the other man said, 'C'mon, we've gotta get outta here," and Mark felt the hold on him weaken for just a moment and he took advantage of it, swinging around fast with his elbow out and his elbow slammed into the man's chest as—

—Mark caught a glimpse of the gun in the man's hand which was held high over Mark's head and he saw it flying downward, growing larger and larger and then—

—nothing . . .

10.

Grunting from the effort, Jordan dragged Mark across the dirt road, his arms hooked under Mark's to Marvin's car, which was parked on the shoulder of Greenbend Road about ten feet away. As Jordan dragged him, walking backward quickly but uncertainly and glancing over his shoulder, Lauren walked with him, wringing her hands and asking, "Is he hurt? How bad is he hurt? Is he breathing? Oh, God, is he *breathing*?"

"I thought you didn't care," Jordan said.

"Oh, shut the fuck up," she snapped as she opened the back door so he could slide Mark into the seat.

"C'mon, Marvin," Jordan called.

Marvin was on his way. The car Mark had been in was still humming, both doors open with the dome light on; the driver lay unconscious on the ground. Marvin had dropped the rock he'd used on the driver and was fishing his keys from his pocket as he walked away when—

—something grabbed his left ankle and pulled hard. Marvin

lurched forward and dropped to his knees, shouting, "Jordy!" He rolled over to see the wiry man he *thought* he'd put out just a moment ago crawling up his legs with painful determination, blood striping his face and clotting his hair. Jordan's footsteps crunched over the dirt as he ran from the car and—

—the bloody man clinging to Marvin's legs opened his mouth slowly, as if he were yawning, and screamed in a voice like metal scraping metal, "*Hellp!* Somebody *helll*—"

Jordan's foot cut the word off with a crack, snapping the man's head back sharply and starting a gout of black blood from his mouth. He rolled the man off Marvin and under the idling car, then helped Marvin to his feet. They were hurrying toward the car when they heard the voice. They couldn't tell how far away or close it was or whether it was male or female, but it froze them in place for just a moment.

"Dave?" the voice called. "Dave? That you? Mark? Something wrong?"

"Let's get the *hell* out of here," Jordan whispered.

They were sliding into the car when the bushes off the road began to hiss and rustle. Someone was moving toward them quickly.

"Now," Jordan said, "let's go now, Marvin, *now*!"

Marvin started the car and had it moving before either he or Jordan had closed their doors. He swung the car around in a U-turn as a figure appeared from the woods beside the road. It was a dark figure, no more than a three-dimensional shadow in the murky evening. As Marvin drove away, pressing his foot on the accelerator, he looked in the rearview mirror and saw the figure standing in the middle of the road, motionless and watchful.

"Looks like somebody got an eyeful," Marvin said uneasily.

"Nevermind that now," Jordan said, picking up the car phone and punching numbers quickly. "I'm gonna call Coogan and tell him we're coming."

Jordan spoke quickly and concisely, telling Coogan to get ready to hide the car when they arrived, then hung up and looked into the backseat, keeping an eye on the rear window for signs of pursuit.

Mark stirred as he lay across the seat with his head in Lauren's lap. He was bleeding from a deep, swollen gash high on his forehead and Lauren held a handkerchief over the wound. She looked at Jordan with a pinched face, fighting tears.

"Is he bad?" she asked. "I mean, is he gonna be all right, do you think?"

"Yeah, he'll be all right," Jordan said, thinking, *But will we?*

When they pulled into the narrow alley behind the store, Coogan and Lizzie were waiting for them beside a dirty white garbage bin that had been pulled away from the wall. Marvin stopped the car, waited for Jordan and Lauren to get Mark out of the backseat, then drove into the manzanita that grew liberally behind the building. That afternoon, he and Jordan had gone into the manzanita with an axe and a saw and had cleared out a space just big enough for the car; Marvin drove into it, killed the engine, sidled his way out of the tight space and helped Coogan and Lizzie roll the garbage bin in front of the car.

In daylight it hadn't worked at all, but the darkness of night added the finishing touch; the car was invisible without a search.

Marvin straightened his glasses and smoothed out his sport coat, then followed the others inside.

"Where were you going, Mark?"

Mark was lying on the sofa with an ice bag on his head. He did not reply.

Lizzie was standing in the kitchen doorway, leaning on the doorjamb. Coogan sat on his ratty love seat with Joan, who had come by late that afternoon after work. Paula was all over the room, fidgeting, pacing, toying aimlessly with knick-knacks.

"Couldn't you at least give him a few minutes to get his bearings?" Lauren asked impatiently.

"No. Mark, where were you *going*?"

He opened his eyes, licked his lips and muttered something unintelligible, then rolled his eyes to Lauren. They were watery and unfocused, but they stayed on her without wavering.

A whirlpool of emotions sucked at her insides as she looked at him. She felt the same compassion for him that she would feel for anyone who had been hurt, but when she looked at him, she saw Nathan and a part of her wanted to start hitting and clawing him until she told her where Nathan was and how she could get to him. But when she looked at him, she also saw their years together and all they'd been through, the times he'd given

her support, the times she'd given it to him, and a part of her
wanted to embrace him, kiss him and cry. She wanted to give
in to neither emotion, so she pulled herself away from Mark's
pleading, confused stare, stood and crossed the room to the fireplace, where she stood with her back to him.

"Okay, Mark," Jordan said, "you're gonna have to start talking. You don't have any choice. You're not going anywhere until
you start answering some questions."

"Ignore him!" Paula snapped. "Don't say *anything*."

Mark shifted his position on the sofa and groaned quietly.

Joan spoke up: "I really don't think this is a good idea, Jordan. I've told you how these people work. You should've gotten
him and just left town. *This* is *not* a good idea."

Jordan faced her. "You think it's a good idea to let him go
trigger a meltdown? Huh?"

"How did you know?" Mark croaked.

Joan sighed, frustrated and afraid. Coogan patted her hand
and whispered in her ear, "If it'll make you feel any better, I'll
go into the store and check the front windows, make sure nobody's prowlin' around. Hell, I'll check *all* the windows." He
got up and went to the front of the house and through the curtains that led into the store.

Mark propped himself up on his elbows and the ice bag
flopped to the floor. "You *couldn't* know about that," he said
to Jordan. "How *could* you know?"

"God told us," Jordan said. He pointed to Lizzie. "See that
woman over there? She *channels* God. He's been telling us all
kinds of nasty things about you people in the Alliance."

Paula cracked her knuckles loudly as she glared at Jordan.

Mark's eyes widened and he sat up straighter. "Is . . . is that
true?" He looked at Lizzie. "Is it? True?"

Lauren and Lizzie began to speak at the same time, their
voices blending together into gibberish.

Lauren rushed to the sofa as if she were about to start beating
Mark, as she'd imagined herself doing earlier, and said in a low,
trembling voice, "Mark, for God's sake, will you wake up and
let go of this shit, these lies, will you just wake up and tell us
what we need to know so we can get Nathan and I can get the
hell *out* of here!" as Lizzie barked, "No, Mark, that's *not* true,
Jordan is just being a *smart*-aleck and I *don't* appreciate it!"

"*Will you people stop!*" Joan shouted.

The room fell silent and everyone turned to see her standing before the love seat, her fists clenched at her sides. Joan's lips squirmed as she spoke, as if resisting the urge to pull back and bare her teeth. "What the hell is wrong with you people? I thought you wanted to do something about this, to try and stop what's happening here in Grover. If I'd thought you were going to be like this, like a bunch of screaming *children*, I wouldn't have gotten *near* you."

Lizzie walked slowly to Joan's side. "You're right," she said. "I'm sorry."

"Oh, it's not just you," Joan replied, looking at the others. "You all seem to bring out the immaturity in one another."

Paula giggled maliciously, enjoying their conflict.

"Okay, look," Jordan said. "Some of us are running on very little sleep and we're all on edge. Let's try to keep that in mind and not let it get the best of us." He turned to Mark again. "Yes, we know you were on your way to Diego to do whatever it is you have to do to trigger a meltdown, and we know you're doing it for Hester Thorne. That covers *what* you're doing and for *whom*, so . . . *why* are you doing it? Just to make Orrin's prediction come true?"

"Prediction? What prediction?"

"You don't know?"

Mark shook his head stiffly. "I'm doing it to usher in the New Age, to pave the way for Orrin's coming on this plane."

"You don't have to tell him that!" Paula shouted. "None of them understand! They're ignorant! They despise the truth and enjoy their blindness!"

Jordan ignored her. "She said nothing about the warning Orrin gave to the press about this? She didn't tell you that she'd already *predicted* it?"

Mark frowned. "No. But she wouldn't lie to me. Hester *can't* lie."

Lauren muttered some profanity under her breath.

"So," Jordan said, "you didn't know that she'd predicted the death of Reverend Barry Hallway and a former member of the Alliance was piloting the reverend's plane when it went down?"

"No, that can't be," he groaned. "That *can't* be."

"Don't listen to them," Paula went on, "don't listen to a *thing* they tell you."

Lizzie stepped over to the sofa, got down on one knee and asked Mark, "Do you get enough to eat there?"

He said nothing.

"Are you required to take frequent enemas?"

He glanced at her then. "Just to . . . clean out the impurities of a lifetime of ignorance."

"Do you get enough sleep?"

"Plenty of sleep. I sleep eight hours a day."

"In increments of two hours, correct?"

He turned his body away from her on the sofa.

"Mark, do you realize what's been done to you? You have been underfed, probably overworked, deprived of sleep, probably required to spend a good part of the day chanting. Your system has been broken down, *you* have been broken down so you could be built up again . . . into the person Hester Thorne wants you to be."

"That's a lie," he muttered.

"Yes!" Paula shouted. "A lie! They're all lies! They're *liars*, all of them, and they're jealous of you because you have the *truth* and they want to turn you away from it!"

Jordan turned to her and was about to tell her to shut up when there was a loud crash from the store, accompanied by an explosion of broken glass. Jordan looked around the room quickly, said, "Where's Coog—" but cut himself off when the lights went out and the cozy living room was replaced with darkness. "Marvin."

"Right here."

"You gotta light?"

Marvin took out the small black flashlight he kept in the pocket of his sport coat and turned it on. Its narrow beam cut sharply through the darkness and cast a soft glow on their faces; they were frightened faces, every one of them.

Jordan hunkered down, reached under the sofa where he'd slid Mark's gun when he came in—it made Joan and Lizzie uncomfortable—and said quietly, "You got yours, Marvin?"

"In my hand."

"Anybody else in here have a light?"

Joan got a butane lighter from her purse, went to the fireplace, and lit two fat candles on the mantel. They sent out a fine golden mist that cast long shadows on the wall.

"Everybody stay in here," Jordan said. "If you need anything, holler. C'mon,'' he whispered to Marvin. They started toward the curtained doorway at the end of the hall as Paula said smugly, "They've probably come to get us.''

Jordan called, "Coogan?''

There was a faint response, an unpleasant *harrumph* sound.

Jordan remembered the first time he met Coogan and how, under stress, the old man had clutched his chest and heaved for breath as if he'd been running. He might have had a heart attack, fallen and, say, slammed a shelf into the fuse box. Maybe . . .

"Coogan, you all right?'' Jordan asked as he pushed the curtain aside and stepped into the store. There was an unpleasant smell clinging to the darkness, the smell of severe body odor and long-spoiled meat. They winced at one another as Marvin's light passed over rows of candy and packaged nuts, cookies and crackers, condiments and loaves of bread, until—

—the beam came to rest on a large potato-chip display that had been knocked over and had slammed into the beer cooler's sliding glass door. From beneath the fallen display case, a beefy arm in a torn plaid sleeve stuck up between two of the shelves.

"Damn,'' Jordan breathed as he and Marvin rushed down the aisle and lifted the display case back into position. Coogan lay on his side, his face bloodied. "What happened, Coogan? Coogan?''

The old man's eyes opened halfway and he made a thick sound in his throat. Jordan knelt beside him, helped him into a sitting position, then asked the question again.

"Duh . . . damned . . .'' Coogan paused to reach up slowly and touch a sore spot beneath his wreath of hair. He said something else, but all they could make out was "ster.''

"Coogan, what—''

There was a sound in the store, a crunching footstep. Marvin spun around and swept the flashlight beam through the store, holding it on the glass door in front. The top half cast a glaring reflection of the flashlight's beam, but below the flat strip of metal that stretched across the door's middle, there was no reflection at all.

Then, three things happened simultaneously.

Marvin said, "Jordan, I think there's something really wr—''

Coogan muttered, "Damned ugly monster.''

And something rose up from behind the row of merchandise beside Marvin. Something big.

Marvin spun to face it, slamming his back into the dairy case and lifting the flashlight to see—

—a chest, an enormous barrel chest, and he lifted the light further until it fell on a hideously deformed face and the odor they'd smelled earlier overwhelmed them in a wave and they raised their guns, but—

—the creature standing before them swept both monstrous arms outward, closing its ham-sized hands around their forearms and effortlessly lifted them over the row of paperbacks, magazines and comic books. The three stubby fingers and fat, knotty thumb dug into their forearms until their hands convulsed and released the guns. Marvin screamed shrilly, Jordan gagged from the awful smell and their minds reeled with the certainty that they were going to die.

Jordan was dropped to the floor, but the creature turned around and tossed Marvin over the row of candy and snacks and against the soda cooler; glass shattered and Marvin dropped to the floor like a swatted fly.

As soon as he was dropped, Jordan began to crawl away from the tree-like legs that towered over him, but the legs turned so that the feet were pointing toward him and the smell worsened, made his eyes water, as the beast bent down, arm outstretched, and hooked a hand under Jordan's arms, lifting him high in the air.

Jordan felt his chest tighten until he thought his lungs would be crushed beneath his ribs. A sound like a faulty fluorescent light began to drone in his head and he knew that if the sound stopped, his mind would stop with it, just shut down and cease to function, because the face he saw—the same face he'd seen in the cave the night before—could not exist.

Something moved just beyond that face and Jordan directed his eyes toward it, happy to look at something else, *anything* else, and saw that two other figures had arisen from the dark, two men wearing black shirts and black pants, their faces disguised by the darkness, but he saw them only for a moment because—

—the arm made a sudden thrusting movement and Jordan found himself shooting backward through the air, saw the distance between himself and the creature growing fast, until—

—his back slammed into the wall and he hit the floor like a rock and the darkness began to get darker and darker. . . .

The living room was thick with anticipatory silence. The

women stared at the curtained doorway at the end of the short hall, waiting, dreading what might happen on the other side . . . except for Paula, who sat comfortably in her chair, certain that someone had come to get her.

Lizzie prayed softly as she watched the doorway; Lauren did the same and was shocked when she *realized* it; Joan had no doubt that the Alliance had found them and she fought the instinctual urge to rush out of the house and get as far away as possible.

Mark lay on the sofa with the ice bag back on his head, still confused and buzzing from the pills Hester had given him.

The silence went on for an unnervingly long time until the screaming and crashing began. Joan bolted out of the love seat babbling, "Oh my God oh my God they found us they're here they're gonna kill us oh my God Jesus Christ," and she started across the room for the kitchen and the back door, but Lizzie stepped in front of her and—

—Mark sat up and the ice bag slid from his head again as he swung his legs off the sofa, muttering, "What's happening here? What's going on?" as Paula giggled in her chair, and—

—Lizzie put her hands on Joan's shoulders and held her firmly, saying, "Calm down, honey. Nobody's going to kill us." She put her arm around Joan, led her to Lauren's side and said, "Keep an eye on her, Lauren?"

Lauren was so terrified her entire body was shaking like it hadn't shaken since she was a little girl. She nodded without conviction and clutched Joan's arm, closed her eyes and breathed, "Oh, dear God, I'm so scared."

Lizzie went to the fireplace, bent down and removed the iron fireplace shovel from its stand and handed it to Lauren. "Will this make you feel better?"

She nodded as she snatched the shovel away from Lizzie and held it in a pale fist.

The noise in the store stopped.

Lizzie turned and beckoned Paula. "Come over here," she whispered.

Paula threw back her head and laughed. "Why? They're here for me, that's why they *came*. Why would I want to—"

There were heavy footsteps and the curtain suddenly disappeared. It was torn away and something else filled the rectangular space, ducked under the top of the doorway, came inside and stood at its full height.

The room filled with a rank smell.

Paula screamed as she fell out of the chair and began crawling away from the thing and toward Lizzie.

Joan and Lauren screamed, too, and the shovel Lauren held clanged against the bricks of the hearth when she dropped it.

Mark stood, swayed, and staggered away from the sofa, but without direction, as he babbled, "What's happening, what's—where did the—what is it, God, what *is* it?" He started to fall, but—

—the creature rushed forward and swept him up in one misshapen arm an instant before he hit the floor, then turned toward the doorway where—

—two men dressed entirely in black stepped in from the store and one of them went directly to the creature and took Mark while the other man shouted, "Everyone on the floor! Now!" He spun around and pointed a finger at Paula, saying, "Except you. Get up and come with us."

Lizzie, Joan and Lauren lay facedown on the floor and kept still.

The second man in black went to Joan's side, got down on one knee, and pulled her head back as far as he could by a handful of hair. "You should know better," he said quietly, calmly, almost pleasantly. He stood and turned to the creature, waved a hand at Lizzie and said, "Let's go."

The creature stomped across the room, leaned forward and struck Lizzie in the head once with what felt like a rock covered with skin, then swept her off the floor. She cried out only once—a sickened and terrified "Oohh!"—and looked up with blurred eyes at the face that hovered over her as the creature held her in its arms the way a groom would hold his bride as they went over the threshold of their honeymoon suite. *Oh, God,* she thought, *what is wrong with him? What is* wrong *with him?*

Then she was carried out of the house, which sounded empty behind her.

SEVEN

INTO THE CENTER
OF THE VORTEX

1.

Although she never lost consciousness, Lizzie had slipped into a numbed daze; she knew she was lying down and that whatever she was lying down in was moving, but she knew little else. Blurry flesh-colored ovals hovered around her, bobbing in and out of her field of vision, leaning close, then pulling far away.

As the daze began to recede, Lizzie realized she was inside a van that was traveling at a high speed. She could smell the poor unfortunate creature who had carried her away, and her first coherent thought since being taken from the house was, *Benjamin Thorne. Lord, please, give me some time with Benjamin Thorne.*

Voices spoke in hushed tones and the van slowed to a stop. Lizzie closed her eyes and listened.

"Is he out there?" Hester asked.

"Yes," a male voice replied.

Hester said, "Okay, now listen, Mark, I want you to listen *very* closely. You're feeling better, aren't you?"

"Yes," Mark answered in a hollow voice.

"You look better, *much* better. Did you take the pills?" She sounded nervous.

"Yuh-yes."

"Good, good, and you feel much better, don't you, of *course* you do, Mark. Now take my hand, take my hand. There. Now listen. Your purpose hasn't changed, do you hear me, it has *not* changed, and you're going to leave now and do exactly what we planned before, do you understand?''

''Yes.''

''And why are you doing this?''

''To speed the coming of the New Age of Enlightenment.''

''Yes, Mark.''

''To pave the way for the coming of Orrin.''

''*Yes*, Mark, and you're going to do that now, aren't you, just as we discussed, just as we planned, *aren't* you?''

''Yes, I am.''

''Good, *wonderful*, Mark, wonderful, now—''

Lizzie heard a long slow kiss.

''—go, Mark, go and perform the duty to which every moment of your life has led you. Do you understand?''

''Yes.''

A door was slid open and Lizzie heard a car idling outside. There was another kiss, then:

''We'll be together again, Mark, after you re-embody. Because we were *meant* to be together, don't forget that.''

Lizzie heard another engine idling outside the van, and after a few moments, the door slammed shut and the same male voice she'd heard earlier said, ''What was *that* all about? You told me that *we* were—''

''Just shut *up* for now.'' Hester took a deep breath, then said, ''I'm sorry. I didn't mean that, I didn't mean to snap at you. I'm just, uh, a little tense at the moment, that's all. Let's talk later, all right? Before the ceremony?''

''Yeah. Sure.''

Lizzie heard movement around her, then a disturbing silence. She opened her eyes and blinked until Hester's face was in focus. She was smiling down at Lizzie benevolently and looked much more at ease than she'd sounded a moment ago.

''Hello, Lizzie. I hope you're comfortable.''

''I'm fine.''

''Good. Good. I'm sorry for startling you back at Mr. Coogan's house, but it was kind of unavoidable. I'm not sure what you *think* you've been doing here in Grover, but I know it's very illegal.''

''Then why didn't you call the police and have me arrested? Why aren't we letting our lawyers work it out? I don't see why it's necessary for you to have your son terrorize a bunch of people then cart me off like a sack of potatoes."

At the words *your son*, Hester flinched and pulled back, her face beginning to twist up with anger; then she calmed, looked relaxed again, in control.

"Why do you do that to Benjamin, by the way?" Lizzie asked. "You use him like the witch in Oz used the flying monkeys, don't you? And worse than that is what I imagine you've done to his mind, how you've twisted him. And on top of it all, you tell everyone he's been dead for years. You use that little sob story to stir up sympathy for you, for all the pain you've gone through. But what about Benjamin's pain, Hester? What about Benjamin?"

Hester smiled, shook her head slightly. "I don't have the vaguest idea what you're talking about, Lizzie. Just lie there quietly. We'll be dropping you off very soon so we can go about our business."

"And what business is that, Hester? The business of spreading your lies? Making more predictions so you can send your other winged monkeys out to make them come true?"

Once again, Hester's face darkened, but only for a moment. She leaned very close to Lizzie and whispered in her ear: "You are pathetic, Lizzie. You don't realize it yet, but you are. You don't have any idea *what* you're talking about or *what* we're doing here. And tonight, I am going to show you exactly *how* pathetic you are . . . and how powerful *I* am." She stood and turned away from Lizzie, saying, "Let's go."

The van began to move again. Lizzie closed her eyes and prayed silently.

Sometime later—Lizzie wasn't sure how long—the van began to jostle over rough terrain; Lizzie guessed it was the dirt road Paula had spoken of earlier that evening. A few minutes later, it stopped and Hester said, "Bring her into the cave." Then the door opened as the van idled.

Benjamin appeared above her, hunching down to avoid hitting his head on the ceiling, but still appearing mountainous. Spittle dribbled over his enormous twisted lips as he breathed through his mouth; the nostrils of his malformed nose were filled with mucous. He leaned forward and picked her up in his arms, carrying her as he had before . . . like a baby. He took her out of the van and into the night.

Lizzie had pity for him, felt pain for Benjamin . . . but she tried to hold her breath for as long as possible, because his odor was unbearable.

She heard footsteps walking behind them as Benjamin carried her across the dirt road and through dense woods. The stars disappeared behind tall trees and she felt bushes and branches brush against her.

In a few moments, the stars disappeared; so did the trees and the bushes. Lizzie felt only damp, cloying air and saw only impenetrable darkness. And yet, Benjamin continued to walk just as steadily and at the same pace as he'd been walking under the night sky.

This must be the cave, Lizzie thought. *And he must know it well.*

The footsteps behind them continued to keep up with Benjamin, but not without a noticeable shortness of breath. Lizzie assumed it was Hester who was following them and smiled, amused by the idea that Hester was having trouble keeping up with her deformed and enslaved son.

She noticed that the darkness began to give way to light, a faint blue light that seemed to come and go, as if it were throbbing. She knew then that she *was* inside the cave of which Jordan had spoken, and the light she was seeing was the light that had so terrified him. As the light grew brighter, she told herself to be alert, to pay attention.

In moments, she began to *feel* the light as well as see it. It slithered over her skin, prodding now and then as if it were looking for entry. She closed her eyes to pray, but—

—she saw, once again, the piles of dead bodies she'd seen on the playground a lifetime ago, so—

—she prayed with her eyes open, asking for protection from whatever it was she was being taken into.

The light grew brighter and her muscles tensed, her stomach churned and she found herself digging her fingers into Benjamin's rock-like arm. Her ears began to ring and she felt a pressure beneath her teeth, as if they were being forced out of their sockets.

The light was behind her now. She could feel it on the back of her head.

Then it was gone. Benjamin had taken her behind a large rock and into an alcove that was sheltered from the light. He leaned forward and placed her on the cool ground. There was still enough light for her to see what was directly in front of her and when Benjamin stepped aside, his mother stepped forward, looking down at Lizzie the same way she might look down at an insect just before she stepped on it.

"Well, Lizzie," she said, "you're going to have to stay here for a while. I have some things to do. You can lie here and pray to pass the time, if you like." She grinned. "Or maybe," she added, gesturing toward the malignant blue light behind her, "you'll see the light."

Hester turned and walked away and Benjamin followed her. Their footsteps stopped and when Lizzie lifted her head, she could see their dark figures standing like shadows in the pulsing light.

"Do *not* take your *eyes* off her!" Hester whispered harshly. "And do *not* listen to a *word* she *says*. She believes in the Great Lie. You remember what *that* is, don't you?"

Benjamin made a pathetic grunting sound.

"Now, if anything goes wrong here while I'm gone, you will be punished."

He whimpered.

She hissed, "You will have to sit in the light for a very long time, do you understand?"

Another grunt, this one frightened and child-like.

Then Hester left, her footsteps sounding like a series of small bones breaking in a staccato rhythm and fading into the distance.

Benjamin turned and started back toward Lizzie. She sat up, pulled herself onto a damp rock and leaned her back against the rough wall of the cave. Benjamin stood in the roughly arched entrance to the alcove and stared silently at Lizzie for a while.

Lizzie pushed from her mind Benjamin's odor and appearance and tried to think of him only as Hester's unfortunate, malformed son whom she probably had kept not out of love or motherly attachment, but simply to use as a tool, a sort of hit man, perhaps even as a kind of pet. Lizzie straightened her posture and gave Benjamin her best smile.

"Hello, Benjamin," she said quietly.

He flinched at the sound of his name, cocked his head and looked at her from the corner of one sagging, runny eye.

"My name is Lizzie."

He rushed toward her suddenly, swiping a hand back and forth through the air as if he were going to slap her. Lizzie held her breath and tensed, but forced herself to show no sign of fear.

Benjamin stood over her, waiting for something—perhaps for her to cringe or cry out—then swaggered past her and went deeper into the alcove, where the darkness was impenetrable. She heard his movements, his noisy, rattly breathing, then a sharp *click* filled the alcove with light and made Lizzie wince. Benjamin had turned on a battery-operated fluorescent lantern. It was perched atop a rock that stood in the middle of Benjamin's possessions, which were arranged carefully on rocks and on the ground. A thin blanket was neatly folded with a single pillow on top. On top of another rock lay a doll that had not held up well over the years; its stuffing had leaked out of holes and tears, giving the dirty body a deflated look, and it was missing some hair and an eye; a small stained rag had been placed over its body like a blanket. On the ground beneath the doll was a toy fire engine; it was obviously old, had a broken ladder and was missing a front wheel, but was just as clean as a new one. Propped against a rock was a rectangular piece of cardboard to which a page from a magazine had been taped; the page displayed a photograph of a misty lake at dusk with two ducks lazing on the surface and dark purple mountains in the background. In the back of the alcove, canned foods were stacked against the cave wall in an orderly manner.

Lizzie was touched, but, at the same time, so indignant that she clenched a fist until her nails dug painfully into her palm.

He lives *here*, she thought. *In a cave. Like an animal.*

And yet, in spite of his appearance and the things he was made to do, he seemed more human than his mother.

After turning on the light, Benjamin went through the small stone room carefully, methodically; he bent down and touched the fire engine, patted at the little blanket on the doll to make sure it was in place, picked up the magazine picture, looked at it a moment, then replaced it, and looked over his collection of canned foods for a long time, as if he might be counting them.

Lizzie cleared her throat, ridding it of the lump that had risen there, and said, "You have nice things, Benjamin."

He hunched down suddenly, looked over his shoulder and made a threatening gurgling sound.

"Don't you think that picture would look better if it were up higher?" she asked, looking around surreptitiously for a place where the picture could be propped up at eye level . . . at least *her* eye level.

Benjamin growled like a dog as he swept the picture up and hugged it to his chest beneath enormous three-fingered hands.

"Up there, let's say." Lizzie stood and pointed to a small flat section of rock jutting out of the wall. "See? That way you wouldn't have to bend down to look at it. It's a very pretty picture," she said quietly. "You should be able to see it all the time."

Benjamin's head turned slowly and he stared at the flat rock, making a curious sound in his throat that sounded like an unarticulated question.

"Here, I'll show you," Lizzie said, stepping up onto one rock, then another, so she could reach the small shelf. "Hand me the picture and I'll set it up here so you can see how you like it, okay?" She reached out a hand for the picture and—

—Benjamin's lips pulled back over his mangled yellow teeth and he roared, taking a step backward and hugging the picture again.

"I'm not going to hurt your picture, Benjamin," Lizzie whispered. "I promise. If you'd like, you can put it up here. How does that sound?"

He stared at her a while, then held the picture out and stared at it a while, then glanced back and forth between the two. He spun away from her suddenly, then began to walk in a slow circle around the lantern, rubbing a hand back and forth over his lumpy head and tugging at his thin, wiry hair. Then he stopped, faced her and made a sound.

It took Lizzie a moment to realize that the sound was a word. Benjamin had said, "Liar!"

"I wouldn't lie to you, Benjamin. What makes you think I'd lie?"

More confused movements, then, in a thick voice that was almost impossible to understand, he said, "Muuhhh . . . Muhver shay . . . you liieee-yerrr."

"Ah. I see. Then why don't *you* put the picture up here. I think you'll like it much better."

Benjamin thought about it a long time, then stepped forward and lifted the picture tentatively, eyeing Lizzie with suspicion. She stepped down from the rock and nodded encouragingly. He placed the picture delicately on the stone shelf, then stepped back to admire it. He moved all around the alcove, looking at the picture from every possible angle, then his already twisted mouth slowly twisted even more into what Lizzie took to be a pleased smile. He looked at her and made a sound like the coo of a *very* large baby.

"See, Benjamin? I told you it would look nice. And I didn't lie to you, did I?" A long pause, then: "Did I?"

He swiped a hand over his face a few times—not unlike the way Curly used to in the old Three Stooges shorts—then bowed his head, shaking it only slightly.

"Benjamin, tell me . . . why do you live here in the cave?"

He began to look around slowly, as if for a place to hide, then seemed to give up and sat heavily on a rock. Slapping a palm to his chest, he said, "Sheee-*cret*."

"Secret? *You're* a secret?"

He nodded, rubbing his bulbous knees nervously.

"And you only go out when your mother lets you, right?"

He started to nod again, then doubled over suddenly as if he were cramping. His hands hung to the ground and his tiny fingernails chittered over the gritty, rocky surface as he mumbled to himself. A string of saliva dribbled from his mouth and plopped to the ground, then—

—Benjamin shot to his feet and rushed her, roaring, his putrid breath enveloping her, and—

—Lizzie screamed.

2.

When Jordan regained consciousness, he heard screaming and crashing coming from Coogan's living room, but it didn't last long. For a moment, in fact, he thought he'd imagined the sounds, but when he heard more voices after a brief silence—quiet, fearful voices—he realized it was not his imagination.

Neither was the pain he felt. It radiated from his back all the way into his head and down through his legs. He was afraid to move because he knew something might be broken, but he *had* to move. His body was not the only thing damaged; apparently the entire situation had been shattered.

Jordan pushed away from the wall and made muffled noises of pain as he used a shelf to pull himself to his feet.

"Mar-Marvin? Coogan?"

There was movement. Pieces of broken glass clinked together. Someone groaned.

"Jordy?" Marvin panted as he stood.

Jordan staggered around the shelf to his side. "Hurt bad?"

"I'm bleeding. And I'm hurting. But I don't think it's bad. Hope not, anyway." He groped around until he found his flashlight, then flicked it on and looked for his glasses. "Shit," he said when he found them.

"Broken?"

"Uh-huh. Oh, well. I've got another pair in the car."

They limped through the maze of toppled shelves and spilled goods until they found Coogan on hands and knees, groaning. Jordan knelt beside him, wincing with pain. "Hey, Coogan. What's the damage?"

"I can't see straight, is the damage."

"Here, we'll find your glasses."

"No, it's not just that. My eyes are crossed. Bastard hit me a couple times. Hard. Right in the head. Looked like he had a big rock in his hand."

"Nope," Marvin said, "just his hand."

"Well," Coogan puffed, trying to get up, "find my glasses anyway."

"Can you walk?" Jordan asked.

"I can try."

Once they'd found Coogan's glasses and got him on his feet, they headed back into the living room. They met Lauren at the doorway.

"Oh, thank God," she said. Tears glistened on her cheeks and her hands quaked as she reached out to help Coogan up the step and through the door.

Joan was right behind her, face pale and jaw slack.

In the living room, Coogan stretched out on the sofa. Lauren clutched Jordan's arm and whispered frantically, "They took him, they took him back, and now he's going to the plant, I know it, I just *know* it."

Jordan put an arm around her shoulder and held her close. "Where's Lizzie?" he asked.

"They took her, too," Joan said. "Her, Mark and Paula."

"What do they want with Lizzie?" Marvin asked, lowering himself into a chair.

"It's not what *they* want with her," Joan said. "It's what *Hester* wants with her."

"Okay, okay, we don't have much time," Jordan said, "we've gotta get moving. Marvin, if he's on his way . . ." Jordan left the sentence unfinished, staring at his friend with a lost look on his face.

"I can try to make it in the car, but if he's taking a plane, he'll get there *long* before me."

"Couldn't we at least *try* giving the plant a call?" Coogan suggested.

Lauren said, "You could try, but I *know* they wouldn't pay much attention to you, and when Mark arrived, they'd just have a big laugh about it."

"Maybe *I* could fly," Marvin said.

"How?" Jordan asked.

Marvin shrugged and looked around the room for any help he could get.

Joan went to Coogan's side and said, "What about Flash?"

"I thought of that, but . . ." He sat up slowly, one hand on his head, his face twisted with pain. ". . . I don't think it would be a good idea."

"Why *not*?"

"Flash?" Jordan asked. "Flash who? Who's Flash?"

"Flash Gordon," Joan replied.

Marvin and Jordan exchanged a glance and Marvin said, "Honey, maybe you better lie down."

"No, *no*, not *that* Flash Gordon," Joan said, animated now, speaking breathlessly. "*Chuck* Gordon. Everybody *calls* him Flash because he flies a *helicopter*. He takes people up for an aerial view of Mount Shasta, and once in a while he uses it for travel."

"Where *is* he?" Jordan's voice had nearly risen to a shout.

"Wait, wait just a minute," Coogan said, still holding his head. "Flash is *not* a good idea. For one thing, he won't have anything to *do* with this. And for another, he's um . . . well, *I* wouldn't go up with him."

"How many other people in this town fly?" Jordan asked him.

"None that I know of."

"Then Flash is our man."

"That's the problem. Flash is *nobody's* man."

"He's temperamental," Joan explained, "and he drinks, but Coogan, he's all there *is*."

"And he's probably three sheets to the wind by now."

"You mean . . . he drinks . . . a lot?" Marvin croaked.

"Every night," Coogan said.

Jordan said, "Well, let's go make Flash some coffee."

3.

The airfield was small and deserted. A few small planes and a helicopter were parked behind a utility shed with rusty corrugated metal siding. The hollow skeleton of an old snack bar stood between the small parking lot and the runway. The driver of the van drove across the parking lot, over a patch of rocky, weedy ground, and right up to the edge of the runway, where a Cessna waited, rotors spinning, lights shining brightly in the dark.

A man sitting across from Mark in the back of the van got up before they'd stopped, unlatched the door and pulled it open. Hester took Mark's arm and led him quickly out of the van to the plane, saying, "I hope you see now, Mark, I hope you *really see* that your wife is not on your side. She is still wallowing in her ignorance, you realize that, don't you?"

He nodded, but said, "I still wish I could have—"

"No, Mark, *no*. No wishing. No looking back now. This is it." They were at the plane and a man inside was holding the door open for him. She stood close to him, one hand placed flat against the middle of his chest. "Remember, Mark, you are your own god. You decide what is right for you to do. You are a part of the Godbody. Right now, you are an extraordinarily important part of the Godbody. And you are going to find the godness within you by doing what you were born to do."

The words *did* make him feel important, made him *want* to do this. But he felt so confused, his mind was spinning so fast. . . .

"Go, now, Mark. And remember to meditate. I want you to chant and meditate during the whole trip." She kissed him, then put her hands on his shoulders, turned him around and pushed him into the plane.

The pilot slammed the door, got into the cockpit, and aside

from telling Mark to strap himself in, said nothing as the plane began to move. Mark stared at his lap for a while, trying not to think, trying to slow down the dizzying spinning in his head. When the plane increased speed, he looked out the window and saw Hester speed by. The ground outside became a blur, then began to fall away, giving him a sickening feeling in his stomach. He closed his eyes, leaned his head back and tried to put himself in a meditative state of mind. It seemed impossible at first, but once he started to meditate—"Gaaawwd-baaawwd-eeeee," he droned quietly, "Gaaawwd-baaawwd-eeeee"—the sound of the plane and the motion of flight disappeared and Mark felt himself floating naked in blissful, silent nothingness.

4.

Benjamin rushed toward Lizzie with a guttural roar, then he stopped inches from her and motioned toward the ground. She dropped to her knees, screaming, but stopped abruptly, angry at herself for losing her control.

He motioned downward again, growling, and Lizzie sat. She watched as Benjamin turned away from her and began stalking around the lantern again, mumbling to himself and slobbering.

Lizzie wondered what she'd done or said to upset him so. She put her head in her hands and prayed silently for the right words, the right actions, *anything* that might win Benjamin's confidence.

She watched him stop his aimless circling, reach behind a thick stalagmite and remove a bulky rag that was wrapped around something. He unrolled it and a spoon, a fork, a rusty can opener and a small comb fell into his enormous hand. He plucked the comb up with a thumb and finger, put the others back in the rag and set them on the ground.

Turning to the doll, he pulled its blanket back and lifted it gently from its stone bed, then carried it to the rock where he'd been sitting earlier. He lowered himself slowly to the rock, staring at his doll, then held the doll in his lap and began to comb its stiff hair. He was clumsy, though, and far too forceful for the task. With each stroke of his hand, strands of hair tore out of the vinyl head and remained tangled in the teeth of the comb.

Lizzie saw that he was using the small end of the comb where the tiny teeth were positioned close together. At the other end, the teeth were spaced farther apart.

He made a sad growling sound, stopped combing and began to fidget on the rock.

"Benjamin?" Lizzie whispered.

Holding the doll to his chest, he stood suddenly, roaring as he shot her a hateful glare. His entire body trembled as the roar grew louder, reverberating throughout the cave, until he threw the comb at Lizzie and stopped. He remained standing for a while, watching her, waiting for her to make a wrong move, then sat again and began to rock the doll slightly in his hands.

Lizzie looked at his hands, with their bulging knuckles, leathery, knotty skin and tiny lumps of fingernails. They were the same hands, no doubt, that had killed, or at least brutalized, the reporter Jordan and Marvin had been looking for before they'd gotten so sidetracked. They were probably the same hands that had killed Joan's friend Paul Kragen and who knew *how* many others. And yet, she watched them now as they rocked an old doll as gently as if it were a living infant. There was *something* inside that hulking body that could be reached, if she could only figure out *how*.

"I know how to comb your doll's hair so it won't come out," she said quietly.

He grunted at her, as if to say, *Shut up.*

"I'll show you, Benjamin." She leaned forward and picked up the comb that had bounced off her shoulder when he threw it. She held it up for him to see and pointed to the large end. "See here? The teeth are farther apart on this end of the comb. That way, the hair won't tangle and pull out."

He leaned back his head to see out from under the thick ridge that slanted downward and stuck out over his uneven eyes. His enormous mouth hung open beneath his flat, lumpy nose as he thought about what she'd said.

He can't decide, she thought. *He can't decide whether to believe me or his mother.*

"I'll show you, if you'd like."

Another grunt, this time with an inflection that said, *I dare you.*

"Do you want me to come over there? Or would you like to bring the doll over here?"

Benjamin stroked the doll as he stood uncertainly. His steps were cautious, halting, and a couple of times he looked as if he were about to burst into another rage. But he finally stood before her, bending down timidly to offer her the doll.

Lizzie lifted herself onto a rock, took the doll as if she were taking someone's baby, and said, "Now watch." She ran the comb carefully through the doll's hair. It worked. The comb moved smoothly as Lizzie tried to cover the bald spot with the hair that was left.

Benjamin made a sound of pleasant surprise. When she looked up at him, she saw that he was *thrilled*. His head was bobbing back and forth and his mouth bent into that mangled smile she'd seen earlier.

"See?" she whispered. "Isn't that better?"

She gave him the doll and the comb and he tried it himself.

"Gently, Benjamin."

He did as she suggested. As he combed the doll's hair delicately, he turned, went back to his rock and sat down again, cooing at the doll and murmuring to himself.

She watched him awhile, enjoying the sight. He seemed so happy. He lifted his head, grinned at her as best he could, and nodded his approval—or perhaps his thanks—then went back to combing. He continued for a long time, acting as if he were alone. Then, when he seemed satisfied with the job, he stood, stroked the doll's hair gently with one finger and put the doll back to bed.

Benjamin returned the comb to the rag on the ground, picked up the can opener and went to his collection of canned foods. He chose a can, went to his rock and opened it. After picking up the fork, he began to eat Vienna sausages noisily.

5.

Flash Gordon's house was dark. Leaning on Joan's shoulders and limping, Coogan led them across the dead lawn, around the broken-down lawn furniture and up to the front door of the rickety shack that was Chuck Gordon's home. Coogan's firm knocking seemed to shake the entire structure.

"Hey, Flash! It's Coogan!" Then, to the others, he muttered, "Boy is he gonna be pissed."

A dog began to bark inside the house.

After a few more knocks, a rough voice shouted, "Awright! *Awright!* But this better be damned good." Stomping feet, more rapid-fire barking, then: "Will you shut *up*, dog!"

The yellow porch light came on, locks clicked and rattled and the door opened on a short, wiry man with a head of thin white hair that was standing up in places, a face as craggy as a walnut shell and the red, bulbous nose of a man whose best friend is a bottle. He wore a threadbare terrycloth robe of indeterminate color and spattered with food stains. At his feet was a four-legged mop with a dirty, matted snout, eyes hidden behind a thick layer of bangs and unwashed hair that was almost the same color as Flash's robe. The dog's tongue bobbed in and out of its mouth as it stared up at them, fidgeting and wagging its tail.

"What the hell do you want?" Flash croaked. Then, after seeing the others with Coogan: "And *who* in thee *hell* are all these *people* at my damned *door* at this *hour*?"

"Well, Flash, if you'll give me a minute, I'll—"

"What the hell *time* is it, anyway?"

"Uh, I don't know, but that's not important right now because we've got to—"

"You wake me up, it sure as hell *is* important! I gotta get outta bed and come to the door and you tell me it ain't—"

Joan shouted, "Shut *up*, Flash!"

He flinched and looked at Joan as if she'd hurt him. "Well, Joanie . . . what're you so rattled about?"

"Flash," Coogan said, "we need your help and we need it *now*. Have you been drinking?"

"In my sleep? *Hell*, no!"

"We need your 'copter," Joan said.

"Nobody flies that chopper but me."

"That's what I mean. We need you to fly somewhere for us."

"In the middle of the friggin' *night*?"

"Can we come in, Flash?" Coogan sighed, exasperated. "Please? I really need to sit down."

It wasn't until then that Flash noticed the bandage on Coogan's forehead and the discolored swelling on his cheek.

"What in *hell* happened to *you*, Coogie?"

"Please, Flash. Let us in."

"Ain't gonna do you no good, 'cause I ain't flyin' nowhere in the middle of the son-of-a-bitchin' *night*."

"We'll pay you," Jordan said.

"Hell, I don't even *know* you."

"My name's Jordan Cross. Two hundred dollars."

"Hell, I can make more'n that in a day of—"

"Five hundred dollars."

"C'mon in."

The dog went into another fit of barking, jumping up on their legs as they filed into the house. Before they went through the door, Marvin leaned close to Jordan and whispered, "I go up in a 'copter with this guy, I'm a *dead* man."

Jordan patted him on the back, but said nothing.

Inside, the air was greasy with the smell of garlic and scorched butter. Flash turned on lights as he led them into his living room.

"Now," he said, flopping into a ratty old easy chair with torn vinyl upholstery, "what the hell's all this about you needin' me to fly someplace?"

"Tonight, Flash," Coogan said. "Right now. We need you to take Marvin, here, to the Silicon Valley."

"Where in the Silicon Valley?" Flash asked.

"Hollis Airpark," Jordan replied. "Unless you can land closer than that to the Diego Nuclear Power Plant."

"Diego? What the hell you want at Diego?"

Joan said, "We can't explain everything right now, Flash, but—"

"We want to stop someone who's planning to trigger a meltdown," Jordan said.

"Call 'em. Tell 'em."

"Do you want the five hundred bucks or not?" Jordan asked.

"Well . . . I don't know. Five hundred might not be quite enough for this kinda—"

"Do you *want* the five *hundred* or *not?*"

Flash wiggled his tongue in his mouth thoughtfully, making a slurping sound. "Well . . ." He turned to Marvin. "You ever been up in a chopper before?"

"No."

Flash smirked. "Okay. Lemme get dressed." He got up, crossed the room, then turned to Jordan. "That gonna be cash?"

"I've got it with me."

Flash left, nodding.

"I'm telling you," Coogan whispered to Marvin, "this isn't a good idea."

"Why not?"

He glanced at the others nervously. "Well, you can tell Flash doesn't make much of a living from his helicopter tours. He doesn't do it for the money. He just, um . . . he likes to scare the piss out of tourists."

Marvin took a deep breath and let it out slowly.

Jordan said, "We'll just have to make it clear to Mr. Gordon that Marvin's not a tourist." He turned to Marvin. "Don't be afraid to show him your gun if you have to. I doubt that Flash has ever had a passenger who could scare the piss right back out of *him*."

They waited in silence until Flash returned, dressed in old baggy jeans and a dirty chambray work shirt. "Okay," he said. "Gimme my pay and we'll go."

"It's in the car," Jordan said as everyone stood. "Half now and half when you get back."

"Hey, wait just a son-of-a-bitchin' minute, you said—"

"We do it this way or not at all. *This* way, we make sure you do a nice, safe job of flying, without causing my friend here too much stress. Understand?"

Flash glared at Coogan, then at Joan, then back to Coogan, as if he knew they'd been talking about him while he was out of the room. Then he nodded before giving a loud whistle and shouting, "C'mon, dog, let's go!"

The mutt skittered down the hall and into the living room, jumping and wiggling with excitement.

"You're not taking the dog," Jordan said.

Flash glared at him, then, standing close: "My dog goes everywhere with me. Or else *I* don't go." He led the way out of the house, turning off lights as he went.

Coogan shook his head slowly as he limped out, muttering, "He loves to have the last word."

6.

"Do you remember your father?" Lizzie asked.

Benjamin gagged on his food, swallowed and growled, raising the fork threateningly.

What does that mean? Lizzie wondered. *He hates his father, or he just doesn't want to talk about him?*

Benjamin continued eating.

"You do remember him, don't you, Benjamin?"

Another growl.

"His name was Mike Lumley. I understand he was a very nice man, and he's—"

He dropped the can and its contents splashed over the ground as he rushed her again, bellowing as he waved his arms. She was ready for it this time; she didn't move, just kept talking.

"—and he's living in a hospital now. He's not allowed to leave, ever, because—"

Benjamin fell to one knee, gripped her shoulders and shook her, screaming in her face.

Lizzie's head was jerking back and forth, but she raised her voice and continued: "—because people think he's very sick, but—"

He pressed a hand over her mouth, pressed hard, and looked into her eyes, lowering his cry to a pleading whimper. He looked around urgently, his eyes wide and frightened. After looking in every direction, he turned to Lizzie again, shook her hard and grunted, "No. *No!*" Then he let her go cautiously, but remained on his knee before her.

Lizzie whispered, "You're not supposed to talk about him, are you?"

He shook his head.

"Why not?"

After looking around again, he said, in as close to a whisper as he could get, "He . . . baaad. Bad and . . . a-and duhh-*dead*."

"Oh, no, Benjamin. He's not dead."

He started to put a hand over her mouth again, but she clutched his wrist.

"It's all right, Benjamin," she whispered reassuringly. "No one's here. No one can hear us."

He pulled away from her, looking around again.

"You're afraid of being punished, aren't you? You're afraid of being made to stand in that light."

Benjamin nodded shamefully.

"Did you know that your father wanted to *protect* you from that light?"

He stood, waving his arms again for her to stop.

"He was not a bad man, Benjamin. What he did was . . . well, it was wrong, misguided, but—"

He screamed at her again and she stopped.

"Aren't you curious? Don't you want to know? Don't you feel *anything* for your father?"

Benjamin looked at her for a long time, his head tilting from side to side thoughtfully. He seemed to be making some sort of decision. Finally, he nodded once and placed a finger over his lips for Lizzie to be quiet. Then he motioned for her to follow him, picked up the lantern and went to the back of the alcove. On his knees, he crawled behind the same stalagmite where he'd stored his comb and utensils. But he went deeper this time, moved aside a few small rocks and dug into the earth with his hands. He produced another cigar box, held it in front of Lizzie, in the light, and opened it.

All she could see were wadded pieces of old tissue paper.

Benjamin burrowed his fingers beneath the tissue and removed a photograph. It was stiff and warped and yellowed around the edges from dampness. In the photograph, Lizzie saw Benjamin as a little boy, his chubby hands pressed together happily before his chest. Mike Lumley was hunkered down beside him, his arm around his son's shoulders.

Benjamin stared at the picture as if she weren't there. He stared reverently.

Lizzie had found a way to reach him.

7.

The moment they arrived at the airfield, Flash changed. He went from grumpy and put-upon to confident and familiar with his surroundings. He was in his element, and his comfort showed.

"I'll fire it up," he said as he got out of the car.

Jordan could see that Marvin was scared. He was fidgety and talking too much. When they got out, Marvin walked around the front of the car, patting his sport coat and fishing through his pockets.

"What're you looking for?" Jordan asked.

"Huh? Oh. Uh, I don't know. The reckless bravery of my boyhood, I suppose."

Lowering his voice, Jordan said, "Come on, don't worry. It'll be fine. Like I said, show him your gun if he starts playing with you. Now. If you *want* to worry about something, worry about what happens when you *get* there."

"Yeah, yeah, that too."

"Remember, put him down if you can. Kill him if you have to."

"Then what? Just dance away tossing daisies in the air? We haven't exactly had a chance to map this whole thing out, you know."

"You know the law. You know just as much about a situation like this as I do. Hell, you got me *into* this shit. This is all your fault."

"What're you gonna do?"

"The question is, what am I gonna do first. I've got an Inner Circle party to crash, I'm just not sure when. Hester's got Lizzie but I don't know where."

"Hey. You get Lizzie out of there. She's a terrific lady."

"Says who?"

"Says me. You take good care of her. After spending some time with her—" He turned to look at the dirty, dark green helicopter that was beginning to putter about ten yards away. "—I'm not gonna feel like an idiot praying up there."

Flash shouted, "Let's go!"

"Scared?" Jordan asked.

"Shitless."

"It'll be fine."

"Hey, if something happens to me up there, do me a favor."

"What's that?"

"Clean your damned office."

Jordan watched his friend jog to the helicopter, duck beneath the spinning rotor and get in. He waved once before he closed the door, and in a moment, the helicopter rose slowly and thudded away. Jordan headed back to the car and said to the others, "Let's go figure out what the hell to do next."

8.

After he'd stared at the photograph for a long while, Benjamin whispered, "Thasss . . . my dad-*deee*."

"It's a very nice picture," Lizzie said. "Do you remember that day?"

He nodded.

"Who took the picture, Benjamin?"

His head tilted first to the right, then the left, and his eyes squinted as he thought hard. Finally: "Muh-my graaah-*maaaww*. Duuhhh . . . Dad-deee hurted Graah-*maaw*. Mu-ver shay . . . he truh-try *kill* Graah-maaw and th-that . . . that he *baaad*." He stopped, winded; saying so much at one time had been an effort. Then: "Muh-make . . . me . . . shad."

"Of course it does. That would make *me* sad, too. But, Benjamin . . . I have some good news for you." She placed a hand on his shoulder cautiously. He was startled, but didn't protest. "Your daddy did not try to kill your grandma. A friend of mine spoke with your daddy recently."

Benjamin jerked away from her hand and faced her, angry.

"Really. He went to the hospital where your daddy lives. Your daddy told my friend all about that day that he hurt your grandma. He feels very bad about it. Even now, after all these years, it makes your daddy very sad that he hurt Grandma. But he didn't *mean* to."

He cocked his head suddenly, like a confused puppy, and looked down at the photograph again, stroking one corner absently with his thumb.

"Would you like to know why I'm here in Grover, Benjamin?"

He nodded uncertainly.

She spoke slowly, praying that he would be able to absorb it all and reach some sort of conclusion. "I knew your mommy when we were both just little girls. We didn't get along. Do you know why? Because even when your mommy was a little girl, Orrin was inside her. She didn't know it then, but he was there. Then she grew up, met your daddy and they got married and went on their honeymoon. That's, um, a little vacation people take when they get married. They came here to Grover. Your daddy says that Mommy went for a walk early one morning, and

we *think* that might have been the day she discovered this cave
. . . and the blue light. And we're pretty sure that you were just
a tiny little seed inside your mommy then . . . growing. She
came to this place every day while she was here and she probably stood in that light. While you were inside her. Benjamin,
we think—'' She stopped, closed her eyes a moment. How could
she put it? She prayed for the right words, looked at Benjamin
and smiled a moment, then said, ''Benjamin, we think that the
blue light out there—'' She gestured over her shoulder. ''—could
have made you . . . the way you are. It could have damaged you
while you were inside your mommy's tummy. Do . . . do you
understand what I'm saying?''

The thick strip of coarse hair that ran along the edge of the
crooked ridge of his eyes knotted in the center and he hunched
forward, frowning at the photograph. He did nothing for a long
time, then put the photograph back in its box and the box back
in its hiding place. When he turned and stepped around Lizzie,
his face was still a dark mask of either anger or deep thought,
she couldn't tell.

''I wasn't finished, Benjamin.''

He spun around and snarled at her.

''Your daddy didn't mean to hurt Grandma. He meant to . . .
well, to kill your . . . your mommy. Because he knew she would
do bad things. Because he knew Orrin would *make* her do bad
things. Your daddy wanted you to have a good life. Not *this*—''
She looked around at the alcove. ''—not a *cave*. Your daddy
wanted you to be happy, like you were when the two of you
played catch with the Nerf ball. Do you remember that?''

Benjamin's eyes widened and his face softened at those words.

''Only he wanted you to be happy *all the time*. He didn't want
you to live in a cave and be punished with blue light and controlled by an invisible spirit that only means you—and everyone
else—harm, like Orrin. He wanted only the *best* for you.''

He turned his head toward the place where he hid the photograph of himself and his father.

''So, he decided to . . . um, to kill your mommy, thinking
that . . . well, that it might ensure you a happy future. He was
wrong, Benjamin, because it's *always* wrong to kill *anyone*, no
matter *what* the reason. But . . . he was thinking of you.'' It
was a small lie, but she hoped it would have big results.

Benjamin stared at the ground a moment, then put a hand on

each side of his head and pressed, clawing his fingers into his hair. He began to walk in a circle again around the lantern, occasionally stopping to kick the large rock on which it stood. Bending suddenly, he swept the tin Vienna sausage can off the ground and wadded it up in his hand like a piece of paper, then threw it blindly. Lizzie flinched as the can bounced loudly off the wall and surrounding rocks. Benjamin continued to circle the lantern, growling softly now.

"Why are you angry, Benjamin?" she asked. Her voice was timid, but her mind was reeling. Was he angry at her? Was he angry because his life *could* have been better? Was he angry at Hester? Or was he just angry because he thought Lizzie was lying again.

No response.

"Are you angry at me? Is it because I said—"

With no warning, Benjamin exploded in a scream— *"Liiieeey-errrr!"*—dove toward Lizzie, gripped her beneath both arms and jerked her off the ground. He lifted her high and began shaking her like a rag doll as he carried her across the alcove to the rock on which she'd been sitting earlier. Then he dropped her.

Lizzie screamed on impact. Hot needles of pain shot up her spine and along her ribs and her scream became a miserable gag as she slid off the rock to the ground.

Benjamin continued to scream, kicking the ground and knocking damp earth and bits of gravel on Lizzie, then he locked his trembling hands together and lifted them over his head, ready to bring them down on Lizzie, but a voice said—

—"That won't be necessary, Benjamin."

Benjamin froze and they both turned to the alcove's archway. Hester smiled.

9.

"No," Jordan said as he stopped Marvin's car behind Coogan's place, "absolutely not. You need to lie down and lick your wounds."

"I'm *fine*," Coogan snapped from the backseat. "Just got a few dings, is all."

"Come on, Coogan," Joan said, putting an arm around him, "take some aspirin, have a drink and go to bed."

Jordan said, "Joan can stay with you for a while."

"Oh, no," Joan said firmly. "I'm going with *you*."

Jordan rolled his eyes.

Coogan pulled away from Joan and leaned toward the front seat. "You tell me Katie's dead, Jordan. Okay, so there ain't a thing I can do about it and when this is all over I'll have myself the biggest cry I've had since my wife died but for now—" His voice grew louder. "—my *grandson* is *alive* as far as I know and if there's a chance he'll be there, *I'm* gonna be there."

Jordan sighed. It seemed endless. Had he known so many people were going to insist upon involving themselves in this case, he never would have taken it. Of course, he wouldn't have taken the case if he'd known a *lot* of things.

"Okay, Coogan," he said, "you can come. But, Joan—" He looked at her in the rearview mirror. "—I just don't think it's . . . well, a good idea for you to come, too."

Joan didn't look angry or even a little upset as she stared out the window beside her. The silence went on so long that first Lauren looked back at her, then Coogan turned to face her.

"You know, I've been telling myself for quite a while that there was nothing I could do about it. And I suppose that, at the time, there wasn't. But you know . . . I never even found out if she was dead or alive. She could still be in there, for all I know. And even if she's not . . . I don't know, maybe this sounds stupid, but . . . I *need* to go in there with you." She looked at Lauren. "Finding your son would be a little like . . . well, I've put up a pretty chilly front these past years, but that doesn't mean I haven't felt guilty. Finding your boy would kind of make up for . . . for what I didn't do."

Jordan closed his eyes before he rolled them this time, then nodded. "Okay," he said quietly. "But keep in mind that I'm not sure *what* we're going to be getting into. We're not gonna be just sneaking through the dark and peeking around corners. This will be *dangerous*."

"Yeah, I know," Coogan said. "And I've got something for that. I've got a *few* things. Come inside and I'll show you."

"We're gonna have to hurry," Jordan said as Coogan got out of the car.

Before they'd gone to Flash's earlier, Coogan had gone to the fuse box in the rear of the store and restored the power, so when they went inside, he flicked on a light.

"I'm a Christian," he said as he led them through the house toward the store, "just like Lizzie. I believe in God and I believe in prayer. But I also believe in being prepared."

Once in the store, the others watched as Coogan went behind the register, reached under the counter and jerked down hard. There was a sharp ripping sound and Coogan pulled out a hand-gun with strips of torn packing tape still attached to it.

"A couple years ago," he said, "some young fella came in here and beat the stuffing outta me for a six-pack of Bud and the cash in the till. So I decided to drag this old souvenir out of the closet just in case it happened again. Army Colt .45. Nice piece of work." He stuffed it under his belt and motioned for them to follow him.

They went through the living room and down the hall to Coogan's bedroom, where he knelt and reached under the bed. He removed a rectangular oak wood box, put it on the bed, turned the latch and lifted the lid. Two Colt .22 target pistols rested in molded depressions in the red velvet-lined bottom of the box.

"My wife bought this set for our thirty-eighth wedding anniversary," he said. "We both enjoyed going out in the woods now and then for a little target practice." He picked lifted them out gently and held one in each hand. "Personalized walnut grips, his and hers." He stood and handed one of the pistols to Joan, the other to Lauren. "Probably won't even have to remember you've got 'em. But . . . just in case."

"Good idea," Jordan muttered.

"Now," Coogan said, pointing a finger at Jordan, "I know you've got a gun, *but* . . ." He went to his closet and began shuffling around. "I used to have quite a collection, but that's about all that's left of it now. But this, *this* baby . . ." He chuckled, still searching. "I only used it a couple times, just for the hell of it, shootin' at the sides of old barns, stuff like that. Mostly, I have it just to have one. I never really—ah, *here* she is." He stood and turned slowly, smiling. In one hand, he held a box of shotgun shells, in the other a sawed-off double-barrel shotgun. He emptied the box on the bed, cracked open the gun and slipped two shells into the barrel. "This," he said to Jordan, "is for Hester Thorne's bad little boy."

10.

Hester walked into the alcove smiling as she looked around. "Looks a bit messy, Benjamin. Has she been a problem?"

Benjamin lowered his hands and stepped away from Lizzie. He grunted noncommittally in response to Hester's question.

"I thought she might be." Hester faced Lizzie as she spoke to Benjamin. "Has she been telling you lies, Benjamin? If she's been *speaking*, she's been telling lies. Did she tell you about her god? About Jesus?" She spat the name.

Benjamin frowned.

"I hope you haven't been listening to her."

Lizzie said, "At least my God doesn't condone the killing of children."

"No. He just sends people to hell when they die."

"No, He doesn't, Hester," Lizzie replied with a gentle smile. "The Bible does not say that and you know it. At least, I *thought* you did. You shouldn't speak with such authority about something you know nothing about."

"The same goes for you, Lizzie. You know *nothing* about what goes on here. And you never will, because you won't let go of your ignorance." She stepped closer to Lizzie. "Tell me a little about your friends, Lizzie? Who sent them? What are they doing here? I know a little. I know that Jordan Cross is a private investigator and I know that Marvin Ackroyd is in the electronic surveillance business."

"Do you know that they found out all about how you killed Reverend Hallway and Edmond Fiske?"

Her eyes narrowed and her cold smile disappeared. "I suspected. I found their little telephone tap."

"Did you know they found out you've been talking with the president?"

Her eyes closed then for a long time. When she opened them, she smiled again and said, "It doesn't matter. They won't be leaving Grover."

'Maybe not. But they know what you're doing. They know what you've sent Mark Schroeder to do. All they need is a telephone."

Hester moved close to Lizzie, squatted down in front of her and grabbed the material of Lizzie's dress in her fists, pulling

Lizzie's face close. "What makes you so superior?" she hissed. "What makes your beliefs so much better? People have never been killed in the name of God? People have never been tortured in the name of Christ? Entire *wars* have been fought for your god! Yet you're still able to worship the way you please. Why not us?"

"Because Christ didn't *possess* anyone and *tell* them to kill for Him."

Hester stood suddenly, her fists clenched at her sides. She spun around to face Benjamin and spoke quickly. "The others will be coming soon. One sound out of her and you're to shut her up, understand?"

He growled affirmatively.

"But don't hurt her *too* badly. She's going to participate in the ceremony tonight. And remember, Benjamin—" She moved close to him and lowered her voice. "—she is a liar. She is *not* your friend. And if I find you've been listening to her—listening to so much as a *word*—you'll be standing out there all night."

Without looking back, she left the alcove.

Benjamin paced nervously, angrily.

Lizzie realized her heart was racing. She took some deep breaths as she watched Benjamin. Finally: "Benjamin, I'm sorry if you're—"

He rushed to her silently and slapped her face so hard that her head knocked against the cave wall. The blow made her dizzy and made her entire skull throb. She waited for the dizziness to subside before speaking again.

"Please, Benjamin, if I could just—"

Another slap, a bit harder this time. She felt blood trickling over her lip. When she looked up, she saw him towering over her, hand raised, waiting for her to say something, waiting for an excuse to strike her a third time.

She bowed her head, closed her eyes and said nothing more. She had lost him.

11.

Two hooded white-robed figures waited just outside the mouth of the cave. Hester came out of the darkness and into the moonlight, smiling serenely.

"Orrin has given me an important message," she said.

The two figures moved closer.

"The usual procedure for finding the Chosen One is to be canceled for tonight. The decision has already been made. It's your responsibility to get the Chosen One and bring him back here. Orrin wants Nathan Schroeder."

12.

Marvin's stomach had never moved around so much in his entire life and he was afraid that, at any moment, it would fly up into his throat and shoot out of his mouth. He clutched the seat beneath him with both hands and his legs were so tense their muscles burned. His head hurt so bad that sometimes it was difficult to distinguish between the throbbing of his headache and the throbbing of the helicopter's rotors.

He wasn't sure how long they'd been up; a few minutes, thirty minutes, an hour or more, he couldn't tell. All he knew was fear.

Flash whistled happily at the controls, but they hadn't spoken since leaving the ground. Marvin was afraid to even look at him; he couldn't bear the *thought* of that angry old drunk piloting him through the air, so he knew the *sight* of it wouldn't help his state of mind.

Between them, the dog sat on its haunches, fidgeting, panting and making excited whining and woofing noises. Occasionally, the dog leaned over and sniffed at Marvin and he brushed it away nervously.

Marvin wasn't sure how long the trip was going to take, so he decided it might be a good idea to ask a few questions. He coughed to clear the fear from his throat, then said, "So, um, how long will this take us?"

"Aaaww, I'd say three and a half hours or so. Mebbe less. Have to stop and refuel, course."

"What?" Marvin asked, turning to him. "Where are we gonna—" He choked on his words when he saw Flash tipping a silver-plated flask to his lips. He stared at Flash open-mouthed until he found his voice and screamed, *"What the fuck are you doing?"*

The dog jumped into Flash's lap and Flash was so startled he rapped his head on the window beside him.

"What in theee *hell* you yellin' about, boy?" Flash asked.

"That!" Marvin shouted, pointing at the flask. "What's in it?"

"Whiskey. Want some?" He held it out to Marvin.

"Yes!" Marvin snatched it out of Flash's hand so hard that whiskey sloshed out of the small opening and filled the cabin with its stinging smell. He put the flask between his legs and held it there tightly.

"Well, ain't you gonna have some?"

"No! I'm keeping it away from *you!"*

Flash stared at him for a long time, frowning, then said, "Oh, no." He unfastened his seat belts and rose a few inches from the seat, leaning toward Marvin and reaching for the flask.

The helicopter leaned sharply to the right and took a sudden dip.

Marvin screamed, sliding down in his seat.

"C'mon, now you give me that," Flash demanded.

"No-no-no!" Marvin shouted, sliding a hand beneath his coat. He pulled out the gun and held it between both hands with the barrel a couple inches from Flash's forehead. "Sit down! *Sit back down!"*

Flash didn't move, just stared at Marvin for a moment; then he eased back into his seat, a smirk curling his lips.

"Just *fly* this fucking thing and *forget* about the *booze!"*

Flash cackled. "There's two things I don't much like to fly without. My dog and my drink."

"How do you feel about flying without your brains?"

He cackled even harder, slapping his thigh. "You shoot me, you gonna go down, boy."

"You keep drinking, we're gonna go down *anyway!"*

"Oh shit, boy. I drink up here alla time," he said, rising again to reach for the flask.

"Not with me you don't, *now siddown!"*

Flash's smirk disappeared. He returned to the controls and straightened the helicopter's course again.

Marvin's hands were trembling and his bladder felt full to bursting suddenly.

Flash glowered at him. "I don't take this shit from nobody in my chopper."

"Most people don't pay you five hundred bucks to take 'em somewhere, either and if you want all of it, you'll stay right there and get us where we're going. *Without* your drink."

He held the gun on Flash until he was satisfied the old man was going to do nothing more than fly the helicopter. Then he slipped the gun back into his shoulder holster, realizing that his fingers were numb from gripping it so tightly, and leaned his head back, trying to relax, trying to calm himself. He couldn't.

Thinking of Lizzie, Marvin closed his eyes and prayed.

13.

The ice-pick beam from Jordan's flashlight pierced the darkness of the woods as they walked parallel to the dirt road that led to the Alliance colony; the others had flashlights, too—they'd taken them from the store—but only Jordan used his. They walked close together, moving slowly, carefully and quietly.

Wildlife skittered and crept all around them.

Wings slapped overhead and an owl hooted.

"We're probably close," Jordan whispered. "If you hear anything that doesn't sound like an animal, freeze."

"Yeah, and *then* what?" Joan hissed.

"Don't worry," Jordan said, "I'm pretty sure the cave is just a little—"

There was a bustle of movement in the woods and it grew louder quickly.

Footsteps and quiet voices.

Jordan flicked off the flashlight, tucked it in a pocket and, just as he had instructed, Lauren, Joan and Coogan froze . . . and looked at him expectantly. He raised the shotgun cautiously, waiting.

Coogan drew his .45 from the pocket of his tan corduroy jacket.

Four people were walking through the woods talking, each of them wearing the same white-hooded robe Jordan had seen during his last visit to these woods. They came close to running into Jordan and the others, but stopped abruptly, startled. A woman gasped and a man touched her shoulder and whispered, "Remember, there is *never* anything to fear." He pulled back his hood to reveal a balding middle-aged face with horn-rim glasses and gave them a guarded smile. "I think you're probably lost, because this is private property. Can I help you?"

Jordan tossed a glance at Coogan, who tossed it right back. Then, an idea: *We could sure use those robes,* he thought. He pointed the shotgun at the man and said, "Don't move and don't say a word." He turned to Coogan and said quietly, "You wanna back me up on this, please?"

"Oh." Coogan aimed his gun and stood straighter, as if trying to be intimidating.

Jordan said, "Now, all I want you to do is take off your robes. Very slowly. Any screaming or shouting's gonna be accompanied by gunshots."

The man who had said there was nothing to fear a moment ago now looked terrified; his mouth hung open and his lower lip trembled. The other three removed their hoods; they were all women.

For a moment, Jordan felt a stab of guilt for holding three women—and even the rather pathetic-looking man—at gunpoint. Then he remembered that these people were on their way to a sacrifice and he felt better.

"Come on," he said. "Take them off slowly."

"This is a big mistake," the man said quietly.

"No talking, just—"

An explosion of pain in the center of Jordan's back sent him to his knees with a sharp cry. But he clung to the shotgun as he rolled over and fired and—

—a man dressed in black left the ground and flew backward as if he were being pulled through the air as the gun kicked back, missing Jordan's face by an inch, and—

—a black running shoe kicked up out of the darkness to Jordan's left and knocked the gun from his hand and sent it clattering over the ground, then the kicker, dressed exactly like the man Jordan had just shot, hurried after the shotgun and—

—Jordan looked at Coogan, who was watching with a face frozen in shock, his gun held limply before him, and Jordan shouted, "Coogan? *Coogan!*" as—

—the man in black bent down, swept up the sawed-off shotgun, and started to run as—

—Coogan blinked his eyes a few times, then aimed the gun and, with the briefest hesitation, fired, and—

—the shotgun was airborne again as the man twirled like a

top, slammed into the ground and dropped heavily, making low, painful growling sounds, and—

—Lauren began to murmur in a panicky whisper that grew slowly louder, "Oh, God, oh my God, what're we gonna—how can we—oh, God, what'll we—" and—

—Jordan tried to ignore the pain in his back as he stood, but cried out anyway, moving stiffly as he retrieved the gun and said, "Calm down, Lauren, right now, do you hear me, just calm down," and then—

—the four people Jordan and Coogan had held at gunpoint just a moment before began to cry for help, the man shouting, "Help! Somebody help us! Somebody help!" and the women simply screaming as—

—Jordan hurried to the man and pounded the butt of the shotgun into his face, knocking him to the ground, and—

—the women ran, their screams cutting through the woods as—

—Jordan put an arm around Lauren and hissed at the others, "C'mon, let's just run, *let's get the hell outta here!*"

They started out at a jog, with Coogan dragging behind a little at first, but catching up as they quickened their pace. Jordan took out his flashlight and used it to guide them around trees and bushes and large boulders sticking out of the earth. The only sounds were their footsteps and their breathing.

Jordan felt panic swelling in his chest. He didn't know where they were headed or what they were going to do; he knew only that they had to get away from there. The car was in the opposite direction, but if they turned around, there were bound to be others gathered around the two men who had been shot.

The flashlight beam zigzagged over grass and tree trunks and wildflowers and—

—a child.

They all stopped so suddenly, they nearly fell in a heap.

It was a little boy. He wore a white robe, hood down, and held what looked, at first, like a stick pointed at them. But once the light was still, Jordan realized the stick was a spear with a deadly sharp point.

There was a whisper of disturbed brush and another child appeared holding another spear.

Then another. And another.

They came from every direction with their spears pointed only in one, white robes shimmering in the flashlight beam, small white faces ghostly and cold, some even cruel. Both boys and girls surrounded them, some with their faces hidden in the shadow of their hoods, and they moved forward steadily and with purpose, the points of their spears drawing closer and closer until they stopped just short of pressing against the four shocked adults.

Jordan held his breath a moment to see what they would do, then, to make sure they saw it, he lifted the barrel of the shotgun slowly.

"Oh, *God*, don't you *dare*!" Lauren hissed. "My *son* could be here, he could be—Nathan? Nathan, are you here?" She started to turn, her eyes sweeping over the children. "Nathan, honey, Mommy's—" She shrieked when the point of a spear prodded her hip.

Jordan ignored her.

'I'm sure," he said slowly in a flat, quiet voice, "that all of you are perfectly willing and able to use those spears. But the problem is, I'm perfectly willing and able to use this shotgun, and if you don't get out of our way right now, I will."

Lauren rasped, "Jordan, you *wouldn't*, my *God*, how could you—"

"Shut up, Lauren," he said through his teeth.

The children didn't move for a long time. Then the boy who had appeared first poked his spear into Jordan's stomach hard and Jordan hitched forward and made a barking sound, half from surprise, half from pain. Then all of the children moved forward a bit.

Lauren began to cry and Joan put an arm around her.

Jordan's voice had a tremor when he spoke again: "I'm only going to tell you one more—"

Another poke in the stomach. One in the leg. The arm.

He almost dropped the gun, but managed to stifle his cry of pain. His anger was overwhelming. He realized that, with the remaining shell, he could get most of them out of the way. But he couldn't. No matter how deeply he reached inside himself for whatever it would take to do such a thing, he couldn't find it. His mind raced as he tried to come up with a solution, an idea, a simple distraction he could toss at them, but—

—when he heard the footsteps approaching from behind, he stopped trying. It sounded like at least three people. Adults.

The children behind them shuffled out of the way as the footsteps neared.

An arm reached around Jordan's neck from behind and pulled hard just once, making Jordan hack.

"Do not move," a deep male voice said into his ear as a hand took away the shotgun. "Do not move even a little."

Similar voices spoke similar words to the others.

"Very good, children," Hester Thorne said. "I'm very pleased. *Orrin* is very pleased. You may go now. The ceremony will begin soon."

The children left quietly and were gone in seconds.

Hester Thorne stepped before them, hands joined behind her back. She smiled and said, "I was expecting you."

14.

They were taken into the cave and past the pulsing blue light to Benjamin's alcove, where they were told to seat themselves on damp rocks.

When they arrived, Lizzie spoke to them only with her face. Her eyes widened and she smiled as if she were about to speak, but when she saw Hester, she clearly thought better of it and simply *showed* them how happy she was to see them.

The three black-clothed men who had taken their guns and brought them to the cave now stood in the alcove's opening holding the guns as their cold eyes drilled into Jordan, Lauren, Coogan and Joan. Hester paced the alcove slowly as she spoke to them, but they obviously had a difficult time concentrating on what she said because their attention continued to be diverted by Benjamin's presence and his odd possessions . . . as well as his odor. The air in the small stone room was damp and cloying anyway, but it was made nearly unbearable by Benjamin's stink.

When Hester realized this, she picked up the doll and the fire engine and threw them to the back of the alcove, where they slammed into the neatly stacked canned foods, knocking half of them over, and snapped, "Will you put this junk *away*. That too," she added, pointing at the picture on the wall.

Benjamin hesitated, glanced for just an instant at Lizzie, then reached up and removed the picture, hiding it behind a rock.

"As I said before," Hester said as she paced, suddenly calm

again, "I was expecting you. But I was expecting *more* of you. One more, to be exact." She stopped in front of Jordan and stared down at him. "Where is Mr. Ackroyd?"

Jordan bowed his head and stared at his lap.

"All right, then." She stepped in front of Lauren. "Maybe you'll tell me where he is."

Jordan took Lauren's hand and squeezed it. It was not an affectionate squeeze; it was a squeeze that said, *Keep your mouth shut*.

"He didn't come with us," Jordan said. "That's all."

"Then where *is* he?"

No response.

Hester glared at the four of them, then hunkered down in front of Jordan and smiled. "I know you're a private investigator. Who are you working for?"

He said nothing.

She kept smiling. "Lawyers, maybe? There's no end to the number of lawyers who would like to prove we're doing something illegal here. For their clients, of course, clients who have relatives and spouses who've found the truth and have left their past lives behind. Or maybe you're working for the press. They just *know* there's a sordid story in the Alliance somewhere. And the tabloids . . . oh, they're the worst. Is that it? The *Enquirer*? The *Globe*? Maybe a magazine, like . . . say, *People*? *US*? *Trends*? Yes, maybe *Trends*. They seem to think one of their reporters disappeared here. I hear Edmond Fiske was very upset about—"

Jordan was already trying hard to control his natural reaction to the situation, but when Hester mentioned Fiske, the smallest reaction slipped by, just a twitch, maybe, a slight flinch or a flex of his jaws. But she noticed.

"Fiske? You're working for Fiske? *He* sent you here?" She looked as if she were about to laugh.

He tried, but he knew he failed to hide whatever minute response Hester was looking for.

She stood, nodding. "But you're not going to tell me where Mr. Ackroyd is, are you?"

He didn't even look at her.

Hester waved for the four men to get out of the archway, then said to Benjamin, "Bring Mr. Cross out to the Center of the

Vortex. And hurry.'' She walked briskly out of the alcove saying to the three guards, "Don't even let them speak.''

Jordan lifted his head then as Benjamin started toward him from the back of the alcove. His instincts told him to defend himself or run, but both were impossible; he didn't have a weapon, and the men blocking his exit *did*.

When Benjamin stood before Jordan, his massive body blocked the light of the lantern and he blackened Jordan's field of vision like an enormous shadow. Benjamin's odor coated the inside of Jordan's nostrils until he thought he'd *never* stop smelling it.

"He's my friend, Benjamin,'' Lizzie whispered.

The man holding the shotgun said, "Quiet.''

Benjamin stood there for a long moment, looking back and forth between Jordan and Lizzie. Jordan found it hard to believe, but Benjamin appeared confused.

Because of what Lizzie said? he wondered. *What has she said to him? What has she done to affect him that way?*

He had no time to think about it, though, because Benjamin bent down, wrapped an arm around Jordan's waist and squeezed, lifting him from the rock and carrying him out of the alcove.

Jordan realized at that moment that what he'd felt up until then was merely tension; the real fear was just beginning to spread through him. He closed his eyes as Benjamin carried him jarringly, holding him like a sack of laundry, until—

—the darkness behind his eyelids began to swirl with color, then exploded with rapid-fire visions—

—a line of naked people falling into a trench after being shot—

—an old woman nailed to a wall with long rusty spikes—

—hands being chopped off—

—and Jordan opened his eyes and breathed, "God, no,'' because it was starting again, the same nauseating headache he'd felt the last time he'd been in the vile blue light that surrounded him once again.

Benjamin finally stopped and set him down on unsteady legs. He tried not to look at anything but his feet, but it really didn't make any difference; the light enveloped him, oozed into his pores and flowed thickly through his veins and arteries. He lifted his head slowly and squinted against the light coming from the crevice just two feet in front of him.

"Oh, God," he groaned as his muscles began to ache and his stomach churned.

"Unpleasant, isn't it?" Hester asked. She stood beside him. "It's always unpleasant for the unenlightened who have not been through the proper preparation."

Staring at his feet again, Jordan spoke in a strained voice. "Like brainwashing?"

Hester laughed. "I'm sure that's how you see it. But *look* at this, Mr. Cross." She swept an arm toward the crevice. "This is *real*. I certainly didn't create it. It's not natural. Not natural in the sense with which we're familiar, anyway. It's *super*natural, don't you think? So why would I need to brainwash anyone? What purpose would it serve? All I need to do is lead them to this and prepare them for the truth that it gives."

Jordan was hunching forward slowly, one forearm across his stomach.

"How are you feeling, Mr. Cross?"

He wanted to close his eyes, but he knew what awaited him if he did, so he left them open and let the throbbing blue light pierce his eyes and fill his head.

"Not well?"

He could still smell Benjamin, who stood near by, and wondered if his theory about the cause of Benjamin's deformities was correct.

"It's only going to get worse, you know," Hester said.

His knees gave way unexpectedly and Jordan went down, groaning at the painful impact. It *was* getting worse. He was afraid he would vomit soon, perhaps even pass out.

"If you'd like to get away from the light, Mr. Cross, all you need to do is tell me where Mr. Ackroyd is. Is he doing something? Running an errand for you, perhaps? Or just watching television?"

His eyelids were growing very heavy and he had to concentrate hard to keep them open. But concentrating wasn't easy because there was a throbbing buzz growing steadily louder in his head.

"I know how much you know, Mr. Cross," Hester said, kneeling beside him. "I know exactly what you've uncovered, and it doesn't mean a thing. It's all been for nothing. I'm taking steps to make sure you've done no damage and to cover your traces so you won't *do* any damage. To do that, I think it would help to know where Mr. Ackroyd is. And you're going to stay right here until you decide to tell me.''

Jordan's teeth clenched and he swallowed repeatedly to keep from vomiting. With a hoarse voice he said, ''Why do . . . you need me . . . to tell you? Why don't you ask . . . *Orrin*.'' He spoke the name with disgust.

''Because Orrin is an Ascended Master and deals in great truths . . . not in the whereabouts of aging salesmen. That's why Orrin has me, to help pave the way for the truth, for his arrival on this plane of existence . . . and to find out where your friend is right now.''

He began to blink and his eyes burned and watered, but he managed to keep them open. In spite of that, however, the images of death and violence he'd seen when he'd closed his eyes began to flash in his mind just as vividly. He leaned forward and pressed his forehead to the ground.

''I . . . I'm gonna . . . b-be suh-sick,'' he rasped.

''I'm sorry.''

He fell on his sides as snakes squirmed in his stomach and gnawed with dull fangs on his insides.

''Please,'' he breathed.

''Where is Mr. Ackroyd?''

A long, low groan rose up from Jordan's gut, then he vomited.

Benjamin stepped forward, making a small sound in his throat, and leaned down to help Jordan up.

''No!'' Hester shouted, looking up at him with shock at his behavior.

Benjamin backed away hesitantly, blinking, shaking his head every few seconds and making irritated coughing sounds. When he saw his mother's furious stare, he stepped forward quickly and kicked Jordan in the back, then turned away. But, although Hester did not seem to notice, the kick was merely a halfhearted gesture.

''Where is Mr. Ackroyd?'' Hester asked again. ''If you tell me, you can get away from the light.''

Jordan clawed at the earth with his fingers as the world tilted and spun around him. ''Heli . . . copter.''

''Helicopter? *What* helicopter?''

''Flash.''

''Gordon? Chuck Gordon?''

He nodded.

"Where is he going?"

"Duh . . . Diiiego."

"The nuclear power plant?"

Another nod.

"He's going there to stop Mark Schroeder, I take it."

"Yuh."

Jordan could keep his eyes open no longer and gave in to the display of carnage that took place in his head.

"All right, Mr. Cross," Hester said, standing. She turned to Benjamin. "Take him back."

Benjamin picked him up and carried him, faster this time, back to the alcove. When he was back on the ground, Jordan lost consciousness.

Hester motioned for the man with the shotgun to join her just outside the alcove. He handed the shotgun to one of his partners and stepped through the archway.

Hester said, "I want you to go right now and find, um . . . find—" She closed her eyes, froze a moment. "—find Luis Jimenez and bring him here to me. Right now. And hurry as fast as you can."

The man said, "Yes, ma'am." Then he turned and left.

Lizzie knelt beside Jordan, who remained still for a minute or so. When he began to move his head, she stroked his hair gently and whispered, "Just lie still for a while."

Hester said, "I'd rather you remain seated, Lizzie."

"Oh? Well, I'm sorry to disappoint you." She didn't move.

Jordan looked up at her with bleary eyes, made a noise that sounded like a chuckle, and croaked, "S'good t'see you."

Lizzie rubbed a hand over his back lightly, up and down, up and down.

Hester said, "Lizzie, you have been doing uncalled for and very unfriendly things behind my back. Your friends have come on my property *armed* with *guns*. Now, in light of all that, I think it's only proper that you *remain seated*!"

Lizzie glared at her a moment, then whispered to Jordan, "Just stay right here until you feel like getting up." Then she returned to the rock on which she'd been sitting.

"Where's my son?" Lauren whispered suddenly, speaking so quickly that the sentence became a single word. She'd been mustering the courage to ask the question since being brought to the cave, but she was so scared that when she finally spoke, the words spilled out in a jumble.

"He's in good hands," Hester said pleasantly. "He's being prepared for tonight's ceremony."

"Cere—prepar—what ceremony? Pruh-prepared *how*?"

"Spiritually. I'll be seeing him soon. He's the Chosen One."

Lauren cried out and her hand went to her mouth. "No. *No!* You're going to k-kill him!"

"Oh, no. There is no death, Mrs. Schroeder. Only re-embodiment. Nathan will be re-embodied, and when he comes of age in his next incarnation, the New Age of Enlightenment will have begun."

"Buh-but why d-do you have to kuh-*kill* him?"

"We're not killing him, but if that's the way you choose to see it . . . You see, Mrs. Schroeder, each person is a kind of human generator. The energy that comes from that generator can move mountains if used properly, it can move *whole worlds*. We're using it to bring Orrin from the spiritual plane to this physical plane of existence, to form a sort of bridge between the two planes and bring them closer together to speed the coming of the New Age of Enlightenment. Your son will be the final Chosen One. Then Orrin will come."

Lauren began to cry, bouncing slightly as if the rock she was sitting on had become hot.

"Just think, Mrs. Schroeder," Hester went on. "Your son will be living his next incarnation in a world with no crime, no addictions, no corruption. People will live in harmony with one another and with the planet."

Lauren's voice grew louder until she was shrieking hysterically and she dove from the rock toward Hester with her arms outstretched, crying, "You *bitch*, you fucking *bitch*, *damn* you, I'll *kill* you!" and—

—the two remaining guards rushed toward her as—

—Lizzie and Joan went after her, followed by Coogan, whose movements were stiff and clumsy, and—

—Hester stumbled backward but not fast enough because Lauren slammed into her, hands clamping onto her throat, but not for long because—

—Benjamin's hand fell between them and pressed on Lauren's chest, pushing her back firmly, but without undue force, until she was standing between Lizzie and Joan, frozen with fear, her jaw slack as she stared straight up at Benjamin.

The guards stopped, but did not retreat.

Lizzie put her arm around Lauren and, as they sat again, said, "Don't do that anymore."

"Very good," Hester said quietly to Benjamin.

After a few moments of silence, Coogan said to Hester, "So what're you gonna do with us? Do we get re-embodied, too? Or are you just gonna *kill* us?"

"As I said before, Mr. Coogan, there is no death, therefore there is no killing. As for what will happen to you, I'm not sure. I'm going to leave that up to Orrin. When he materializes here tonight, he will make that decision. It's appropriate that you will be waiting here for him because his whole purpose for coming is to cleanse the earth of those who close their minds to the truth and those who actively stand in its way."

"Satan doesn't cleanse," Lizzie said matter-of-factly. "He decays, corrupts and destroys."

Hester turned an icy gaze to her. "Please, Lizzie. Keep your biblical mythology to yourself."

The guard Hester had sent away returned to the alcove and said, "He's just outside, Ms. Thorne."

Hester left the alcove, but they could hear her voice just beyond the archway.

"Luis," she said, "I'm very sorry to disturb you, I can tell you were sleeping, but I'm afraid something's come up with which you can help me."

Luis said, "Oh, that's, uh . . . no problem, ma'am."

"Good. Now . . . if I'm not mistaken, you were a police officer in San Jose before coming here, right?"

"Yes, ma'am."

"And San Jose is very close to the Diego Nuclear Power Plant, am I correct?"

"Yes, ma'am. They're neighbors."

"I'm wondering . . . do you still have friends on the force there, Luis? People you still talk to, keep in touch with?"

"Yes, ma'am."

"Ah, good. Very good. I think you might be able to help me."

15.

Marvin had to urinate.

It had begun as simply an ordinary, low-grade urge to relieve his bladder, but he'd ignored it back then. He'd been ignoring it for well over an hour now. Under normal circumstances, he would be able to ignore it awhile longer. But not under *these* circumstances.

His entire body felt knotted with tension. He thought that, if it were physically possible, his hair would be clenched. The helicopter flew in a single direction, but it went up and down and left and right, bouncing around the sky like the little white ball in an old-fashioned movie-house sing-along as Flash whistled to himself and sang songs, swaying in his seat to the off-key tunes.

Jordan thought better of insisting that Flash knock it off—maybe this was the best he ever flew, maybe it was a lot worse when he was frightening tourists—for fear of pissing him off and giving him any reason to start *really* playing around with the controls. So he'd been silent, holding the flask between his thighs while perspiration soaked his palms and dribbled down the middle of his back and his bladder grew like a water balloon being filled slowly. He realized that he was actually squirming in his seat like a little boy. About the only thing he *wasn't* doing was—

He put a hand over his crotch and squeezed. It was getting worse fast. His penis was beginning to ache.

"The hell's *wrong* with you, boy?" Flash asked, interrupting a round of "Someone's in the Kitchen with Dinah."

"I've gotta go," Marvin rasped.

Flash squinted at him, puzzled. "What? You gotta . . . you mean you gotta—" He threw back his head and let out a long string of staccato cackles. "Number one or number two?"

"If you mean do I have to urinate or defecate, *I've gotta take a piss*! How long before we stop to refuel?"

Flash was too busy laughing to answer, and as he laughed he looked out his window to the ground below and—

—the helicopter made a sudden dip to the left and Marvin felt his insides rising quickly and he was sure he would throw up. They were going down. Dropping. Fast.

Marvin screamed, *"Aww God Jesus save us please save us*

*we're goin' down we're goin' down please Jesus Christ save us
don't let us—"*

They touched down.

There was no more movement except inside Marvin's abdomen and skull. He was slumped down in the seat, hugging himself and panting.

Flash was hysterical.

"Duh-did we l-land?" Marvin asked.

"Yeah, we lan—" He stopped to laugh some more. "—we landed, bucko. We're in a—" More laughter. "—a field, so you can get out and drain your lizard." He went on cackling.

Marvin didn't move for a while, just tried to concentrate on slowing his dangerously rapid heartbeat and catching his breath.

"Lizzie w-was right," he whispered. "A planeful of atheists *will* pray on the way down."

He removed his seat belts, set the flask on the floorboard, opened his door and peeled himself out of the seat. Ducking more than he needed to, he hurried out from under the rotor, his feet shooshing through tall dry weeds that danced in the swirling air. The dog followed him happily, yipping and snapping at his ankles.

Marvin's weak legs abandoned him and he dropped to his knees, still wheezing a little. He realized he didn't feel the need to relieve himself anymore and looked down to see a large wet spot over his crotch and left thigh. The dog stuffed its nose between his legs and sniffed voraciously. Some of the tension in his gut let go and he began to giggle, then laugh loudly. But in seconds, his laughter ended with a dry, hollow sob. Then he stared at his knees silently.

He still had a fair chance of dying, either in the helicopter or at Diego. Of course he could always tell Flash to head back and just forget the whole thing, or have Flash drop him somewhere in San Francisco and he could take a cab home.

And abandon Jordan and Lauren and Lizzie.

And let Mark Schroeder carry out his assignment at Diego and kill everybody within the zip code and then some.

Actually, he thought it would be nice to stay right there in that field. The ground was cool and he liked the sound and smell of the weeds.

Marvin thought of Lizzie again and closed his eyes.

"God, if you're there . . . and boy, I hope you are, 'cause

I'd hate to think I was doing this all by myself . . . give me a hand here, would you? I don't want to kill this Schroeder guy, but I may have to. And I sure as hel—I-I mean, I sure don't want to get killed myself, but—" A chuckle. "—I might. So, um . . . yeah, just give me a hand with this. Thanks. Um . . . amen."

Brushing at the spot on his pants, he stood and went back to the helicopter, where Flash was laughing even harder. The dog jumped in and nestled in between their seats again.

"Wuh-wasted stop, huh?" Flash cackled, looking at the spot on Marvin's pants.

Marvin got in, reached for the flask on the floorboard, and——it was gone.

Flash's laughter exploded. His face was bright red, his eyes glistening with tears.

He held the flask in his hand.

"*Damn* you!" Marvin shouted, snatching the flask away.

It was empty.

"Well," Flash said between laughing fits, "you didn't seem to want any."

Marvin slammed the door and buckled up. They got off the ground, then went back down as Flash continued to convulse with laughter. He tried again, and again he failed. After giving his laughter a little time to die down, Flash tried again.

As they left the ground, Marvin whispered, "Please, God . . . *please* give me a hand with this."

16.

A few minutes after stepping out of the alcove to speak with Luis Jimenez, Hester returned and said to the guards, "I'm going to need both of you." Then, to Benjamin: "Do *not* let them move." She turned to her guests and smiled. "You just make yourselves comfortable. There's nothing at all for you to worry about. All you have to do is wait." To Jordan: "I've taken care of *everything*." She left, flanked by the two men in black.

No one said anything for a while. They were all afraid of Benjamin. All but Lizzie.

He sat on his rock, watching them, his fingers fidgeting with one another between his knees.

"Benjamin," Lizzie said cautiously, "do you mind if I speak?"

He growled, but nothing more.

"I'd like you to meet all of my friends," she went on, smiling now. "Would you like that?"

He scratched his head vigorously, still a bit rattled by his exposure to the blue light.

Lizzie put a hand on Lauren's shoulder. "Benjamin, this is my friend Lauren. Say hello to Benjamin, Lauren."

Lauren stared at Lizzie with teary-eyed disbelief.

"Go ahead," Lizzie whispered in her ear. "He's just a child. A big, frightened child who does what he's told. We need him to *like* us."

Lauren turned to Benjamin slowly, almost *unwillingly*, looking as if she thought she were about to be slapped, and murmured, "Huh-hello, Ben-Benjamin."

"Do you know why Lauren is here?" Lizzie asked. "Because her son is here. She came to find him. But your mommy doesn't want—"

Benjamin made a sound that was unintelligible to the others, but Lizzie recognized it as "No."

"It's all right, Benjamin. She's not here, she can't hear us. And we'll talk quietly, okay? See, my friend Lauren came to find her son and take him home because she wants her son to have a good, happy life, just like your daddy wanted *you* to be happy. But your mommy won't let her take him. Lauren isn't even allowed to *see* him. He's being forced to stay here, away from his mommy, who loves him. Just like you have to stay here in this cave, with no one to love you, just a little ways from that bad, ugly light. And tonight, Lauren's son—his name is Nathan—is going to be killed in that light. That's not very good, is it, Benjamin?"

He scratched his head again, stroked his cheek and muttered to himself.

"And this is Joan. Say hello, Joan."

Joan managed a smile. "Hello, Benjamin."

"Joan used to have a daughter, but she had to *leave* her daughter here, Benjamin. It wasn't safe for Joan to stay here, so she left and got help to come back and get her daughter. But her daughter was gone. Your mommy lied and said Joan had left *with* her daughter. But Joan has never seen her little girl again.

Don't you think that's sad, Benjamin? Wouldn't you have felt bad if, when you were a little boy, someone had come along who wouldn't let you play catch with your daddy? If someone had come along and taken the Nerf ball away . . . and then taken you away from your daddy?''

"Nuuhh-*Nerf* baawwwl," Benjamin growled as he slapped his palms on his thighs again and again and rocked back and forth. He was getting agitated; he was frowning and the cords of muscle in his neck stood out tautly beneath his knotty skin.

"And these two men are Jordan and Coogan. They've come to help Lauren find her little boy. Say hello to Benjamin."

"Hi, Benjamin," Coogan said with more warmth than discomfort. "It's nice to meet you."

Jordan stared at the hulking figure rocking and fidgeting just a few feet away, then glanced at Lizzie. "Uh . . . hel-hello, Benjamin." He looked at Lizzie again, amazed, and whispered, "That's incredible, Lizzie, absolutely incredible."

"There's nothing incredible about it," she said happily, smiling at Benjamin. "He's my friend, aren't you Benjamin?"

He stood and began circling the lantern, massaging the back of his neck with one hand and scratching his chest with the other. He looked angry and confused and hurt at once.

Lizzie said, "He's a very nice young man who likes beautiful things and misses his daddy."

Benjamin exploded. He roared and kicked the rest of the cans over in a clatter of tin, then continued to kick at the stone wall behind them once they were scattered around him.

Lizzie whispered nervously, "He's just . . . a little temperamental."

He turned and swung his fists again and again, roaring. Lauren screamed and they all ducked out of the way.

Then, after Benjamin had stopped and sat with his back to them and his head in his hands, they were quiet.

17.

Insects chittered and crawled inside Benjamin's skull.

Part of the cause was the residual effects of the blue light, but there was something else at work as well, something so foreign to Benjamin that he didn't know how to handle it.

Lizzie had been just another liar when she was first brought into the cave. His mother frequently brought people in for him to watch over for a while, or sent him out to get them, if not hurt them. She always introduced them to him as liars, as enemies of the truth and of Orrin, and they always huddled against the wall, paralyzed with fear. They never moved from their place and they never *ever* spoke to him. Most of all, no one knew his name; even his mother didn't use it anymore.

But Lizzie had been different. She'd spoken to him, called him by name, and she'd even been *nice* to him. No one was *ever* nice to Benjamin, not even his mother. Of course, he saw very few people besides his mother, but he had a feeling that, were he to meet more, their reactions and behavior would be no different.

But Lizzie's behavior was *very* different.

Benjamin feared his mother. Sometimes when he slept, he had nightmares in which he relived the times his mother had become angry at him, screamed at him and made him kneel in front of the crevice and bathe in that awful blue light for hours at a time. When he was awake, he lived in fear of it happening again. But in spite of that, he couldn't help wondering if perhaps she'd been wrong about Lizzie.

And if she'd been wrong about Lizzie, how many *other* people had she been wrong about?

How many lies had she told him?

How many times had she told him to do things that *she* said were good, when perhaps they had actually been bad?

These thoughts swirled all around him, allowing him to catch an occasional glimpse of them, but remaining just out of reach. His muddled thought processes frustrated him, made him angry, and that was why he burst into tantrums of shouting and hitting. Lizzie's friends seemed nice, just like her. They all spoke to him, said hello. He liked that. It was so nice for a change, to hear other people speaking his name and actually being polite. But they stirred confusion in him, made him think about things he'd never thought about before and he didn't know what to do, how to react or what to believe or *not* believe. That confusion infuriated him and made him scream at them, made him want to hit them, pick them up and throw them. He tried hard to control himself, but he felt that control slipping. He didn't want to think about it anymore, about Lizzie or her friends or any of the things they put into his head.

So he sat with his back to them, closed himself off from everything, and just tried to rest.

18.

"Hello, Nathan."

"Hi, Ms. Thorne."

"How are you?"

"Fine."

"Everything is all right? You're ready for tonight's ceremony?"

He nodded, but he was confused. Yes, he was indeed ready for the ceremony. But why had he been separated from the other children? Why had he been taken into the woods? And why was he here now before anyone else?

He asked Hester none of the questions.

"You're probably wondering why you're here now," Hester said, putting a hand on the back of his head and walking slowly toward the cave. In her other hand she held a penlight that sent a needle-thin beam into the darkness.

Nathan looked around them. The man who had brought him here was gone. The others would be gathering soon for the ceremony, but they were alone now.

"I know you've only been here a little while, Nathan, but you've learned so quickly. It takes most children *twice* as long to pick up the things you've learned. You're a very bright young man. That's why I'm sure you'll have no problem dealing with what I'm about to tell you."

Nathan looked up at her then, not sure whether he liked the sound of that or not.

"Tonight's ceremony is going to be different. We won't be going through the usual procedure to find the Chosen One."

"How come?"

She hunkered down in front of him and put her hands on his shoulders. "Orrin spoke to me earlier tonight, Nathan. He told me that *you* are the Chosen One."

A wave of numbness passed through him at first, then an almost uncontainable rush of excitement.

"Me?" he breathed.

She grinned. "Yes, *yes*. Isn't that *wonderful*?"

"B-but . . . how come? Why me?"

"Because Orrin *himself* has *chosen* you, Nathan. You're a very special boy. Orrin has seen something in you that he's seen in none of the others. He's seen in you an energy the others don't have. And tonight, when that crystal enters you and releases that energy, it's going to help Orrin enter this plane. *You*, Nathan . . . you are going to bring Orrin to us, then re-embody into the New Age of Enlightenment."

Just a moment ago, he'd felt a gnawing hunger—the servings at each meal were small and there was never anything he really wanted—and he'd been exhausted—it had been *so* long since he slept, and he was only allowed to sleep a little bit at a time—and achy—he'd worked hard every day since he'd gotten there—but now he felt ecstatic, full of electricity. *He* was the Chosen One.

He wondered what his mother would think. She came to mind very seldom, and then only in a vague detached way. He was sure Mom wouldn't understand. Hester was always telling him how ignorant his mother was, how she was swimming in the lies of the unenlightened and willfully closing her mind to the truth. Hester said his mother would do nothing but hold him back and keep him from learning, from becoming enlightened, and therefore it was necessary for him to put her behind him, make her a part of his past and move on.

He decided to say nothing about his mother and even found it easy to put her out of his mind and give in to his excitement. Normally he would have been much more animated—perhaps jumping up and down, clapping his hands and laughing—but he was just too tired.

"You understand completely what is required of you as the Chosen One, don't you, Nathan?"

He nodded, smiling.

"Good. Now." She stood, took his hand and said, "I want you to come into the cave with me before the others arrive. There's someone I want you to see."

19.

Lauren felt herself shrinking away. Everything around seemed to grow gradually larger as she grew smaller. She sat beside Joan, head in hands, as Joan rubbed her back comfortingly, although she didn't feel it.

It was obvious that they had failed. They hadn't come close to getting Nathan, hadn't even *seen* him; for all she knew, he was already dead. If so, they would be joining him soon. She tried to feel bad for the others if not for herself, but she couldn't feel *anything*. As for herself . . . she was glad it would be over soon. With Nathan gone, death was far more appealing than going on with her life.

Lauren heard Jordan and Lizzie whispering to one another and she tried to focus her mind on them, hoping it would eclipse her dark and weighty thoughts.

"We had a talk before you came," Lizzie whispered.

"A talk?"

"Yes, a talk. He can speak. We talked about Mike Lumley and why he did . . . what he did. I think it got to him."

Lauren realized they were talking about that creature sitting in the corner with its back to them. She lifted her head and glanced at Benjamin. He was paying no attention to the whispering, just rocking back and forth and grumbling.

"How much did he already know?" Jordan asked.

"Almost nothing. I got the impression our talk started him thinking, maybe asking himself some questions he'd never asked before. I think he might be—"

Benjamin suddenly stood, spun around, rushed to Lizzie, grabbed a handful of her hair and leaned forward to bellow an incoherent threat into her face. Then he returned to his rock, facing them this time and watching very carefully.

"You were saying, Lizzie?" Jordan muttered.

Footsteps sounded outside the alcove and every head turned to the archway.

Hester appeared and smiled at them. "There's someone here I'd like you to see before the ceremony, Mrs. Schroeder. I think it will help you . . . help *all* of you . . . to see just how wrong you've been." Pointing to Lauren, she said to Benjamin quietly,

"Make sure she doesn't move from that spot." Then she stepped out of the alcove.

Benjamin stood and his footsteps crunched heavily over the ground, stopping behind Lauren, who was suddenly tense, staring at the archway, wondering if maybe . . . if it were possible . . .

"Come with me, Nathan," Hester said just beyond the archway.

Lauren's gasp sounded almost like a scream. She was off the rock and diving toward the archway, crying, "Oh my God Nathan honey where are you please come to me Natha—" but—

—Benjamin's hands fell on her shoulders, pulled her back and pressed her body down hard onto the rock, and—

—Lauren fought, giving no thought at all to Benjamin's size and strength, just swinging her fists back over her shoulders, slamming her head and elbows back into his abdomen and trying to pull away from him at the same time, then—

—Nathan appeared in the archway, standing in front of Hester, and—

—Lauren froze, paralyzed by the sight of her son. He looked like a different boy altogether. He was so thin and pale with hollow cheeks and cavernous eyes. Even his hair looked thinner and lay flat against his head as if it were wet.

"Nathan," she said, but her voice was weak now, so weak that she said nothing more for a while, just looked at him, drank in the sight of him.

"Mom?" Nathan said. "Zat you?"

"Yes, honey, *yes* it's me."

"And these," Hester said, waving toward the others, "are some friends of your mother's. They've all come, Nathan, to take you away from here. From me. They think you're being held here against your will, that you're being harmed somehow."

"Really? How come, Mom?"

Lauren didn't respond; she was in too much pain to speak. Nathan didn't seem happy to see her at all; he didn't come to her or sound excited or even smile, just stared at her with those flat eyes and spoke to her in that flat voice. She couldn't believe it, didn't *want* to believe it.

"Nathan," she whispered, "are you all right?"

"Uh-huh."

"You're sure? You don't . . . look well, honey." Tears came

and she didn't try to stop them. "You look tired and . . . and thin."

"I'm fine." He smiled for the first time—although it wasn't his usual smile—and finally showed a hint of life in his eyes and excitement in his voice as he said, "I'm the Chosen One, Mom! Did Ms. Throne tell you? *I'm* the Chosen One and my energy's gonna bring Orrin here! Tonight!"

"Oh, Nathan," Lauren sobbed. Hot blades sliced through her insides and she was blinded by her tears. "Nathan, what has she done to you?"

He looked disappointed, even hurt. "Nothing, Mom. Ms. Thorne's just been teaching me. The truth."

"My God, Nathan, don't you know that she's going to *kill* you tonight? That's why we're here! To keep her from killing you like she's killed so many others! You're going to *die*, Nathan, *please* don't let her *do* this to you!"

Nathan stared at her for a long time, his expression of disappointment growing even worse, until he finally looked up at Hester.

"See?" Hester said, getting down beside him. "It means nothing to her or to any of them because they have closed themselves off from the truth, just like I told you. They're not like you, and you can no longer consider yourself one of them. Because you have important things to do. You have a purpose."

Nathan looked at his mother, who was sobbing uncontrollably.

"Who is she, Nathan?" Hester asked.

He thought about it a while, then shook his head sadly. "Just some lady named Mrs. Schroeder."

"That's right." Hester stood, flashing a bright smile at Lauren, at all of them.

"You fucking bitch!" Lauren screamed, throwing herself at Hester. Benjamin held her back effortlessly, but that didn't stop her from kicking and hitting at the air, jerking convulsively in Benjamin's hold as if she were having a seizure.

Hester's smile did not even waver. She patted Nathan's back. "Let's go, Nathan. I think you've seen enough."

They left the alcove.

Even after they were gone, Lauren's fit continued, until she was exhausted. Benjamin let her go and she slid from her rock to the ground, limp and panting as she cried.

While the others tried to calm Lauren, Jordan watched Benjamin carefully.

He went back to his rock and sat down, picking up a stone about the size of a child's head. He growled as he crushed it.

20.

Since they'd stopped to let Marvin answer nature's call, he'd calmed considerably. He was not relaxed—he would *never* be relaxed in that helicopter with Flash at the controls and the smell of whiskey in the air—but at least he was able to think with more clarity than before. And he'd been thinking about time.

He didn't know what time Mark had left Grover, but it had presumably been well before Marvin and Flash had left, which probably had been about ninety minutes; with luck, it had been *shortly* before they'd left. He would have felt more comfortable if he knew how long it would take to get to the plant once they'd landed. He wasn't even sure if he could *find* the plant.

Having taken all of that into consideration, Marvin could feel his doubts swelling fast. He decided that, if he *did* manage to head Mark off at the plant's gate, it would be a freak accident.

But he would have a better chance if they didn't lose another second.

"How long before we refuel?" he asked.

Flash said, "Comin' up in just a few minutes."

"How long does it take?"

"Oh, half hour or so."

Marvin thought a moment, then: "Do you know where Hollis Airpark is?"

"Yep."

"Can you make it there without refueling?"

"Nope."

"Not a chance?"

"Nope."

Marvin sighed, disappointed.

"Might be able to make it to that *nuke*-yoo-ler plant, though."

"What?"

"I say, if I don't refuel, I *might* be able to make it to that *nuke*-yoo-ler plant you're headed for. But that's a *might*, now, not a for-*sure*. Then, a course, you gotta worry about where to land. Can't just set this ol' girl down on *any* ol' thing, you know. And it'd cost you extra for the risk *and* for the pain in the ass of gettin' refueled out in the middle of nowhere.''

Marvin thought about it and the thought chiseled away at the calm he'd managed to maintain for a while. If they ran out of fuel, they'd go down. Naturally. But what if Flash kept a close eye on the gauge so that, if they got too close to running out before they got there, he could *set* them down. They'd be closer to the plant then and if they weren't quite close enough, Marvin could catch a ride or hotwire a car. Hell, he'd steal one at gunpoint if he had to.

"Headin' down for a pit stop," Flash called happily.

"Don't."

"What?"

"Keep going."

"You *shittin'* me?"

"No. Keep going."

Flash began to cackle again, long and hard. "Well, now, if *this* don't beat the pants off a dyke! If I thought you was talkin' serious, I wouldn'ta told you we might be able to make it without refuelin', and remember I said *might*."

"Well, I *am* talkin' serious. Keep going."

"Do you know what you're *sayin'*? We could crash and burn! Whatta you think it *means* to run outta fuel?"

"You're going to make sure that doesn't happen. Watch it close and when we get too low, land."

More cackles. "You don't know what you're talkin' about! You just wet your pants for *nothin'* and you want me to—"

"*Yes!* And if you wanna see my gun again, I'll *show* it to you!"

The cackling died and he stared at Marvin with a cold sparkle of fear in his eyes.

"I said it'd cost more, so you'd better—"

"Fine, we'll pay you whatever you want, but Jordy's got the money, so you'll have to wait to afterward."

"We might be *dead*!"

"Then you won't *need* it!"

Flash turned away from him slowly.

They kept flying.

21.

White figures appeared from the woods steadily, joining those who had already come just outside the cave. Light from lanterns and flashlights bobbed through the darkness.

Nathan was the center of attention. As word spread that Orrin himself had named the Chosen One, they came to congratulate Nathan, one after another, shaking his hand, patting his head, hugging him. All thoughts of his mother—or, as Nathan had begun thinking of her since seeing her in the cave, Mrs. Schroeder—were gone.

"You're so fortunate, Nathan," a doughy, aging woman said, kissing his forehead.

A man shook his hand firmly and said, "You'll be talked about for ages to come, son. People will speak your name with reverence."

A young woman knelt and embraced him, holding him tightly for a long time. "My husband wouldn't let my little boy come here with me," she said solemnly. "I haven't seen him in almost three years. But if he *had* come, and if this had happened to *him*, I would have been *so* proud. I'm very happy for you, Nathan."

They continued to come with their congratulations and praise. Hester watched proudly, smiling. When Nathan had a free moment, she leaned over and whispered, "I hope that visit with your mother didn't upset you. Just remember that everyone *here* understands what you're doing and, as you can see, they all love you for it."

More came, forming a line that led to Nathan.

"Ms., uh . . . Ms. Thorne?" a faint voice hissed. "Ms. Thorne? Psst!"

Hester squinted into the surrounding darkness, moving away from Nathan so she wouldn't steal any of the attention from him. She saw Luis Jimenez standing a few yards away and went to him.

"Yes, Luis?"

"I called, Ms. Thorne. It took me a while to reach my old partner, Frankie, but . . . well, I told him everything and—"

"You gave him the description of Mr. Ackroyd?"

"Yes, yes, and he wrote everything down. He said they

couldn't do anything because the plant is outside the city limits, but it's still in Santa Clara County. So he said he'd call the sheriff's department and see that they took care of it."

"So they'll be there? Waiting for him?"

"Unless he gets there before them."

Hester nodded, then took his hand. "You have no idea what you've done, Luis. Someday you will, but for now, please accept my gratitude and Orrin's."

"Yes, ma'am. I'm happy to help. Um . . ." He looked around, puzzled. "May I ask what . . . what's, uh . . ."

"You mean what's going on here?"

"Yes. If you don't mind my asking."

"Not at all, Luis. Surely you've heard of the Inner Circle."

"Of course, but I didn't know—"

"Tonight is our last meeting." She put an arm around him and began leading him toward the cave. "And after what you've done for us tonight, I think it's only appropriate that you join us."

22.

"Do you hear something?" Jordan whispered, asking no one in particular.

Lizzie and Joan were flanking Lauren on a long flat stone, watching her closely; she had become unnaturally still since Nathan had gone. Jordan had gotten off the ground and seated himself beside Coogan. Benjamin watched them, but kept a distance, fidgeting, pacing and grumbling to himself incoherently.

They listened closely in response to Jordan's question and when they spoke, they whispered, hoping to avoid another explosion from Benjamin.

"I hear *some*thing," Coogan said, squinting, "but my ears are lousy, so I can't tell what it is."

"Voices," Lizzie said. "Outside the cave."

Joan listened for a moment, then said, "I hear laughing. It sounds like a cocktail party."

"They're gathering," Jordan said. "They'll be starting soon, I suppose."

That got a reaction from Lauren: "Starting? Th-the ceremony? Are . . . are they killing Nathan?"

"No, honey," Lizzie said, one hand on Lauren's shoulder, "not yet, and we hope to try to stop them."

Lizzie got a glare from Jordan for that.

"I said we *hope* to," she reminded him, "that's all."

Jordan said, "I think that, under the circumstances, even that's a gross exaggeration."

"The voices are louder," Joan said. "I think there are more of them now."

"They're coming to see Nathan die," Lauren whispered in a flat, tear-dampened voice.

The silence that followed Lauren's remark was thick with frustration and fear.

Lizzie looked at Lauren's blank, puffy, wide-eyed face, at Joan's nervous and fearful twitches, at Coogan's weary sadness and, finally, at Jordan's demeanor of frustrated surrender.

She inhaled slowly, then released an explosive breath, her fists clenched. The voices *were* growing louder; more people *were* coming. They didn't have much time left. She closed her eyes, whispered a short prayer—"Lord, you know the situation. We need Your help. In Christ's name, amen."—then stood.

Jordan watched her with an annoyed expression.

Lizzie started toward Benjamin and, as she walked past Jordan, said, "You shouldn't give up quite so easily."

Benjamin was sitting down and leaning forward, his forearms dangling between his spread knees. He heard Lizzie's footsteps and sat up suddenly, growling.

"Benjamin, I have to speak with you. Please listen to me. And please don't get angry, because there's no reason for it. You *know* I'm your friend and that I don't want to hurt you. So will you please just listen?"

His lumpy, fat lips pulled back over his teeth and gums as he stared at her, then he finally made a small, hoarse sound.

"In a little while, your mommy is going to kill the boy who was in here," she said slowly and solemnly. "She is going to stab a sharp crystal in his body and *kill* him, then feed him to that bad blue light out there, do you understand?"

Benjamin's head made jerky movements and he said, "Ruuhh . . . reeee-embaawwdy."

"No, Benjamin, she is *not* going to re-embody him. Nathan will not be reborn in another body. He will be *dead*. There is *no* re-embodiment, there is *no* reincarnation. What she is going to do to Lauren's little boy is *bad*, do you understand? You at least have this cave and your things here—your doll and your fire engine and your picture, and your photograph of you and your daddy—but when your mommy is through with Nathan, he will have *nothing*. He will have no toys, no home, no vision, no hearing . . . *nothing*. He will be *dead*, Benjamin.''

He slapped his hands over his face several times, then stood, pushed her out of the way and began circling the lantern again, his broad shadow falling over them again and again as he moved.

''I think you're wasting your time,'' Jordan said. ''And probably risking your life.''

Her frustration turned to a fiery anger, which got the best of her. Lizzie spun on Jordan and snapped, ''How can you *possibly* be so glib? *You're* going to be dying, *too*, doesn't that *mean* anything to you.''

''Lizzie,'' he said calmly, but with a slight tremor in his voice, ''it scares the hell out of me. I just don't see what we can possibly do about it.''

She had nothing to say to that because she understood perfectly; she was fighting to hold onto her faith and let go of her fear. She reached out and grabbed Benjamin's arm as he passed and said sternly, as a mother would, ''Benjamin, *stop*. Listen to me. We need your help. You *have* to help us, otherwise—''

The blow came quickly and when it hit—a backhand to the right side of Lizzie's head—her feet left the ground and her back slammed against the stone wall. Bombs exploded in her head and she was suddenly sick, falling over on her side and vomiting on the ground.

Jordan shot to his feet but watched, helpless—he knew that to do anything else would be useless and suicidal—as Benjamin went to Lizzie and picked her up. Lizzie made another retching sound as Benjamin shoved her against the stone wall and began hitting her in the face.

Benjamin stopped suddenly, froze with his arm raised to strike again, and stared at Lizzie.

Her nose and mouth were bloody and one eye was already swelling. She managed to speak, but her words were almost as unintelligible as Benjamin's.

''Puh-peeeze, Bennumun. Peeeze . . . hehhp ush.''

Benjamin threw her to the floor and uttered an anguished cry before retreating to the corner and squatting on the floor, facing them. He watched as Jordan and Coogan went to Lizzie and moved her away from him. And, as he watched, he knocked his head against the stone wall hard, again and again and again.

"Ahm okay, Ahm okay," Lizzie sputtered as Jordan and Coogan moved her gently to where they'd been sitting. "Really. I'm okay." Her speech was clearing up quickly and she pulled away from them to sit up on her own. "Anybody have a rag? A hanky?"

Coogan pulled a handkerchief from his back pocket and said, "It's clean, too. You're lucky."

"Thanks." She dabbed at her cheeks, her mouth, running her tongue over her teeth to check for damage. "Teeth're fine," she said. "My lip's cut, though. And I bit my tongue."

Her lower lip was swelling rapidly; her right eye was nearly swollen shut.

"Nose isn't broken, is it?" Coogan asked, leaning close to take a look.

"No, it's just—" She touched her bloody nose and winced. "—just injured, is all."

"Look," Jordan said, one hand on her arm, "I know what you were trying to do. But don't. Do it. Again. He's liable to kill you next time. And for *nothing*. It's not doing any good. Okay?"

"I know, I know. You're right. I won't do it again. I'll still think he didn't mean to hurt me, though."

"What, he beat the shit out of you by *accident*?"

"No, no. He's just confused. *I'm* confusing him, I think. I'm making him *think*."

"Yeah, well, if he'd thought any harder, we'd be peeling your skull off that wall. Let's just sit here quietly and leave him alone, and if something comes up, I mean, if we see a chance to do something, we'll *do* it. But not until."

A hand fell on Lizzie's shoulder from behind and she looked up to see Lauren leaning toward her.

"But thank you," Lauren said. "For trying, I mean."

They did just as Jordan had suggested; they stayed quiet and ignored Benjamin.

Until Hester arrived.

She stepped into the alcove with her mouth open, about to speak, but stopped when she saw Lizzie. She smiled.

"Ah," she said, "I see you upset him." To Benjamin: "Very good. Keep it up, if necessary." Then she looked at the others again.

She didn't see Benjamin turn his back to her, didn't see his fists clenched at his sides.

"The ceremony will begin soon," Hester said. "As I told you before, I'm going to wait until Orrin has materialized before deciding exactly what to do with you. I have a pretty good idea what *he* will do, but I'm going to wait just the same. In the meantime, I don't want to hear a sound from any of you. It's a very important ceremony and I won't stand for interruptions. I'll wait for Orrin to re-embody you, but I will punish you myself if you step out of line. If you'd like to watch the ceremony—" She smiled at Lauren. "—and you really should, it's a beautiful ceremony—you can watch it from right here." She gestured to the archway. "But do *not* go any further." To Benjamin again: "Did you hear me? You can let them watch if they want, but do *not* let them go any further than right outside. Do you understand? And they are not to make a sound. If they interrupt the ceremony in any way, I will punish *you*, too."

"Why, Hester?" Lizzie asked. "Why are you destroying the plant? Why do all those people have to die? How can you *live* with yourself knowing you're responsible for so many deaths?"

"Re-embodiments. It's impossible for you to understand as long as you cling to such a barbaric concept as death. They will live again. As for the plant . . . the moment it happens, every network and television station in the country—in the *world*—will cover it. Countless people will see it. It will be linked to Orrin's warning. And they will believe. Then Orrin will come." A slow, heartfelt grin. "Isn't it wonderful to live in a time when things happen so *fast*."

Hester turned and started for the archway, but Lizzie called her name and she stopped and turned.

Lizzie said, "Do you *know* about the demon that's inside you?"

"*What?* I don't know what you're talking about. You mean Orrin?"

"Orrin is a lie. It's name is not Orrin. Do you know that it's there? Do you know where it comes from?"

Hester glared at Lizzie for a long time; for a moment, she looked as if she might step forward and strike Lizzie. Instead, a cold smile grew slowly on her face and her eyes narrowed. When she spoke, it was not with her voice. It was the same deep, hoarse, male voice that had spoken to Lizzie before. "I can see by your face that your god is not doing a very good job of protecting you. Perhaps you should get another."

Then she left, humming a quiet tune that faded as she headed for the mouth of the cave.

23.

Hester came out of the cave and clapped her hands three times. The chattering voices silenced instantly and all eyes turned to her.

"Come inside," she said. "I think we're about ready to begin."

As everyone entered the cave, Nathan stood and stared at the cave's yawning black mouth as it swallowed all those white-robed believers, adults and children alike.

Hester saw that he wasn't going in with the others and went to him.

"Will it hurt?" he asked.

She hunched down in front of him. "Of *course* not, sweetheart. Would I want you to do something that would *hurt* you?" She waited for an answer, then: "Well, *would* I?"

He shook his head slowly.

"You've watched the ceremony before. You haven't seen anyone hurting, have you?"

He shook his head again.

"You'll feel no pain," she said, holding up her penlight. "It'll be over . . . like *that*—" She flicked the light off. "—and then, just as quickly—" She turned it back on. "—you'll be starting all over again, a healthy baby boy who will have the privilege of growing up in the New Age of Enlightenment. So. Are you ready, Nathan?"

There was a long pause before he nodded, then he took her hand and they went into the cave.

Inside, light from the lanterns danced over the glistening cave walls. In the smooth curves of the rock formations, Nathan imagined that he saw faces, hands, eyes, grinning mouths. Drops of moisture clung to the tips of stalactites, sparkled like diamonds, then dropped. The whispered voices and crunching footsteps echoed through the darkness.

By the time they reached the Center of the Vortex, the voices had silenced and everyone began forming half-circles around the glowing crevice: first the children, then the adults.

A small pixieish young woman with a fluorescent lantern came to Nathan, smiled and said, "Hi, there." Her voice was high-pitched and tiny, like Tinkerbell's; Nathan liked it.

Hester said, "Nathan, this is Angela. She's going to prepare you. She will bathe you, then lead you in a brief meditation and chant. Go with her now and, when you come back, it will be time for your re-embodiment. Okay?"

He nodded.

Angela took his hand and led him away.

24.

"I think we'd better go down," Flash said, frowning at the gauge.

"How much do we have left?"

"How the hell am *I* supposed to know?" Flash shouted.

"Well, doesn't the gauge say how much is left?"

"The damned gauge doesn't go by *ounces*!"

"So how far do you think we can get?"

"I don't *know*!"

Marvin looked down. He saw car headlights gliding silently over a freeway with buildings lit up on either side. He recognized miniatures of familiar signs: 7-Eleven, Denny's, BP, 76.

"Where are we?" he asked.

"Headin' into San Jose pretty soon."

"Where do you want to put it down?"

"There's a field up here 'side the freeway that'll do me."

Marvin remembered pictures he'd seen of Chernobyl right after the meltdown at the Russian power plant—the burned bodies, the blackened landscape—and of the surrounding area and people years after the accident—hideously deformed cattle and babies—and he thought of what *this* area would be like if he failed to stop Mark Schroeder. He realized the chances of success were slim, but they were much slimmer if he didn't try, didn't push himself—and, if necessary, Flash—to the limit.

"Keep going," he said.

"You are *crazy*! Do you hear me? You are out of your fuckin' *mind*!"

"Fine. Just go a little further."

"*A little further?* Just what in thee *hell* does *that* mean, a little *further*?"

"It means just what it says."

"I'm puttin' her down," Flash growled with determination. They started down and the dog began wriggling excitedly.

"You do and you'll have to deal with this on the ground." Marvin aimed the gun at him.

"What, you're gonna *shoot* me?"

"If you don't keep going."

Then Flash surprised Marvin. He started to cry. He shook his head, sniffling, wiping his nose on his sleeve and muttering, "Shit. Sheee-*yit*. Son of a *bitch*. I shoulda stayed in m'damned *bed*. Don't know who in the *hell* you think you are, but . . . shee-*yit*."

They kept going.

25.

Mark was sitting perfectly still in the plane, eyes closed, head back, hands joined in his lap. He was chanting under his breath, lost in meditation; his mind was focused sharply on what he was about to do.

The plant. The task. The purpose.

He could not hear the plane's engine or the pilot's voice. He couldn't even hear his own breathing. There was nothing but his task and its purpose and—

—a tiny insect-like voice. It was deep inside him, in the deepest, most private, secret part of him. He'd been able to quiet the voice a little, but he could not silence it.

What if she's wrong?

So he tried, instead, to simply ignore its words.

What if death does exist?

He increased the speed of his chant.

What if you really will *be killing all of those people?*

He deepened his meditation.

Ending their lives . . . murdering them . . .

And still the voice went on. Unstoppable. Undeniable.

What if they're landing?

He chanted faster, a little louder.

We'll be killing them soon.

Mark's chanting stumbled. He didn't understand the voice now. It wasn't making sense.

"I said, we'll be landing soon. Mr. Schroeder?"

The plane's engine roared in his ears suddenly. He felt the rumbling vibration all around him and reality rushed in on him in an instant. Mark opened his eyes and turned to the pilot. "I'm sorry?"

"We'll be landing in a while. I thought I'd let you know."

"Oh. Yes. I see. Okay."

His body felt numb. His head ached and his mouth tasted like old pennies.

But he had a task, a purpose, a destiny. He would let nothing stand in his way. Not even that voice . . .

. . . the small, irritating voice of the one thing that had terrified Mark relentlessly since the day he'd left Lauren: doubt.

26.

They had all heard the voice that had spoken through Hester a while ago and they had spoken little since, leaving one another alone with silent thoughts.

Jordan's fear grew more intense as he imagined the kind of future Hester and Orrin—or who or whatever it was—had in mind for the world . . . unless Marvin succeeded in stopping Mark Schroeder.

Lauren thought only of Nathan and wondered what he was doing at that moment.

Coogan thanked God his wife was not alive for all of this, and wondered what mistakes they could have made in raising Paula that would make her want to join such a vile group and turn her back on her own children.

Lizzie wondered if maybe Hester wasn't *meant* to succeed, if perhaps God had other ideas, and she prayed for the strength to overcome such doubts.

Then the voices outside the cave drew closer. Footsteps resounded in the cave and voices rose and fell, then silenced. Only the sounds of movement and an occasional reverent whisper could be heard as the Inner Circle gathered outside the alcove.

"Oh, God," Lauren whimpered. "They're out there. Nathan is with them, he's out there somewhere. My baby, oh, God . . ."

"We need to pray," Lizzie breathed. "That's all we've got left."

"Amen," Coogan said. "He's done *bigger* things. No reason he can't change *their* plans." He nodded toward the archway.

Lizzie stood and went to him. "Anybody want to join us?" she asked.

Jordan ignored them.

Joan looked at Lizzie cautiously and said, "Look, I walked away from the Catholic church for good reasons, and I—"

Outside, Hester said, "The circles are complete. We are ready to begin."

Lauren stood and stumbled to the far wall of the alcove that faced the group outside. She pressed her palms to it first, then her cheek, her entire body, and whispered, "Oh my God, my baby, my little boy."

Benjamin growled at her for moving so close to the archway.

Lizzie grabbed Coogan's hand, then Joan's, closed her eyes and said rapidly, "Dear Lord, we come to You in desperation. The best we can do is put this in Your hands, but we *need* your *help* and we need it *now*. Nathan needs Your help, Marvin needs it, wherever he—"

"And now," Hester said, "we will focus our energies on the wholeness of the Godbody and begin the chant to call on the Guardians."

Following Hester's lead, they began to chant: "Gaaawwd-baaaww-deeee. Gaaawwd-baaaww-deeee . . ."

"My little boy," Lauren murmured, "my little boy, my son, my baby, what are they doing to my baby. . . ."

Benjamin growled at them again, louder this time, moving toward them threateningly.

The chanting went on relentlessly.

Lizzie continued to pray.

And although he appeared to ignore her, Jordan's eyes were closed and he was following intently Lizzie's every word, because he knew there was nothing else he could do.

27.

Nathan was embarrassed.

Angela had led him away from the group and down a long narrow branch of the cave to a room with a black pool in the center. Drops of moisture fell from the long narrow stalactites hanging from the narrow ceiling and sent constant ripples over the pool's surface; the gentle dripping echoed through the room and down the passage behind them.

Angela had set her lantern on a flat stone the size of a large barrel and, in one unexpected movement, slid Nathan's robe up and off, pulling his arms over his head.

That was why Nathan was embarrassed; except for his sneakers, he was naked.

Then Angela took off *her* robe.

Nathan's face burned.

She took his hand and led him into the pool until the water was up to his waist.

"There are crystals in this pool that Hester has treated and energized," she said. The echo in the room gave her soft voice a magical quality. Nathan found it relaxing, calming. "Bathing in this water will increase and purify the energy you already possess. And if Orrin chose you himself, you must have a lot of very *special* energy."

Putting one hand on his back, she cupped the other and scooped the cold water onto his chest, running her hand down his abdomen, then repeating the gesture two more times.

Nathan watched her closely. He watched the way her shiny blond hair began to fall slowly around her shoulders as she moved, the way her tiny round breasts shifted slightly now and then, the way her eyes sparkled and her hands felt on him.

"Now," Angela said, "I want you to lean back and relax. Don't worry, I won't let you fall."

He leaned back into the crook of her arm.

"Hold your breath," she said, placing a hand on his chest.

She dipped him under the water and pulled him back up.

When he opened his eyes and saw her pretty smile, her bright eyes and her hair falling down around her face, he realized she was one of the last people he would see in this life.

28.

"I'm takin' her down," Flash barked decisively.

"How much farther?" Marvin asked.

"I don't give a *shit* in the *morning* how much farther, I'm *takin'* her *down*, and if you don't *like* it, you can *shoot* me when we *land*, but I'm *not* gonna—"

The engine coughed.

"Oh, shit," Flash groaned.

The engine began to sputter.

"What's wrong?" Marvin asked, panicking at the sounds from the engine.

"We're outta fuel that's what's wrong you son of a bitch!"

Marvin felt sick. He clutched the edges of his seat and muttered, "Oh God, this is it, this is it, this is it. . . ."

They began to descend quickly, but the engine was still wheezing and struggling; it hadn't died yet. Flash was trying to get them as low as possible before that happened.

Then it stopped.

Silence.

"Glide us in glide us in!" Marvin screamed.

"Helicopters don't *glide* you asshole they *drop*!"

And they dropped .

29.

"We're landing," the pilot said.

Mark blinked several times, then nodded and said, "Good. That's good." But his words did not hold the confidence he'd intended and it made him nervous, agitated. There was no more time to chant or meditate, no more time to think.

Maybe, Mark thought as the plane descended, *that's just what I* don't *need . . . time to think.*

The wheels of the plane shrieked as they scraped the runway.

30.

Impact was deafening.

Marvin and Flash had both screamed all the way down, Flash holding his barking dog to his chest while Marvin leaned forward with his face between his knees, then—

—the slamming shock of the helicopter landing, the crunch of metal and—

—the helicopter's curved Plexiglas broke in several places, forming sharp, transparent fangs that surrounded the two men, and then—

—cold.

Marvin didn't move for a long time. His lower back felt as if someone had driven over him in a car. His eyes were clenched shut. All he could feel was the cold and something moving on his lap. He opened his eyes slowly to see the dog perched on his thighs, jittering happily as if it wanted to go back up and do it again. Marvin turned to Flash, who was leaning forward in his seat, shaking his head and scrubbing his face with his palms.

A fine white mist curled all around them.

The helicopter had fallen through the ceiling of something, taking out a good portion of two walls as well.

"Oh, boy," Marvin sighed. He pushed the dog off his lap, unbuckled his belts and tried the door. It was stubborn, but he managed to get it open after a few tries. When he got out, his body still stiff from the tension of the drop, he stumbled over several hard objects lying loose on the floor around him. He looked down.

Cornish game hens.

Marvin looked all around them and realized where they were: inside a long, rectangular, refrigerated shipping container. They were surrounded by frozen Cornish game hens, chickens, steaks, hamburger patties, hot dogs and fish, all wrapped in plastic.

He leaned into the helicopter to tell Flash he was going outside, but stopped. Flash was hugging his dog and sobbing.

Marvin turned and sidled through the opening in the wall, careful to avoid the jagged, torn aluminum, and hopped down onto the pavement.

He heard footsteps and voices rushing toward him and he thought fast. If he was found, he'd *never* get to Diego on time.

There would be questions to answer and police to talk to and he could not afford that, so—

—he turned away from the voices and saw more shipping containers, six of them all together, grouped neatly around him behind a large building. He limped to the back of the one they'd landed on, then ducked around the corner and headed for the back of the next container. Hurrying along the wall of the building, he went around the corner and realized where he was.

Ahead of him was a lot filled with eighteen-wheelers. To his left, trucks were lined up at a fuel island.

They'd landed at a truck stop.

The footsteps and voices drew no closer; they'd stopped at the helicopter and he could hear several people talking at once.

"—call the police and get a—"

"—calling an ambulance now, so—"

"—just dropped right out of the sky, just dropped like a damned—"

Trying to conceal his limp, Marvin headed for the fuel island to look for a ride, comforted by the weight of the .38 beneath his sport coat.

31.

Mark stepped out of the plane and onto the runway. He was surprised by how weak his knees felt.

The airpark was well lit but small, and there appeared to be no one around except himself and a man standing beside a dark sedan several yards away. The man started toward him, taking broad steps but not hurrying.

Mark turned and looked into the plane. The pilot smiled and nodded toward the man with the car, saying, "He'll take it from here." Then he leaned over and pulled the door shut.

"Mr. Schroeder?" the man behind him said.

Mark turned to him and tried to smile, but he knew it was a clumsy effort.

"I'm your driver," the man said. "You're to come with me."

Mark followed him to the car, willing his legs to hold him up and trying to ignore the speed of his heartbeat.

In the car, the man smiled and asked, "Did your flight go well?"

Mark looked at him and thought, *They're all so calm. So at ease.* Then: "Um, the flight? Yes, the flight, uh, went fine, just fine."

The man started the car.

"Um, how far do we have to go?" Mark asked.

"Oh, it's a little drive. Not bad. I have something for you to listen to." He pushed a cassette into the tape deck.

"Hello, Mark," Hester said.

Her voice startled him and his back stiffened.

"I think I know what you're thinking right about now," she said, "and I want to ease your mind. You're probably having doubts, aren't you?"

He almost responded, but pressed his lips together tightly.

"You're human, Mark. Humans have doubts. Just keep remembering a few things to fight those doubts. Remember the Center of the Vortex and how wonderful that light made you feel. Remember Orrin and the things he's taught you. And remember *me*, Mark. When you've re-embodied, we'll be together again. Orrin will see to it."

Mark could feel the tension bleeding from him as she spoke. Her voice alone was enough to calm him, but her words gave him strength.

She went on: "You're heading now for your destination. I want you to relax and chant with me, Mark. Focus all your thoughts and energy on your task, and remember . . . we'll be together in the New Age."

Mark relaxed in his seat, leaned his head back against the headrest and began to chant quietly with Hester.

32.

The fuel island was busy. Attendants were filling trucks while drivers walked back and forth between their trucks and the main building where they paid for the diesel.

Marvin approached the island slowly, cautiously. He didn't know what he was going to do or how he'd do it without drawing attention to himself, he only knew that, no matter what, he *had* to get a ride to the plant.

A man walked by him wearing black jeans, a soiled white shirt and a white turban. The man walked hurriedly as he stuffed papers into a large fat folder. He was tall and very thin and looked jarringly out of place among the truckers in their plaid shirts and blue jeans, some with bellies hanging over their belts, all looking weary. This man moved briskly and, in spite of his dirty shirt, appeared fresh and alert.

When he reached the fuel island, the turbaned man said something to one of the attendants, then waved and went to a blue-and-white eighteen-wheeler parked beside the pumps. He reached up and opened the door.

He's a driver! Marvin thought, surprised. He quickened his pace, wincing at the pain in his back. He decided he would try the turban first.

The Indian was climbing into his truck when Marvin reached him.

"Excuse me, excuse me," Marvin shouted above the thunder of all the other trucks.

The man looked down, slightly annoyed. "Yes, yes, what is it?"

"Which direction are you headed?"

"I can't take any passengers," the man said, shaking his head.

"No, please, wait, listen to me, I'm in a real bind. My car's broken down and I really need to get someplace. I don't think it's very far from here. If you could just—"

"No, no, dat would not be possible, I can't take any passengers." He reached out to close the door.

"No, *please*, it's not very far. If you're going by the Diego Nuclear Power Plant, you could just drop me off in front of—"

The man flinched. "What . . . what was dat you said? Diego? Is dat where you're going?"

"Yes," Marvin said, sounding relieved.

The man leaned out the door just a bit, scrutinizing Marvin. Then he pulled himself in suddenly and slammed the door.

"Wait!" Marvin called, knocking on the door. "It's not very far, really. I'll give you money if you want." He knocked again, more insistently.

The truck's engine growled to life.

Marvin looked around quickly. There were plenty of other truckers. But there wasn't plenty of time.

He grabbed the railing and hiked himself up on the step. Slipping his right hand under his coat, he opened the door with his left.

The Indian jumped, eyes bulging, and opened his mouth as if to cry out, but when he saw the gun he simply froze.

"I'm sorry, but I'm afraid you're gonna have to take a passenger tonight. Now, I'm going to step over your legs and you're going to start driving. Just get us out of here. When you get to the exit, you're going to turn right. You're not going to shout. You're not going to do anything to get anyone's attention because I've got this." He raised the gun until it was aimed at the man's face. "Nod if you understand."

He nodded.

"Okay." Marvin stepped over the man's legs, around the gearshift and sat in the passenger's seat with a grunt; ground glass crunched between his vertebrae. "Now. Close the door and let's go."

As they were driving through the lot toward the exit, the Indian kept looking at Marvin, his lips parted, his eyes still wide. Finally, he said something Marvin didn't understand.

"You're duh man."

"What? I'm sorry?"

Then he said something that horrified Marvin.

"You're duh man. Duh man dee police are looking for."

"Whuh-what man?"

He pointed to a rectangular black box on the dashboard. A strip of small red lights flashed on and off on its face. "On duh police scanner. I hear duh sheriffs say dey are looking for a man who . . . who looks like you . . . and who has a gun . . . and who is headed for duh nuclear power plant. A possible terrorist, dey say. Named, uh . . . Ackroyd."

Marvin was speechless. Had Hester arranged it? And if so, how the hell had she managed to do it?

"Jordan," he muttered. Hester might have found out from Jordan or one of the others. She couldn't have found out from Lizzie because Lizzie knew nothing of this particular plan. She *had* to find out from one of the others. Which meant she *had* one of them. Or all of them.

Marvin slipped his thumb and forefinger under his glasses and rubbed his eyes hard. It seemed that the sensible thing to do was apologize to the nice man with the turban, have him drop Marvin off at the nearest pay phone, call a cab and get the hell away from there as fast as possible.

He dismissed that thought immediately. Even before receiving

this news, he'd known it was going to be difficult to impossible—
leaning heavily on the impossible side—and had committed to it
anyway. He wasn't about to back out now. He turned to the
driver.

"I'm sorry about this. I really am. I just don't *do* this sort of
thing. But . . . well, these are unusual circumstances. If I tried
to explain them to you, you'd think I was crazy." Marvin looked
at the gun in his hand and chuckled without a smile. "You probably think that now. I just don't want you to think . . . well, that
I'm doing this for . . . oh, I don't know, for some . . ." He
sighed. "Just drive."

33.

"Gaaawwd-baaaww-deeee. Gaaawwd-baaaww-deeee."

The chant went on. Every few minutes, following Hester's
lead, the pitch of the voices rose a bit and the speed of the chant
increased.

But there was something else.

Jordan heard the same rhythmic flapping he'd heard in the
cave the night before. He stood and walked toward the archway.

"Where you going?" Coogan asked.

"I want to take a look."

Coogan joined him.

Lizzie was on her knees, praying silently. Joan was staying
close to Lauren, who stared at the stone wall and occasionally
joined in the chant under her breath. Her voice was as distant as
the look in her eyes; she sounded confused, lost.

Benjamin had been pacing but stepped in front of Jordan and
Coogan when they started toward the archway. They looked up
at him, both trying to conceal their fear.

Speaking slowly, Jordan said, "We just want to watch the
ceremony."

Benjamin grunted and walked backward out of the archway,
watching them. He gestured for them to come out and lifted a
hand to let them know they'd come out far enough.

They turned toward the blue light throbbing from the enormous crevice, where Hester stood facing the two semicircles of
white-robed chanters.

Coogan gasped when he looked over the heads of the crowd and saw the mottled, reptilian creature flying in slow circles.

"There's only one," Jordan said. "There should be more."

Sure enough, something appeared in the crevice. It was just a dark spot at first, but grew as it oozed out of the crevice until it resembled an enormous, long piece of human excrement sliding slowly out of a giant rectum. It was not quite out of the crevice when it spread first its arms, then its wings, and shot out into the air, joining the other one in flight as a third began to ooze out of the crevice.

"Good God," Coogan breathed tremulously. "What . . . are they?"

"Mark called them angels."

"He was right," Lizzie whispered. She'd joined them silently and stood behind them, a frown further darkening her already bruised and bloodied face. "They are angels. But—" She shook her head slowly. "—they are *not* angels of God. . . ."

34.

A cool hand touched Nathan's cheek and he stopped chanting abruptly and opened his eyes. In his robe again, he was sitting Indian-style on the ground beside the pool where he'd been chanting. When he opened his eyes, he saw Angela kneeling before him, her sweet, smiling face just a couple inches from his.

"That's enough," she whispered. She stayed there for a while, her hand on his face, smiling at him. Ghostly echoes of the ceremonial chanting drifted into the room and the gentle dripping over the pool seemed to stay in sync with its rhythm, which had been growing steadily faster.

Nathan thought it would be nice to stay right there, looking at Angela's smile and listening to the dripping, maybe even nicer than being the Chosen One.

"You're a very special boy, Nathan," Angela whispered. Then she kissed him on the forehead—a slow, lingering kiss—then stood and reached out her hand. "Come on, now. It's time to go."

Nathan stood and took her hand and they started toward the chanting voices.

35.

The tape stopped abruptly and Mark's eyes snapped open with surprise.

"Are we there?" he asked.

"Not yet, Mr. Schroeder," the driver said. "Just a few more minutes. There's something I need to tell you. Ms. Thorne called me on the car phone shortly before your plane landed. She wanted you to know that there will probably be police officers at the plant when you arrive."

"Police? At the plant? I don't understand. Do they know I'm coming?"

"They don't. But *someone* does. Someone named Marvin Ackroyd. He's armed and hopes to stop you before you get inside. The police know nothing of your reason for coming to the plant, and because the guard at the gate will know you, they'll let you through with no problem. But they will be waiting for Mr. Ackroyd, and they will stop him."

"But how did he . . . I mean—"

"She also said that you're not to worry about it. She has everything under control."

Mark thought about that. If Hester said there was nothing to worry about, then it was wrong for him to worry. His anxiety would only drain him of much-needed energy and make it difficult for him to focus on his task.

But . . . police? Mark got nervous around police when he was doing *nothing;* how would he react to them now, knowing what he was about to do . . . and knowing that he had a gun under his coat?

"It'll just be a few more minutes, Mr. Schroeder," the driver said. "Would you like me to rewind the tape and replay the beginning?"

Mark's voice sounded a little breathless when he spoke: "Oh, yes, please. Please."

The driver rewound the tape, said, "Remember, we're on Diego Road now, so it won't be long," then pushed the button.

As he listened to Hester's voice, he thought of how she looked, how she felt and smelled and tasted. But even her voice and those thoughts could not completely silence the nagging voice deep inside him. The voice was different now. It was no longer the tiny, insect-like voice he'd been hearing on the plane.

Now it was Lauren's voice.

Think, Mark, she said. *Think. Think about what you're doing. Think. You're not thinking, Mark. Think.*

Hester's voice and Lauren's voice. Speaking at the same time. Directly to him.

Suddenly Mark felt sick, felt like the car was spinning in circles, and he closed his eyes, afraid that if he didn't, he would see the world outside go around in a grey blur, and he wanted to open the car door and throw himself into the night, screaming, just to get away from those two lovely, smothering voices, and his trembling hand was on the door's handle, the fingers hooking under the plastic to pull, and—

—he realized the car was slowing and he opened his eyes to see that three deputy sheriff's cars were parked at the plant's gate just fifty yards off of Diego Road.

The driver stopped the car, then the tape, then smiled at Mark and said, "We're here."

36.

The Diego Nuclear Power Plant was twenty-eight miles southeast of San Jose, just off U.S. 101.

And they were close. Just two exits away. Marvin had to think fast.

"Okay, okay," he breathed to himself, looking out the window.

The Diego exit would put them on Diego Road, which ran parallel to 101 and also led to the plant. Beyond the shoulder of the freeway was a sharp embankment that dropped down to a barbed-wire fence, beyond which was a barren strip of land covered with dead weeds. A hundred yards beyond the first fence was another. Beyond that, Diego Road.

Marvin could see the plant up ahead. Its corpse-grey glow rose above the oak trees that surrounded it.

If he had the driver drop him off on the freeway directly in front of the plant, Marvin could go down the embankment, climb the fence, cross the field and show up on foot. It would be a hell of a lot less conspicuous than showing up in an eighteen-wheeler.

"See where the plant is up there?" he asked the driver.

"Yes, I see."

"I want you to skip the Diego exit and pull over right across from the plant."

"You want me to stop?"

"That's right."

"Duh Highway Patrol might come."

"You'll just be there long enough to drop me off, that's all."

When the driver pulled over and stopped, Marvin turned to him and smiled. "I'm sorry for the inconvenience. I really appreciate the ride."

"Oh, my pleasure, my pleasure." His eyes were still as wide as they'd been since Marvin had first pulled his gun.

Marvin looked around until he spotted the driver's CB radio mounted overhead above the windshield. "Um, I'm sorry about this, too," he said as he reached up, clutched the radio's microphone firmly and jerked down hard. The cord tore out of the radio.

Smiling at the driver again, Marvin said, "I wouldn't want you to make any noise about me. Drive carefully."

Holding the microphone in one hand and his gun in the other, Marvin got out of the truck and used his shoulder to push the door shut.

Moving slowly at first, the truck pulled away.

Marvin threw the microphone into the field and waited until he heard it land.

The plant was an enormous, threatening structure surrounded by several smaller buildings. Floodlights towered over Cyclone fences topped with rows of barbed wire.

Gritting his teeth against the pain in his back, Marvin started down the embankment.

37.

Nathan stood beside Angela, holding her hand, just a few yards from the group. He watched Hester closely, impressed by her tight mask of intense concentration; this was the first time he'd ever watched the ceremony rather than participating in it and he found it fascinating. For a little while, he completely forgot that he soon *would* be participating.

A man came to Nathan's side and smiled down at him warmly. Under his right arm, the man held the rolled-up mat upon which Nathan would lie.

The Godbody chant had reached a fever pitch and would be ending soon.

Four of the Guardians circled overhead while two more watched from ledges high up on the cave walls. One of them looked down on him, its face serene, lips stretched into a beatific smile. Nathan's chest swelled with pride as he smiled back, and—

—the chanting stopped abruptly, startling Nathan. His eyes darted from the Guardian to Hester.

She turned slowly to Nathan. Her voice was warm and maternal as she nodded once and said, "Bring the Chosen One. . . ."

38.

When Hester spoke, Jordan glanced over his shoulder at Lauren in the alcove.

"Make sure she doesn't come out here," he said to Lizzie. "She's liable to lose it completely if she sees this."

Lizzie said, "I don't think she can even hear."

Coogan turned his back on the ceremony suddenly, shaking his head.

"My *God*," he hissed, "I can't take this. There's gotta be something we can do, something we can try. We can't just stand here and watch her *kill* that boy. C'mon, Jordan, I'm game if you are. We don't have a whole lot to lose."

Coogan was right. They had to at least *try* something. But what?

Nathan was escorted to the front by two people. The mat was rolled out. The young woman at Nathan's side said, "He has been bathed and cleansed."

"Thank you," Hester said.

The escorts joined the semicircle.

Hester turned Nathan to face the group and put her hands on his shoulders from behind, saying, "On this very special night, we will perform the Chant of the Masters before the re-embodiment. Focus your energies on the Ascended Masters and help the Chosen One to bridge the gap between the planes so that we may finally open the door on the New Age of Enlightenment.''

They began to chant the names of the Ascended Masters.

Lizzie faced them, but was not watching them or even listening. Her face was turned up toward the jagged and uneven ceiling of the massive stone cathedral as she prayed harder than she had ever prayed before. Reflected blue light sparkled on the beads of perspiration that clung to her creased brow.

She was praying for forgiveness of her sins, for the cleansing of her soul. She knew her slate would have to be clean before she could possibly attempt what she planned to do: invoke the name of Jesus Christ to command the demon that possessed Hester Thorne to leave.

39.

Mark stood with his back to the car until it drove away.

Two of the deputies leaned on one of the squad cars while three more stood at the guardhouse with Clay, the security guard, a short, bullet-shaped black man. They were all bathed in the sputtering glow of the mercury vapor lights that illuminated the grounds all around the plant.

Mark had seen the deputies stiffen when he got out of the car. They watched him cautiously, ready for the worst.

He started down the drive toward the guardhouse.

The two deputies by the car moved away from it, unsnapping their holsters casually.

Mark was closer . . . closer . . .

One of the deputies standing at the guardhouse said something to Clay, who shook his head and responded.

. . . closer . . .

Clay took a step forward and said, "Can I help you?"

The inside of Mark's mouth was fuzzy, his tongue felt thick, his throat swollen shut. He kept walking, swallowed hard, cleared his throat and called, "Hey there, Clay."

Clay watched him a moment longer, then said, "Mark? Schroeder?"

"Yeah." Mark reached the guardhouse and Clay shook his hand, grinning.

"Well, what the hell're you doing here? I thought you moved to the country."

"We did, but . . . well, that didn't work out the way we'd planned."

"Oh, sorry to hear it."

Mark glanced at the deputies. They watched him with cold suspicion. Clay seemed to have forgotten they were there.

"So, what are you doing here?" Clay asked.

"Well, I was thinking about getting a position on graveyard. I thought I'd come see Mitch while he's on and ask about an opening. Mitch is here tonight, isn't he?"

"Sure is."

Another glance at the deputies. They hadn't budged.

"So, uh . . . what's going on here, Clay?" Mark asked. "Some kind of problem?"

Clay made an annoyed gesture with a hand the size of a thick slice of prime rib. "Oh, some tip they got. Right, boys?" he asked the deputies.

One of them nodded.

"But you don't have to worry about Mark," Clay said, grinning. "He's a friend of the family, here." He turned to Mark and asked, "By the way, how is your family, Mark?"

Mark's throat froze into a solid tube of ice and, for a few seconds, his lips moved, but no sound came out. He coughed once, then said, "Fine. They're fine. Yeah, that was my wife who dropped me off. She'll be back in a while." He looked back toward Diego Road where the driver had dropped him off and—

—he saw movement on the other side of the road. At least, he *thought* he did. It could have been anything really: a dog, a bird, *anything*. But it gave Mark a chill. He remembered what the driver had told him. *He's armed and hopes to stop you . . . he's armed and hopes to stop you . . . hopes to stop you . . . stop you. . . .*

"So, what went wrong in the country, Mark?" Clay asked.

He braced himself; he would have to make more pleasant conversation while hiding his fear and the fact that *he had to get inside*. He smiled and talked some more with Clay.

40.

From the embankment below the freeway to the fence across Diego Road from the plant, Marvin had been cursing his decision to leave the real-estate business. The landing in Flash's helicopter had thrown something out in his lower back and the pain had crawled all the way up to the base of his skull; his knees ached and his stomach burned and the combination of it all was beginning to make him feel weak and a little dizzy.

Those kinds of things had never happened to him while he was selling houses.

Oak trees grew beside Diego Road and Marvin got behind a fat one before climbing over the barbed-wire fence. Staying behind the tree, he peered around the trunk at the plant's gate across the street and saw the three squad cars, the deputies, the security guard and Mark. They were talking. Marvin could even hear laughter now and then.

It was obvious the deputies weren't going to stop Mark.

Even if Mark were standing clear of the others, Marvin couldn't possibly hit him from that distance. And if he tried to get any closer, the deputies would change his plans. Even if they didn't stop him, what would they do once he'd fired a few shots into Mark? He thought it unlikely that the deputies would demand explanation.

He could run, of course . . . providing he was *able* to run. He could go down the road a bit, then run across at an angle to the gate and maybe—just *maybe*—surprise them enough to do what he had to do.

But the outcome would be the same for *him*.

He sat on the ground, leaned his shoulder against the tree trunk and scanned the surrounding area. There wasn't much around the plant. On the way there in the truck, he'd noticed a couple of buildings—colorless, blocky structures—a mile back, maybe less. Other than that, the plant was surrounded by flat land divided by barbed-wire fences.

But he knew that, beyond that empty space, there were houses, neighborhoods and towns filled with people. A lot of people.

He let out a breath through puffed cheeks, stood and hobbled down the road.

"God," he whispered, "I hope Lizzie's right about you listening to anyone who speaks to you, because I want you to be listening when I say I hope I'm doing the right thing. I don't approve of killing, but I think it's justified in this case. Of course, I've been wrong before. Anyway, I think you'll be the only judge I explain it to, so if I *am* wrong, I hope you'll show me some mercy. I'll need it. Um . . . amen.''

He stopped and turned back toward the plant's gate. He watched it for a moment, bracing himself for the pain to come, then pulled out his gun and began to run as—

—Mark tried to wrap up his conversation with Clay. The deputies were talking among themselves as Clay went on and on about his last camping trip in the Mount Shasta area. Mark fidgeted, nodded, smiled and every time Clay paused, Mark started to say that he had to be going, but Clay always interrupted him. One of the deputies bailed him out.

"Excuse me," he said. "I think we're gonna take off. It looks like we got a lousy tip. We were told it was from a good source, but . . ." He shrugged.

"Well, it *was* just a tip, remember," another deputy said. "I've never taken them too seriously, myself." He smiled at Clay and said, "I'll be sticking around a little while longer, just in case."

"Yeah," Clay said, "we get that kinda crap all the time here. Phone calls, notes, bomb threats from environmentalists, from nuts, you name it."

Clay launched into one of his stories and Mark tuned him out. The four deputies who were leaving headed for their cars. Mark stepped around Clay and headed for the plant when he heard a sound.

He stopped and turned, listening intently.

Tapping . . . it sounded like a rapid tapping that grew steadily louder.

"No," Mark breathed when he recognized the sound as footsteps. "No . . ."

The deputy listening to Clay's story heard Mark and turned to him, frowning.

Mark took a few steps backward as—

—Marvin ran diagonally across the street, gun in hand. Pain shattered his back each time a foot struck the pavement, but he bit his lower lip to keep from crying out and tears streaked down his cheeks and—

—the sound grew louder, *closer*, and Mark felt panic rising in his throat like a bad meal as he stumbled backward, but he remembered what Hester had told him—that no one, absolutely *no one*, could stand in his way because what he was doing was right and *had* to be *done*—and he stopped as—

—the deputy looked suspiciously in the direction Mark was staring and asked, "Is something wrong?" But—

—Mark said nothing to him, but whispered, "For me . . . coming for me," as he watched the road and started to walk slowly in that direction as—

—the deputy motioned for the others to get out of their cars as—

—Marvin's pain became so excruciating that it was something more than pain now, but he didn't care, *couldn't* care, because his attention was focused completely on the corner of the Cyclone fence that drew closer and closer and closer as—

—Mark raised his voice slightly and the others heard him as he continued to say, ". . . for me . . . he's coming for me," as he reached beneath his coat, and—

—one of the deputies said, "Hey, listen to that, somebody's com—"

Marvin rounded the corner, heading straight for them in a staggering run, his gun clasped between both hands as—

—Mark drew his gun and aimed and—

—the deputies shouted curses as they clumsily unholstered their guns and—

—the night exploded with gunfire. . . .

41.

Jordan was still standing with Coogan just outside the alcove staring at the ground to avoid looking directly at the blue light when the chanting was joined by a ululating wail. It was Lauren.

With one sweeping gesture, Benjamin swung an arm through the air and scooped Jordan, Coogan and Lizzie—who had been leaning against the wall praying silently—into the alcove like three children. Jordan's foot struck something and he fell through the archway as Benjamin lumbered quickly to Lauren.

Joan was beside her, shaking her and hissing into her ear,

"Sh-sh-sh! Stop Lauren please stop he'll *hurt* you he'll hurt *all* of us *please* he'll—"

Benjamin slapped a hand over her face, closed his fingers on the front half of her skull and lifted her to her feet; he put his mouth to her ear and growled quietly.

Beneath his palm, her muffled cries stopped. When he let go of her, she collapsed in a heap. Joan and Lizzie rushed to her side and helped her back onto the rock.

On hands and knees, Jordan looked back to see what had tripped him up. It was a rock. But it wasn't like all the other rocks on the ground in and around the alcove. It was a *perfect* rock. It was about twice the size of Jordan's fist and it was still rocking back and forth slightly from the impact of his foot.

It was loose, unattached.

It was a weapon.

He got to his feet as Benjamin went to the archway and peered out to see if anyone had heard Lauren's cry.

"I'm sorry," Lizzie said to Lauren. "I'm sorry he did that, but you scared him. He was afraid his mother would hear us and—"

"Why the hell are you apologizing for that thing?" Jordan hissed.

"Because he can't apologize for *himself*. And he is not a *thing*."

He watched Benjamin standing in the archway. He looked like a thing to Jordan. His left foot was inches from the rock Jordan had tripped on . . . the rock Jordan *needed*. . . .

"Coogan," he whispered. "See if you can get him back in here. Divert his attention."

"Who, Benjamin?"

Jordan nodded impatiently.

Coogan looked at Benjamin a moment, then turned back to Jordan with deeper wrinkles in his forehead and around his eyes. "Well, I . . . I-I . . . how would I—"

The chanting stopped.

Deafening silence crashed down around them suddenly.

No one in the alcove moved; only their eyes darted from face to face, waiting. Then, outside in the chamber, Hester spoke.

"You understand what you are about to do, Nathan Schroeder?"

A small young voice said, "Yes."

Lauren stood and staggered toward the archway blubbering, "She said his name, she said hi—he's out there right now, he's out—oh God oh my God—"

"You are fully willing to enter your next incarnation?" Hester asked. "You *want* this?"

"Yes."

Joan threw herself on Lauren, hushing her and keeping her from rushing out of the alcove.

"Then," Hester said, "we're ready."

Lizzie spun around and walked straight for the archway, muttering to herself, ". . . *knew* what it was all along, I shouldn't have *waited*, I *shouldn't* have, I should've just *done* it. . . ."

"Lizzie?" Jordan said. "Where are you go—Lizzie, what're you *doing*?" He stood and followed her.

She stopped in front of Benjamin, placed her hand flat over the center of his chest and said, "Benjamin, you *know* I'm your friend. And I *know* you won't hurt me."

Then she was gone.

"Oh, shit," Jordan said.

Benjamin stood gawking after her for a moment, his face managing to register surprise in spite of all that twisted flesh and cartilage, then made a gurgling groan as he went after her.

Jordan saw his chance.

He rushed to the archway and swept the rock up in both hands without stopping and went after Benjamin as—

—Lizzie headed for the altar purposefully, her back straight, her steps broad, with Benjamin closing in behind her until—

—Jordan closed in on *him*, first running, then jumping, then, during that split second off the ground, slamming the rock down on the back of Benjamin's large and misshapen skull.

Rock met bone with a crack that resounded through the enormous chamber.

A few heads turned away from the ceremony to see what had happened.

An explosive grunt escaped Benjamin before he hit the ground. More heads turned.

Jordan ducked into a shallow triangular depression in the wall and watched.

Lizzie hadn't lost a beat. She stalked up the incline, broke through the line of adults, then between two of the children, until she faced Hester, who stared in disbelief.

Hester said, "What are you—"

Lizzie pointed a steady index finger at her and said loudly, "In the name of Jesus Christ—"

Hester flinched.

"—I command the demon that is in you—"

Hester's upper lip curled back into a sneer, her head dropped forward and she glared up at Lizzie from beneath deeply furrowed brows.

"—to *come out*!"

Gasps rose from the onlookers and a hiss of confused whispers floated through the chamber like a mist.

On the ground at Hester's feet, Nathan lay naked on the mat, afraid to move. The two women towered over him like giant pine trees in the woods outside.

Jordan kept an eye on Benjamin, who still lay on the ground; he stirred and made retching sounds, but he didn't get up. Jordan stayed in his hiding place, furious at Lizzie for doing whatever the hell she was doing when they *could* be getting out of the cave. When Lizzie began shouting at Hester, Jordan stuck his head out of the small shelter and turned back toward the alcove.

"Coogan!" he hissed. "Coogan! Hey!"

Coogan stood just inside the archway, terrified. He'd watched Lizzie walk out, then Jordan, and he could hear the commotion outside, could even hear someone—he assumed it was Jordan—calling his name. But he was afraid to move. He felt weaker and older than he'd ever felt before.

Joan was still holding Lauren down, but she couldn't quiet her.

"Look out there, please," Lauren sobbed. "See what's happening, see what they're doing to my son."

Trembling, Coogan moved forward slowly, stepped through the archway and turned to his right. He saw Benjamin on the ground. He saw Lizzie and Hester glaring at one another, bathed in blue light.

"Coogan, over *here*!"

And he saw Jordan's head sticking out of a low opening in the wall.

"Go!" Jordan rasped. "Take the others, get the lantern and go. Now! *Go!*"

He couldn't move. His body was numb, his heart had stopped and he wasn't breathing.

"Dammit, Coogan, get outta here!"

It took tremendous effort, but Coogan broke out of his paralysis, went back in the alcove and grabbed the lantern.

"C'mon, c'mon," he said.

Joan whispered, "What? What are we doing?"

Coogan turned the lantern off, deciding he wouldn't use it until they left the light behind, then said, "We're leaving."

Once again, Lizzie began, "In the name of Jesus Christ—"

Hester stepped around Nathan.

"—the son of God—"

She slapped a hand on Lizzie's wrist and closed her fist tightly.

"—I command the demon—"

Lizzie's voice trembled from the pain of Hester's grip.

"—thuh-that is in you—"

"Lizzie," Hester breathed, jerking Lizzie close until their noses almost touched, "listen to me, Lizzie . . . I don't *want* it to come out." She inhaled deeply, then let it out slowly, and suddenly her breath smelled of excrement and her throat sounded filled with phlegm. For an instant, her face looked swollen, as if it were going to split open and reveal something horrible underneath, something that was trying hard to get out. When she spoke again, she whispered, but not in her voice: "I told you many years ago that she was *mine*, but you didn't believe me. Happy now, cunt?"

Hester backhanded Lizzie with the strength of a large man and Lizzie flew backward into the semicircle of children.

Several women cried out in shock.

One of the children shrieked.

Nathan held his breath, shivering from cold and fear. Overhead, he saw the Guardians spiraling downward until they lighted gracefully. One of them landed beside Nathan and smiled down at him. Nathan felt better suddenly. He knew the angels would protect him.

Coogan hustled the women out of the alcove, saying, "Move fast, maybe we won't be seen that way. Everybody's pretty distracted."

"What about Jordan and Lizzie?" Joan asked.

"Nathan, what about *Nathan*?" Lauren cried.

"Shh! You've *got* to be quiet. Jordan and Lizzie are gonna get Nathan, Lauren. They're gonna . . . do their best, now come *on*!"

Pointing to Lizzie on the ground, Hester shouted, "This woman is an agent of the Great Lie! She has come to stop this ceremony and prevent the coming of the New Age of Enlightenment. She knows that—"

Hester stopped when she saw Benjamin lying on the ground a few yards from the alcove. Just beyond him, she saw Coogan, Lauren and Joan hurrying out of the chamber.

She pointed at them and said, "Stop them."

Every head turned in the direction she was pointing, but no one moved. No one needed to. Instead, they watched the Guardian that stood beside Nathan spread its beautiful wings and lift itself from the ground gracefully. A few children cooed and some of the adults smiled as they watched the sleek, glowing creature glide just a few feet over their heads, but—

—Jordan *didn't* smile. He saw the slimy beast flying toward Coogan and the two women and, still clutching the rock, he stepped out of the small shelter and shouted at them, "Run! Run! *Get out now!*"

They ran, Coogan and Joan pulling Lauren by her arms as she began to scream, "Nathan! Nathan, please—let me *go*, let *go* of me—Nathan, please, come with us, please—"

Her words dissolved into a ragged scream and Joan's scream joined hers as the winged creature landed in front of them silently and spread its black and grey wings to block their path. It moved toward them slowly, backing them against the wall.

Jordan turned toward Hester and her followers and—

—he cried out in horror. One of the creatures stood directly in front of him, its wings opening, as if to embrace him. Close up, the creature's skin and wings looked diseased; what appeared to be open sores drained thick dark yellow fluid while a clear, viscous substance clung to the creature's wrinkled black-and-grey hide. Its eyes were almond-shaped and pure black, its snout running with snot from its flat round nostrils. Sharp yellowed fangs jutted from beneath its thin, grinning lips. And more thick, yellow fluid dribbled from the tip of the creature's enormous erection.

It clutched his shoulders and pushed him against the wall. After that, it didn't move, didn't even blink. It just held him there and stared into his eyes.

Jordan looked to his left at Coogan, Lauren and Joan. The creature before them hadn't moved, either.

And they're not going to, Jordan thought. *They're just holding us for Hester until she's done with her ceremony.*

"Please, *please,*" Hester called, raising a hand, "pay no attention to them. The Guardians will see that we finish the ceremony uninterrupted." She finally regained the attention of her followers. "Continue chanting as I perform the re-embodiment."

They followed Hester's lead and, once again, the chamber echoed with the sound of their voices, their eyes closed, heads lifted slightly.

Once they were well into the chant, Hester knelt at Nathan's feet. His eyes were wide with fear and confusion.

"I'm very sorry about all of that," she said softly, "but it's taken care of now. Are you ready, Nathan?" She smiled.

He nodded as—

—Lizzie opened her eyes. Her head was in a vise and her jaw throbbed. She felt disoriented, the way she used to feel when waking up from a long drunk. Groaning, she lifted her head, sat up slowly, struggled to her feet and muttered, "Oh, dear God."

Hester was kneeling beside Nathan on the alter. Her lips moved as she raised her arms slowly, her hands joined around the long crystal spike.

Lizzie opened her mouth to shout at Hester, to stop her, or at least stall her, but—

—a dark figure appeared before her from above, wings spread wide, lips quivering around its jagged, uneven fangs. It slapped its gnarled hands onto her shoulders and dug its curved, black claws into her back just enough to hurt her as it began to push her backward.

Speaking quickly, Lizzie growled, "In the name of Jesus Christ get your *filthy* claws *off* of me!"

The creature doubled over and shot backward, vomiting explosively on itself as it landed in a black heap on the ground.

"Thank you," Lizzie breathed as she looked up at Hester and saw her arms stretched high above her head, the crystal spike sparkling in the blue light as—

Lauren screamed, *"Naaathaaan! Naaathaaan!"* and—

—Lizzie knew she was too late, too slow, she could never get to him in time, and she felt weak, too weak to stand, until she saw something that made her want to laugh with joy as—

—Hester chanted quietly, her arms still, ready to swing downward hard and drive the spike into Nathan, but—

—someone behind her screamed, then someone else, and the chant began to die out as other voices rose in horror and someone shouted, "Get back!" and another cried, "What is it?" and a little girl shrieked, "Get away get away!" and then—

—Hester smelled him as she brought the spike down with all her strength, but—

—strong hands gripped her wrists, jerked her to her feet and spun her around.

Hester looked up at her son. "What the *hell* are you *doing*?" she rasped. "Let go of me. Let *go* of me right *now*!"

He didn't let go. He stared down at her with cold scrutiny. Tears rimmed his eyes.

Hester separated her hands, holding the spike in her right hand, and tried to jerk from his grasp, snapping, "Go back! Go back to your place right *now* or your punishment will be even wor—"

He let go of her left wrist but tightened his grip on her right. Then he tightened it even more.

"Let go. You're hurting me. Do you *hear*, you're—" Her voice rose quickly until it began to squeak. "—hurting me . . . hurting me, let go, you're—" Her hand began to shake and her fingers loosened around the spike and—

—he plucked it away from her.

Hester's wrist cracked like a stick in his grip and her head fell back as she screamed.

Holding the spike in his right fist, Benjamin punched it into her stomach hard, lifting her off the ground with the force of the blow until he held her above him, the spike buried deep in her abdomen, and—

—terrified screams filled the chamber as Hester's followers backed away from the altar, some of them falling and tripping up others as—

—a man backed into Lizzie and knocked her to the ground and—

—the creature standing before Jordan suddenly broke into a wet, gurgling scream that made its entire body quake and it fell away from him, dropped to the ground and began to writhe and vomit, quickly spreading a puddle around itself, and when Jordan looked around, he saw that the others were doing the same as—

—Lauren broke away from Coogan and Joan and ran toward the altar screaming her son's name.

Nathan was screaming, too. He was too terrified to get up or even move, so he closed his eyes and screamed as Hester's blood spattered on his naked body.

Hester tried to scream but could only retch as blood dribbled from her mouth. Her arms and legs were limp and her head lolled forward.

Benjamin looked up at his mother and said, "Shtay in . . . the luh-liiight . . . long tuh-time."

He shoved her into the crevice, then backed away.

The screaming died out. Even the four Guardians had fallen silent as they lay quivering on the ground. For a long time, no one moved.

Something was wrong.

The air changed, became thick, stifling.

The blue light ceased to pulsate; it simply glowed for a while, until—

—a flash of white light from the crevice made everyone shield their eyes. It was painfully bright, blinding, and—

—it happened again, but this time, thin veins of the blinding light stretched out into the cave and—

—Jordan felt his hair shifting on his head, heard it crackle with electricity, and then—

—he felt the wind.

It was hot and dry and began gently at first, swirling through the cave. The blue light actually swirled with it, beginning to form a glowing tornado.

Lizzie clambered to her feet and hurried toward the altar, dodging the white-robed people who staggered as they looked around the cave, perhaps for friends or spouses.

Benjamin met her halfway. Nathan was in his arms, his eyes wide and staring at nothing, his mouth open, tongue working frantically.

"Give t-to . . . muh . . . maw-meeee," he said.

With a tremendous, gut-wrenching crack, the crevice opened, lengthening itself up the wall of the chamber. Pieces of the cavern began to fall away from the walls and ceiling. A large stalactite dropped to the ground with an impact everyone felt beneath their feet; a chunk of the stalactite broke off and it fell on its side with another *clunk*.

Several women screamed. Men began to shout.

The wind suddenly doubled in force, but it was no longer swirling.

It was blowing into the crevice.

Lizzie thought it felt like the earth was inhaling as the force of it threw her into Benjamin. He began walking, pushing her away from the crevice and placing Nathan in her arms. He turned her around and began pushing her, crying, "Go! Gooo! Guh-*goooo*!"

Jordan was at her side suddenly, his arm around her, pulling her with him toward the others who waited by the alcove.

"Benjamin!" Lizzie screamed, but her voice was a distant whisper. "Where's Benjamin?" She turned, pulling one shoulder away from Jordan and—

—she saw Benjamin just a few feet behind them, stumbling against the force of the wind until—

—a hysterical man who was tearing away his white robe ran in front of him, fell, and—

—Benjamin tripped over him, started to get up quickly, but—

—an enormous stalactite with a base the size of a tree trunk broke away from the ceiling. For a moment, it seemed to Lizzie that it was falling in slow motion and she opened her mouth to scream at Benjamin, thinking that she might have enough time to warn him, but—

—the hulking, slow-moving boy disappeared beneath the piece of stone as if he had never been there.

"No!" Lizzie screamed, letting go of Nathan's legs. "Please, God, *no*!"

Jordan took Nathan from Lizzie and pulled her to him roughly, shouting, "Come on Lizzie come on *now*!"

Lauren ran to meet them, her arms outstretched, crying.

Pieces of stone were flying around the chamber like sand in a windstorm. They stung Lauren's skin, made Lizzie hunch forward to protect the boy. The wind became deafening. Screams were swallowed by the powerful current of hot, sucking air. A chunk of the ceiling dropped to the ground and a section of the chamber wall collapsed on several of Hester's terrified followers. The earth beneath them reacted to each piece of stone that fell on it as the cavern chamber collapsed.

The bodies of the fallen Guardians slid across the ground, then flew through the air across the chamber and disappeared into the crevice.

Jordan leaned forward heavily as he hurried Lizzie out of the chamber, but he still felt himself being pulled backward. And it was getting worse.

"Hurry!" he shouted, pushing them, pulling them. "Go! Go!"

A few of the white-robed believers were struggling out with them, but only a few. The screams behind them combined to become a single agonized wail.

Coogan still had the lantern and turned it on as they left the deadly light behind them.

The wind began to lose its strength as they neared the mouth of the cave. They could hear again, although their ears were ringing. The cave echoed with cries, and they could still hear the scream of the deadly wind behind them.

Outside the cave, they stopped running. Coogan and Lizzie fell to the ground. Lauren took Nathan in her arms, crying hysterically. Joan leaned against a tree trunk, hugging herself and taking slow, deep breaths. Jordan paced.

Perhaps a dozen of Hester's followers came out of the cave and ran screaming into the woods. Jordan waited, watching the mouth of the cave, but no one else came out.

"We'd better get back to the car," he sighed. "Pretty soon, this place is going to be a madhouse."

42.

Jordan drove. Lauren sat beside him with Nathan lying in her lap wrapped in Jordan's sport coat. She spoke to him soothingly, stroking his hair and telling him how much she loved him. He had not yet stopped shaking.

Lizzie, Coogan and Joan were silent in the backseat.

"We're gonna have to get out of this town right away," Jordan said. His voice was unsteady. "We'll go to the motel and get our stuff, then—" He glanced in the rearview mirror at Coogan and Joan. "—if you two have things you want to pick up, we can—"

"I'm not going anywhere," Coogan said softly.

"What? You have to come. You know what this town is gonna be like in a few hours?"

"I can't." He shook his head slowly. His voice was hoarse

and flat. "I don't know if P-Paula or Jake were . . . in there. I need to find out."

"I'm going to stay, too," Joan said, taking Coogan's hand. "Nobody's going to connect us to that. Why would they?"

Jordan couldn't answer. She was right.

"And don't worry," Coogan said. "If we do get dragged into it, we won't bring you up."

"You're both sure?" Jordan asked.

They said yes.

At the motel, Jordan gathered his and Lauren's things together quickly. He checked out and drove to Coogan's. The car idled as they said their good-byes.

"Will you keep in touch?" Lizzie said to both Coogan and Joan.

"Sure will," Coogan said. He looked much older; his shoulders hunched forward as if carrying a great weight.

Joan was sturdier. She smiled as she stepped forward and hugged Lizzie, then Jordan. Lauren was still in the car with Nathan.

"Thanks for your help," Jordan said, shaking Coogan's hand.

When Lizzie hugged him, Coogan broke down. His shoulders quaked, although he fought to hold back his sobs.

"They're dead," he whispered, his head hanging over Lizzie's shoulder. "I just know they're dead. My family . . . my whole family . . ."

Lizzie held him and said nothing; there was nothing to say. When he'd finally calmed and pulled away from her, she held his hand and said, "We're going to see each other again, Coogan. Okay?"

He nodded.

"We'll see each other again either here or there."

He smiled then and nodded again.

Jordan and Lizzie got back in the car. Lauren waved at them as Jordan backed out and drove away.

Joan put her arm around Coogan and squeezed and said, "Whatta you say we go inside and get drunk."

He chuckled, sniffling and wiping his tears on his sleeve. "It won't help," he said. "But it won't hurt. . . ."

43.

The sky was grey with the first sign of dawn when they heard the news.

They'd spoken little since leaving Grover and, tired of the silence, Lizzie had turned on the radio and found a San Francisco news station several miles back. The Grover story was out already. According to the newscaster, a cave behind the Sleeping Woman Inn had collapsed with an unspecified number of Alliance members inside. The newscaster promised to report any further details as the story unfolded.

But there was another story. . . .

"A bizarre story has come out of the Silicon Valley," the newscaster said. "At about three o'clock this morning, three men were killed in a senseless shooting at the Diego Nuclear Power Plant."

Jordan sat up behind the wheel and listened.

"A few hours earlier, the Santa Clara County Sheriff's Department received a tip that an armed man would be arriving at the plant soon. No reason was given, but it was made clear that the man intended to kill someone. Five deputies, a security guard and a former worker at the plant, Mark Schroeder, were standing at the gate when the gunman, Marvin Ackroyd, arrived and began shooting wildly. The deputies drew their weapons—and so did Schroeder. Deputy Michael Watson was shot in the head and died instantly. Schroeder, also dead, was shot three times. Ackroyd was shot in the chest and died in the ambulance on the way to the hospital. No further details are available. An investigation is under way."

Jordan's entire body weakened. His foot let up on the accelerator and the car slowed on the freeway. He eased the car onto the shoulder and put it in park. He stared out the windshield for a while, not moving. Then he pounded his fist on the steering wheel three times. Then on the dashboard, again and again and again. He threw the door open, got out and kicked the tire, pounded his fists on the hood, kicked at the ground several times and spread dirt and gravel. Then he leaned on the hood, let his head hang down and breathed slowly for a long time.

Lizzie got out of the car, walked around to the driver's side, got behind the wheel and closed the door. She waited patiently until Jordan got back in, then she pulled back onto the freeway.

They drove to Redding in silence.

44.

Morning sunlight glared harshly through the filthy windows.

"You earthlings *taste* good . . . but you play lousy pinball," the pinball machine said to no one in particular. Several explosions sounded over the tinny speaker, then the machine's lights flashed off and on. After that, it was silent for a while, then: "You earthlings *taste* good . . ."

A teenage girl was slumped on a bench a few feet away from the pinball machine. She had stringy dirty-blond hair and was wearing clothes that looked like they'd been worn too long without a wash. She was crying quietly and she was very pregnant. Every three or four minutes, she looked up at the clock over the ticket counter.

Behind the counter, an enormously fat man with greasy hair, a thin, patchy beard and a small, almost Hitler-like mustache read a paperback book called *Love's Angry Passion*. The bus that was getting ready to leave rumbled and coughed behind the building, but the man seemed not to notice. He looked up from his book when the door opened, looked for a moment at the man and woman who walked in, then returned to his story. He put the book down when she came to the counter with her suitcase and purse and said, "I'd like a round trip ticket to Irving, please."

Jordan went to a bench and sat down heavily, wearily. A few minutes later, Lizzie joined him.

Lauren was in the car with Nathan. She was afraid to leave him alone. Besides, he had no clothes.

"So," she said, "this is your hometown."

"Yeah." He wasn't paying her much attention because he really didn't feel like talking.

"Did you enjoy growing up in Redding?"

He chuckled and said distractedly, "I didn't much enjoy growing up."

"Ah. Um, about that, Jordan . . ."

He turned to her. "What about it?"

"Well, you were very upset when you learned Marvin had

told me about your childhood. Well . . . he was just trying to prepare me for the way you might react to me . . . to my beliefs.''

"Yeah, I know what he was doing. He was *always* doing things like that.''

"He was . . . a peacemaker,'' she said. "And I'm glad we had him. We didn't exactly hit it off.''

Jordan laughed softly.

"I'm sorry he's gone, Jordan.''

"Me too.''

They were quiet for a while and Lizzie watched the pregnant girl on the opposite side of the bus station.

"So,'' she said finally, grinning at Jordan, "have you changed your mind about any of the things we discus—argued about?''

"*Hah!*'' He shook his head slowly. "Well, Lizzie, I have to admit that, for the first time since I was a little kid . . . I prayed. I mean, I *really prayed*. And I meant it more than I ever did as a child.'' He thought about that awhile, looking surprised at himself, then: "But the hand of God did *not* appear and smack Hester Thorne in the mouth. Where was He? Why didn't He answer?''

"But He *did!*'' she laughed happily. "You're expecting Cecil B. DeMille stuff, special effects, but . . . like I said before, God works through people. He used Benjamin. Benjamin was our Eskimo.''

"Our *what*?''

"Eskimo. Let me tell you a story. There were these three guys talking over drinks in a bar. Two of them were talking about why they believed in God. The third one said, 'There *is* no God. He doesn't exist.' The others asked why he thought that and he said, 'A few years ago, I was exploring in the Arctic. I got lost, ran out of food, and I was dying. I prayed to God to save me. If he saved me, I promised I would stop screwing around, give up booze and go to church every week. I prayed and prayed and prayed.' The others asked if God had saved him and he said, 'Hell, no. Some Eskimo found me and took me home.' '' She smiled at him. "Benjamin was our Eskimo.''

They fell silent again. Lizzie watched the pregnant girl.

Jordan stood. "I should go. Sure you don't want to ride with us?''

"No sense in you having to drive all the way to Irving. Hey

. . . keep an eye on Lauren. She's going to need someone now. She and Nathan both.''

"Yeah, I will.''

"And let's keep in touch, okay? I may need a private detective someday.''

"Well . . . keep it simple, if you do. No more Satan shit.''

She laughed and gave him a hug.

Jordan went to the door and looked back once. Lizzie was seated next to the crying pregnant girl, speaking softly, her arm around the girl's shoulders.

When Jordan got to the car, Lauren was asleep in the backseat with Nathan in her arms. She was completely relaxed and, as a result, her face looked different than it had since he'd met her; all the tension and fear were gone. She was, he realized, quite pretty.

He started the car and headed for the freeway.

45.

It was on the radio the whole way to San Francisco.

"Hester Thorne was a very dear friend of mine,'' Sheila Bennet said. "But her loss will be felt by those who have never even met her. This fall, I will begin production on a two-part television movie on Hester's life. I will be playing the part of Hester Thorne. I want the world to know the Hester that I knew. I want the world to know what she was trying to do for *them* when she formed the Universal Enlightened Alliance.''

The president released a brief statement: "Hester Thorne was clearly a leader for our time. Her work addressed the concerns that are unique to this era. Her message was one of unity and peace, of the value of this earth and the value of each and every individual living on it. I only hope that, although Hester has been taken from us in this horrible tragedy, her work will live on and accomplish the things to which Hester Thorne devoted her entire life.''

Jordan sighed behind the wheel. "That . . . is what I'm afraid of . . .''

JOHN SAUL

*John Saul has produced one bestseller after another:
masterful tales of terror and psychological suspense.
Each of his works is as shocking, as intense and as
stunningly real as those that preceeded it.*